Countess Athena & Godfather's Twins

For radio or media interviews, book
signings, or personal appearances
Email: info@GlobalWorldPublishing.Ltd

Countess Athena & Godfather's Twins

Lewis Barton

Library of Congress Control Number: 2021918019
ISBN: Hardcover 978-1-6641-9839-5
Softcover 978-1-6641-9838-8
eBook 978-1-6641-9837-1

This is a work of fiction. Names, characters, places and incidents either are the product of the author's imagination or are used fictitiously, and any resemblance to any actual persons, living or dead, events, or locales is entirely coincidental.

Any people depicted in stock imagery provided by Getty Images are models, and such images are being used for illustrative purposes only.

Print information available on the last page.

Rev. date: 11/05/2021

To order additional copies of this book, contact:
Xlibris
844-714-8691
www.Xlibris.com
Orders@Xlibris.com
837194

Contents

Castellammare & Cornino Family Tree

Baron Felix 1857 - Murdered — **Baroness Roseanna** 1849 - Died in Childbirth

Fraternal Twins

Baron Vittorio 1865 - Died in Accident

Baroness Vittoria 1928 - Died of Natural Causes

Marries

Mario

Fraternal Twins

Baron Santino 1889 - Murdered

Countess Sophia 1952 - Died of Natural Causes

Marries - **Count Maximo**

son of Count Don Carlos - Arranged marriage by Count Don Carlos & Baroness Vittoria

Fraternal Twins

Count Santino 1895 - Drowned as a child

Countess Athena 1973 - Died of Natural Causes

Fraternal Twins

Countess Florence

Marries

Baron Antonio

son of Baron Teodoro & Baroness Theresa

Duchess Maria

Marries

Duke Vito

son of Duke Don Vito & Duchess Sabrina

Countess Athena, Duke Don Vito, and the Baron and Baroness of Brescia arranged these marriages

Fraternal Twins

Duke Vito Jr. 2012 - went off the grid

Duchess Marie

Marries

Lewis Barton

Arranged marriage by Duke Vito & Baron Antonio

Fraternal Twins

1982 - **Danny & Antonio**

1983 - **Mary & Janella**

1984 - **Sophia & Marie**

1985 - **Athena & brother**

2001 - Countess Florence & Baron Antonio, Duchess Maria & Duke Vito, and Duchess Marie & Lewis Barton's four sets of fraternal twins disappeared, except Athena.

2012 - Duchess Marie or possibly one of her doubles; unsure of her whereabouts, or possible death

Preface

Countess Athena & Godfather's Twins is the first book of a four-book series. This book series illustrates one hundred and forty three years of Sicilian family life - their love and devotion, traditions, commitment and loyalty, royal families merging, wealth, survival, and crime with the first book covering the first eighty years. All these factors had an influence on the world, both in America and abroad.

The author began to research and document five generations of historical events in an effort to learn what happened to Duke Vito and Duchess Marie Cornino twenty years ago, along with their eight grandchildren who were four of the five sets of twins, and the great-grandchildren of Countess Athena Marie Castellammare; and Duke Don Vito Cornino, the godfather of Palermo, Sicily. Baron Tony and Countess Florence Zibelli, along with seven other family members and their security, domestic, and medical staff, as well as their two pilots, were last seen in Zurich, Switzerland in August 2001, while doing some banking business. They mysteriously disappeared and no one has seen or heard from them since. Rumors have spread that they were in a plane crash; others say they were in a shipwreck; and still others have said they are on a private island in the South Pacific . . . another theory is they were kidnapped by the Russian Mafia.

It all begins in 1857 in Castellammare, Sicily, with Baron Felix Castellammare sitting on the porch of the 1,000-acre Castellammare Villa Estate overlooking his fields, olive groves, and grape vineyards. Baroness Roseanna, Countess Athena's great grandmother has passed, leaving eight-year-old fraternal twins, Baron Vittorio and Baroness Vittoria. A revolt was brewing in the village and Count Don Carlos was going to use the revolt to take Castellammare Villa Estate from him by force.

What happens to the Baron and the twins is told and we follow them into tragedy and bitterness as they reclaim the Castellammare family treasure hidden in the castle.

Someone new arrives on the scene, Duke Don Vito Cornino, the Godfather of Palermo, Sicily, and the grandfather of Vito Jr. & Marie Cornino. He organized the Castellammare area, which became one of the strongest Mafia areas in Sicily in the late 1800s, and was then introduced to the United States in the early 1900s

Baroness Vittoria, Countess Athena's grandmother, arranged the marriage of her fraternal twin daughter, Countess Sophia, to Count Don Carlo's son in order to take back Castellammare Villa Estate. Countess Athena, a fraternal twin born in 1888, arranged her twin daughter, Countess Maria's marriage to Duke Don Vito Cornino's son, Duke Vito Cornino, the Godfather of godfathers.

In this book . . . you will follow the lives of five generations of royal twins. You will also learn how, where and when the Kennedys became millionaires. Baron Tony's family is killed and Duke Don Vito comes to his rescue. For his safety, the young boy is hidden in a wagon under hay to sneak him away from the killers and get him to a steamboat headed for America. Walk in Baron Tony's shoes and discover how the phrase 'concrete boots' came about and is known world-wide.

Discover the true murderer in the Valentine's Day Massacre and why Al Cappone was innocent.

You will also learn about the deal between President Roosevelt and Duke Don Vito which allowed the United States military to go through Sicily to Europe in World War II.

In 1936, Duke Vito and Duchess Maria Cornino purchased a pre-civil war plantation home on the Mississippi River near New Orleans as their winter home, where fraternal twins Vito Jr. & Marie Cornino were born in 1939.

The plantation home is where the mafia triangle was incepted.

To commemorate the 75th anniversary of the last victory of the Battle of the Wilderness in the American Civil War, a Plantation Ball was planned and was one of the finest affairs of that time and remembered for years to come. The theme was inspired by "Twelve Oaks" from the "Gone with the Wind" novel. Why Murders Inc. decided to use hit-women as well as hit-men is revealed during the Ball.

Following the Plantation Ball, Duke Don Vito & Duchess Sabrina and Count Mario & Countess Athena remained at the Plantation awaiting the birth of Duchess Maria and Duke Vito's baby, or babies, as was common in the Castellammare family. During this time, Countess Athena spent several hours each day sharing the Castellammare history with her daughters, Duchess Maria and Countess Florence. The legacy of the Castellammare family was passed down generation to generation and was told to the author, Lewis Barton, 40 years later.

This book was inspired by real people, places, and events.

Some of the names in this book have been changed to protect the guilty.

The Plantation Ball

The Plantation Ball of 1939 was quickly approaching. Countess Athena was packing her steam trunk and getting everything ready for her trip to America to help her twin daughters, Duchess Maria and Countess Florence with the preparations and offer suggestions to ensure that the Ball would be a great success. The Plantation Ball was no ordinary party or gathering. It was one of prestige. Dignitaries and everybody who was anybody attended.

The day had arrived and Duke Don Vito & Duchess Sabrina and Count Mario & Countess Athena, along with their bodyguards and the crew boarded Duke Don Vito's private Douglas DC-3 Skytrain from Palermo, Sicily, bound for New Orleans. The airplane, one of the first private custom airplanes ever made had been tailored to suit its owner's taste and comfort. The seats which could accommodate from 21 to 32 passengers had been removed and replaced with two beds, a food and bar gallery, comfortable reclining seats, and a bathroom with a shower. The propeller-driven airliner had a cruising speed of 207 mph which allowed them to travel in a fraction of the time from one country to the other. The other option of transcontinental transportation at that time would have been by steamship, which traveled at 21 mph. Considered one of the safest built to date, the DC-3 airplane is still being used today, over eighty years since its first flight in 1935.

The plane landed in New Orleans and the two couples were picked up by a private chauffer in a black Packard Limousine and driven to the Seventeen Oaks Plantation. Duchess Maria rushed out to greet them. As Countess Athena hugged her daughter Duchess Maria, she reached down and patted her protruding stomach.

"They're excited about the Ball too," Duchess Maria chuckled, "They haven't stopped kicking."

Her mother hugged her again and they walked into the plantation house arm-in-arm, excited to get settled in and begin with the preparations.

Duke Don Vito and Duke Vito greeted one another with an embrace as they kissed each other on both cheeks. Shortly afterward, the two men proceeded to take a walk around the plantation and discuss business as they enjoyed the beauty of their surroundings.

In 1936, Duke Vito and Duchess Maria Cornino purchased the pre-civil war plantation home on the Mississippi River near New Orleans for their winter home. The plantation home is where fraternal twins, Vito Jr. & Maria Cornino were born in 1939. The duke and duchess chose the plantation because the temperatures resembled those in Sicily during the winter months.

Vito and Maria also had a summer home in Chicago, which was akin to the temperatures they enjoyed in their grand villa located in the Italian Alps.

During this time, people suspected that the mafia triangle was New York, Chicago, and Miami. This was not correct. The actual triangle was New York, Chicago, and New Orleans. The plantation near New Orleans was the main meeting grounds, particularly in the winter months and in Chicago during the summer months.

This is the plantation where the final plans were made and executed on John Kennedy's assassination.[1] It was also where Duke Don Vito's men obtained World War II secrets from Benito Mussolini's office. Many of these secrets included Hitler's plans which were in action and plans for future actions. Secrets were transcribed from secret codes that had been developed and used by Duke Don Vito and Vito over twenty years earlier. Because Duke Don Vito was constantly under surveillance by Mussolini's men, he was restricted in what he could do or say. Countess Athena was a successful businesswoman and exported her wines and olive oils to America. The plantation's location on the Mississippi River gave it access to have its own dock where her goods could be delivered and unloaded. Since Countess Athena was never

---

[1] Story of JFK's election and his assassination are in Book 3 of series

under scrutiny, she was able to place the secrets transcribed by Duke Don Vito into false bottoms in the wooden crates of her exports and send them to Vito, who would then decipher them and forward them to President Roosevelt by military couriers.

Preparations were completed and the day of the Ball had arrived. Countess Florence went to her appointment at the hairdressing salon where her hairdresser, Maggie, did her hair in a style befitting the theme of the Ball. While she sat under the dryer waiting for her hair to set, Rosalie proceeded to do her manicure. Maggie was very talented in her field and not very talkative while she worked. Rosalie, on the other hand, loved to gossip and was not discreet about discussing everyone else's business. As she worked on Countess Florence's nails, she proceeded to tell her about a client who had just left the salon.

"You should have heard her," Rosalie said, "She was furious because her boyfriend, Tristano, was taking his wife to the Grand Ball instead of her. She couldn't believe that he would choose his wife over her!"

Rosalie proceeded with her story, "She said that there's going to be big trouble at the Ball. Tristano hates Duke Vito and he's going to shoot him!"

Countess Florence reacted to Rosalie's story with a courteous interest, but without any emotion or urgency as to cause Rosalie to suspect Countess Florence of knowing the unsuspecting intended victim or that she could possibly thwart Tristano's quest of shooting Vito. Countess Florence finished her appointment and rushed back to the plantation house to tell her husband, Baron Tony what she had just learned at the salon.

Baron Tony walked through the plantation house with Duke Don Vito, amidst servants scurrying around making final preparations and past the kitchen staff who were busy assembling the dinner which was to be served. Duchess Maria was in her room making sure all of her themed attire was ready and no detail would be omitted. Tony asked one of the servants where he could find Duchess Maria and after receiving her response, they bolted up the stairs to the sitting room, finding Maria relaxing for a bit before the Ball would begin and guests would be arriving.

"Maria!" Tony blurted out, trying to catch his breath, "One of your invited guests - a man named Tristano - you invited he and his wife to the Ball and dinner?"

"Why, yes we did," responded Maria, "He's a business associate and friend of Vito's."

"Well, the only business Tristano is interested in is killing Vito. Countess Florence was at the salon and Tristano's girlfriend, in her anger, impulsively blurted out his plan because he was taking his wife and not her to the Ball."

Maria's anger seethed as she turned and looked at Tony and Don Vito. "I'll take care of this," she said, "I know exactly what I'm going to do."

"Are you sure Maria? In your condition?"

"Yes, I am sure," Maria calmly responded. Tony and Duke Don Vito could see the dark coldness in her eyes stemming from this man's deceit. This coldness and seething anger they had only witnessed before with her great-grandmother, Baroness Vittoria, who spent her life full of bitterness and rage that ran deep within her soul because of the injustice and pain she had suffered at such a young age.

The Plantation Ball was celebrating the 75th anniversary of the victory of the last southern victory of the Battle of the Wilderness in the American Civil War. The theme was perfectly represented in the plantation's décor which was inspired by the "Twelve Oaks" in the "Gone with the Wind" novel written in 1935, by Margaret Mitchell. Tony was in charge of the bands. As the guests arrived by automobile and horse and carriage, one of the bands was set up and playing on the front porch of the plantation, which flaunted its seventeen grand columns and overlooked the Mississippi River with its private dock where guests arrived by paddle riverboat. The other band was set up and playing on the back porch where guests would meander around engaging in conversation and enjoying cocktails. To the delight of the arriving guests who were all dressed in their pre-civil war attire, Tony set the perfect stage for the Ball to begin with his carefully choreographed performance. He arrived wearing a Civil War Confederate officer's uniform, riding on a white horse. As he approached the plantation, two civil war cannons were shot off, and the bands played "Old Dixie" as he dismounted from his horse and greeted the guests.

The Ball had begun. Although more than 200 people had been invited, only a select few were invited to have dinner at the main dining table which seated twenty people. Due to Duchess Maria's knowledge of the impending trouble, seating arrangements were adjusted. Countess Florence sat at one end of the table, while Duke Vito sat at the head of the table on the other end. Everyone liked Maria, so the seating changes caused no problem. The unaware 'would-be' assassin sat next to Tony and across from Maria. Don Vito sat beside Maria in case she needed any help. A side table was placed directly beside Maria's seat which had covered platters ready to serve the guests - in hers was a .32 derringer. Most of the dinner guests had been served and were enjoying pleasant conversation when Tony saw Tristano reach into his jacket pocket. He signaled Maria who quickly but discreetly uncovered her dish, grabbed her pistol, and shot Tristano in the temple across the dinner table. It was a perfect shot, even though it was only five feet away! Tristano dropped over dead into his dinner plate. His wife jumped up from her chair and stepped back from the table looking at her dead husband. The rest of the dinner guests just sat there, shocked at what had just happened, but not really horrified. One of the dinner guests seated at the table was a 95-year-old Civil War Colonel dressed in his Civil War uniform. He stood up, pulled out his pistol, and shot it in the air claiming, "I ain't never had this much fun since the Wilderness!"

The guests quickly moved to the parlor where they enjoyed an array of desserts while the dining room was cleaned and Tristano's dead body removed.

Tony was amazed at what he had just witnessed. Maria's demeanor was cool and calm as she took care of business. Remembering this moment, it was 10 years later when he decided to use hitwomen in Murder, Inc., and it was another 10 years before anyone figured out that Tony had made women members. Duke Don Vito had confirmed his decision with something he had said to him years before, "Italian women are more dangerous than shotguns."

Vito was shocked at his wife's behavior, not knowing that she had stopped the man who was planning on killing him.

"Maria!" Vito said, running to his wife's side. "What . . . ?" He glanced over at Tony who was still sitting in his chair smiling.

Maria looked up at her husband and said, "Don Vito told me from the time I was a child, 'The strength of a family, like the strength of an army, lies in its loyalty to each other.' You are my family and Tristano's plan was to kill you."

Vito looked surprised, but then said, "Fake people don't surprise me anymore. Loyal people do. And, you know, the saddest thing about betrayal? It never comes from an enemy."

The Ball continued with bands playing, dancing, and spirits flowing, until the wee hours of the morning. The Reel Dance was popular in the *Gone with the Wind* movie and highlighted at the Ball. Everyone had a wonderful time, and the Ball would be talked about for years to come.

Duke Don Vito & Duchess Sabrina and Count Mario & Countess Athena planned on remaining at the plantation awaiting the birth of Maria's baby - or babies as was common in the Castellammare family.

Vito and Duke Don Vito spent hours talking and watching the boats load sugar and cotton and receiving Countess Athena's wine and olive oil when they arrived at their dock.

Countess Athena, Duchess Sabrina, Countess Florence, and Duchess Maria shopped for blankets, clothes, and everything a new baby and its mother could possibly want or need. The nursery was perfect and ready for the new addition.

"I still think we should buy another crib, Maria," Athena said.

"And if there's only one?" Duchess Maria laughed, "And - if they are twins, they can share the crib for a while. They're small!"

Countess Florence looked at Duchess Maria's stomach and said, "He, she, or they don't look very small!"

Countess Florence and Duchess Maria cherished the time that they were spending with their mother, Countess Athena, and spent many hours over many days intently listening to her stories about the Castellammare family's history from the memories her grandmother, Baroness Vittoria had shared with her.

And the story began . . .

Baron Felix Castellammare

Baron Felix Castellammare sat in the shade of his porch that late summer afternoon, sipping on an ice cold glass of Castellammare wine while enjoying the richness of his land and even more so, the cool, crisp wind which was blowing up from the Sicilian coastline. The Castellammare estate spread out below him, carpeted with wheat fields and cornfields, dotted with olive groves and terraced with vineyards along the hillsides. The afternoon wind swayed gently in the golden wheat as men worked in the olive groves and vineyards. All was quite peaceful in the Baron's world.

Beyond the low, rolling hills that fringed the immediate estate, even steeper hillsides rose up, jagged with rocks as if creating a fortress around the estate with a lone mountain peak poking even higher up into the clear blue sky. Further off, its rocky flanks were splashed with green foliage. Below the estate, the turquoise sea sparkled like a jewel in the blustery late afternoon wind, and there, tucked beneath the seaside cliffs, stood the ancient fishing village of 166, though the Baron could only see a few of its rooftops.

At some distance behind Baron Castellammare and his sprawling stone villa, a massive outcropping of rocks jutted out from the side of a hill in that direction. Perched precariously to one side of that outcropping was a castle by the sea that also belonged to the Baron. This explained the name of the family and of the village, Castellammare. Whether the village had been named after the family or the family after the village was a question lost so far back in antiquity, probably no one could answer it properly. The point being, though the castle remained a fine place for the children to play and provided a safe place to retreat in times of danger, it had never been a particularly comfortable place to live, so the Castellammare family had long ago built and occupied the villa.

Baron Castellammare was a large man in his early fifties, overweight, but not in any grotesque sense of the word. He simply displayed the body of someone who quite clearly enjoyed good food and the wine that went with it.

He wore khaki pants, finely made Italian boots, both of which were dusty from walking in the fields that day, and a loose, white cotton shirt, opened at the collar. His sweat-stained hat sat on a table nearby, as did a chilled glass of wine. In 1857, the Baron was able to enjoy chilled wine because his peasants dragged ice down from the nearby mountains, which he then stored in his cellar. The Baron took great pride in serving chilled drinks to his guests, in whatever fashion they liked them, and in fact, had considered making a new business of supplying ice to local merchants, but the demands on his time were already too great.

The Baron had been sitting there for some time that afternoon when he noticed dust rising up on the road that ran further up the coast towards Trappeto. Some minutes later, a man on horseback appeared out of the dust and the Baron cursed to himself quietly. He watched and waited and sipped his Castellammare wine.

A few minutes later, the man and horse arrived and were prancing about in front of the Baron's front porch. It was a fine Arabian horse, but the Baron did not think so highly of his rider.

A horse ridden by an ass, he thought, although he did not say this out loud.

The man was Count Don Carlos, a fellow landowner and Bourbon dandy, who was dressed more fittingly for a royal court than for the fields of Sicily, with skin-tight white pants on his relatively slender and tall frame, knee-high leather boots, a frilled white shirt, a red waistcoat, and a riotously colored tasseled waistband to accent all the rest. Otherwise, he had a close-cropped beard; eyes that seemed to be forever squinting from the sun and clearly thought far too much of himself.

All he's lacking is one of those foot-high pompous hats, the Baron thought.

"Baron Castellammare!" Don called out.

"Welcome, Count Don Carlos. Would you care for something to drink?"

"Some of your late wife, Roseanna's famous burgundy?"

"If that is your wish, I will have Angelina bring some."

"No, no. I do not have time to sit and talk today, God rest her soul. I can still smell her homemade perfume and see her beauty."

Baron Castellammare stared. Count Don Carlos kept prancing around on the restless horse.

"What can I do for you today, Count Don Carlos?"

"I came to see again if you will sell me your land?"

"It does not occur to me as something I would like to do."

"Why not? . . . I know, don't tell me. Because your family has owned this land for hundreds of years. As did the Spanish before them, and the Maltese knights before them, and Crown of Aragon before them, and the Hohenstaufen kingdom before them the Normans before them and . . ."

"You are forgetting the Romans."

"No, of course. I was coming to them, and the Greeks before them and the Phoenicians..."

"Yes, indeed. It goes on and on."

The Baron slightly raised and tipped his glass of wine and drank to Count Don Carlos' knowledge of history. The Baron knew it all too well, even though Count Don Carlos had omitted a great deal of it in his abbreviated version of things. The Papacy, for instance, had raided Sicilian estates on a whim over the centuries; where their Inquisition and the wicked men behind it could find nothing better to do in this life than to deform men's bodies on the rack or exact their tortured screams at the stake; and how the Bourbons followed in the wake of all the centuries-old plunder and destruction, gaining power, only to uproot the ancient feudal system by selling off their land to pay for their self-indulgences, until chaos and lawlessness had ensued, leaving landowners to hire private armies or be left to the whims of roving bandits. And there they were, with men like Count Don Carlos maintaining their own private group of thugs, and men of honor like Baron Castellammare making allegiances with what bandits he could find up in the hills who maintained their own code of honor.

You could state it in ancient terms that were simple: Either you brought about order by means of suppression, or you brought about order by offering dignity to all those who struggled for something decent in this world.

Count Don Carlos had chosen the former method, Baron Castellammare the latter. It was among these latter that the term 'omerta' had sprung up because men like Count Don Carlos could not be trusted, no more than you could trust the local officials so that in the end there was no one else whom you could depend to resolve your grievances than an honorable bandit.

Of course, not all bandits were honorable and the whole conundrum had the Baron shaking his head as if tormented by gnats. He sipped at his wine with Count Don Carlos still parading around in front of him.

"So, what do you say to that, Baron?" he asked.

"I say that Caesar's troops marched upon Gaul eating bread made from Sicilian corn, and we will still be here making that bread long after everyone else has tired of Sicily and gone home. You included."

Juan Carlos scoffed.

"It is only fair to warn you that Ferdinand is planning a new invasion in Naples this very minute and when he retakes Sicily, all those who have corroborated with those bandits up in the hills will have their heads handed to them."

Count Don Carlos pranced a bit more, smiling.

"Eh, don't try to kid me, Baron Castellammare. The hills have eyes and I know you associate with these people. There are some working here in your fields right this minute."

He nodded at the villa itself, still smiling.

"Maybe even some inside those walls ... Oh, it's fine. Your secrets are safe with me. Omerta, as you Sicilians say, but it will not go so well with you when Ferdinand returns. Better to sell me your land now, while it is still worth something to you."

The horse reared up and pirouetted, forcing Count Don Carlos to settle him down with his reins. When the horse turned back, the Count was still smiling.

"What do you say, Baron? I will pay you handsomely."

"If you are so sure of getting it for nothing soon, why bother paying me anything at all?"

"Because I am an honorable man."

The Baron almost laughed. Honorable man. Honor to Juan Carlos was a word, without any noble deeds attached to it. He ascribed nobility to his name while conducting himself like a scoundrel.

The Baron tipped his glass to Juan Carlos and drank.

"Shall I be frank, Count Don Carlos?" he said.

"By all means, Baron."

"I would rather be robbed at the hands of King Ferdinand than to sell my lands to you at a profit."

A dark cloud fell over Count Don Carlos' face. His horse reared up again and again he settled him as he sat there upon his restless horse, not smiling now.

"You are being a fool, Baron. The people of the village are preparing to revolt again. There is talk of independence again and new government, and without an army to protect you, as I have, everything you own will be left smoldering in ruins."

The Baron shrugged and sipped his drink again.

"Are you sure you won't have some wine, Count Don Carlos?"

"I have come here attempting to be fair."

"I have no doubt that you did."

Count Don Carlos stared.

"Then consider yourself warned. A wildfire is being whipped up among the peasants right this minute and I cannot protect you from it."

"You are right, Count Don Carlos. I have been warned."

He tipped with his glass and drank. Count Don Carlos pirouetted with his horse while staring, then whipped the horse and galloped off.

The Baron took another drink from his chilled wine, hoping to wipe the bad taste out of his mouth.

At that very moment, Teresa Saccaro was marching up the steep, dusty path from the ancient fishing village of 165. Her long, urgent strides leaning far forward with her hands used against her knees in order to catapult herself all that much more swiftly up the cliff. She wore a long, black peasant skirt, a black blouse, and sandals, with a black scarf tied over her black hair. She was a handsome and proud woman, but by the way she dressed and by the worried look on her face, you had no doubt she was a peasant. If someone had told you, "Teresa has no husband and four starving children at home," you would have believed it, though in fact, she was childless and did have a husband at home; one of those bandits Count Don Carlos had mentioned.

The dusty path zigzagged this way and that up the cliff, for the most part, a goat trail, with crude steps carved into the rock here and there, winding back and forth, back and forth and ever higher, until the village had fallen away and there were no longer any homes clinging to the steep hillsides around Teresa. Eventually, the path crested the hill and the vast Castellammare estate came into view, with its wheat fields and cornfields and olive groves and vineyards terraced along the rugged hillsides.

In the far distance, Teresa saw the castle clinging to its crag of rock and closer to her, the sprawling stone villa. She marched in that direction along the dusty road with grim determination. The afternoon wind swayed in the golden wheat around her, and the men working in the vineyards and olive groves called out to Teresa, but she paid no attention to them. There was trouble afoot that day and she felt it was her duty to warn the Castellammares.

Of course, trouble was nothing new in Sicily. There was always some kind of trouble in Sicily. There had been some kind of trouble in Sicily for thousands of years, but Teresa knew this threat was immediate and a grave danger to the Baron. The entire village was brewing with revolt, and with no seeming purpose other than to find an outlet for its fury.

Having sat there for a spell, sipping his wine and considering the visit by Count Don Carlos, the Baron noticed a small, black speck appear over the crest of the hill from the direction of the sea. Curious, he watched that speck grow, until at last, he realized it was Teresa. He watched her with continued interest until she, at last, arrived at his porch and stopped in the hot afternoon sun, bending over to catch her breath.

"Teresa, please, come up here and rest in the shade." "Angelina!" he called out over his shoulder. Promptly, a stern-looking, middle-aged peasant woman appeared through the opened door. "Angelina, please, bring Teresa a glass of cold wine. She is trying to kill herself out there in the hot sun."

Angelina looked stonily at Teresa and disappeared back into the old villa. Baron Castellammare patted the seat beside him.

"Teresa, please, come here. Have a seat before you expire from this heat."

Reluctantly, Teresa ascended the stone steps and sat down. Her long, dark hair was parted in the middle and braided on both ends with the brow of it sitting somewhat low on her forehead.

"What on earth has gotten into you? Why didn't you come on a donkey or have one of the men bring you up here in a cart?"

Teresa looked warily at the open door and back at Baron Castellammare.

"What? Speak, Teresa. You're acting as if Ferdinand and his invading army have just landed in the harbor."

Seeing Angelina come out the open door with the glass of cold red wine, Teresa waited until she had disappeared back inside the villa and even then, drank from the wine with continued wary glances at the open door until she felt absolutely certain that Angelina was not listening from the inside.

"The people in village have been whipped into a frenzy today and over what I do not understand."

"No doubt because those bastards over in Naples have suspended our constitution again."

"It is something else, Baron Castellammare. I heard anger today about everything and toward everyone."

Baron Castellammare scoffed.

"Since when is that news in Sicily?"

"But this time it is different." Teresa leaned forward and spoke in a hushed voice. "If you own land, suddenly you are a Bourbon and there is talk of revenge."

"Teresa, have another wine. You worry too much. Angelina! Honestly, Teresa. You know I have no use for the Bourbons, either."

Angelina appeared and the Baron gestured for her to bring more wine. Angelina disappeared and Teresa again waited until she was certain this peasant woman was no longer listening before she leaned closer to the Baron.

"My husband Enzo told me to come to warn you. He also sent word to Ernesto."

"Enzo? What does he know of this business?"

Teresa leaned forward and spoke in even a more hushed voice now.

"Enzo is working at the docks today and overheard Giuseppe talking to some of the other men. He said that they are coming specifically after you tonight."

"Giuseppe? That brigand? To hell with him. Don't tell me he's still angry because I caught him stealing my cattle. He should be thankful I did not have him hung."

"Baron Castellammare, please! I don't know why it is different this time, but it is. You can say it is King Ferdinand and this constitution business in Naples with the frustration built up by 50 years of war and insurrections, but I'm here to warn you. Your life is in danger. People in the village have been worked up into a frenzy and they are coming after you tonight."

"Please, drink your wine, Teresa. It will help you to calm down."

The Baron sighed and looked out over his land. The day had grown late, and the wheat had turned a honey color in the dusky light, as it waved in the wind off the sea.

"Teresa, have I ever been anything but kind and generous to the people of Castellammare?"

Teresa looked down and shook her head.

"And you. Do I not pay you well?" he asked.

"Of course. No one can ever question your generosity, Signori Castellammare."

"I am generous with everyone. Is that not true?"

"No one can deny it, Signori Castellammare."

He sighed again, pulled a handkerchief from his pocket, and wiped his brow.

"Too generous, my late wife used to tell me, God rest her soul."

"God rest her soul," Teresa said and crossed herself.

Angelina appeared with two more chilled glasses of wine. The Baron took his, saluted to Teresa, and drank. When Teresa failed to drink from her glass, the Baron encouraged her with a wave of his hand.

"So, tell me why I should worry today," he said once Teresa had set her glass down.

"I came here to warn you. The men are gathering torches, broken bottles, and knives, and they will be out tonight with an earnest inclination to kill. Now that you know, it is for you to decide what you will do about it."

The baron looked out again over his fields of rolling wheat, the vineyards and the olive groves with the late afternoon sea sparkling in the background.

"And I tell you, they will do nothing to harm the Castellammare estate."

He looked over at Teresa with a restrained smile.

"Or my family."

Just then, the sound of laughter echoed from inside the sprawling villa and the twins came rushing out.

"Zietta Teresa, Zietta Teresa!" they said upon seeing her and rushed to her arms. "Have you come to watch us tonight?"

"Vittorio, Vittoria," the Baron said, "Behave yourselves. Teresa has come to share a glass of wine with me and nothing else. Now go back inside and clean up. Angelina will be serving us dinner very soon."

They groaned.

"Go!" the Baron said as he shooed them off.

Once they had disappeared, he sighed and looked back out at the fields.

"They have grown more and more unruly without a mother. God knows they need one."

"So, marry again."

"And what? Lose another wife?"

"Marry young."

"Roseanna was young."

"They don't always die in childbirth."

The Baron hoisted his glass of wine.

"To Roseanna. This was her own special blend of wine, as you well know."

He drank and looked back out over his estate. The sun had set behind the mountain and darkness quickly rushed over the land.

"At least hide the children tonight," Teresa said with a look up at the castle.

The Baron scoffed.

"We will be lighting candles in the church tonight for Roseanna and taking confession. Don't tell me this mob of yours is prepared to kill Father Antonio as well."

"I don't know where they will stop. I fear they would crucify the Good Lord in their present mood."

Teresa crossed herself again. The Baron scoffed at her again. After a moment's reflection, he finished his wine and patted Teresa on the hand.

"One moment, please. I have something for you."

The Baron disappeared inside and returned a minute later with a vial.

"Some of my wife's homemade perfume."

"No, I couldn't," Teresa said.

"Of course, you can. Here. I'm sure she would have wanted you to have it."

Teresa took the perfume vial and clutched it in her hand without speaking. Her eyes nervously darted from the Baron up to the castle and back again.

"Please, Signori. At least hide the twins up there tonight. Even better if you take everyone up there and bar the gates."

The Baron waved her off.

"Angelina!" he called out, "At least allow me to get a wagon to take you home."

"No!" Teresa said with a reach for the Baron's hand.

Angelina appeared and Teresa quickly pulled her hand away.

"Never mind, Angelina. Never mind."

The Baron waved her off. Angelina exchanged an icy look with Teresa and disappeared back inside. Teresa stared at the door warily for a long moment before standing up.

"I don't dare go home in your wagon, Signori," she whispered. "And you should tell no one I was here."

She nodded her chin at the door.

"But they will know anyway. These walls have eyes."

"Honestly, Teresa. You would make a saint nervous today with your talk."

"I beg you again, Signori. Take the twins and seek safety tonight."

Teresa looked at the vial clutched in her hand.

"Thank you," she said and strode off.

The Baron watched her as she walked away. The wheat was waving in the wind with the dust rising up in the road. The men were working in the vineyards as the sea began turning dark in the final light of the day. The Baron thought, "How could there be anything wrong in this world?" It was nonsense.

When Teresa was again but a black speck on the horizon, the Baron rose with a grunt and went in to have a small meal with his young twins, a son and daughter.

Sins of the Father

Baron Felix Castellammare had returned to stand on his front porch after they had finished eating and watched twilight turn to velvet over the land. His gaze was in the direction of the sea, which was darker than the land that lay before it as if the land gave off light from the heat of the day that was slowly dissipating into the cooling sky. The Baron saw no mobs with torches making their way up from the village. Everything was quiet. As he had suspected, the business about an uprising was Teresa's imagination running away with her and nothing else.

He pulled out his pocket watch, checked the time, and calmly placed the watch back into his vest pocket.

"Angelina," he called quietly back into the house. "Where are you? What is taking so long? Hurry and bring the twins. We are keeping the good Father."

A few moments later, Angelina corralled the two children out the door and looked nervously at the Baron, as if something was not right. Having sensed this energy, the Baron almost asked Angelina the same thing he had asked Teresa earlier in the afternoon. What on earth is wrong with you? Instead, he tapped the twins on their shoulders and waved with his hand.

"If we are ready, then let's go."

In his leisurely but confident stride, the Baron stepped down from the porch and walked around to the road at one side of the villa and headed up it towards the church at the top of the hill. The church was visible as a darkening silhouette against the still pale sky, a half-mile away. This was not a grand building in any sense of the word, nothing even close to a cathedral, just a simple country church, but it had been solidly built of stone by local craftsmen and was handsome for all its modesty.

As was his fashion, the Baron went out ahead, leaving Angelina and the twins to trail along behind him. To him, the twins were precious, the future and legacy of the family, but not something to be fawned over. You let them sit on your knee now and then, but otherwise, life was a serious and demanding business. The Baron had little time for fun and games. When the twins grew up, they too would understand this.

From a distance, the Baron could see Father Ramone standing on the front steps of the church and waved as he drew near. Father Ramone waved back. Being that the Baron was a man of wealth and prestige, who gave generously to the church, the Father was all too happy to arrange these private communions and confessions for him and his family. If nothing else, it gave the Father additional opportunities to groom and nurture their relationship and at the same time, exact more money from the Baron.

"Welcome," Father Ramone called out as the Baron neared.

"Good evening, Father."

The Baron bowed and genuflected ever so slightly, and the Father made the sign of the cross. Angelina and the twins were not far behind the Baron and they too received the Father's blessing.

"Please, come into the home of our Lord," the Father said as he encouraged everyone to go in ahead of him.

They each stopped to dip their hands in holy water and cross themselves then followed the Father up the aisle. The Baron, Angelina, and the twins stopped at the second pew from the front, genuflected, crossed themselves again, and took a seat. Father Ramone went forward to the altar, lit more candles, spoke some words in Latin, said a blessing for Roseanna, blessed those present again, and proceeded to give communion, after which he went to the confessional box. The Baron nodded at Angelina, who led Vittoria into the confessional first. A few minutes later, she returned with Vittoria, looked nervously from the Baron to the front door of the church and back, then finally took Vittorio by the hand.

When she returned with Vittorio a few minutes later, the Baron insisted that Angelina do her confession next, but she refused.

"Please, you go, Baron Castellammare. I will watch the twins and go last."

Studying Angelina for a long moment, the Baron, at last, nodded his head and proceeded to the confessional. The minute he had disappeared inside, Angelina whispered for the twins to stay put and hurried on quiet feet to the doors of the church. With a look back at the twins, she peeked out, quickly closed the door again, and stood there with her back pressed against it for a long moment. You could have mistaken the look on her face for one of torment, or one of anger, or both. Whatever Angelina was feeling, she quickly crossed herself and disappeared out of the front door.

When the Baron stepped out of the confessional and saw that Angelina was missing, he calmly proceeded over to the twins and knelt beside them.

"Where is Angelina?" he whispered.

"We don't know, Papa," Vittoria said.

Though a girl, she had always been the more precocious and confident of the two children.

"What do you mean, 'you don't know'?"

"We don't know, Papa. She told us to wait here and went towards the door of the church and never came back."

The Baron looked in that direction and over at the confessional.

"You wait here," he said and went to inform the Father.

The Father appeared from the door of his booth and also looked around with concern.

"Perhaps she had a call of nature," the Father said.

"I doubt it. The twins said she went towards the front door."

"Then let us go have a look."

When the Father threw open the doors to the church, he gasped and shrunk back, clutching his cassock. There, on the road leading up from village, a mob of hundreds was marching towards them, carrying torches.

"God help us," he said.

After a moment, he grabbed Baron Castellammare by the arm. "Come, let us take the twins and retreat to your castle."

"Nonsense. What are we? Jackals? Besides, this is the house of our Lord. Do you really think they would dare to enter and defile it, or you, a messenger of God?"

"We should all fear for our lives before this mob, Baron Castellammare. At least let us think of the twins. I beg you again. Let's take them and run."

The Baron started down the stone steps of the church.

"I will run from no one. What would I have if I did? To abandon all that my family has worked for over the centuries. No!"

"Then at least allow me to take your twins to safety."

The Baron looked back.

"Do as you must but I promise you. I will go and turn this mob aside."

The Baron walked some hundred paces towards the approaching torches and stopped, his feet spread apart as if bracing against a stiff wind. As the mob drew near, it gathered new momentum, like a magnet to steel, seemingly drawn to engulf and overwhelm the Baron. Giuseppe, the leader, was first to reach him and held out his arms as if to restrain and silence the mob. The two men stood face to face, Giuseppe as tall as the Baron but twenty years junior and with a large, flat grim face that immediately encouraged mistrust. He seemed to be scowling at life, an appearance that his one glass eye only enhanced.

"Why do you come here to the house of the Lord in this manner?" the Baron asked.

"The house of the Lord, you say?" Giuseppe looked back at the mob with a derisive sneer. "How much will you bet the Father is in there right now with his whore?"

Giuseppe turned back.

"Don't talk to me of the house of Lord. Even if we forgive the Father for his blasphemies of the flesh, he's a whore for money too and is in bed with the Bourbons."

"You talk much of righteousness for a man who stands here, displaying none."

"To hell with you, Baron."

"Fine, to hell with me, but I ask you again. Why have you worked these men into a frenzy and come here in this manner?"

At hearing these words, the mob erupted in jeers and threats. Giuseppe gestured with his hands for them to be quiet again.

"Why? Do you not read the news? Have you not heard how your Bourbon compatriots have torn up our constitution and stripped us of our rights?"

The Baron looked over Giuseppe's shoulder at the mass of people with torches behind him, and then back into his eyes.

"What have I to do with this Bourbon filth? I am a Castellammanian. I am a Sicilian, like you. Like all of you!" he shouted.

"Then prove it."

"How shall I prove it?"

"By sticking a knife into that scum of a priest and helping us to clear the land of everyone who has consorted with these Bourbon scoundrels."

"I ask you again not to speak of our Father in this manner."

"Our Father." Giuseppe spat and glanced back at the increasingly restless mob. "I already told you. Our Father has long whored himself to his Bourbon masters, he whores himself to whoever will fill his coffers and he whores himself with whatever women will have him. What man of God is that?"

"So, you ask me to defile the church in order to save it."

"I am asking you to help us cleanse this church of that vile scum."

"No, I will not take up arms against God's house or any of His servants. If you don't like the way this church is run, appeal to the local bishop. If you don't like the way the land is managed, address your concerns to the village mayor."

"We did!" someone shouted from the crowd. "And he's dead!"

There was laughter. The Baron peered into the glare of the torches and back at Giuseppe.

"Do you not see what you have done now?" he said loud enough for the entire mob to hear him. "Whether today, or tomorrow, or the next day, there will be a new government, and you will have to answer for your deeds."

"We are the new government," someone shouted.

"And we are taking justice into our own hands!"

"Because we will never have justice from these Bourbon pigs!"

With these words, the mob grew incensed and surged forward. Giuseppe held out his arms to hold them back, but his efforts were no longer sincere.

"Get out of the way, Baron, or suffer their wrath."

"And I tell you!" the Baron shouted out. "Go home, before the earth is painted red with your own blood!"

It was the Baron's sincere effort to save these men and women from their own hands, but it did nothing but incite the mob further.

"Go on, get out of our way," Giuseppe said and shoved the Baron aside.

The Baron braced himself from this first blow, but then another man shoved him, and another man until the Baron had fallen to the ground and was being trampled by the mob. In a growing state of frenzy, those passing by took to kicking the Baron and finally they beat his head with the butt of their torches.

Having witnessed the mob disintegrate into violence through the cracked front door of the church, Father Ramone, tried to flee out the back door, but the mob caught up with him and dragged him back to his altar. As if in a final defense, he reached for his cross and staff, but Giuseppe pushed him down.

"On your knees, you bandit."

The Father began to pray in Latin.

Moments later, the mob was dragging the Father's concubine out of his sacristy, her hair disheveled, her clothes half torn. She was shoved to the ground next to the Father.

"Where are these twins?" Giuseppe demanded to know.

As if in a final act of redemption, the Father shook his head and refused to answer.

"Where are they!?" Giuseppe shouted.

Again, the Father shook his head.

Giuseppe grabbed the woman by the hair and shook her violently. "Where are they!"

"She does not know anything," the Father said.

Giuseppe struck him across the face with the back of his hand.

Angelina appeared from the mob and restrained Giuseppe.

"I will find them. They are here, and if not, they cannot have gotten far."

"Then find them. We cannot afford to leave one single trace of the Castellammare blood alive or there will always be a curse upon us for what we have done here."

"I will look in the vestry," Angelina said. "Someone, go check the confessional."

Giuseppe looked back at the Father.

"Only God can save you now, Father. The same with you, you whore."

They both kneeled there with their heads hung abjectly. The woman was crying, but the mob took no pity on her. There were cries for both their deaths until someone finally broke through and thrust a knife into the Father's gut. As he slumped over from the blow, another man slashed the Father's throat and kicked him over. The woman had cowered away in fright, but someone grabbed her by the hair and slit her throat, and the blood from both of them spurt forth in a fountain. It quickly gathered on the wooden floors, as if someone had spilled a bucket of red paint. In their rush to destroy the church and the altar and everything associated with it, men stumbled over the bodies and slipped in the blood and fell but continued about their work cursing. Giuseppe went to find Angelina and the twins.

Moments earlier, Teresa's husband Enzo had slipped into the storeroom at the back of the church and stood there warily in the darkness, listening to the bedlam out front, his long face accented on top with a tall forehead and below by a square jaw. With his strong nose, he was ruggedly handsome. With his clear eyes, he was seemingly kind. Knowing he had a minute at best, he hurriedly went about looking among all the crates and barrels. As he neared one corner, he heard rustling and turned a barrel out of his way.

"So, there you are."

The twins sat there hunched down, staring back. The boy put his hands up to his face and started crying, so Vittoria slapped him.

"Shut up," she said.

Vittorio continued weeping, but quietly. Little Vittoria did not like the smell of the garlic, cheese, and wine on the man's breath but sensed that she could trust him.

"Yes, the female blood was always the strongest in your family," Enzo said. "Well, I would just as soon leave you to the mob, but we owe your father. And your mother, God rest her soul, so I will save you."

He rummaged around and quickly found a heavy, cloth sack.

"Now listen to me. They are looking for twins all over the countryside and they will be looking for twins for years to come, so I must hide one of you. And since you are the strongest, young lady, it is best if I hide the boy. Do you understand?" he said bending down to look at Vittorio. "I am going to place you in this sack and carry you with us. I will take you up into the hills where you will be safe for now. And then once everything has died down, we will take you to live with a family. And then my debt to your family will be over."

He showed the boy the sack.

"All right?"

The boy looked at his sister and she nodded.

"We understand."

"All right. Let's go. We have no time to waste."

Enzo stuffed the boy into the sack, tied it shut, threw it over his shoulder, and waved for the girl to follow him. At the back door to the church, Enzo peeked out, saw people rushing this way and that among the nearby fields, but quickly realized it was mostly in a frenzy to destroy things. They were so enflamed with their passions; they were not alert to everything around them.

The minute Enzo felt no one was looking his way, he grabbed the girl's hand and hurried with her to a nearby grove of trees where two donkeys were tied, hidden from view. Enzo set the sack down, told the girl to wait with the donkeys, and went back to see if anyone had noticed them. The mob, in its frenzy of destruction, had set fire to the church but no one seemed to have paid any attention to them at all. Satisfied that they were safe for the moment, Enzo placed the girl on one donkey, strapped the sack over the other donkey, and started up into the hills among the cover of the trees.

The night was clear and warm. The hills smelled of sage and rosemary. The sky was dancing with stars. Against this peaceful setting, Enzo looked back down from the crest of a hill and shook his head. A half-mile away, the church was on fire. The whole scene reeked of madness.

Enzo led the donkeys higher and higher along a narrow trail that wound up into the rocky hillsides. They went over a rise and down into a small valley, then up over another rise, but always higher until they came to a cave near the crest of a peak. Looking back, you could see the lights of the small villages here and there along the land and then farther off still, the dark sea and the lights of more villages along the ribbon of its coastline.

Men with rifles laughed and called to Enzo as he approached.

"Your new girlfriend, Enzo?"

"Aren't you getting them a little young these days?"

"What, did your wife kick you out of the house?"

"Shut up," Enzo said and passed by them on his way towards the mouth of the cave.

To one side of the entrance, he tied off the donkeys and undid the straps that were holding the sack. With the guards still chuckling to themselves and making wisecracks, he led the girl into the cave and set down the sack.

A man met Enzo there with a cigar in one side of his mouth. He was bald with an egg-shaped head and hooked nose and was anything but handsome, but there was a sincerity in his dark, watery eyes that at once commanded your respect and made you feel safe. This was a man who knew the value of life.

"So, you brought them?" Ernesto said.

"Yes," Enzo replied, untying the sack.

The boy came out, rubbing his eyes against the torchlight in the cave and looking scared. The little girl stared at Ernesto. He tussled her hair gently.

"And?" Ernesto said to Enzo.

Enzo shook his head. A hint of sadness passed over Ernesto's face.

"Do they know?" he said quietly.

Again, Enzo shook his head.

"Go bring your wife. We will keep them safe."

Enzo went out and started to untie one of the donkeys.

"What's the matter, Enzo? Did Ernest steal your girl now?"

"Shut up," Enzo said as he climbed upon the donkey.

Soon, Enzo had disappeared, and Ernesto came out to the mouth of the cave.

"Not a word is to be spoken of this. To anyone. Am I clear?"

The men fell silent and stared. Ernesto nodded ominously and disappeared back into the cave.

The Twins are Hidden in the Cave

Enzo steered clear of all villages and settlements on his way down from the hills. Eventually, he came to a modest stone house on a knoll overlooking a valley. Having heard the rustling outside, Teresa rushed to open the door, saw the grave look on her husband's face, and knew it was not good.

"The Baron?"

Enzo shook his head.

"My God," she gasped and crossed herself and quietly spoke a prayer.

"And the girl and boy?"

"They are safe with Ernesto."

"Thank God for that."

"Come. I believe he wants you to explain to them about their father."

Teresa started back in towards the stove.

"I will bring them soup," she said over her shoulder.

"It is not necessary, Teresa. There is food there already."

"Not that rot Ernesto's men cook up."

"It is fine. Come. We have no time to waste."

"I will bring them food," she said and began to ladle soup into a small tin pot. When she was done, she screwed on the lid. "This will not slow us down."

"Fine, but let's go before Count Don Carlos learns the twins are missing and sends out patrols all over the countryside."

Teresa did not comment and went about her business as if her husband wasn't there. She finally gathered some bread and some of the twins' clothing.

"There, we are ready," she said as if Enzo had been the one holding things up.

Outside, Teresa climbed onto the donkey and Enzo led the way back up into the hills from where he had come. Early on, Teresa had asked Enzo to explain what had happened, but he made it clear with a sharp gesture of his hand that it was not the time to discuss it. Occasionally, they saw groups of men milling about among the villages, but no men on horseback or anything to suggest that Count Don Carlos already knew or that he had sent his men out looking, at least not this far yet.

Eventually, as Teresa with Enzo neared the mountain sanctuary, they were met with men bearing rifles. Seeing Teresa, they bowed out of respect. There were no more jokes about young girlfriends.

As before, Enzo tied up the donkey near the mouth of the cave, and as before, Ernesto came out to greet them. Teresa took his hand.

"God bless you, Ernesto. The Lord will watch over you for looking after these twins."

"I am more concerned with those who would kill me for doing so."

"Men such as that would kill you for far less."

Ernesto acknowledged this truth with a nod of his head.

"I have brought them soup and bread," she said.

"I did not feed them, knowing you would." Ernesto looked over his shoulder at the twins, now seated on some blankets along one wall of the cave. "I have left it for you to decide. If and when to tell them."

"Thank you, and may God bless you again."

Ernesto stood out of the way and allowed Teresa to go to the twins. She squatted down and took both of them into her arms. She cried and the effect of it was to make both twins cry too, the boy more so than the girl.

Finally, Teresa pulled back and looked into their eyes.

"Your father is dead."

The boy looked confused. The girl stared intently, seeming to understand.

"I am sorry, but I will take care of you now. Enzo and I will take care of you, but you must stay here for a little while. You will be safe, but you will have to play a little game if someone ever comes looking for you, okay? You must pretend that you are not brother and sister. Do you understand?"

The two children nodded. Again, the girl seemed to grasp things more clearly than the boy.

"If anyone recognizes you as twins, they will know who you are, and they will try to kill you too."

"We're hungry," Vittoria said, speaking for both of them. "Father had told us not to eat before confession because we would be having a big, splendid meal upon returning home."

"I know," Teresa said. "Wait here and I will bring you both a bowl of soup."

Once Teresa had found two bowls and cleaned them and had gotten the twins settled with their soup and a big piece of hard crust bread, she joined Enzo and Ernesto near the mouth of the cave.

"Now you can tell me what happened?" she said a whisper.

"What is there to tell you? They killed him. Father Antonio too."

"Was this not your job? To protect the Baron, at the very least?"

"He insisted he was safe," Ernesto said. "Or so you told us."

"I also told you to send men down there to protect him. You saw the people in the village today, Enzo."

Enzo shrugged.

"My God. The incompetence."

Teresa crossed herself and sent a kiss heavenward.

"Are you not going to tell me anything? Were they shot? How did it happen?"

"It doesn't matter," Enzo said. "They're both dead and we owed this debt to the Baron, so here we are. We can only hope it doesn't get us killed too. How are you going to keep this a secret down in the village?"

"Never mind. I will find a way. Just none of you say a word. Ever."

"Do you think we don't know how to keep silent?" Ernesto said.

"I know you do."

"Then let's not talk of it anymore. I'm sure Count Don Carlos will suspect us, but he will not dare come up here looking. Not without that devil Ferdinand at his back. The twins will be safe here for now.

What you do with them down there," Ernesto nodded his head at the villages below, "That is your business."

"What madness," Teresa said. "Of all people, murdering Baron Castellammare."

"He was a good man, or we would not be here helping."

Teresa crossed herself again and looked over at the twins. They were seated in the shadows and eating their soup and bread by candlelight as if nothing had happened. How *would* she hide them? Twins were a signature of the Castellammare blood, particularly male and female twins. The Baron had been a twin and his father before him and his father before him. If any of Teresa's neighbors or anyone in the surrounding villages saw the twins, they would believe they were Castellammares, whether they were or not.

One of them, alone, Teresa might say 'a friend of mine in Palermo passed away and left behind this orphan', but the minute the village people got wind of there being twins in the village, the rumors would spread and the men who had killed their father would come looking for them too.

For one night at least, they were safe.

Teresa walked back over to them as they sat on their blankets.

"Are you full now?"

"Yes, thank you, Zietta," Vittoria said. "When can we go home?"

Teresa smiled sadly.

"Someday, but not right now. Someday you will go back and reclaim the Castellammare estate, but for now, we must pretend that you are off to see the world. Doesn't that sound like fun?"

Vittorio began to cry, so Teresa comforted him. Vittoria sat and watched as though she understood, but never said a word about her thoughts.

"Come you two, let's sleep."

Teresa took their bowls and made them comfortable under the covers.

"God is looking out for you. Don't forget to say your prayers and thank Him each night."

"We won't forget, Zietta Teresa," Vittoria said.

"Good. I don't know how long you will have to stay here, but I will come to see you as often as I can."

She kissed them both on their foreheads.

"Now try to sleep."

Teresa tucked them into their covers and went out to stand with Enzo and Ernesto at the mouth of the cave.

"Are they all right?" Ernesto said.

Teresa nodded.

"As well as can be expected. No sign of torches?"

Both men shook their heads.

"The bigger the fire, the faster it burns out," Enzo said. "That mob will have burned itself out long before it reached the next village."

Teresa looked at both men.

"It is best if I go. The neighbors will get curious."

"I will go with you," Enzo said.

"No, stay here with the twins."

"No, you are right, Teresa," Ernesto said. "The neighbors will get curious."

"Then we are off," Enzo said and embraced Ernesto.

Teresa embraced Ernesto too.

"Thank you again."

He nodded and watched them both go out and gather their donkey and start down the hill. Teresa and Enzo traveled in silence for several miles.

"I still don't see how you will keep this a secret from the village," Enzo said. "Hide them in the cellar?"

"Don't worry yourself, Enzo. I will find a way."

Enzo could not see how but did not say another word.

Along the crest of the hills that cradled the seaside village of Trappeto, a man on horseback rode hard against the stars and did not stop until he had reached the front steps of Count Don Carlos' estate. As would be expected, the man on horseback had seen armed guards out at the gate and all along the road leading up to the villa itself, but these men recognized him and did nothing to stop his progress.

At the front of the house, a livery boy took the horse while another man opened the door and let the rider inside. In the foyer, a servant met the rider and led him to Count Don Carlos' study. The Count looked up from his desk and studied the man in the lamplight. The rider had an unusually tall, narrow forehead, which had the effect of making his whole face seem very long. It was a mostly rectangular looking face, but the round chin and tuft of fluffy hair sprouting up on the top of the head like a carrot top was parted down the middle. more or less, making the face look rounder than square. The eyes were strangely offset, one seemingly lower than the other and his ears, which sat very low in relationship to the entire head were, like the eyes, not quite symmetrical in relation to each other, or to the head. A goatee offset everything else. All in all, he was not a foul looking man. The overall effect of all these features was a one-part comedy and one-part curious sadness.

The man took off his satchel and pulled out a roll of parchment.

"The deed, as you asked."

Count Don Carlos quickly unrolled the parchment, nodded, and looked up at the man.

"You do not look happy, Romano."

"I have some bad news."

Count Don Carlos gestured for Romano to sit down.

"And what is the bad news, Romano?"

"I should say, there is good news and bad news. The Baron is dead, as is that pimp of a priest, but we did not find the twins."

Count Don Carlos slapped his palm on his desk and cursed.

"You fools! How could you have let them slip away?"

"Giuseppe swears they were not at the church."

"Of course, they were at the church. The Baron would not have been there if not for taking the twins to communion."

Count Don Carlos cursed again.

"That fool. I knew I should never have trusted this mission to him."

Count Don Carlos looked out the windows, fuming. Romano sat there silently, not wishing to speak, lest he enrages the Don further.

"And the rest of it?" he said, looking back.

"There is not much to relate. The mob burned down the church and then burned itself out by the time the men had reached the next village. They have all gone home now."

Count Don Carlos cursed yet again.

"Find them! Use your contacts. I will give you however many men you need but find them."

"And if they are up in the hills, with Ernesto and his band?"

Count Don Carlos looked back out the window. The warm summer night was turning cool now. The air was wet with the scent of the sea.

"I cannot afford to start a war with them yet. Not until Ferdinand lands here with his forces."

Count Don Carlos looked back.

"But turn over every stone in the meantime. Just don't make me any new enemies in doing so. Not unless it means finding those twins. And if you find them, bring them to me. I personally want to spill their blood onto the earth."

Romano nodded.

"That's it. Send out riders everywhere. Offer a reward. Quietly, of course, but let it be known that the new Baron of Castellammare will be very generous with anyone who helps."

Romano nodded.

"Go. Waste no time. I don't care about the hour. Night and day, I want men searching. Those little wretches cannot have gotten far."

Romano nodded and got up to leave.

"And Romano."

"Yes, Count Don Carlos?"

"Make sure and contact Leone, the mayor in Castellammare. Inform him that the Baron had sold his estate to me just before his untimely death. We regret his loss greatly, but the business must go on."

"Yes, Count Don Carlos."

With Romano gone, Count Don Carlos turned in his chair and looked back out the windows, his hands joined, his thumbs busy twiddling. He had sat there stewing for a good time before his anger suddenly erupted to the surface again and he let out with a curse that could be heard far out into the summer night.

The next day, an older man named Gino sat at the mouth of the cave with a rifle in his hands, a cigarette in the corner of his mouth and his legs dangling over a rock ledge. His job was to maintain a vigil on the countryside below him. Gino's lean, square face suggested he had been handsome in youth, but that face was now gaunt and wrinkled from the years. His already long nose had grown in the direction of his mouth and his lips had grown thin from the travails of existence. Nonetheless, there was a sparkle of mirth and kindness in Gino's weary old eyes and a measure of his handsomeness still showed through.

The twins had been instructed never to come out together, only one at a time and the little girl was the first one to show her face that morning.

"Ah, our little princess," Gino said.

"My father calls me signora."

Gino nodded sadly.

"I can see why."

Vittoria studied the man and looked down past the hills towards the sea.

"Someday I will go back and reclaim what is ours."

Gino's first impulse had been to nod sadly again but the statement had been made with such charming seriousness, he had to suppress a laugh.

"How long do you think I will have to wait?" Vittoria asked.

"That I do not know. At least until you have grown up."

"And when will that be?"

Gino considered his words.

"A girl becomes a woman at eighteen."

"And never sooner?"

"Sometimes."

"So, I will have to wait for at least ten years. Or perhaps a little less if I am lucky."

"Perhaps."

She nodded knowingly.

"Very well. I must go tell my brother."

"I think you absolutely should."

Vittoria nodded proudly and disappeared back inside.

The morning passed and Gino maintained his vigil in the countryside below. From time to time, he remembered the girl and smiled. She would be something to meet at eighteen, all right.

Towards late morning, Gino saw little Vittorio near the mouth of the cave, studying him. Gino pretended not to notice and went about his business, wondering when the little man would finally gather the courage to come outside.

Some minutes later, he finally did.

"Ah, so our little soldier has finally come out to see the world today."

Vittorio stared.

"Where's your sister?"

Vittorio pointed back inside the cave.

"That's right. You don't ever come out together. See, you're already getting smart. Come, sit down," Gino said and patted the rocky ledge next to him.

Vittorio did so.

"So, what do you think of this beautiful day?"

Vittorio shrugged.

"That's right. Who knows? Maybe you're going to fall in love today."

Vittorio stared.

"You see, that is the way of life. You never know what is going to happen from one day to the next, so you have to be ready for anything."

Gino gestured abruptly with his hands.

"Like a tiger, eh?"

The boy jumped and got big eyes.

"Not too big on talking, eh?"

Just then, Ernesto came up the trail with two of his men.

"What are you doing?" Marcello, one of the men said. "Starting a family or watching for trouble?"

"I'm giving the kid an education, okay? Then, he gets into trouble, he knows what to do."

"He's already in trouble, and so will you be if you keep screwing around."

"Who's screwing around?"

Suddenly, the two men were arguing back and forth with each other with a great deal of cursing. Then, just as suddenly, they were having a big laugh.

Ernesto and Marcello and the other man disappeared into the cave.

"Hey, bring us some lunch and a glass of wine!" Gino called after them.

"You want the antipasto with that?" Marcello called back.

"Screw you! Just bring the meal! And one for the boy too!"

Gino made the tiger gesture again and again the boy jumped. Gino laughed and patted him on the knee.

"That's okay. You make sure you're ready for anything and we'll be okay."

Marcello came out a minute later with two bowls of stew and some bread.

"Where's the wine?"

"The boss says you're on duty."

Gino let out with a string of foul epithets directed into the cave, to let the boss know what he thought of that directive. The boy stared with big eyes. A moment later, Ernesto appeared with a half glass of wine.

"Take it easy."

"I'll take it easy. What do you think? I'm going to fall asleep over one glass of wine. It helps me to concentrate."

"Then eat and concentrate on what's going on down there. That bastard Carlos has men combing the countryside."

"You don't worry. They know enough not to come up here."

"Yeah, well. Just in case. Pay attention."

"I was paying good attention until you two started screwing with me. Excuse me, young man."

Ernesto smiled and patted Gino on the shoulder and went back inside. Gino broke off a piece of the bread and handed it to the boy.

"Eat," he said with his mouth full of stew.

Vittorio stirred his spoon around in the stew aimlessly.

"You don't play with it, you eat it."

Vittorio had a spoonful and nibbled at the bread and stared down at the countryside falling far, far below them.

"Would you shoot someone with that gun if they came up here?"

Gino looked up from his meal and smiled.

"If it's someone who doesn't belong up here, I shoot them."

Gino patted the rifle.

"That's the idea."

"Someday I will shoot the man who killed my Papa."

Gino studied the boy, nodded, and patted him on the back.

"That's right. You find that son of a bitch and you put the gun right there."

He put his finger at the boy's head.

"Boom! Just like that, and he doesn't give you no more trouble."

Gino made the tiger gesture again, and this time, instead of flinching in fear and staring in fright, Vittorio made it back.

Gino laughed long and hard.

"Good boy. See? You're already learning. Now eat your stew."

The Baron's Death is Avenged

The following afternoon, a young man with ringlets of light brown hair and a pale, square handsome face came charging up the hill towards the cave in a great rush. Not yet eighteen years of age, he had that kind of youth about him, but his nose had been broken at some point in the past and was slightly bulbous at the end, marring what was otherwise a still innocent face. The broken nose aside, by his countenance and the grave expression on his face that day, you would have thought the young man much older than his years.

Gino, who was sitting outside with Vittoria and maintaining his usual vigil of the Sicilian countryside, became aware that someone was coming up the hill well before the young man appeared. The men stationed down below whistled at regular intervals. Gino could tell by the whistles whether it was friend or foe and how fast this individual was coming by the intervals.

On this day, the men were also having a good time at Mario's expense.

"What's the matter? Your girlfriend catch you with another gal?"

"That's okay, Mario. We'll ship you over to America. No gal is gonna catch you way over there."

Having heard a slew of comments along these lines, and the associated laughter, Gino was not surprised to see the grim look on Mario's face when the young man burst through the last bit of brush below the cave. It seemed as if his first impulse was to start a fight, or at the very minimum, to tell Gino to shut up. In fact, Gino had been thinking about having a bit of his own fun, but before any of that could happen, Mario's eyes came to rest on young Vittoria, and he stopped in his tracks. Though a few years shy of blossoming into full womanhood, there was no escaping Vittoria's beauty or the fact that she seemed much older than her age.

Mario stood there with his boots locked to the ground, and with all his attention focused on Vittoria for several seconds before he turned to Gino.

"Don't say a thing, old man."

As Mario started into the cave, Gino laughed and looked over at Vittoria. She had turned her head to watch Mario disappear inside.

"Ah, so both of you got it, eh? Well, maybe someday you two are gonna hear the wedding bells."

Gino called into the cave.

"I think you're sunk, Mario!"

"Just do your job old man," Ernesto called out from inside.

Gino looked back at the girl, patted her on the knee, and laughed again.

"You'd better hurry up and grow into a big, beautiful woman or you lose him, eh?"

He laughed once more and returned his attention to the countryside below them. It was a warm summer morning, but still early enough that there was a coolness in the wind and a bit of dew on the ground.

Inside, Ernesto took Mario aside and listened to his son's news in private.

"The word is it was that bastard Carlos. He paid Giuseppe to stir up all that trouble."

"And who told you this?"

"Salvatore. The one with the meat shop in Castellammare."

Ernesto nodded. He knew Salvatore. The man was honest and practical.

"Go on. How does he know?"

"Salvatore heard it through some other men in the village. Giuseppe was throwing money around, trying to stir people up and get them to join him. It was all about getting the Baron out of the way so Carlos could take over Castellammare."

Ernesto stared at his son.

"He's not the kind of man to lie, Papa."

Ernesto nodded.

"I know."

"There's more, Papa."

"Go on."

"A woman in the village heard Angelina talking. You know, the one who worked for Baron Castellammare?"

Ernesto nodded.

"She was taking money all along to keep Carlos informed of the Baron's business."

"Why would she do such a thing? The Baron always paid his people well."

"I don't know. They say she had a thing for Giuseppe."

Mario made a lewd gesture.

"You know. When a woman falls in love, she'll sell her children for a man."

Ernesto looked hard at his son.

"You know too much for so few years."

"It's the way it is, Papa."

"All right. We'll deal with this Giuseppe. And this Angelina."

"They say she fled to Palermo with her money."

"Eh. We'll find her. No one can hide from us in Palermo."

"They say she is taking a boat to America."

"No one can hide from us in America."

Ernesto patted his son on the shoulder.

"Are you hungry?"

"No, I ate in the village."

"Then go take this over to Gino and tell him to come in here. I have something I need to be done."

"And what about that bastard, Carlos?"

"Don't bite off more than you can chew."

"I'll chew him up myself if you'll let me."

"You will do nothing of the sort."

Ernesto put a hand on his son's shoulder as if to guide him back outside, but Mario pulled away.

"Why do you leave that bastard alive? He has men all over the countryside searching for us. Searching for the boy and the girl. If we don't kill him first, he'll come for us."

"No. He will never dare to come up here."

"No. He'll simply pick us off one by one down there."

"Listen to me, Mario. The man has too many friends in Naples. We need to wait and see how things play out with Ferdinand. Without Ferdinand, I would take Carlos in a second, but we must be sure not to overplay our hand."

Ernesto stared at his son and saw how his blood boiled with the need for revenge.

"You listen to me and you listen well. You never act when you're hot like a bull. You take time. You think and act only after you have considered every angle. Otherwise, you will find your own head lying on the ground."

Seeing his son still filled with rage, Ernesto slapped him gently on the cheek with both hands.

"You think you are alone? We were all like this when we were young. Ready to fix the world with a gun, but it takes brains too."

Ernesto slapped Mario on the shoulders.

"Don't worry. Someday, we will fix that bastard Carlos but now is not the time. Trust me. When Carlos sees what we do to this Giuseppe, he won't have enough men on horses to cure his fears."

"Then let me kill Giuseppe."

"No. You do not send a stallion to plow a field."

Ernesto slapped his son gently on the face again with both hands.

"When the time comes, I will let you take care of Carlos. Focus your mind on that and forget this other thing, okay? Now go tell Gino to come in here."

Mario did as he was told and watched resentfully as Gino disappeared into the cave with his father, so intent in his rage that he was completely unaware of Vittoria for several seconds. When he looked over at her, he saw she was staring at him.

"What?" he said, as he sat down several feet away.

"Are you going to kill the man who killed my father?"

Mario darted a glance at her and looked back to where the hills fell away down towards the sea.

"Don't ask so many questions," he said.

"I only asked one."

"And I told you to shut up."

The two stared at each other. The look on Vittoria's face was every bit as fierce as Mario's. When Mario looked away, Vittoria kept staring.

"Look somewhere else," he told her with a wave of his hand.

"If you won't kill him, I'll do it myself."

"I said, shut up!"

Mario looked back down at the valley below, still stewing. Some moments later, his father came out to the mouth of the cave with Gino, and Mario felt his blood boil all over again.

"Take whatever men you think you need," Ernesto said softly.

"I'll take Pascal. The two of us will be plenty."

"Fine but keep it quiet. We don't want any fingers pointing up here."

"We'll be plenty quiet."

"Good. Then go."

Gino started down the hill with a shotgun slung over his back.

"Oh, Gino," Ernesto called after him.

"Yeah, boss."

"Send someone up to relieve Mario so he can get some rest."

"I don't need any rest."

Ernesto studied his son for a moment and nodded his head at Gino.

"Okay, go."

Ernesto looked back at Mario.

"And your mother?"

"She says if you don't show up at home soon, she's moving up here."

Ernesto scoffed. Mario looked up from the countryside.

"Anyway, she was cooking food like mad and plans to ride up here with all of it."

"When was she planning this?"

"Tomorrow, I think."

"Then you'd best take some men and donkeys and go escort her."

"I'll go tonight."

Ernesto studied his son.

"And don't forget."

"How am I going to forget?"

"Because you're young and impetuous and that's what young, impetuous men do."

Mario scowled. Ernesto nodded and disappeared inside the cave.

Time passed and Mario's emotions calmed. The blood in his eyes receded a bit. He became aware of Vittoria there next to him, swinging her legs over the rock ledge as he stole a glance at her. Like Mario, she had ringlets of hair with a noble head and her beauty was sweet. It was the kind of beauty that made your heart smile inside. It made you want to lie down with her and dream.

When Vittoria turned to meet Mario's gaze, he quickly looked away. Then, realizing that she was still staring at him, he grew resentful.

"Look at something else," he said.

"Then you look at something else," she said.

Mario was starting to hate her. He hated that she was so beautiful. He hated that she was so beautiful and arrogant and proud.

"If you want to be useful, go bring me some lunch."

"I'm not your servant," Vittoria said and got up to go inside the cave.

A minute later, her brother appeared at the mouth of the cave.

"Hi, I'm Vittorio Castellammare."

"Oh, shut up and go sit down over there," Mario said.

Late that night, Giuseppe was alone drinking wine in a bar in Castellammare. He had taken his favorite whore upstairs an hour earlier, and now satisfied, he was seated in a corner, looking morose and drinking. Giuseppe heard people whispering around him, and being of a suspicious mind, suspected it was about him. The whole village was talking about the Baron and the Father being murdered and all the trouble that had been stirred up, but Giuseppe didn't care much what any of them thought. He only cared that the twins had gotten away. Count Don Carlos had paid him handsomely to do his job and he did not like that he had failed, even if it was only in part of it. He tossed back his wine and waved for the proprietor to bring him another one, wanting to wash away the lousy feelings.

While the proprietor was busy pouring the wine, the door to the bar opened and a man named Lazzaro came in. Everyone in the bar stopped what they were saying and watched Lazzaro make his way over to Giuseppe's table. With a look around the bar, he sat down and whispered into Giuseppe's ear.

"There is word that Ernesto and his gang of bandits are hiding them."

Giuseppe snapped a look at Lazzaro, just as the proprietor came and set the glass of wine down on the old wooden tabletop. Both men were silent until the proprietor had left.

"Has anyone seen them?" Giuseppe said quietly.

"No, but someone we know said that they had seen Enzo pass by that night with a little girl and a sack strapped over his donkey."

"So, what? You're saying the boy was in the sack?"

"What else could it be?"

Giuseppe nodded and drank from his wine.

"Plus, someone reported seeing Enzo go down and drag his wife Teresa back up into the hills later that same night."

Lazzaro shrugged.

"What else could it be?"

Giuseppe cursed and looked away.

"I understand your frustration," Lazzaro said. "There is no going up there without starting an all-out war."

Giuseppe nodded.

"Does Count Don Carlos know?"

"I did not tell him, nor do I know of anyone who has told him."

"All right. Keep this quiet and I'll go speak with him in the morning."

Lazzaro nodded.

"We will find them." Lazzaro patted Giuseppe on the hand. "We will find them and be rid of them very soon."

Lazzaro stood up and walked out of the bar.

Unsettled by this news and suddenly feeling weary, Giuseppe tossed back the rest of his wine, left some money on the table, and got up to leave. The stone promenade and seawall of the small harbor were just outside the door. Giuseppe went along the waterfront on that summer night, hearing the insects sing in the hills and the boats tied the seawall slurping from the slap of waves against their sterns.

The village went up into the hills and Giuseppe's home was up there at the backside of all the others. His mind was busy with a thousand thoughts. There were Count Don Carlos, the twins, his whore, and that wheat deal he had been trying to arrange in Palermo along with countless other things that needed to be done the next day. It would be a busy one and heading up the backstreets from the harbor, his mind was consumed, working out all the details. The wine, too, had dulled Giuseppe's reflexes so that he was totally unprepared for Pascal's powerful arms as they suddenly grabbed him from around the corner of a building. A hand went over his mouth and Gino dug a knife into his guts. He pulled it out and dug in again, higher this time and closer to the heart, and again, the knife sounding as if it had been stabbed into a sack of flour. Giuseppe struggled briefly to free himself, then went limp. All his cries of pain had been completely silenced by the coarse, hairy hand over his mouth.

"There, you foul, ugly son of a bitch," Gino told him. "The Baron is avenged, and you got exactly what you had coming to you."

With that, Gino dug the knife up further under the rib cage and found the heart. There was one last jerk of the body and Giuseppe expired. Gino and Pascal dragged Giuseppe down an alley between two buildings, where Gino added the additional insult of poking out Giuseppe's eyes and cutting off his tongue. The murder itself was a message to Count Don Carlos and anyone who would work for him. The eyes and tongue were a message to anyone who had witnessed the killing. Keep silent and pretend you saw nothing, or you will be next.

With their work done, the two men dragged the body back out into the open and disappeared up a street into the hills.

Ernesto, who left little to chance in life, stood pacing by the mouth of the cave late into the night, waiting for news. When he heard a whistle from down below, he stopped pacing. A minute later, he heard another whistle. Then, another minute later, Gino appeared. He nodded at Ernesto and leaned his rifle against the wall of the cave. Ernesto snapped his fingers and a man appeared from inside the cave.

"Bring Gino a glass of wine and a bowl of stew."

"Just the glass of wine," Gino said. "I ate on my way up from the coast."

The man disappeared. Ernesto looked at Gino.

"You idiot. I told you to come straight back with the news."

"Eh. It looks better. Pascal and I were having a meal at an inn. What did we know?"

"You'd better hope."

Gino's eyes rested on Ernesto.

"When I tell you no one followed me, you can count on that."

When the man came out with the wine, Ernesto whispered in his ear.

"Go down and make sure everyone is on alert. I would not put it past Count Don Carlos to retaliate when he hears the news."

"No one will miss that pig, Giuseppe. I can guarantee it."

"Perhaps not, but go down and tell the men anyway."

Gino drank from his wine. Ernesto watched the other man head down the hill before turning back to Gino.

"So, nothing?"

"I have slaughtered lambs that gave up more of a fight."

"I mean, you saw no one and no one saw you."

"No. If they did, I left them a message they won't soon forget."

Ernesto nodded and studied Gino.

"All right. Go get some sleep."

"I'll drink my wine. You know how it is, boss. You kill a wild beast, and the mind is up all night, telling itself wild stories."

"I know how it is."

He patted Gino on the shoulder, thinking he was a fine old man and a good soldier and regretting that it had been necessary to call on him in this way.

"Try to get some rest," Ernesto told him as he looked out over the land for a moment before disappearing back into the cave.

By the next morning, news of Giuseppe's death had already raced through the village of Castellammare. By noon, Romano had gotten wind of it out in the countryside and galloped in to gather whatever additional information he could. Having questioned a number of people and being satisfied that he had learned everything there was to learn, he galloped at full speed back out to the Castellammare estate. Count Don Carlos was already there, arranging to have the place remodeled and redecorated. The grounds bristled with armed men everywhere. The men and women working the fields went about their duties with grim faces and resentful looks.

Seeing Romano, Count Don Carlos excused himself from the carpenter he was speaking with and went over to speak with Romano at the far end of the room. Romano, with his long, sad square face and its offset eyes and a crop of hair like a carrot top parted in the middle, whispered in his ear and Count Don Carlos listened, then stood back with the eyes of someone who has just been told he has a fatal illness. After a long moment, he went to look out the window of his new study and stood there with his hands working restlessly behind his back. Another long moment passed while Count Don Carlos considered things and Romano stood there staring at his back.

Finally, Count Don Carlos turned to face Romano and spoke quietly.

"It was to be expected. They don't want war right now. We don't war right now, and now they have their petty revenge, so we leave it alone. Tell everyone to mind their business and pretend this never happened."

"As you wish, Count Don Carlos."

"For now, that is the way it has to be. The dumb bastard probably deserved it anyway."

Romano shrugged.

"This taking possession of Castellammare has stirred up enough trouble. I don't need to stir up any more right now."

"As you wish."

"And the twins?"

"As far as we know, they are still up in the cave with Ernesto."

"All right. Be discreet about it, but I want eyes everywhere. If any children should suddenly spring up here or there, I want to know about it. Ernesto is not dumb. He will probably separate them, so don't look for twins only. Be aware of any children who seem to appear out of nowhere, and just keep looking."

"We are, Count Don Carlos. The people are not cooperative, but we have eyes."

Count Don Carlos walked Romano out onto the porch, where only the previous day, the Baron had been sitting, fanning himself and talking to Teresa. Now the place was overrun with guns and dangerous-looking men.

"You're a good man, Romano. You know what to do. Take care of this thing and I will reward you handsomely."

"We will find them, Count Don Carlos, and I will deliver them to you like little piglets in a sack."

Count Don Carlos smiled and patted Romano on the shoulder.

"Go in peace, my friend. I am here for you if ever you need anything."

Count Don Carlos stood there watching Romano as he rode away, reviewed the workers in the field and his guards, and walked back into the villa.

Life in the Cave & The Twins are Separated

That afternoon, Gino heard a whistle from far below. It was some time before he heard the next whistle, and again before he heard the next whistle. Ernesto came out to the mouth of the cave, suspecting as Gino did, who it was.

Fifteen minutes later, Ernesto's wife, Constantina, appeared through the brush on the back of a donkey. Mario was walking beside her, leading two other donkeys that were bearing heavy packs.

Ernesto jumped down from the rock ledge to greet her. They kissed as older couples often do, on the cheeks.

"You should not be out like this," Ernesto said.

Constantina had a regal face, not beautiful, but kind and pleasant to look at and filled with warmth. She was robust, as older Italian women frequently are, but only slightly overweight with breasts the size of melons. She smiled at everyone in sight and gestured with a finger at Ernesto.

"While we're telling people what to do, a man should come home to his wife from time to time."

"Please, Constantina."

"Don't please Constantina me. Where are the twins?"

"They're inside eating."

"Then help me up."

Ernesto and Mario both helped Constantina up over the ledge.

"And bring the food," she said to Mario before going into the cave.

Seeing the twins, she went over to give them a hug. They knew her, but only vaguely, and were both a bit shy in responding.

"What is this junk?" she said, looking at their plates. "Mario!" she called over her shoulder. "Get that food in here. What? Are you trying to poison them?"

Ernesto gestured as if besieged and waved for the men to accommodate his wife. Once she had fed the twins and was satisfied, she sat alone with Ernesto farther back in the cave.

"Umberto is flexing his muscles in the village again."

"So, I have heard," Ernesto said.

Umberto was the leader of another group of men, that like Ernesto, offered protection and settled debts and disputes. Only, Umberto was not nearly as honorable as Ernesto. He cared nothing about the peasants. His only interest was in working for the landowners because the landowners had the money. Umberto was not against making a deal on both sides of the bargain either and often did so. What's more, he was young and aggressive and always feeling as if he ought to own Ernesto's Maggietory too.

"So, what do you plan to do?"

"Start a war, I suppose you want me to say."

"There is starting a war and there is sending a signal."

"So, what signal would you have me send?"

"I don't pretend to do your business."

Ernesto made a face that said, and what do you call this?

"Clip his wings, Ernesto. Before he becomes too emboldened."

Ernesto nodded.

"And what other business did you have for me today?"

"Someone stole three of Signori Assante's donkeys, and Signori Marzano has never been paid for the land he sold to Signori Scarpati."

Ernesto threw up his hands.

"These stupid fools. Life was simple under the feudal system. At least we did not have as many headaches to fix."

Constantina stared.

"I'll have someone look into it," Ernesto said.

She continued staring.

"I'll have to send someone to clip Umberto's wings. Anything else?"

"Come home to your wife someday."

"I'll try. Forgive me. With this Castellammare business." He thumbed his chin at the twins. "Who knows when things will calm down again."

Constantina stood up.

"Then I will go."

Ernesto started out towards the mouth of the cave with her and waited while she showered the twins with hugs and kindness again.

Outside, Ernesto nodded, and several men came to help Constantina down from the ledge and onto her donkey.

Ernesto nodded again as a gesture for them to go with her and the caravan of donkeys. The men started down the hill with a final wave from Constantina.

With his wife gone, Ernesto called in Mario and three other men and gave them instructions about the three stolen donkeys and this land business. They stared at him when he was done as if expecting more.

"That's it. Don't get any ideas about starting a war right now."

The men went away disgruntled, particularly Mario.

The minute they were gone, Ernesto took Pascal aside.

"My wife tells me that Umberto is growing bold again. Take some men, however many you think you need, and send them a message. I don't want any wars. Just piss along the boundaries of our Maggietory enough so that they have second thoughts about muscling in."

Pascal nodded and left. Ernesto trusted Pascal and his judgment. As big and strong as he was, Pascal had no need for bravado. He would whack Umberto hard but discreetly. We're still here. Don't get any ideas.

Ernesto went back into the cave and sat down to some of his wife's cooking.

The following morning, Gino again sat near the mouth of the cave maintaining his vigil over the valley below, while Vittorio sat by Gino's side maintaining his vigil of the old man. When Gino tossed a pebble down the hillside, Vittorio tossed a pebble. When Gino played with the stubble on his chin, Vittorio played with his chin. When

Gino cleared his throat and pushed the cap on his head back, Vittorio pretended to be pushing a cap on his head back. It was all done with unconscious flair on the boy's part and Gino did not miss a bit of it.

"So, tell me, Vittorio. What are you going to be when you grow up?"

"I'm going to have a gun and watch over the world and make sure that nobody makes any trouble, just like you."

"Yeah?"

"Yeah."

Vittorio was very serious, so Gino was very serious with him.

"I think the world will be a very safe place then."

"People will know that if they make trouble with Vittorio Castellammare, boom! Just like that. I fix them good."

Gino nodded and did everything he could to keep a straight face.

"That's a good boy," he said. "You make sure everything's right in this world."

Vittorio nodded somberly and looked down over the countryside.

A minute later, Gino heard a whistle down the hill. Then another one. A minute later, Enzo appeared through the brush. When Vittorio saw him, his eyes got big. Enzo nodded cursorily at the boy, reached out to shake Gino's hand, and in the same motion repositioned the rifle over his back.

"How goes it?" Gino asked.

Enzo nodded.

"The boss is inside."

Enzo nodded and went into the cave. Vittorio followed his movements with the same big eyes.

"What's the matter, Vittorio? You gonna fix him good too?"

Vittorio shook his head, clearly startled by the reappearance of this man who had saved him and by the things he did not understand.

"You see young man, no one can save the world all alone. It takes many. When you work alone, you can move fast, sure, but then there is more danger. When you work together, it takes more time, but then you are surer of getting things done right."

He tousled the boy's hair.

"Here, let's toss another pebble."

They each took one, tossed them, and watched them skip down the hill.

Inside, Ernesto was receiving the latest report on Count Don Carlos's activities.

"And what of Ferdinand?"

"There are rumors that Garibaldi plans to attack him here, then take the mainland."

"Attack him here? You mean *here* or in Sicily or at Castellammare or what?"

"No, they say he plans to land in Marsala and then head to Palermo and try to defeat Ferdinand's forces there. But they are only rumors."

"Then he will pass this way and no doubt make trouble."

"Why bother with us up here? Maybe someday, but not now. He will have his hands full with Ferdinand."

"You know much."

"It is only what I hear. And think."

Ernesto nodded.

"No, you are probably right. It makes sense. Take Palermo, then Messina on the way to the mainland. If he achieves his grand unification, then he will come back and try to clean up any loose ends."

"So, we wait and see. Perhaps they won't be the same kind of bastards."

"Perhaps."

The two men studied each other.

"Speaking of Palermo, I need you to go there and do a job."

Ernesto explained about Angelina. Enzo nodded.

"My wife knew she was a traitor."

"You knew this and didn't tell me?"

"The Baron was free to hire whomever he wished."

"And so, what if it costs a man his life, eh?"

Enzo shrugged.

"Just the same. Next time you tell me."

Enzo shrugged.

"So, you want this Angelina back here? Or you want her to disappear?"

"Find out what you can learn about her first, then make her disappear."

Enzo nodded.

"And what does your wife know about dealing with these twins? We can't leave them here forever."

"She has a friend who's a widow in Palermo. She's childless. We were thinking, bring her here and say the twins were hers."

"We can't leave them together. The minute someone sees twins, there will be talk, and soon after that, Count Don Carlos will know."

"So, we take one of them and deal with the other one later."

"Take the girl first."

"Now?"

"No. When you come back from Palermo with the widow."

"She will need a place to stay."

"Have her stay with you for now."

"Too many eyes, Ernesto. She will be safer somewhere else."

"All right. I will arrange a place. Near you. And I will send a man. I don't dare leave her or the child alone." Ernesto shrugged. "We'll say it's her brother."

"Better to say it's her husband. No one here knows she's a widow."

"As you wish."

"Just not with us."

"All right. When you come back, I'll have everything arranged and you come to take the girl."

"As soon as I'm back from Palermo, I'll see you."

The two men shook hands and hugged.

"Get her before she gets on a boat."

"I will."

Enzo started to leave.

"Oh, and send the boy in. It's time for the girl to get some fresh air."

Outside, Enzo told the boy to go inside but he did not want to leave Gino's side.

"Go," Gino said. "Take your nap and dream of killing all the bad guys and saving the world. I'll be here when you return."

He hugged the boy and sent him inside.

"Too bad for all this trouble. You could take him home with you and adopt him."

"I would. He's a good kid. He reminds me of when the world was a simpler place."

"When was that?" Enzo said.

"I don't remember. A long time ago now."

"You're dreaming, Gino."

"Yeah, we're all dreaming. Screw you. Go on your way to Palermo."

Enzo shook Gino's hand and started down the hill.

A moment later, Vittoria appeared from inside.

"There she is again," he said.

Vittoria looked at Gino as a princess would look at an unwelcome beggar, and then out over the countryside.

"I hope you have already killed the men who killed my father."

"One of them. I did. Yes."

Vittoria looked over at Gino with great interest, then her mood darkened.

"Why only one of them?"

Gino chuckled to himself.

"Your brother's a lot more fun than you."

"That's because he's not as smart as me."

"Ooohhhhh, I see," Gino said. "So, when you're smart, you're no fun."

"That's not what I said."

"Then what did you say?"

"Don't be silly. When will you kill this other man? Or will I have to do it myself?"

Gino stared at Vittoria for a long moment and broke out in laughter. She stared indignantly.

"When I take Castellammare back, you will not laugh at me."

Gino nodded with a wry smile.

"Young lady, if you can take Castellammare back, no one will be laughing at you. Not me or anyone."

"Well, I will! Someday soon I will."

"And I will be waiting for the news."

"I know. Because you won't be there to help me."

Gino laughed loudly again and got back to his work.

The next day, an enormous mob of people descended upon the church in Castellammare for Baron Castellammare's funeral, such that most of the crowd was left standing outside in the street. When the service was over, those inside the church filed out and those in the streets joined them and the entire procession started off in a plodding march towards the cemetery. Several men went ahead carrying an enormous icon of Jesus on the cross, while six men bore the coffin behind them. Other men held the icons of various saints aloft. Horns blared, women dressed in black wept and men followed along with their heads hung down. The village was drenched in sunlight. Everyone was dressed in black and looked weary from their grief as much as from the heat.

As was the unwritten law in these matters, a brief truce was observed between all parties and the members of the various gangs held to their separate places in the procession and did not mingle. There were guns visible everywhere and a smoldering tension in the air but nothing much came of it until some of Ernesto's men got into a fracas with some of Duke Don Carlo's men. Shots had been fired in the air and the men pulled apart.

When the cemetery was finally reached, dirt was being tossed on the coffin, and the funeral was over, the men with their guns melted back into the countryside and everyone knew that the truce was no longer in effect.

Pascal, the man whose arms had held and rendered Giuseppe helpless while Gino stabbed him, had attended the funeral and reported back to Ernesto later that night. Pascal was of those voluminous men whose weight somehow did not offend you. Perhaps because it was not flabby weight. That was certainly the case with Pascal. He was built like a bull.

You would never have thought to call Pascal handsome, but you would not have called him ugly, either. He did not seem particularly kind or mean. If anything struck you about Pascal, it was his serious demeanor. Seeing Pascal did not inspire one to crack jokes.

He along with a group of men had gathered around a fire in the cave to discuss the funeral and relate what else they had learned that day. A bottle of wine was being passed among them. Teresa had come up to see about the twins and had led them further back in the cave when the other men began to arrive, safely out of harm's way. They were at a distance, where the twins could see the proceedings, but not hear what was said. Both of them appeared eager to learn what was going on among the men, but Teresa kept them at bay.

"Did you see Count Don Carlos today?" Ernesto asked Pascal.

"I could have shot him if certain parties had not forbidden it."

"I told you. We will not be the ones to start the war. Not yet. If Garibaldi comes, we let that fire burn itself out. Then we'll see."

Pascal was not happy, nor any of the others. They knew that someone would have to pay for Giuseppe. It was only a matter of time, and who and when.

"What else do we know?"

Pascal took a drink and spoke.

"Giuseppe's funeral is tomorrow. I would shoot him too, but he's already dead."

Some of the men laughed. Pascal looked around at them. He did not seem particularly upset about their laughter, but neither did he look amused.

"What else?" Ernesto said.

"Romano is running around the countryside, prying his nose into every little thing." Pascal nodded over his shoulder. "Looking for them, I presume."

"Does he know?"

"Why don't we ask Romano?"

"Don't get smart."

"Don't ask foolish questions. Of course, he knows, and the sooner you get rid of these twins, the safer it will be for all of us."

"I will take your advice into consideration."

Pascal grunted.

"Don't get smart."

Some of the men smiled, but not Pascal or Ernesto.

"So, what else?" Ernesto said.

"I heard from some of the fishermen in town that Garibaldi has sailed from Sardinia. I'll shoot him too if you'd like."

"You keep shooting at things and eventually you shoot yourself in the foot."

Pascal made a face like he didn't think that was too bright, or funny.

The men talked for over an hour, during which time they finished their bottle of wine. Then some of them melted back into the countryside. Others went down the hill to relieve the guards. Some of them stayed and slept. The twins sat there watching it all by the light of the fire.

Once the meeting had broken up, Teresa helped the twins to bed and made her way back down the hills towards home through fields and groves, worrying about her husband as she did. She knew Enzo was in Palermo on a job. What job, she had no idea, nor any guarantees that he would return home. It was part of the life they lived. The danger was always present, and there were never any guarantees about anything. You might be alive tomorrow, you might not. With a mark on her head, Teresa had no guarantees she would survive the walk home but arrived safely a little after midnight and slipped in the door. Enzo was not there.

An hour later, she heard rustling outside and grabbed the shotgun they kept by the bed. She stood there with it pointed at the door. Then she heard the front door unlock and knew it was Enzo.

"Enzo?" she whispered just to be safe.

"I'm here."

Hearing that, Teresa put the gun down and went out to greet her husband. They were poor and never had much, but they were in love and always kissed as new lovers do.

"Have you eaten?" Teresa said, pulling away.

"No."

"Sit," she told him and lit the stove.

Enzo poured two glasses of wine and cut the bread. A few minutes later, he was eating a warmed plate of pasta with sausage. Teresa watched him without speaking. She never asked her husband where he had been or what he had been doing.

"I went up to see the twins," she said when Enzo was almost done with the pasta.

"You shouldn't have done that."

"They need attention, Enzo. They are only little children. No school. I don't think they've taken a bath."

"You could have waited. Francesca will be here tomorrow."

"But only the girl."

"Ernesto is right. We cannot afford to keep them together."

"It will break their hearts."

"Better broken hearts than coffins."

Teresa stared at her husband without speaking.

"I think the girl will take it easier."

Enzo nodded, wiped up the last of his meal with a piece of bread, chased it down with a gulp of red wine, and wiped his mouth with the back of his hand.

"I spoke with Gino the other day. According to Gino, the boy has already adopted him as his new father."

Teresa shook her head.

"What?"

"Then it will break his heart, even more, when they have to separate them."

"So, there will be a lot of broken hearts around here."

Teresa turned her head slightly and smiled without showing her teeth.

"Jerk."

Enzo nodded and got up to place his dirty plate on the counter. When Teresa got up to take care of the dishes, Enzo spun around and swept her off her feet. She squealed like a schoolgirl.

"I'll show you a jerk."

Teresa jumped into Enzo's arms, staring into his eyes and running one hand through his hair, as he carried her off to bed.

Very early the next morning, Enzo had coffee with bread and jam and headed up to report to Ernesto. As always, he had a rifle slung across his back. Nearing the cave, he came across the guards and they greeted him with a handshake and a bump of the shoulder.

Gino was out front with Vittorio when Enzo walked up.

"Careful, or you know who here will give you the Sicilian kiss. Boom. Isn't that right, Vittorio?"

Vittorio held out his finger, mimicking a gun, and said "Boom."

Enzo barely smiled and went inside the cave. Ernesto met him there and gave him a hug. The two men looked at each other and Enzo nodded.

"What did she tell you?"

"Not much. She loved Giuseppe and would have done anything he asked."

"Love is blind."

"You'd have to be blind to love that guy."

"So that's it?"

Enzo shrugged.

"As best I could tell. She didn't do it for money. I don't think. She cried when I told her that Giuseppe was dead. Anyway, I got tired of hearing her scream and having her spit in my face, so I put a bullet in her head. She sleeps with the fishes now."

Ernesto slapped Enzo on the shoulder.

"And Francesca?"

"She's coming today. She'll be here before dark."

"So, how do we handle this thing tonight?"

"Best if you slip her away without the boy knowing it."

Ernesto shook his head and looked to the heavens.

"I'll be glad when we're done with this chore."

"I wouldn't take the boy down there now. At least not for a few weeks. It might be best to leave him up here."

Ernesto scoffed.

"Give him a gun. The sooner he learns to use one, the better his chances."

"That's an image. The little godfather."

Enzo smiled.

"So, what do you want from me today?"

"Go give Pascal a hand. A farmer named Carmine came up and complained that some of Count Don Carlos' men have been keeping him from getting his crops to market. Take a couple of the young men with you and escort Carmine to bring back whatever food he has to offer us."

"You got it, boss. See you tonight."

Enzo went out whistling.

"You want a few more of those?" he asked Gino as he jumped down from the ledge.

Gino swore at him and Enzo smiled.

"I'll see you tonight," he said.

The two men nodded at each other, knowing what that meant.

Late that night, Enzo shook Vittoria quietly where she lay in bed. She opened her eyes sleepily. Ernesto and two other men were standing nearby. Vittoria looked back at Enzo. He put a finger to his lips and waved for her to follow him. She got up and did so with a look back at her brother. Enzo waved more emphatically and encouraged Vittoria along with his hand.

"What are we doing?" she whispered when they were outside.

"We're taking you down to live with a family," Enzo whispered back.

Ernesto and the other men had come out and stood around them. Vittoria looked from face to face and back at Enzo.

"What about my brother?"

"We can't have you together right now. When the time is right, he'll be taken to live with another family. Someone nearby. You'll see him again, but not right now."

Vittoria looked from face to face again.

"We don't have time to lose," Enzo said. "If someone sees you and your brother together, nobody's going to be seeing anybody."

"Why can't I say goodbye to him?"

"Because. He will cry."

Vittoria nodded and looked around again.

"And no donkey?"

Enzo scoffed.

"Wait here and I'll bring you the royal carriage. Come on," he said and pretended to offer her the royal treatment as he motioned down with one hand and bowed. "I told you we don't have time to lose."

"I have to pee first."

"Then go pee."

Enzo helped Vittoria down and she went off behind the bushes. The men stood there looking at each other. A moment later, she returned.

"All right, let's go. Your carriage is right down the hill here."

Ernesto made a gesture with his hands as if to say, calm down. Enzo nodded back as if to say, he had his own ideas about who should calm down.

With a final wave, he started down the hill with Vittoria beside him. Two of the men had gone out in front of them. Two of them fell in behind. Each of them had a rifle slung over his shoulder. They moved forward silently but steadily on a moonless night. A few times, Enzo had everyone stop at the edge of this or that grove, or on a ridge overlooking a valley and sent two of the men out to scout the countryside first, and once they saw a man on horseback, forcing them to hide and wait for half an hour to be sure, but otherwise they saw no one at that late hour and made it to the small village where Enzo lived without further incident.

Teresa was waiting for them at Francesca's new home and rushed to hug Vittoria as everyone came inside.

"God bless you, child. This is Francesca, and her husband Paolo."

Paolo nodded. Vittoria seemed unsure of herself, so Francesca just held out her hand.

"It's a pleasure to meet you, Vittoria. I hope you will be happy staying here with us."

Vittoria nodded and stared at Francesca. It was easy to do. She was beautiful, the kind of beauty that stopped men in their tracks, that drove them mad, the long neck and heart-shaped lips, the shock of long hair and fair eyes and kittenish nose that would fill them with longing and be a cradle to their dreams, but Vittoria saw something else. She saw a face that was sincere and noble and inspiring. It was as if Francesca smiled and wept for the world all at once. It was a face that had known pain and suffering and from those things had distilled a great kindness and compassion. But more than anything, it was as if in Francesca's beauty, Vittoria finally saw the mother she had barely known.

Having stared for a long moment, and feeling a secret joy in her presence, Vittoria suddenly threw herself at Francesca's skirt and hugged her tightly. Francesca smiled sadly at Teresa over Vittoria's shoulder as she rubbed the girl's back.

While she stood there hugging Francesca, Vittoria stole glances at Paolo in the shadows. He had a fine, square face with a clear forehead and a straight nose, sensuous lips. and oiled hair combed back. His mouth was bordered by two lines which made it seem as if his mouth had been clipped off on either end, and his eyes were a bit too close together, but they were honest, sincere, and intense eyes. All in all, he was a very handsome man.

This being the first time Francesca had seen Paolo, she too stole glances at him in the candlelight, and Paolo stole glances back.

When Vittoria pulled away, Teresa got down in a crouch.

"Do you understand? You have to pretend to be Francesca and Paolo's daughter. You're from Palermo and came to live here with your parents and to everyone in the village your name will be Cecilia now."

"But Zietta Teresa," Vittoria said. "When can I see Vittorio again?"

"Soon, soon."

"But I worry about him."

"I know, but we are only thinking of your safety. Don't you think you will be happy here with Francesca and Paolo?"

She looked up at Paolo for a moment then spun around and fell back into Francesca's arms. Teresa tussled her hair and shrugged at Francesca.

"You are okay for the night?"

Francesca nodded.

"Paolo will be here with you and there will be two men watching from our house. We are only right there across the street. I have told all the neighbors and they will confirm your story if anyone asks."

Francesca stared with a look that said she might be confronted with mortal danger at any moment, so Teresa reached out to hug her.

"Thank you," she whispered.

"Don't worry. Go home and rest. It's been a long night."

Teresa nodded and shook hands with Paolo.

"Thank you, too."

Paolo nodded and shook hands with Enzo. Nothing more was said. They left and Paolo, Francesca, and Vittoria were alone.

"Did you want a glass of wine?" Francesca said.

Paolo looked at her with those dark eyes of his that seemed to be burning.

"Yes, thank you. A small one, please."

While Francesca went off to pour it, Paolo leaned his rifle against the wall and pulled the curtains back to peek out the window.

Vittoria Begins a New Life

When Vittorio awakened the next morning, the first thing he noticed was that Vittoria was not there. He walked out towards the mouth of the cave expecting to find her sitting outside with Gino. When Vittorio saw Gino sitting alone, he went searching further back in the cave, where sometimes he and his sister had gone exploring together. Still failing to find Vittoria, he grew frantic and ran towards the mouth of the cave. Ernesto intercepted him with one of his big hands.

"Your sister's not here anymore."

Vittorio immediately began to cry.

"Don't be a baby. We don't cry around here. She's safe but we had to take her to live somewhere else."

Vittorio wept even more now and ran outside and threw himself into Gino's arms.

Inside, the other men stared at Ernesto

"What's the matter? You can't be nice to the kid?" one of them asked.

Ernesto grumbled under his breath, but said nothing.

Outside, Gino let Vittorio cry until he had mostly spent himself.

"Okay, are we all right now?" Gino said, holding the boy's chin up.

Vittorio shook his head adamantly from side to side and wiped at his sniffles. Gino stared.

"What, we're not men now?"

Vittorio stared. Gino punched him gently in the chest.

"What kind of bad guys are you gonna shoot in that condition, eh? We'll be overrun with bad guys if we all sit around here crying all day."

Vittorio stared, his tears stopped, but his anguish remained unabated.

"Listen to me young man," Gino said, leaning down into Vittorio's face. "You and me, we got each other, right?"

Vittorio nodded.

"So, what's the problem. Being here with your old Gino is not good enough for you anymore?"

Vittorio stared for another long moment before falling apart and throwing himself into Gino's chest again. Gino patted his back and waved with the other hand for someone to bring him something to eat. A man brought out bread with jam and some warm milk. When he could gather himself, Vittorio nibbled on the bread and drank some milk, but he remained distraught all day. Gino stuck with him and talked about guns and battles and of being men, and before long it was time to tuck Vittorio into bed. He awakened once in the night, afraid and crying for his sister, but by the next morning, he seemed to have turned the corner. He went and sat with Gino and searched the land below as if expecting to see his sister appear at any moment, but he did not cry anymore.

"You know how to use this?" Gino said, patting his rifle.

Vittorio shook his head.

"Okay. Maybe it's time for you to learn."

Gino put the safety on and handed the rifle to Vittorio. The barrel end immediately fell to the ground and the butt-end fell away from his shoulder.

"Not like that," Gino said. "What's the matter with you? You going to shoot yourself in the foot? Get it up here."

Vittorio struggled with the weight but finally had the rifle in position again.

"That's good. Now look down the barrel. You see?"

Vittorio nodded.

"You get that sight pointed at somebody's chest and, boom! That's the last thing he remembers."

Vittorio tired of the weight and put the rifle down. Gino took the gun back and stared out at the countryside. Vittorio looked up at Gino.

"How do you know when it's a bad guy?"

"You know. Usually, it's because he's pointing one of these back at you."

Vittorio stared for another long moment.

"What happens to you when you die, Gino?"

"You go with God." Gino looked over. "Or you go down there?"

"So, when we shoot a bad guy, he goes down there?"

"Eh. Who knows? All I know is, he's not around here to bother me no more."

Gino smiled and patted Vittorio on the back.

"All you need to remember is, we're the good guys, okay? We're here to help the people, so you see somebody giving somebody trouble, you step in and make sure there's not going to be any more trouble. Those fools with the government, they're not going to do anything to help us, that's for sure."

Vittorio looked down over the countryside and set his chin.

"Okay. I'll make sure no one makes any trouble for the people."

He was very serious now, so Gino was very serious with him.

The days flew by. Those days quickly turned into weeks, and those weeks into months and the young twins mostly forgot about each other. Vittoria's days were consumed with the demands of peasant life, where she became more and more like Francesca with every passing day, simply by virtue of association – proud in her bearing, firm in her dealings with people, grave in her awareness of life's unending struggle, but above all else, kind to those she met. It was a struggle to grow your own crops, raise animals, haul your goods to market each day, and carry water from the well, but Francesca did it with quiet dignity and Vittoria unconsciously emulated her.

In all this, Paolo lent a hand and looked out for the safety of his supposed wife and daughter, and not so secretly, the two fell in love. They were for the most part discreet, but Vittoria saw their furtive gestures of affection, whether in the kitchen or in the garden or along the road to the well, she would catch them secretly touching each other's hands. Just a brush in passing, but it spoke more of sincere love than all the poetry that man had ever written.

Meanwhile, Vittorio was busy learning to be a man and a soldier, and was becoming more like Gino with each passing day, quiet but determined, relaxed but always attentive, serious but quick to laugh. At his age, the humor in life was not always so evident to Vittorio, but he pretended to laugh along with the men and was at least very good at the serious part.

Vittorio would think to himself, "God help Ferdinand's armies if they should ever run into me." Gino would secretly watch the boy with all his seriousness and smile.

After much consideration, it was decided that Vittorio's safety was inextricably intertwined with that of Vittoria's and that there was no way for the two of them to be safer than if Vittorio remained living in the stronghold. Even apart, the twins simply resembled each other too much for a mere separation of miles to have fooled anyone. If you spotted one of them one day and spotted the other one the next, the identity of both would have been quickly compromised.

So, the months flew by and turned into years, and two young twins were never afforded an opportunity to see each other. They entered puberty and began to blossom into adulthood, and throughout it all, Count Don Carlos remained relentless in his efforts to ferret out and kill these two legitimate heirs of Castellammare. Early on, Romano had brought back news of this newly arrived couple from Palermo and their young daughter, and being made aware of their existence, Count Don Carlos assigned men to watch them day and night, but Francesca had cut Vittoria's hair short in order to hide her signature curly locks and called her Cecilia wherever they went, so in the end, Count Don Carlos could do nothing. Without conclusive proof, he did not dare spill blood and raise the ire of the peasants even further against himself, but he never lost his suspicions about this young Cecilia.

These immediate concerns were soon set aside, as the fate of everyone involved, including Vittorio and Vittoria, were soon swept up in the torrents of history. The reasons for the trouble reached so far back in time that no one could have pointed to a specific event or to an hour and say, there, this is where it all began. But, with the breakdown of feudal society in Italy and with the yearnings for democracy sweeping across Europe, it was only a matter of time before the revolution reached the shores of Sicily.

When Conte de Cavour, the Sardinian Prime Minister, signed a Treaty of Defensive Alliance with Napoleon III provoking the Austrians to attack northern Italy, the calls for Italian liberation and unification became even more urgent. The Austrians, Sardinians, the Papal Army, and the French were at each other's throats north of Rome. Insurrections against the Bourbon rulers had erupted in Messina and Palermo. While the latter was easily suppressed by loyal troops, these distant events had caught the attention of Giuseppe Garibaldi, who had raised a ragtag army to liberate his native Nice from the French, but now saw a more intriguing and feasible opportunity in these Sicilian rebellions. Rebranding himself a zealot for Italian unification, Garibaldi landed his army of roughly a thousand Italian volunteers near Marsala, west of Castellammare, and was soon joined by a gathering band of citizens.

Ernesto and his men met in the stronghold one night to discuss the situation.

"Pascal," Ernesto said. "What do you know of Garibaldi's intentions?"

"He attacked the garrison outside Alcamo."

"I know that. The bastards are right under our noses. I said his intentions."

Pascal shrugged.

"The word is he's proclaimed himself dictator of Sicily and is advancing on Palermo."

"The dictator of Sicily," Ernesto muttered.

"Wait till he gets there," Enzo said. "They're already battling from barricade to barricade in the streets, and General Lanza sits in the harbor with some 25,000 troops and a flotilla of ships waiting to bombard those fools into oblivion the minute they reach Palermo.

"Does anyone know the strength of his forces?" Ernesto asked.

"I heard 4,000 men," Mario said.

"4,000 men? Alone or with these local fanatics?"

"All told," Pascal said, "as Enzo said, 'they'll be slaughtered.'"

"Good, then everyone stay out of the way. Enzo, you take a horse and ride to Palermo. You also must stay out of the way, but see what happens and bring back word."

"I say we use this opportunity to rid ourselves of Count Don Carlos once and for all," Pascal said.

"We don't make trouble with 4,000 troops marching around."

"So? The minute they pass, boom! We take him out. You think Garibaldi's going to turn his little shit army around to rescue one landowner?"

"We wait," Ernesto said.

"Christ. When it comes to that bastard, that's all we do is wait."

The men grumbled behind Pascal.

"When Garibaldi is in Palermo, we'll talk about it."

"Yeah, we'll talk about it."

"That's it," Ernesto said. "Get on with your business."

The men went out grumbling among themselves and had soon slipped back into the night.

Two nights later, they were gathered again with the freshly returned Enzo.

"What is this I hear? That Lanza's troops surrendered and fled back to Naples?"

"It's true. The word is a British admiral intervened and prevailed upon Lanza to spare Palermo. Those Bourbon bastards are all gone, and Garibaldi is on his way to Messina."

"A wildfire soon burns itself out," Ernesto said. "As I had predicted. So how are things in Palermo now?"

"Mostly quiet, but when the locals saw Garibaldi's beacon-fires at the outskirts of the village two nights ago, you should have seen the madness."

Ernesto nodded in thought.

"So, what are we waiting for?" Pascal said. "The government in Naples will collapse in a matter of weeks, if not days. I say we go after that bastard, Count Don Carlos without delay."

"No, we wait until we hear what happens on the mainland," Ernesto said.

Pascal bolted to his feet and cursed out loud in one motion. The men watched him go outside and then looked back at Ernesto.

"Let's see what happens on the mainland. Then we'll talk."

The men grumbled and Ernesto knew he was losing their respect, but he still believed that caution was the best policy.

Two weeks later, word came that Garibaldi had entered Naples by train and was being hailed as a national hero. The next day, he surrendered all his successes to Victor Emmanuel, who was crowned the new king. A contingent of carabineers arrived from the new government a week later and quickly set about protecting the old Bourbon landowners.

Pascal was beside himself with fury. Ernesto had called a meeting and Pascal could hardly sit still.

"Go ahead, say it!" Ernesto said.

"What? I told you. We should have struck while we had a chance."

"And what? These new bastards in power. You don't think they would have come to root us out? We just sit there on the porch of Castellammare and offer them a glass of wine? No one was home, so we moved in?"

Pascal sneered as he listened.

"Think smart," Ernesto said, "Maybe it's never the time to go after Count Don Carlos, but this definitely isn't it."

Ernesto looked around at all the men.

"Besides, we have bigger problems to worry about. With some of the old aristocracy collapsing, there is increased lawlessness, with more and more lawless gangs. We need to recruit, just to stay strong and defend our own Maggietory. Let's everyone focus on bringing in some fresh blood. Meanwhile, I'll put out feelers with these new magistrates and see where they stand."

The men melted into the night and were back talking two nights later.

"Anybody got someone to shoot," Pascal said while passing around the bottle of wine. "I need to burn off a little frustration here."

"Stop screwing around," Ernesto said.

"I'm not screwing around," Pascal said. "What did we find out? These new jerks in power turn out to be even more corrupt than the old ones, which means I'm going to be looking at that bastard Count Don Carlos sitting on his throne up there for the rest of my years. So, I feel the urge to shoot someone. It's only natural."

"Look at it this way," Gino said. "If they weren't corrupt, we'd be out of a job."

"I'm not complaining. I'm only looking for pleasant working conditions."

"You want pleasant working conditions, I know a tailor who's hiring down in Palermo," Ernesto said.

Pascal gave him a gesture.

"All right, let's quit fooling around and get down to business."

"Three thousand years," Pascal mumbled to himself. "This way and that. The tides of history sweeping through Sicily and look at what we got. Everything just the way that it was."

"Are you done over there, Cicero?" Ernesto said. "I'd like to go over this list of new recruits before the sun comes up."

Pascal gestured again, drank from the wine, and leaned back on his elbow.

"I vote for the little godfather here."

He rubbed Vittorio's head and waited for Ernesto to continue.

Vittoria Visits the Cave to See Vittorio

All through that fall and into the following spring, the residents of Castellammare watched as fresh boats docked in the harbor and new magistrates and judges disembarked, accompanied by scores of carabineers, all of them representing the King of Sardinia and promptly offering protection to the old Bourbon landowners, or anyone else who would kiss their boots and shower them with gifts, Count Don Carlos included. Thus, with all that had changed, nothing really had. Things continued more or less as they had for centuries; and just as it continued, the common people of Sicily did not bother much with these new authorities and showed them little respect. The troops marched along the roads to Marsala or Palermo, but the minute they ventured up into the hills or made any trouble for Ernesto and his gang, shots were fired, and the troops would retreat.

Now fourteen and a young woman in bloom, Vittoria had watched these events with renewed frustration. Her hopes of reclaiming Castellammare had been dashed again. Having seen in Garibaldi an anarchist as many did, she had expected him to sweep away the old Bourbon royalty, to no avail.

Having nowhere else to turn, Vittoria realized it was now time to seek the help of her brother. She had never forgotten about him. In fact, she had thought often of Vittorio, but had never considered violating their imposed separation until now.

One day, with the excuse of going into Castellammare on business, she headed instead up into the hills. The farther she traveled, the more the way became unfamiliar to her. Plus, things had changed with the years, a new home here, an old one had fallen into ruin, but an instinctive memory from her trip up to the mountain guided Vittoria back and she eventually came to the slope directly below the cave and Ernesto's stronghold.

A young man with a rifle quickly intercepted her.

"Where do you think you're going, little beauty?"

"I am looking for my brother, Vittorio."

The young man made his face long with a knowing look and nodded his head.

"And you are?"

"Vittorio's sister. Don't be stupid."

"I would be stupid to admit I know anything about a Vittorio, let alone to allow you to pass up this hill."

"Then tell Ernesto I'm here to see my brother. You know Ernesto, don't you?"

"I have heard of him."

"Don't be stupid. And don't think I'm stupid. I know who you are now. You're Ernesto's son, Mario."

"Hmm," Mario said and nodded. "And I seem to remember you. But you don't look quite the same without all the curly hair."

"It stopped being curly. I don't control such things.

Vittoria stared seriously at Mario. He studied her back for a long moment and then whistled at someone up the hill. A minute later, another young man appeared out of the brush and trees.

"Take my place. I need to escort our lost little bird here up the hill."

The man nodded while staring at Vittoria.

"Come," Mario said to her and started up the hill with his rifle slung over his shoulder.

Vittoria followed along holding up her dress as they trudged up the hill. They passed a man, then two more, then another two, stationed at set intervals along the hillside. After several minutes, they scrambled up the last of the slope and came to the ledge of rock that guarded the entrance to the cave. As had been the case six years earlier, Gino sat there maintaining a vigil on the valley below, and though he was older and grown wiser with age, he was still kind, gentle, and patient-looking behind his craggy face.

"Guess who I have here?" Mario said.

Gino nodded, studying Vittoria.

"You are a long way from home, young lady."

"I have been a long way from home since that day Enzo swept me up and carried me away from Castellammare. I want to see my brother."

Gino nodded at her and looked at Mario.

"He's inside eating."

"Wait here," Mario said.

He leaped up over the rock ledge and disappeared inside. A few moments later, he reappeared with Ernesto.

"You shouldn't be here."

"Well, I am."

"I see that."

Vittoria saw a familiar looking face appear in the shadows behind Ernesto. When their eyes met, Ernesto looked over his shoulder and back.

"You'd better come inside."

Mario reached down and helped Vittoria over the ledge. Inside, she was face to face with her brother now. Her eyes adjusted to the darkness and she saw the similarities you could not ignore, the same straight, clean nose, the same sensuous lips, the upper lip slightly smaller than the lower, the same dimple above the upper lip, the same cheeks that seemed as if they had grown ever so slightly inflated, the same serious but sensitive eyes, though Vittorio's had narrowed a bit and his skin had darkened, perhaps in both cases from being out in the elements so much. Conversely, Vittoria's skin remained fair and light and her eyes still had that almost unnatural fullness of a child's.

As if drawn by their ancient bond and common chemistry forged in the womb, they both stepped forward and embraced.

"It is good to see you," Vittoria said.

"It is good to see you." Vittorio replied.

Vittoria looked around at the men in the cave.

"Come, I need to talk with you in private," she said to Vittorio.

When she encouraged him to join her in the furthest depths of the cave, the men all looked to Ernesto for instructions. He stared, his watery eyes flashing this way and that until finally, he nodded to say, it's all right. Let them go.

When they were some fifty feet away, Vittoria turned and looked to make sure no one had followed them or was listening before she spoke.

"We must take Castellammare back ourselves. No one is going to help us."

Vittorio nodded.

"Do you understand?"

"Ernesto tells us to wait for the right moment, so we wait."

"He is always waiting for the right moment. He will always be waiting for the right moment. When this or that new leader comes and the stars are aligned. We are always waiting for the perfect hour to strike, but that moment will never come."

Vittorio stared silently and without passion.

"Vittorio. I'm telling you. Either we take Castellammare ourselves or we'll never see it again."

"How can we go up against Carlos's army?"

"I don't mean now, this very minute, but we must start planning. We must plan and prepare and be ready to strike when the opportunity presents itself."

Vittorio stared.

"What?" Vittoria said.

"I don't know. I don't share your passions."

"Vittorio, how can you not? It belongs to us. It belonged to our ancestors. Our family has lived there for hundreds of years, and we would be now if that bastard had not come and stolen it from us. If for no other reason, we must do it to honor our father's name. He must be turning in his grave."

"What do you propose to do?"

"I don't know. I just wanted to see you and make sure you were with me. And to agree to start planning."

He shrugged.

"I'm willing to try, but I don't have much hope."

Vittoria placed her hands on Vittorio's shoulders.

"Don't think like that. Trust in me and I will give you hope. This is not a sin we commit. It is our God-given right and we will have it back."

"I said I'm willing to try."

"Okay."

Vittoria smiled a bit and brushed the hair back from Vittorio's forehead.

"I knew you would grow up handsome."

He looked away, seemingly embarrassed by the comment.

"You are. I'm so glad to see you again. I have thought of you often. Have you thought of me?"

"Of course. Many times. I have thought to go down and find you, but there is danger everywhere. I have no right to drag it to your doorstep."

Vittoria hugged her brother.

"We will dispense with this *danger.* Someday we will dispense with it once and for all."

They heard stirrings at the front of the cave and looked that way.

"I should probably be getting back."

Vittoria started that way but suddenly stopped and grabbed Vittorio by the arm.

"We must figure a way to meet again."

"Here?"

"No. I will talk to Paolo. He will help us. Somewhere in between. I know a place where we will be safe."

Vittorio started back and again Vittoria grabbed him by the arm.

"Oh, there is one other thing. Mama once told me of a secret place where she had hidden all her jewels. If we can somehow get our hands on them, we will have the money we need to hire men to get rid of Count Don Carlos."

"Why do you think it's still there?"

"It's still there. It's in a place where no one would ever think to look."

"And you remember where."

She nodded.

"Someday, when we are ready, I will tell you."

Ernesto eyed them suspiciously when they returned to the mouth of the cave.

"So, you have your conspiracy all worked out."

Vittoria looked at Ernesto in the way she would always look at common people, as one who feels superior to them.

"You forbid me seeing my brother for six years and now you argue with us talking alone?"

"Time has failed to teach you manners, I see."

"I have lived with your manners. I know your manners. We talked. Don't make too much of it."

"People who have nothing to hide don't go off and talk in secret."

"This from you, the man who has lived in a cave for thirty years."

"I live because of this. When people start dying because of your scheming, then we will see who looks wise and who looks like a fool."

Vittoria nodded and started to leave.

"Don't come here again. You endanger yourself and you endanger all of us."

"I will heed your words. Goodbye, Vittorio."

She hugged him again, gathered her skirt, and jumped off the ledge on her own. Mario fell in with her.

"I don't need your help," she said.

Mario looked back at Ernesto.

"Go with her as far as Calatafimi."

With an indignant look at both Ernesto and Mario, Vittoria started down the hill at a resolute pace. Every so often, she would turn her head back and glower indignantly again at Mario. He kept some distance back, so as not to be too stung by those looks.

At her present age, Vittoria was often governed by powerful emotions, but she was cunning above all else, and the thought eventually entered her mind:

"How can I use this person?"

Accordingly, she slowed her pace and finally turned to wait for Mario while they were in the shade and cover of a grove.

"This is silly, walking apart," she said.

"It was my thought too."

"So," she said and started forward again but alongside Mario now.

Every few paces, she looked over at him. When he looked back, she held his gaze, knowing the power of her beauty and seeing it work readily on Mario. As a bull set loose in a pasture with cows, his tail had gone up. His nostrils had flared. Vittoria studied his every unconscious signal and waited until he seemed on the verge of snorting before she tapped lightly on his manhood.

"I remember being a foolish little girl and having a crush on you."

Mario looked over.

"And now?"

She studied him for a long moment and let the slightest hint of a smile cross her face.

"I no longer have time for being foolish."

She left her beguiling smile on him for another long moment before looking forward, assured that the hook had been set and seeing the evidence in her peripheral vision. Mario fidgeted with the buttons of his shirt. He ran a hand through his hair, cleared his throat, and held his chin up.

Without warning and without looking Mario's way, Vittoria reached over and held his hand. When they had walked in this manner for several paces, Vittoria squeezed a little harder.

Her cunningness had become what it was as she had studied very carefully Francesca's stealth touches of the hand of Paolo, and the other little gestures of endearment they shared.

She had witnessed on regular occasions the look in Paolo's eyes as he looked at Francesca, and she saw that same look in Mario's eyes now.

It was all she could do to keep from smiling to herself.

On the outskirts of Calatafimi, she turned to face Mario, still holding his hand, and with her body as close as was possible without touching his. Though he was eight years her senior, Mario stared back, as dumb as an ox now.

"Perhaps I'll see you again," she said.

Seeing he was about to charge forward, she put a finger to his lips. "I'm just a girl, remember? But someday, I won't be."

She let that thought stir the Mario a bit and reached up to kiss him on the cheek.

"Thank you," she said. "For watching over me."

She turned and walked away, and Mario stood there, helplessly watching her. A hundred yards down the road, Vittoria looked back without stopping, waved, and headed on her way.

Not until she had disappeared around the bend did Mario finally turn and head on his way home.

That spring, the new government held a referendum on unification. The authorities in Sicily cherry-picked who was allowed to vote, and the measure passed with a resounding seventy-five percent. Again, no one much believed in the results of the vote, and the way people felt about it was of little consequence. The new King and his government were entirely focused on the north, fighting with the Austrians and attempting to unify the northern part of Italy. All of their resources were focused to that end, leaving the people of Sicily impoverished and left to govern themselves once again.

So, the carabineers and new magistrates put on a show and the people allowed it. The only thing that had changed substantially was the color of the uniforms.

One of the magistrates, Bernardo Altobelli, turned out to be a sincere man and made an overture to Ernesto. "Let us meet. On neutral ground. I'll come alone."

Through his intermediaries, Ernesto was assured of Bernardo's sincerity and agreed. They were to meet at a particular crossroads. It would give Ernesto and his men an unobstructed view for miles. Any attempt to ambush them with troops or carabineers and his men would simply melt back up into the hills.

Somewhat to Ernesto's surprise, Bernardo rode out alone on horseback. When he arrived at the crossroads, he dismounted and stood there waiting. Ernesto and his men were hidden among the brush and trees nearby, watching and waiting.

After several minutes, when it became clear that Bernardo had nothing up his sleeve, Ernesto and three of his men rode down to meet the man.

"I am Ernesto," he said from his horse.

The man bowed his head slightly. Ernesto stared, wary, but he liked the man. He had a big, handsome face with a tall forehead, a receding hairline, a straight, strong nose, intense, sincere, furrowed eyes, and a caterpillar mustache.

"What is it you want from me?"

"Peace, if it can be had."

"What peace can be had when your government is so at odds with the interests of our people?"

"I understand your concerns and I share them, but I am only one man. If we can find no way to build trust and deliver results, eventually they will come after you and everyone else up there in the hills and it will not turn out well."

"They have been coming to look for us for 2,000 years."

"It is different now, Ernesto. The world is changing. You go on like this and you will become like those natives over in America. The modern world will run you over."

"What do you propose?"

"To achieve small victories together."

"Why do you choose me? There are hundreds of men up in the hills."

"Because I am told you are honest."

Ernesto nodded.

"So, what is your plan?"

"You tell me your complaints. I will see what I can do to address them. If we can go about it in this way, everyone wins. If we fail, we will have lost little but our efforts to try."

Ernesto studied Bernardo, thinking.

"Count Don Carlos continues to make threats and hamper the people I protect from getting their goods to market. Make him stop and you will have gained a bit of my trust."

Bernardo nodded.

"I will see what I can do."

"We will all see what you can do."

The two men nodded respectfully at each other and Ernesto rode off with his men. Bernardo watched them for a long moment before mounting his horse and riding back towards Castellammare.

Vittoria Falls in Love

In those days, one of Vittoria's jobs was to deliver eggs, fresh produce, and meat to the local merchants and collect the funds. So, every morning she set out in a small wagon, wearing a peasant dress and straw hat. Along the road, she would see the carabineers here and there as she went, and being shrewd, she had learned to be cordial and flirt with them until she had them eating out of her hand.

Francesca and Paolo initially kept a close eye on Vittoria as she went out into the world, but came to trust in her shrewdness, especially since they had a guard watching over her, and they frequently used her absence to satisfy their passions.

So, it was that early summer morning, Francesca returned to the house carrying a basket of zucchini and eggplant. A few moments later, Paolo took off his hat, wiped his brow with the sleeve of his shirt, squinted up at the sun in the sky, and headed towards the front door.

When he entered the house, Francesca rushed to greet him with a long kiss and embrace.

"I am worried," Francesca said.

"About what?" Paolo asked her, while still holding her in his arms.

"I keep seeing a young man along the road when Vittoria goes out."

"Yes. What about it?"

"I'm worried that he's following her."

"Why are you worried? She has a guard," Paolo replied.

"I know that," she said. "It's someone else."

"Oh that," he said. "It's Mario. Ernesto's son."

"So? What are you trying to tell me?"

"Oh God, Francesca. Use your head. I think they're in love."

Francesca was shocked by Paolo's response and he reached out and embraced her again.

"For God's sake, stop worrying. I told you. If I am not watching her, someone else is."

"So why haven't you stopped them?"

"What? Were you never young and in love?"

Francesca tried to break free, but Paolo held her.

"Let me go."

"What are you going to do? Go out there and make a scene for the carabineers to see? You'll be lucky if Count Don Carlos doesn't hear you up in Castellammare."

"I said, let me go."

"And I said, stop it."

Paolo had said this as he held Francesca close to him.

"I know everything she does."

Francesca stared, as curious for answers as she was furious.

"I saw them kiss once, okay? But that's it. If for one second it looks to go beyond that, I'll stop them. Otherwise, who cares?"

"I care."

"For Christ's sake, Francesca. She's a young woman. It's going to happen. Sooner or later, it's going to happen and better with someone like Mario. He's a good kid. He comes from good blood and at least he can look after her."

"What are you, a breeder all of a sudden?"

"Oh, you are a beautiful, silly woman."

Paolo held her close.

"God, I love you," he said. "You are so beautiful. If I could be here in your arms forever and nowhere else, I would."

She looked up at him and smiled, but a moment later, Francesca was pulling away.

"I need to go find her."

Paolo grabbed her by the arm and pulled her back.

"Like hell, you will. She's safe. There is always a man watching her, and Mario. You go out there and make a scene and the news will be all over Sicily."

"Let me go."

Paolo smiled and kissed her tenderly.

"You go and I'll go after you and we'll turn this whole village into a circus."

Francesca stared.

"Come on," Paolo said. "Let's go to work in the garden. Your daughter is safe. So, she's falling in love. Quit fighting life and let it be what it is."

Francesca made a mocking, half comical face at Paolo.

"The great philosopher now. Eh."

He laughed and grabbed her rear. She slapped at his hands and pulled away.

"All right, the great Cicero. Let's see you go pull weeds."

Paolo laughed again.

"I came in here to get a glass of chilled wine," Paolo said.

"And got distracted."

"Yeah, I did."

He smiled a big white smile and headed down into the cellar.

"Here, I poured one for you too," he said, coming back up.

They drank, and when Paolo set his glass down, he grabbed Francesca around the waist.

"I'm getting distracted again."

"Get away from me, you big gorilla."

Francesca slipped free and Paolo chased her out the door.

Down in the village, Vittoria had finished distributing her goods and collecting her funds and had stopped at a store to look at dresses. There was one that had come from Naples via Palermo and Vittoria touched the fabric longingly.

"Only twenty piastres," the women said.

Only twenty piastres. It was more than Vittoria made in a month.

She felt the fabric again, thanked the woman, and left. It was hot so she slipped around to the back of the buildings and walked into a nearby orchard. She was deep among the trees when Mario revealed himself. Vittoria stopped and stared. Mario stared back, hungering for what he could not have. Vittoria had turned 15 that spring and was full of womanhood, like a rosebud, bursting at its petals and ready to bloom, but Mario could not have her yet.

He came forward and she allowed him one kiss. She knew he wanted more, so to soften his frustrations, she placed a gentle hand to his face.

"Dear Mario."

"Dearest Vittoria. Someday I will marry you."

"Oh, Mario. Have you forgotten what I said?"

"No. I have not forgotten."

"And yet you bring me no news."

"What news can I bring you? Count Don Carlos has licked the boots of these Sardinian bastards and is stronger than ever. We must wait."

"Always wait. I know. That's what your father always says."

"It is not only because my father says it. It's the prudent thing to do. As long as he is protected, you'd be a fool to touch him."

"Yes, there was a time we could have struck. When all was chaos. Who would have cared then? But your father is always a cautious man, and now..."

Vittoria pulled away and walked. Mario rushed to catch up with her.

"Vittoria, please. Someday, I will kill that lying thief Count Don Carlos myself and return Castellammare to you. I promise. But you must be patient."

Vittoria glared sidelong at him.

"You talk to me of patience? I have been waiting for six years now. Patiently. That is nearly half of my life and I have run out of patience. What I need are courage and bravery."

"Oh, Vittoria. Please, be patient."

She bristled anew at hearing that word again.

"I mean, at least show some understanding. What are we going to do? If we strike Count Don Carlos right now, we'll have these carabineers all over us. I will find a way, I promise you, but we must wait until the time is right."

"Of course. Be patient."

She pulled away and walked in the other direction. When Mario caught up with her again, she had tears in her eyes.

"Oh, my love."

He stopped her and wiped the tears from her cheeks. She let Mario stew in this vision of grief for a long moment and allowed him to one more brief but tender kiss from her lips before pushing away.

"I must go now. My mother will be worried about me."

"Please don't go yet."

"No, I must." She touched his face tenderly. "Please come see me again. Soon."

"I will. I love you."

She smiled and touched his face.

"I must go."

"Let me walk with you."

"No. If Paolo sees me with you, he will be very angry."

"I don't care."

She put a finger to his lips.

"I do. I have to live with him."

She gently stroked Mario's cheek.

"Soon, okay?"

He nodded, still helpless before her.

Vittoria walked off with a secret smile, feeling as a puppeteer feels, pulling strings. Taking her time, she did not arrive home until very late that afternoon.

Turning the latch on the front door, Vittoria was about to open it when the door flung open from the inside. Hearing the wagon arrive, Francesca had been waiting there and dragged Vittoria in by the arm. Had Vittoria's hair been more convenient, Francesca probably would have used that instead. She slammed the door shut and embarked on a tirade. Vittoria listened without the slightest sign of intimidation or anger. Several times, she glanced over at Paolo, who sat sheepishly over in a corner.

"You cannot stop me," Vittoria said when Francesca was done.

Francesca raised a hand, but Paolo intercepted her.

"Enough. You've made yourself clear."

Francesca shook herself free and went to sit at the kitchen table. When Paolo tried to comfort her, she shoved his hands away. He went down to the cellar and brought back a liter of chilled wine. It was not really chilled, just far cooler than the hot summer day. He poured two glasses full and shoved one over to Francesca's side of the table. She drank from it like it was lemonade.

Vittoria sat down at the table too.

"Eh, maybe it's time for a little wine for you too."

Francesca eyed Paolo as he poured a third glass full. He shrugged at her and pushed the glass over to Vittoria. Vittoria sipped at it once and stared at Francesca.

"Don't look at me," Francesca said.

"I will do anything to regain Castellammare."

"Anything? Does that include whoring yourself?"

Vittoria stared until Francesca looked at her.

"You can't possibly think I'm that dumb."

Francesca stared and nodded.

"No, you're right. I learn more every day about how cunning you are. Pity this poor Mario."

"When we regain Castellammare, he will be the Baron Mario, and who will have regrets then?"

Francesca raised her eyebrows in mock admiration and drank from her wine. Paolo drank from his and poured both glasses full again. He seemed to be holding back a smile.

"Funny, eh?" Francesca said to him. "Maybe I should have held out for someone with a bit more money."

"Maybe you should have."

Now they were both trying to hold back smiles.

"I still can, you know." She wiggled the fingers on her left hand. "Nothing's yet etched in stone."

"I'll go out tonight and see if I can rob someone."

"Someone rich."

"There's not much point in robbing the poor."

"You're smarter than I thought."

Now they were both trying to hold back laughs. Francesca looked at Vittoria, who was smiling wryly.

"Don't you think we're going to paper over what's happened here. I catch you with this Mario and, bam, right to your grave."

Vittoria stared, completely unintimidated.

"At least marry him before..." Francesca made a gesture with her hands. "You know."

Vittoria nodded.

"I know. Like you two do in here every day when I go into the village."

Francesca eyed Vittoria over a drink of her wine.

"Maybe I'll smack you right now."

Vittoria sipped at her wine without responding.

"If you give your blessings, I will marry Mario when I turn sixteen."

"Oh. Just like that. You're getting married."

"You're the one who suggested it."

"Better that than losing your honor is all I meant."

"So, I'll marry him."

Francesca gestured with exasperation at Paolo and looked back at Vittoria.

"Like you have any idea what's good for you at your age."

"Of course, I do."

"Of course, you do. And what would that be?"

"A man who will help me to regain Castellammare."

"My God. Is that your only criteria?"

Vittoria shrugged.

"And how do you know he's willing to help you?"

"Because."

"Because what?"

"Because I've been grooming him for the past two years."

Paolo burst out laughing. Francesca looked from him to the heavens and crossed herself.

"My god, you're like a little monster here."

"No, I just know what I want."

Vittoria stood up.

"Did you bring water today?" she asked Paolo.

"I brought water."

"I'll go water the plants before it gets dark."

Francesca watched her leave and turned to Paolo, shaking her head.

"I don't know if I dare go to sleep at night."

"That's why I'm here. To protect you."

Paolo laughed again and drank his wine.

The following spring, Mario and Vittoria were married. Teresa was there along with Enzo, Ernesto, and his wife Constantina, Pascal, Gino, and of course Vittorio. There were armed men everywhere until it seemed there were more of them than the people attending the wedding.

A band played. The wine was poured. People drank and danced, and flowers were thrown.

On the outskirts of this celebration, Romano and some of his men watched all that took place and reported back to Count Don Carlos. Count Don Carlos had long believed this young woman named Cecilia, who had mysteriously appeared shortly after Baron Castellammare's death, was in fact, his daughter Vittoria, and he additionally had reason to believe that a young man growing up among Ernesto's band of thieves was, in fact, Baron Vittorio, but like Ernesto, Count Don Carlos had yet to feel emboldened enough to strike. He knew that Ernesto, after fending off a number of misguided incursions by carabineers and the Italian army and picking off a stray soldier here and there to show his strength, had entered into a pact with Bernardo Altobelli, acceding to the rule of law and promising to maintain peace, as long as the interests of the local populace were respected and Ernesto was otherwise left alone.

Had Count Don Carlos handed over the head of Ernesto on a platter a few months back, it would have been welcomed, but now a war with Ernesto was the one thing the local authorities did not want. When there was peace, everyone prospered. When there was war, everyone suffered.

Besides, it was only a matter of time before men like Ernesto went the way of the dinosaur. A train line was being built from Palermo to Lercara. Another one from Messina to Leonforte and from Messina to Catania. The world was growing smaller. Soon there would be troops everywhere and few places left for people like Ernesto to hide.

But on that spring day, things remained as they were. Because of neglect by the government in the north, Sicily remained impoverished and people were boarding boats every day, bound for the new world, and those that remained behind still needed the protection of men like Ernesto.

As the wedding came to a close, Ernesto took Mario aside.

"Remember what I have taught you. We fight as a team. We survive as a team. I know what she wants, and I tell you as before. Wait. The time is not right yet. I don't want to find I have a new daughter-in-law and a dead son."

"I want his head as much as she does, Papa, but I have told her we have to wait. She doesn't like hearing it, but I told her we have to wait."

"Good. You are smart."

Ernesto patted him affectionately on his face with both hands.

"Don't ever let all your brains go out . . . you know."

Mario smiled and hugged his father.

That night, when the festivities were all through, the newlywed couple retired to the small home that Ernesto had built for them behind Francesca's cottage.

Hidden Treasure in the Castellammare Castle

It wasn't long after their wedding that Vittoria was pregnant and busy on every front. She had expanded her meat and produce business to include a line of olive oils, which she took to Palermo each week for export. While there, she often took time to buy herself a new dress or new earrings or something that had caught her eye in the finer clothing stores. Where others were failing and fleeing to America, she was buying up their land and prospering. And all the while, she remained obsessed with regaining Castellammare.

One day, she arranged to meet with Vittorio in a grove outside of the village. Ernesto was ever vigilant, with himself and everyone who worked with him, but the truth was, the old vendettas had lain dormant for so long, no one had much stomach for reviving them. Peace was better than war and there was little to gain from fighting.

Of course, none of this satisfied Vittoria, and she immediately brought up the subject of Castellammare once she and Vittorio had embraced.

"I have given up hope," Vittorio said.

He was laid back. She was the complete opposite.

"I will never give up," she said.

"I can see that."

"It was *ours*, Vittorio!"

"So, you are busy buying up the countryside. Build a new Castellammare. In the end, it's just another piece of land."

"I can't believe I'm hearing you say this."

Vittorio shrugged.

"I want to get married someday, have kids, and enjoy a happy life. If I start a war with Count Don Carlos, I will soon be one of three things. Dead, in jail, or on the run."

Vittoria sighed heavily and looked off through the grove. It was an autumn day and very pleasant with golden light and a cool breeze off of the sea.

"Well, it seems that everyone is resigned to the way things are, so I must resign myself to being the one who kills him."

"Don't be foolish. You're pregnant. You'll get yourself killed."

"I won't ask you to do it again. Please don't tell me how to live my life."

"I don't want to see you dead."

"Yes, well. At least I'll die with my honor."

Vittorio shook his head.

"Look, I would only ask you for one thing."

"And what is that?"

"Remember the jewels I told you about? The ones Mama had hidden in the castle?"

Vittorio nodded.

"I want you to go retrieve them for me. That way I can hire men to get rid of Count Don Carlos. And then I will ask nothing more of you."

"It's madness."

"This one thing."

"Never mind hiring someone to kill Count Don Carlos, you don't even know if the jewels are there."

"They are." She waited.

Vittorio sighed heavily.

"All right. Where?"

"Do you remember the old grotto in the basement?"

He nodded.

"And the arched opening that led into it?

He nodded.

"There are two keystones. Right and left, above the arch. The jewels are hidden in a purse behind the one on the right. When you go there, you will see five small stones missing on that side of the arch. They were footholds placed by Mama so she could easily access the jewels."

"And you believe all this."

"Why wouldn't I? My mother told me."

Vittorio nodded.

"So, will you go? Or must I hire someone else to do it?"

Vittorio sighed again.

"All right. I will go. But it will take time. I must go there and watch and make sure of all the activities and routines before I act. And I have other duties, you know."

"I know."

Vittoria got up on her toes and gave Vittorio a hug.

"Thank you. Someday, when I have Castellammare back, you will thank me."

"We shall see. If either one of us is still alive."

"We are Castellammares, Vittorio. We are great people. Noble people. The ages can come and go but nothing can keep us down."

Vittorio looked down at Vittoria's belly.

"How are you?"

"I'm good. I can feel them kicking."

"Them?"

"Of course. It's in our blood. First one goes. Then the other."

Vittorio shook his head.

"What?"

"You're pregnant. There is peace. Why would you want to disturb that?"

"This one thing."

"Yes, I know."

He hugged her.

"I must be going."

Vittoria stared plaintively.

"Don't worry. I'll let you know."

"Thank you."

Vittoria started back through the grove, feeling optimistic. Vittorio went on his way, feeling a strange sense of doom.

A few nights later, Vittorio took up a position overlooking the castle and settled in to watch. He had a bit of bread and cheese with him, and a pear.

He had been there for perhaps fifteen minutes when he heard a pebble come cascading down from the slope above him and jumped to his feet with his rifle pointed. It was Mario and he held up his hands.

"Oh my God, Mario. I could have killed you."

"You could get yourself killed, hanging around here like this."

"And what? Are you following me now?"

"I know my wife. I know what she does. I figured something was up."

"Yeah, well. It's not what you think."

"It looks a lot like what I think," Mario said.

"Well, it's not."

The two men nodded knowingly at each other and Mario sat down. Vittorio settled back into his position and explained about the jewels.

"I don't know, Vittorio. It sounds like nothing but trouble to me. Even if we get the jewels, what the hell is she going to do, hire an assassin?"

"*We?*" Vittorio said.

"Sure, you don't think I'm going to let you go in there alone."

"Why would I drag you into this, Mario? It can only complicate things and I risk leaving my sister a widow."

"Eh. You worry too much. Look down there. There's not a soul around that castle. All the Don's men are down there at the villa, and out in the fields."

"We'll wait and see. Or have you learned nothing from your father?"

"I learned enough to follow you."

"Something you may come to regret."

"Nonsense. Let's watch."

Vittorio pulled out the bread and cheese and Mario had a sack with wine and the two young men sat there eating and watching men and torches come and go around the Castellammare estate. For Mario, these observations were completely objective. For Vittorio, they were suddenly subjective. He became aware of distant memories and began to experience long-suppressed emotions. Vittoria was right. As much as he hated to admit it, the attachments to Castellammare were deep and impossible to ignore.

Nothing much happened until midnight when a man rode out on horseback to check on the castle. Mario and Vittorio watched him check the doors, circle around to inspect the grounds, and stop for a cigarette under the moonlight before he rode back down to the villa.

The two men waited for another hour and when nothing else happened, they left.

The next night they were back, and the night after that, but the routine was the same. Each night around midnight, the same man rode out to check on the castle, smoke a cigarette, and ride back down to the villa.

"Let's go in tomorrow night," Vittorio said once the man had disappeared around to the stables at the far side of the estate. "I'll bring a torch and a key."

"All right," Mario said. "But I say we keep the jewels. I don't dare give them to my wife."

"I made her a promise."

"So did I. Our wedding vows."

Vittorio smiled sadly.

"Let's get the jewels. Then we can decide."

The next night, the two young men arrived just after dark, waited for half an hour, just to make sure there were no surprises and slipped down from their perch atop the great, towering outcropping of rock. The castle was built to the side of it towards the sea and as they came around the base of the castle, they could smell the sea mist. Then the lights of the villa came into view again.

Mario held the unlit torch. Vittorio took the big iron key and fiddled with the lock. After some effort and frustration, the lock finally turned and both men looked back down at the villa as the door creaked open. With a final look that way, they closed the door from inside, turned the latch, and lit the torch.

"I assume you know the way," Mario said.

Vittorio pointed and started off towards an arched hallway. It led to a heavy wooden door that opened onto a stone stairway. The stairway spiraled down into the bowels of the castle. It was very musty smelling.

On the next level down, they were looking up at the great beams and floor planking of the main floor. At the end of a large room with its low, wooden ceiling, they came to an arched opening. The five missing stones were just where Vittoria had said they would be.

"This is it," Vittorio said.

He handed the torch to Mario and started up with his foot in one opening and his hand in the next one up.

"Hold the torch up here higher," Vittorio said.

Mario did.

"Ouch. Not so close."

Mario chuckled and did as asked.

Vittorio eventually had one hand in the highest foothold and was trying to free the keystone with the other.

"Let me place my other foot on your shoulder," he said to Mario.

Mario obliged him and moved the torch to his far hand. He could hear and feel Vittorio struggling above him. Some moments later, he heard the scraping sound of the keystone sliding out.

"Damn it! Look out!" Vittorio shouted.

All in one motion, he let go of the heavy stone and repositioned his free hand in the opening it had left behind. Mario had jumped out of the way and the stone crashed to the stone floor. A great, thunderous sound echoed through the castle.

"Sorry," Vittorio said. "I couldn't hold it."

"Well? Are the jewels there? We need to get out of here. I'm sure they could hear that all the way down in Palermo."

Vittorio had reached his hand in to search and quietly cursed.

"All right, forget it, Vittorio. If it's not there, it's not there. Let's get out of here before we end up in a gunfight with Count Don Carlos' men."

Vittorio was still struggling with his whole arm inside the opening, stretching that little bit further, when his fingertips finally felt what seemed to be a beaded purse.

"I think I've got it. Give me your shoulder again."

Mario did and Vittorio inched the purse his way until he could grab it whole.

"Got it," he said and started to scramble down.

Back on the ground, he pulled on the string and opened the purse.

"Jesus," Vittorio said. "Diamonds and gold. It's a small fortune."

"All right, it's a small fortune," Mario said. "Let's get the hell out of here."

"What do we do about the stone?"

"Screw the stone. We'll be lucky to get out of here alive. Come on!" Mario said to Vittorio, who was still staring into the purse.

As if transfixed, he finally pulled the string closed and slipped the purse inside his satchel. The two men raced up the stairs and heard the sounds of men coming.

"There must be another way out of here," Mario said in a panicked voice.

Vittorio stood there thinking.

"Well, is there?"

"Yeah, towards the back but we'll have to jump."

"Well, that's fine, so let's start jumping."

They ran down to the end of the long, arched hallway and hurried up a long flight of stairs. With the main floor vaulted, the second floor was twenty feet up in the air. Vittorio led the way through several chambers and antechambers until they came to a small nave and an opening with a wooden shutter.

Mario opened it and looked out. The opening faced an edge of the granite outcropping, with a narrow walkway between that and the end building. Here and there, the jagged ends of granite encroached from the outcropping.

"We're going to kill ourselves, just jumping." He looked back at Vittorio. "There's no other way?"

"Not except in front, and I'm sure they'll be waiting."

"All right, I'll do it! I'll go first."

Mario grabbed Vittorio's shoulder, as if they would never meet again, crawled up into the opening, paused for one second, and jumped. Vittorio hurried to look and saw Mario land with a splat a second later.

Mario cursed under his breath and got up on his feet sorely. With a look up, he waved, as if to say, I've got you. Vittorio dropped the torch, climbed up into the opening, and too paused before jumping. Just as he did, he heard the sounds of men rushing feverishly through the castle behind him. It was just enough to distract Vittorio so that his boot caught on the ledge and he tumbled over, headfirst. In trying to right himself, his head smacked into the granite, and then he just fell as if a sack of onions. Mario caught him as best he could, but his head hit again.

"Vittorio! Talk to me."

Vittorio groaned. Blood was streaming down his face and his hair on the back of his head was soaked with it. Mario looked around, hearing voices from somewhere inside the castle and fearful about how long they had to get away undetected.

A moment later, Vittorio opened his eyes.

"Vittorio! Can you walk? We need to get out of here!"

Vittorio shook his head, no.

"Take the jewels. Go. It's what my sister wanted. I've done my duty now."

"No, Vittorio! I'm not going to leave you here."

"No, you must go."

He shook his head and closed his eyes as if needing to go to sleep.

Mario looked around and cursed.

"No, I'm not going to leave you here, Vittorio."

He quickly slipped Vittorio's satchel around his own neck, hoisted Vittorio over his shoulder, and started off down the curved, narrow corridor. The castle rose up on one side of him, the outcropping of rock on the other. Just before the curve of the castle brought Mario into view of the villa, the rock wall gave way to the wooded hillside, with a wooded ravine and Mario slid down that slope, still holding Vittorio over his shoulder as best he could. In the background, he heard voices, more frantic now, and worried that someone might have seen them. He could only hope not. With Count Don Carlos' horses, they would easily outrun Mario. His only chance was to stay hidden and perhaps find shelter inside the cottage of some peasant they had helped in the past.

At the bottom of the ravine, Mario ripped off a part of his shirt, tied it around Vittorio's head and started circling around the hill, away from the castle and Count Don Carlos' men, always working his way slowly downward, always keeping well hidden in the woods and brush. The burden of carrying Vittorio's dead weight was so great that Mario was forced to stop every few hundred yards to rest. At one point, he sat staring at Vittorio's bloody head resting in his lap and wept.

"You stupid fool," he cursed under his breath at his wife. "Look what your greed and obsession have done to your brother."

Vittorio groaned and Mario wished that he could do something to help but he knew could not.

It was nearly an hour before he reached a valley and the home of someone he knew he could trust. When old man Bertolli opened the door, he looked nervously both ways and quickly waved Mario inside. Bertolli's wife appeared, saw the blood, crossed herself, and helped to get Vittorio on a bed.

"Bring fresh water and some cloth," she told her husband.

She was stout, like most old peasant women, but not entirely unpleasant to look at and had her long, gray hair tied up on her head. As a midwife, she had common sense in such matters. She was well acquainted with blood and didn't flinch when she unwrapped the bandage and saw Vittorio's head. But Mario could read her pessimism instantly. He could see the reasons for it in Vittorio's wound. His head on the backside was no longer rounded as it had been before his fall, it was now flattened and crushed from his fall. The sight of it made Mario shudder.

When the husband came, he too saw the wound and assumed a very somber look, with his flat, plain face expressionless, his small mouth pursed up in grim recognition. Even with the finest surgeons up north, Vittorio would probably not live.

Regardless, Mrs. Bertolli took scissors and cut away the hair, washed the wound carefully, and rewrapped the head loosely, so as not to add any pressure. When she was done with that, she knelt and prayed. Then she covered Vittorio and encouraged the two men out into the front room.

"You should take him to Palermo, but I don't think he would survive the ride. Perhaps you can bring someone here, but..."

Mario nodded. The three of them looked at each other somberly and understood. They shouldn't ask how it happened. Mario shouldn't hope for a happy ending."

"I'll go home and bring my wife back. His sister."

Mrs. Bertolli nodded.

"I am sorry," she said.

"No, thank you. Thank you both. You will be rewarded."

"No, please. You have done enough for us already."

Mario nodded.

"Thank you again."

He cracked the door, looked both ways, and slipped off into the night.

When Mario entered the house and saw Vittoria, he knew her for what she was, forever planning and scheming and manipulating and he hated her. Even her sincere concern at seeing blood on his shirt disgusted Mario.

"Your brother is mortally wounded."

She gasped. Mario pulled the beaded purse out of the satchel and dropped it on the table.

"Here's the price he paid with his life. Your treasure."

Vittoria shook her head very slowly from side to side. There were tears in her eyes.

"No, no, no, no, no! Where is he?"

Seeing her grief, he found compassion for her, but not love. He held her while she wept.

"Get your shawl and I will take you to him."

Vittoria went away and returned with a blank face as if she were in shock. Mario guided her out the door with one hand on her back but did not touch her any further as they walked through the fields. It took most of an hour to reach the Bertolli's cottage. Mario knocked quietly and this time Mrs. Bertolli opened the door, reached out and embraced Vittoria.

"I am sorry," she said. "Come."

Mario did not bother joining them. He knew what the outcome was going to be. There was nothing he could add to help Vittorio.

"A glass of wine?" Mr. Bertolli said.

"Please," he nodded, "Thank you."

Mario bowed his head in appreciation and drank when the wine came. Mr. Bertolli did not have a glass and the two men sat there in silence. Mario thought he should go up to the stronghold and tell Ernesto the news but there was his wife. He couldn't leave her, even though he really didn't love her.

Mrs. Bertolli came out a few minutes later.

"Your wife asked about a doctor."

"And what about her?"

"She can stay here. It might not..."

Mrs. Bertolli stopped in midsentence, but Mario filled in the blank. Vittorio might not die right away. It might take a day or two. There was no real point in the doctor, but Mario agreed to go find one.

He went off again and did not return until almost three in the morning. The doctor came in, expressionless, though his face was full of it, from the bushy, arched eyebrows, to the owl-like deep eye sockets, the sparkling eyes, the nose like the end of a summer squash and the pursed lips.

He nodded and asked where he could find the patient. Mario followed him into the back room. The doctor did not say a word but sat down on the bed and immediately unwrapped the bandage. The grim look that came over him was all he had to say.

After probing a bit with his fingers, he rebandaged the head, took Vittorio's temperature, checked his pulse, and went back out front with his bag. Everyone followed him.

"His skull is seriously fractured and is putting pressure on his brain. At a minimum, he needs to be in the hospital in Palermo, though I'm not so sure anyone there can help the young man. He would need surgery to repair the fracture and then hope to keep the pressure on his brain relieved until the bones heal."

The doctor looked from face to face.

"He has no hope here, so if you have no plans of moving him, I suggest bringing a priest."

Vittoria broke down sobbing in her grief. Mario walked the doctor to the door.

"Thank you for coming."

"I am sorry that I could not do more."

He left. Mario went back and stared at Vittoria as she buried her face in her hands, sobbing in her grief.

"What do you want to do?"

"Can we take him to Palermo at least?"

Mario nodded and left to bring back a wagon. He did not return until after daylight and Vittorio was already dead. As much as his whole being rejected the idea, Mario went to comfort Vittoria. The Bertollis were making coffee in the kitchen. Vittoria looked up at Mario through her tears.

"I'm sorry," he said.

"He awakened once. Just before he went."

Mario nodded.

"Do you know what he said?"

Mario shook his head.

"I brought you the jewels. Now you must go take back Castellammare, for my sake. Don't let me have died in vain."

Vittoria stared for a long moment and broke down in tears again.

Vittorio's Funeral & Santino's Murder

The funeral was held in the small village where Ernesto's wife lived. The bandits came down from the hills and the carabineers and magistrates stood around uneasily as the old stone streets swelled with their ranks. The church overflowed with a great mass of people all dressed in black. At the end of the funeral, the procession of people walked from the church towards the cemetery with horns blaring and their heads hung down in grave despair. Nothing was openly said about this being Vittoria's brother, for they all knew Vittoria as Cecilia and conducted themselves as if *omerta* applied to this fact, but there were rumors and people whispered.

When the funeral and burial were finished, the women dressed in black ceased praying over their rosary beads and offering comfort to those who did or did not welcome it, and they returned home to their own lives. Vittoria sat alone at the end of that autumn day, content to be alone and brood in her twisted heart. That is what life does to people. It twists and bends them like the gnarled trunks of old trees, until they do not resemble at all the fresh young saplings they had once been.

Some people went on to become saints out of such hardship as if sprouting leaves to provide shade to the weary from life's capricious cruelty, but some turned to poison, and that was what quickly became of Vittoria, especially once Ernesto sent word through her husband, Mario. Forget this Castellammare business or you'll find yourself in a grave.

Vittoria was six months pregnant and like a crocodile in a pit, silently awaiting its next victim.

When she gave birth to fraternal twins that winter, the whole village was abuzz, and the old rumors were renewed. Twins were the mark of the Castellammare blood. Was this not true?

Of course, Count Don Carlos believed it to be so and was convinced that Vittorio had been killed retrieving something from behind that keystone in his castle and he longed to know what that was. He otherwise remained obsessed with stamping out that old Castellammare bloodline, but no less than Vittoria was with regaining what she knew Count Don Carlos had stolen from her and her family.

Count Don Carlos brooded. Vittoria brooded. The moment of confrontation remained simmering in the background of their lives.

Having named the twins Sophia and Santino, Vittoria went through all the expected rituals. The twins were baptized, and Vittoria breastfed them. She took them for walks and changed their diapers. From all external appearances, Vittoria was doing what every mother was expected to do, but she may as well have been lifeless inside. She put no more heart into it than she would with gutting a fish.

Francesca and Paolo watched Vittoria and knew that something had changed. Mario watched her and knew something had changed. He began to feel like a widower at twenty-one, but Vittoria would not talk to him or anyone about her feelings and Vittorio's death.

It is a strange thing, this ball of emotions we call the heart. It has the capacity to blind a person from their past and what really drives them, and Vittoria was increasingly driven by ancient forces she did not understand. One could say that she had abandoned her obsession to regain Castellammare and had distilled those failed efforts to control life into bitterness and hatred. That would have described things well enough, but in fact, that obsession had not left her. Vittoria had simply placed it inside some hidden chamber, where that witches brew of emotions went on twisting and warping her once tender heart.

If anything, Vittoria was now like a viper, flicking its tongue and waiting with eternal patience for the right time to strike.

The years passed and the times grew increasingly hard on the common people. Public and church lands and the old feudal commons had been gobbled up by the wealthy like Count Don Carlos, and their crops and meats were now being sent to Palermo or the mainland for greater profits, causing the price of local food to rise and forcing many desperate peasants into petty theft in order to survive.

The ensuing chaos and hardship led to an even greater network of bandits and private armies, the latter hired by rich landowners, and leading to the expected results. The wealthy got richer amidst a booming economy. The peasants who had stolen were regularly brought to trial and punished, but the villages remained too impoverished to maintain permanent police forces and bring about actual justice.

The Palermo National Guard had made efforts from time to time to crush what was now being called the mafia, clumsy efforts that had only served to alienate the local populace further since honest men like Ernesto and his gang took the brunt of the punishment. The cattle thieves, smugglers, and the vilest of all the criminal elements who had been hired by the wealthy landowners to protect them were left to operate with impunity.

As to the term mafia, the men it was meant to describe did not embrace it and no one was quite certain from where the word derived. The Sicilian adjective *mafiusu* implied swagger and bravado, and quite possibly had roots in Arabic words like *mahyas*, meaning the same, but more likely than not, the term mafia had been popularized in the wake of a play titled, *The Mafiosi of the Vicaria*, which had played throughout Italy to great success.

In the play, the words mafia and mafiusu were never uttered once, but the play did portray a mafia-like prison gang, whose members spoke of *omerta* and *pizzu*, the latter being a Sicilian term that meant 'wetting the beak,' which was a secret code word for extortion. These were terms this sect of thieves did embrace, as they did *cosa nostra*, which was how they referred to themselves and their own enterprise. This was our thing, our interest, our cause.

Amidst this ongoing corruption and strife, Vittoria's business interests had suffered badly. It was as if Vittorio's death had placed a curse on her and everything she touched now turned to stone. She had begun life with ambitious and long-range plans. Now she was simply struggling to get by each day and was brought to her knees by poverty.

Bitterly, she sold enough of the jewels Vittorio had brought her to keep her family afloat and struggled on.

Yet, despite these hardships, Vittoria maintained her grace and dignity and was admired. She may have been cheerless, but royal blood still stirred in her veins and she had not forgotten, nor shed entirely, the lesson she had learned early on from Francesca. Act kindly towards people, give generously, and be fair, even if you were not in a position to do so and your heart isn't in it.

Though Vittoria felt a deep loathing for herself that she did not dare to admit or articulate; she was greatly embittered by her lack of success. She was still a beautiful young woman and admired by the people around her. There was even talk of restoring the rightful blood to the Castellammare estate. As if recalling a fairytale, people spoke of a time when the land was rich, people prospered, and Baron Castellammare treated all who worked for him with kindness and dignity.

Whatever else could be said of life in rural Sicily, it was rapidly changing. With the advent of trains, walking was now akin to crawling, and where men had once felt lucky to have a donkey, many owned horses.

Paolo, Francesca, and Vittoria were among these, with Paolo having built an expansive corral and stable between their two homes, some of their income was now stemming from the sale of their foals. For the young Sophia and Santino, these huge beasts were a great fascination. Santino in particular had gotten the bug and prevailed upon Paolo to teach him to ride when he was only five years old. By eleven, he had his first horse and by sixteen, he was the proud owner of a spirited white stallion.

It was perhaps Vittoria's one joy, watching him parade around the village as if he were a prince. With his mother's brooding, sensitive eyes, and his father's sensitive mouth, set in a lean, finely boned face, and with a shock of dark, wavy hair, he had that quiet authority about him. He owned the world, or soon would so it seemed.

Vittoria would watch and allow herself a fleeting encore of her long-buried dreams. "Someday," she thought, "he will help me to recapture Castellammare."

Vittoria was no less proud of her daughter, a beauty without compare, with long, wavy almost auburn hair and pale, rose petal skin, and features that could not have been more finely chiseled. She was so perfect, it seemed she was more of a drawing than an actual person, her nose so fair, it disappeared into the face, leaving behind only the two dots of her nostrils. But Sophia did not possess any of Vittoria's ambitions, and for that, she took second place to Santino in Vittoria's heart.

One particular day, Ernesto and his men were sitting around the stronghold in mourning. Pascal had been killed the previous night in a raid and a bottle of wine was being passed among the men in his honor. Fidelio, a wiry man with a gaunt, pinched face, big, flat ears, a pencil-like mustache, and lines deeply etched into his receding hairline, blew out smoke and held up the bottle.

"To Pascal."

"To Pascal," everyone said.

Giancarlo, the man sitting next to Fidelio put his arm around him and held up the bottle again before drinking. Giancarlo looked like a beat-up playboy. His watery eyes had taken a beating. His skin had taken a beating. His hair seemed to be the only thing left intact from his younger days. Both men were smoking, and a bit drunk, and reeked of the barrooms where they had been drinking.

"And to hell with the carabineers," Giancarlo added.

As was the case from time to time, a local magistrate had sent a patrol of them out, with instructions to hunt down Ernesto and otherwise put on a show of power. It was time to put these gangs in their place. Pascal had been killed in the ensuing skirmish, and Ernesto had ordered one of the village officials to be killed in retribution.

As had been the case with much of Italian history since the fall of Rome, punched back in this manner, the magistrates quickly lost heart for the fight and called a truce. We took one of yours. You took one of ours and let that be a lesson to you.

For Ernesto's men, the matter wasn't over. Tensions spilled over from time to time, sure, but they suspected there was more behind this incident.

"It's that Carlos," one of them said to Ernesto. "He won't be satisfied until he kills you, Mario and Vittoria, and those two twins.

"That bastard is haunted by the ghosts of his own conscience," Fidelio added.

Ernesto nodded.

All the men stared at him, waiting.

"Is that all you're ever gonna do?" Giancarlo asked. "Nod? We get whacked and we sit here nodding?"

"We whacked them back."

"But we're not getting to the root of the problem. You know those sons of bitches down in Castellammare don't want any trouble with us."

Ernesto shrugged.

"Yeah. So, something is stirring them up."

Ernesto shrugged again.

"Jesus Christ. Maybe it's time for some new leadership around here."

"So, you take over, Giancarlo."

Giancarlo smirked and looked away.

"Yeah, if we could get you out of those bars and away from your whores, you'd make a great leader."

"I'm there whenever you need me."

"No one questions that you are a good man, Giancarlo. But a leader?"

Ernesto made one of those incomparable Italian gestures.

"Yeah," Giancarlo said.

"Yeah?" Fidelio said.

"Yeah, you bunch of crazy men," Ernesto said. "So now what?"

"So, now we still got problems," Giancarlo said.

"So, you're the big leader, you figure them out," Ernesto said.

Someone held up the bottle.

"To Pascal."

"To Pascal," everyone said, and the men drank.

Two days later, Giancarlo and Fidelio were riding down the mountain on horseback when they came across a crew of men who claimed to be repairing the road. It was a very narrow stretch, where the mountain fell off steeply on both sides and where men had lost their lives in the past. Not recognizing these men, Giancarlo inquired as to who they were and how they had come to be there.

"What do you care?" the leader of them asked.

Giancarlo looked over at Fidelio and back at the man. Giancarlo could joke with the best of them, but you didn't mess with him.

"I care," he said. "The men I work for care."

"Yeah, yeah. We know you work for Ernesto and we work for Count Don Carlos. So what?"

"So, when I ask you a question, you answer me. That's what."

"Yeah? Well mind your own business. Don't stick your nose where it doesn't belong."

Fidelio started to pull the shotgun from his back, but Giancarlo held up a hand.

"We'll be back tomorrow, and you'd better have a better answer for me."

"Or what?"

"Or you'll end up down there, with the dead."

"Yeah, yeah."

Giancarlo smiled.

"Go on, get back to work, you bunch of monkeys."

"Get out of here," the man said.

"Yeah, just get back to work."

Giancarlo and Fidelio started off.

"And make sure you do a good job for us," Giancarlo called back.

The workers gestured obscenely, and the two men rode off slowly, glancing back several times and laughing to themselves.

That night, Giancarlo reported this business back to Ernesto who drummed his fingers while he listened, smelling something rotten, but not knowing what.

"Check on them again tomorrow and see if they've made any progress. If not, run the morons off before Count Don Carlos gets any ideas."

Ernesto had learned to put up with the jerk on his own estate, but he wouldn't put up with him anywhere else.

That next morning, Vittoria asked Santino to accompany his sister into the village with their goods.

"You go with her. I have men's things to do."

"Like riding your white horse all over the countryside."

"Be thankful. I know everything that goes on and can tell you when there is danger."

"All you know is what girl lives where."

Paolo had come by to repair a gate and did his work with a big smile.

"What?" Vittoria said. "Why don't you talk some sense into the boy?"

"Don't mess with women, Santino. You see what it gets you."

"Why you..."

Vittoria went after Paolo with her foot and he dodged out of the way, laughing. Meanwhile, Santino had gotten up on his horse and was prancing around, watching this scene.

"Go on, get out of here," Vittoria told him. "Go do your *man* things."

Santino tipped his hat and trotted off at a brisk pace. Vittoria watched him for a long moment, unable to suppress her love for the boy. He was so tall and straight and proud, and she felt certain that someday he would be a great man.

"Come," she said to Cecilia. "Let's get to market before Count Don Carlos' men beat us there."

Having heard the many stories about Castellammare from his mother, Santino often rode that way, and on this day followed a narrow donkey trail that led up along the backside of the castle. The path rose and rose until it eventually came to a pass, where he could look back down to the castle far below him, perched to the side of the massive rock outcropping, and from there across the Castellammare estate where it rolled off towards the sea and in that moment, he shared his mother's ambition. What a beautiful place, and the man who had killed his grandfather and stolen that land from his family would someday have to pay with his life at Santino's hands.

Without any hurry, he turned and headed further up the mountain until he came to the road that led down from Ernesto's stronghold. On occasion, he rode up there too, but on this day, he remembered he had not eaten breakfast and decided to head home for lunch. On his way, he came to that narrow stretch of road where the men were working and was aware of them acting nervously and overly cordial, but thought nothing more of it and continued on his way.

He was halfway across the gorge when he sensed movement behind him and turned to find a man running very fast the other way. In that split second, Santino became aware of the burning fuse and realized the man had left dynamite on the road. Santino spurred his horse, but it was too late. The blast went off, the horse bucked wildly, and Santino was thrown into the abyss. Spooked, the horse lit off for home. The four men working on the road hurried over and peered down the steep mountainside. Santino's body was at the body of the gorge, torn up and lifeless.

Two of the men mounted their horses and raced down the mountain towards Castellammare. The other two men set off another charge, where a large rock formation encroached on the road and they worked feverishly to cover up their deed.

An hour later, Bernardo Altobelli rode up with Count Don Carlos and two carabineers. The men explained that they had been using explosives to clear some rocks and had not seen the boy. The men showed the carabineers where it had happened and apologized profusely. Count Don Carlos expressed his remorse. What a Maggieble thing.

Bernardo stared at all of them, not believing in Don Carlos' sincerity and not knowing what to think of the explanation he had heard. It sounded reasonable enough, but Bernardo did not believe much of anything when it came to Count Don Carlos.

"You," Bernardo said to two of the carabineers. "Go down and tell the family the news and bring them up here."

They saluted and left. Bernardo cringed at the thought of having to face a bereaved mother, or whoever would be coming.

An hour later, a hysterical Vittoria arrived, along with Mario, Paolo, Sophia, and Francesca.

When Vittoria saw the body, deformed and lifeless, and looking tiny at the bottom of the gorge, she went after Count Don Carlos.

"You did this, you bastard."

She got at his face with her nails and nearly pushed him into the gorge before the carabineers got hold of her.

"I am sorry, Cecilia," he said, as everyone knew her in public. "It was a Maggieble accident, which I would do anything to undo."

Vittoria, who was weeping hysterically, yelled, "Then die, you bastard!"

Bernardo gestured to one of the carabineers, who restrained her. Bernardo took the lead carabineer aside.

"Please, at least remove the women to a safe distance. It would be better if they returned home, but I do not want them watching this gruesome business of dragging the body back up. If they insist on staying, arrange a wagon or some other place for them to sit."

The lead carabineer nodded and went to speak with the family.

In the end, Vittoria refused to leave, so the women were led to a place a good distance from the gorge where they were safe but could still see the activities along the road.

Sometime later, a group of men arrived from town, and the laborious process of rappelling a man down to the body with ropes began. It was close to an hour before they began dragging the body back up. Vittoria came running over when she saw it and could not be restrained. She wept and wept over her son and called his name and cursed Count Don Carlos and swore vengeance and it ended only when a wagon arrived, and the body was loaded on to it. Vittoria climbed in with the body, her eyes dead to the world now, her heart black. Sophia, Francesca, and Mario climbed in too and rode back into the village.

Paolo stayed behind and watched Bernardo further interrogate the men, studying their eyes, their hands, their every gesture and mannerism, until he felt sure who was most guilty. Then he rode without haste up to Ernesto's stronghold to bring the news.

The Slaughter for Santino, a Message to Count Don Carlos

Paolo knew that Ernesto would already have heard the news as he raced up the mountain towards the cave. In Sicily, news traveled on the wind, especially bad news such as this, and the somber looks on the faces of the guards stationed along the hillside confirmed his suspicions, as did the way Gino nodded at him gravely at the mouth of the cave.

Inside the cave, Paolo found Fidelio and Giancarlo seated with Ernesto, along with several other men.

Ernesto nodded.

"Sit down and tell us what you have learned."

Paolo sat and looked around at the men.

"It was Lanzo and Vincenzio who did it. Two other men were there and took part, but they were basically kids doing what they were told."

"The same could be said true of Lanzo and Vincenzio," one of the other men said. "They did not wander up there on their own. They were told to do this thing."

"You should have let me shoot them when I had the notion," Fidelio said to Giancarlo.

"You're right. I should have let you shoot them," Giancarlo said.

"So, we shoot them now," Paolo said.

Ernesto held up his hands and scratched at the three-day-old growth on his neck. He stared out towards the mouth of the cave. Someone would have to pay with his life. Maybe more than one, but you had to go about these things judiciously. With a calm mind, not acting out of revenge.

"An eye for an eye," he said, looking back at the men. "We don't go about killing indiscriminately.

"Two eyes for an eye," Fidelio said with a draw on his cigarette.

His gaunt, deeply lined face could look jovial at times, but at moments like this, he had the look of the razor's edge about him.

Several men had murmured behind him. Ernesto shook his head in response.

"An eye for an eye."

The men murmured again.

"It was a boy," Giancarlo said.

This brought on more whispered, restless voices among the men.

Ernesto held up a hand and sat there thinking again.

"All right," he said. "I don't know that Count Don Carlos will miss either of those bastards."

"Now you are thinking right," Fidelio said.

"All right, you two sons of bitches, take care of this. And take Benito with you. I don't want to see anyone else dead."

"We can take care of this ourselves, but that's fine boss," Giancarlo said. "Benito can shoot the bastards in the knee caps, Fidelio in their guts and I'll put one in their heads."

Ernesto nodded.

"Go on," he said. "And don't get carried away. We don't want reprisals for a reprisal."

"Don't you worry, boss," Giancarlo said. "When we get done with them, nobody's going to be in the mood for any more reprisals."

Ernesto nodded skeptically at him. Giancarlo would have been a brilliant tactician if there wasn't next week. If you waited long enough in Sicily, there were always more reprisals.

As Giancarlo and Fidelio were getting up to leave, the men heard whistles from the guards down the hill, then more whistles. By the sound of them, they knew it was friend not foe, but still the men tensed up in unison and got their rifles ready.

A moment later, Mario came rushing in.

"Why aren't you with your grieving daughter and her mother?"

"What am I, a babysitter that I should hang around with the women when there is work to be done?"

"Watching after our women is work too."

"So, I left two men down there and I am here, ready to put a bullet into the heads of these bastards."

Ernesto wanted to look to the heavens but didn't, lest he stir up his son even further.

"Go on," he said to Giancarlo and Fidelio again. "And be quiet about it. We don't want any evidence left behind."

"Why do they get to go do the killing and not me?"

Now Ernesto did look up to the heavens.

"You talk like it's a privilege." Ernesto slapped his son gently on the face. "Sit down and try to learn something."

Enraged, Mario stalked the cave, steaming. Giancarlo and Fidelio went out smiling with the young man Benito trailing out of the cave after them.

"Oh, what? And he gets to go?" Mario asked about Benito.

"I told you to sit down and listen," Ernesto said.

Outside, Gino was smiling as the three men passed by.

"Going off to make more widows?"

"We are in the business of delivering playmates to the devil," Giancarlo said with a big smile of his own.

"He's going to be having one big party tonight," Fidelio said with another big smile.

"And maybe Count Don Carlos is crying tonight instead."

"You guys are a laugh," Gino said. "Just remember, we have to put up with the resulting shit."

"Don't you worry. We will catch all the crap for you this time, old man."

The men saluted sarcastically, but also showing loyalty.

With the three men gone, Ernesto turned to Paolo.

"Take six men and my ambitious son here and keep an eye on the widow. Round the clock. I don't think Count Don Carlos would dare to do anything right now, but we don't want to take any chances."

"Come," Paolo said to Mario, who brushed his hand aside and left with a fierce look at his father.

On the way down the mountain, Paolo picked out six more men and they rode like the wind until they had reached the village, where they found women dressed in black, weeping, and banging pans. At the house, Paolo gestured to Mario.

"Go, set everyone up."

Not liking to take orders, Mario barked at the men. "Get the horses in the corral. Take up positions here and there around the property. Hurry up. Let's get to work! The men went off about their business sullenly, the same way Mario would have reacted if someone was barking at him.

Francesca had come out of the house as Paolo rode up.

"What is it with all these men?" she whispered when he came to the door.

"You need to ask?"

"I'm asking."

"Don't be foolish." Paolo nodded at the house. "How is she doing?"

"How do you think? You think she was black before? For her, the whole world is over."

"You really think he would come?" Francesca said.

"Who knows? You don't take chances. Especially when it comes to you."

Paolo grabbed Francesca's backside and gave her a kiss. She shrieked in response and pushed him away.

"You crazy man."

Paolo nodded.

"Yes, I am. Now please get this crazy man something to eat. I haven't had food since morning."

"Go next door," Francesca said. "You don't want to be a part of this mourning."

"You're right. I'll see you at home."

Paolo grabbed her backside again, and again she pushed him away.

Later that night, Giancarlo, Fidelio, and Benito stood in the shadows of downtown Castellammare, waiting for Lanzo and Vincenzio to finish eating at the café and come back outside. They heard music and voices and laughter from inside, and would have liked to go in and enjoy the revelry too, but they waited outside in the shadows and counted the minutes. They had pig skin filled with wine and some bread and salami. They passed around the food at one point while they waited. Men and women came and went from the café. but there was not one sign of Lanzo and Vincenzio.

Later in the evening, Fidelio yawned.

"When are those two morons going to have enough of their wine and whores."

"Ssshhh," Giancarlo said. "Speak of the devil. Here they come right now."

The two men came out looking well lubricated, but still wary. First Vincenzio then Lanzo took a look both ways before they were satisfied and headed up the street. Knowing where they had tied their horses, Giancarlo pointed around the back way.

"You wait for them up there. I'll follow around behind."

Fidelio and Benito disappeared up a back street. Giancarlo waited until Lanzo and Vincenzio had turned the corner and then hurried up the street towards the café. When he came to the lighted windows, he made sure to act nonchalantly as he went past. A man with a shotgun over his back was nothing unusual in Sicily. Although, a man with a shotgun and in a hurry was another thing. Plus, you never knew if a carabineer or two might be in there drinking.

Giancarlo slipped past the café like he was on his way home and then hurried to catch up with the two men. They were just about to enter a man's corral and barn when Fidelio and Benito confronted them. Lanzo and Vincenzio went for their rifles, but Giancarlo was right behind them.

"Uh, uh," he said as he put the barrel of his shotgun up against Lanzo's head.

Fidelio put the barrel of his shotgun in Vincenzio's guts and Benito relieved the two men of their guns. With that done, Giancarlo smacked Vincenzio, then Lanzo in the back of the head with the butt of his rifle. Both men groaned and collapsed to the cobblestones. Hearing the sounds outside, the proprietor came to his door to see what was happening. When he saw the men and the bodies, he disappeared back inside.

Giancarlo quickly had both men gagged and tied up

"Help me get them onto their horses," Giancarlo whispered to Benito.

Together with Fidelio, they soon had both men strapped face down over their saddles, as if they were dead. Quietly, they led the horses out of the corral, closed it, and walked slowly up the street; the clip-clop of the horses' hooves followed them out of the village. At the base of the hills behind the village, they untied their own horses and rode up the narrow trail into the hills and followed them until they were at the outskirts of the Castellammare estate. From their vantage point, they could see almost everything that went on down below and stood there watching until they heard first Lanzo, and then Vincenzio awakening.

"Get them on the ground," Giancarlo said to Benito.

He did so roughly. Sensing where they were and what was about to happen to them, both men stared with wide eyes. Perhaps it was anger as much as fear, but what you saw was the fear in their eyes. Neither man had a face that encouraged sympathy or compassion. Lanzo had that look of a ruthless killer—narrow, wide-set eyes, a long narrow nose, jowls like mutton, and a hard mouth. Vincenzio looked to be the dumber of the two with his big ears, putty nose, and long chin, but his piercing, dark eyes and tall, wide forehead suggested intelligence.

"That's right," Giancarlo said. "Have a good look around, because it's the last you're going to see in this world."

He chuckled with Fidelio. Benito had a shotgun pointed at the two men, in case there was any trouble. Giancarlo shrugged at Fidelio.

"Which one first?"

"This bastard," Fidelio said.

Lanzo desperately tried to back away on the ground until Giancarlo kicked him in the head with his boot.

"Take it like a man, you stinking dog, and remember what you did to the boy. You're lucky we don't find your son and feed him to jackals too."

With that, Fidelio slit Lanzo's throat and stood back to watch him die. Lanzo struggled mightily for half a minute or so, in a last desperate attempt to stop the bleeding and survive, as a man will always do under such circumstances, despite the futility.

With the cobblestones wet with blood, Fidelio now turned his attention to Vincenzio, who, having witnessed this butchery, had tried to get to his feet and run, only to be knocked down by a blow from the butt of Giancarlo's shotgun. He now laid there with the barrel to his head.

With a sigh, Fidelio performed the same 'throat operation' on Vincenzio, slitting his throat and then spitting at him.

"That will teach you to take a boy from his mother."

Fidelio looked over at Giancarlo, who had been watching him.

"What?"

"Nothing. Just remind me not to call you when...you know..."

Fidelio smiled and looked over at Benito, who was standing there with a shocked expression on his face.

"What the hell's wrong with you? Are you feeling sorry for the poor sons of bitches now? Quit screwing around and let's get them on their horses."

A minute later, they had both men again tied off across their horses and walked them down through the grove towards Count Don Carlos' vineyard. They found a gate in the fence, led the horses through it, gave them both a good slap on their hindquarters, and watched the horses gallop off in the direction of the corrals.

"All right, let's get out of here before we have any trouble," Giancarlo said.

The men hurried back to their own horses and rode off as fast as they could into the hills.

Ernesto was waiting for them and looked from face to face when they returned. He gave special attention to the blood on Fidelio's clothing and looked back at his face.

"I cleaned up a bit before coming to see you," Fidelio said.

"I can see that."

Ernesto stared at him, thinking.

"Did anyone see you?"

"Carmen, the teamster but he won't say a word."

Ernesto nodded.

"We hope."

"Trust me, when word gets out about those bodies, memories will vanish."

"Go warn the men. Be on full alert," he told Benito.

Benito went out. Ernesto looked at Fidelio again.

"Must you be such a butcher?"

Fidelio shrugged.

"You want a job done. I make sure no one forgets."

Ernesto looked at Giancarlo, who shrugged too.

"Don't look at me. I don't pretend to control him."

"All right, go get something to eat. And remember in the future. I have to answer to Bernardo about all of this."

"You know what I say about Bernardo?"

"Yeah, I know what you say about Bernardo."

"Yeah."

"Yeah, except Bernardo is the only one standing between us and all-out war. And our cooperation with him is the only thing keeping him on our side."

Fidelio lit up a cigarette with a smile.

"All right, go on, get the hell out of here," Ernesto said.

"I think I'll have some of Gino's stew first."

"You son of a bitch. How can you eat?"

"I'm hungry."

Ernesto shook his head.

"Don't you worry, boss," Fidelio said. "I take good care of you."

Fidelio went to grab something to eat. Ernesto sat down with Giancarlo and talked about what they would do tomorrow.

In the morning, Romano rode in early to tell Bernardo about the deaths and the magistrate received the news with a grim demeanor. He sat considering things for a long moment, sighed, rose out of his chair, and announced to his subordinate that he was riding out to Count Don Carlos' estate to view the bodies. Not looking forward to the task, Bernardo let his horse walk at a leisurely pace the entire way.

At Count Don Carlos' instruction, his men had placed the bodies in a stall of the main barn, but otherwise left them the way they had been discovered. One of Count Don Carlos's men pulled the sheet back and Bernardo stared. After a moment, he hung his head, closed his eyes, and put a hand to his chin.

"Why did you leave them in this manner? It's an insult to God."

"It's an insult to God to leave them like this. I wanted you to see what these savages will do. It's an insult to God to do this to a man."

Bernardo waved a hand.

"All right. That's enough. Cover them up. Clean them up and return these bodies to their wives and families."

Bernardo turned to leave. Count Don Carlos went after him.

"So, what are you going to do?"

"What am I going to do? I'm going to see what I can learn about who did this."

"We already know who did this."

"Of course, and if I go to Ernesto and his men and tell them, I know who did this, do you know what they are going to tell me?"

Count Don Carlos stood there staring.

"They're going to tell me, 'and we know who is responsible for the death of Santino'."

Count Don Carlos scoffed.

"The one was an accident. This," Count Don Carlos waved a hand at the covered bodies. "was a slaughter."

"Was it an accident, Count Don Carlos?"

"Are you accusing me of planning this unfortunate explosion?"

Bernardo stared, nodding in answer.

"I'll tell you both the same thing. You need to find some way to bring peace. Otherwise, you'll both be in the ground. Either that or I'll have you both behind bars."

"Tell this to Ernesto and his gang."

"I'm telling you now."

Bernardo stared for another long moment before he turned and left.

Again, he was in no hurry and rode along in a slow trot with the sea off to his left and the mountains off to his right. The sea was very blue that day and the mountains were high against the blue sky. Bernardo could not help but think of what a shame it was that people could not live in peace in this beautiful land.

In Vittoria's village, he took note of the armed men scattered here and there but pretended not to notice much and said nothing. If anything, he offered a very slight nod of respect in passing.

At Vittoria's house, he dismounted, took hat in hand, and went up to knock at the door. Paolo answered, looked back once at the women inside, stepped outside, and closed the door. Mario, who had been sitting by the door to the barn, came over as one who is expecting trouble.

Bernardo nodded at Mario and looked back at Paolo.

"What can I do for you, Signore Altobelli?" Paolo said.

Bernardo sighed, looked off, and tapped his hat against his leg.

"I came to offer my condolences, first and foremost."

"If you want to offer your condolences, you can have that Count Don Carlos arrested and hung."

Paolo held up a hand and gestured at Mario, who fumed but shut up.

"I thank you for that, Signore Altobelli. And what would be the second reason you came to see us?"

Bernardo sighed again.

"I wondered if you or Ernesto know anything about the two murders that took place in Castellammare last night?"

Mario started to speak and again Paolo held up a hand to him.

"We have not heard a word about this. Why would we know something?"

Bernardo nodded and looked off.

"I did not think you would tell me anything, even if you did happen to know, but I would be failing at my duties if I did not come out here and ask you."

Paolo nodded.

"So now you have asked, Signore Altobelli, and I have given you my answer."

"And would you be answering for Ernesto as well?"

"I don't know what Ernesto does or doesn't know. I live here."

Bernardo nodded.

"Well, if by some chance you happen to see Ernesto, will you please tell him that I wish to speak with him?"

"If I happen to see him, I will."

Bernardo nodded and started to leave.

"Oh," he said, stopping. "Please do give my condolences to Vittoria. It is a shame, her boy. A shame."

"It is a shame," Paolo said.

Bernardo nodded and left.

The minute he was out of sight, Paolo turned to Mario.

"Go and inform your father of Bernardo's visit and ask him what he would like us to do?"

Finally provided with some semblance of a gallant task, Mario walked back to the barn, quickly saddled his horse, and rode off in a gallop. Paolo watched until he had disappeared, opened the door of the house to check on the women one more time, closed the door, and went off to feed the horses.

Santino's Funeral

That afternoon, with Santino's body prepared, the door to the house was opened and the wake commenced. The peasants came in ones, twos, and groups down the dusty streets and passed through Vittoria's front room as Fr. Columba was there to bless each and every one of them. The women closest to Vittoria remained gathered around her and there was much weeping, prayer, and consoling of the grieved.

As promised, Bernardo came to pay his respects and Ernesto made sure that he arrived at more or less the same time. When Bernardo saw Ernesto, he acknowledged him without a word. The men sat apart in the front room, their heads held high above the grieving, yet paying their respects.

Later, Bernardo sighed and rose to his feet and offered Vittoria and the entire family his condolences one last time. Ernesto rose to his feet a moment later and followed Bernardo outside. Bernardo had waited on the porch alone and the two men came to be standing there, side by side, gazing off at the distant mountains.

"Where can we talk alone?" Bernardo said.

"This way," Ernesto said and led him around to the back of the barn.

Against the wall, there was a heavy wood plank set upon two tree stumps and the men sat down. It was a minute or so before Bernardo finally spoke.

"I cannot promise peace if this sort of thing continues. Already, there is talk of the army mounting a campaign to clean up the hills, once and for all."

"Of course, and nothing will be done about Count Don Carlos."

The men glanced at each other.

"We both know what we think we know, but I can't possibly prove his guilt in a court of law. Not without witnesses, and witnesses have a strange way of disappearing in Sicily. In fact, two of them disappeared just last night. In a most gruesome fashion. Of course, I will presume you know nothing about that, right?"

Ernesto stared at Bernardo for a long moment before looking out over the rolling countryside. It was dry and dusty in some places, but rich with crops here and there and generally very pleasant to look at.

"I heard something," Ernesto said. "But Count Don Carlos has made many enemies over the years. It's hard to say which one of them got angry with him this time."

"In this, you speak at least part of the truth."

Bernardo sighed and tapped the toes of his boots on the hard soil.

"Count Don Carlos has made many enemies. Who got angry with him this time? I don't believe that is so hard to determine." Bernardo sighed again. "In any case, as I said, if this keeps up, I cannot promise you anything. No matter what I think about justice, there are those who are eager to go after you, and they are the ones with the money and the power..."

"And with that money and power, there is no justice for those who don't have money and power."

Bernardo sighed again.

"In your heart, I know you are a good man, Ernesto, so I have tried to help right the wrongs, but there is a point at which I am powerless to do anything on your behalf."

"I understand. You have been a fair man with me. I have tried to be the same in return."

"I have no doubt that's true."

With a final sigh and a slap of his knees, Bernardo stood up.

"By the way, have you heard anything about a man named Duke Don Vito?"

Ernesto looked up and away again at the countryside.

"There are many Vitos in Sicily."

"Indeed, there are. This one happens to be from Palermo, and he's made contact with a number of prominent landowners over the past few weeks in a not entirely pleasant way."

Ernesto looked up again.

"Are you asking me if I have anything to do with this Duke Don Vito?"

Bernardo sat there nodding his head slowly, as if in deep thought.

"No. I'm simply telling you this for your own good. This role you play of being a guardian for the simple people, it has turned into something very different in the city and we have knowledge that these men are now planning to flex their muscles out here in the countryside."

"You think I should be worried about these men?"

"I think everyone should be worried. You included. These men have shown themselves to be ruthless, beyond anything either one of us can imagine."

Ernesto nodded.

"You will tell me if you hear of anything."

Ernesto nodded again.

"And I will do the same for you."

Bernardo pretended to dust off his hat on his pant leg.

"Let's do what we can to keep the peace. I am doing what I can to hold off a full-scale war, but one more dead body and things will spin out of my control."

He nodded his head at Ernesto and walked around towards the front of the barn. Ernesto remained sitting there in thought for several minutes before he rose to his feet and followed.

The next day at noon, nearly the entire village poured into the church for Santino's funeral service, and Fr. Columba had barely gotten the gathering quieted when a great murmuring erupted at the back of the church. Heads turned and word spread that Count Don Carlos had arrived outside with several of his men. When Vittoria learned of his presence, she screamed and marched towards the entrance. Mario raced out ahead of her. Paolo attempted to stop Vittoria, but she would not be dissuaded.

Outside, several of Ernesto's men had Count Don Carlos surrounded with their shotguns pointed at him. Bernardo, who had come for the funeral, hurried out to get between the men.

When Vittoria appeared, Count Don Carlos offered her a cordial nod.

"Get away from here, you pig, before I claw your eyes out."

Vittoria went after him but was intercepted by two of Ernesto's men.

"I came to offer my condolences, that is all."

"Condolences. You killed my son and now you want to pay your respects and say you're sorry for your vile deed?"

Vittoria tried to grab one of the shotguns and was again dissuaded.

"I will not be satisfied until I can spit on your grave, you lying bastard."

"Please, you have offered your condolences," Bernardo said. "Now it is best to leave. There will be no peace with you here."

Bernardo encouraged Count Don Carlos's horse away, but he spun it around to face Vittoria again.

"I know nothing I say can undo the loss of your son or bring him back, but I can offer you something else. Something that I believe will help to take the sting out of your pain."

Vittoria, who was weeping uncontrollably at this point, waved a hand violently and Sophia and the other women continued trying to comfort her. Meanwhile, Father Columba had come out and he, along with Bernardo and the other men, were hustling Count Don Carlos away.

"Please consider my offer," Count Don Carlos called back. "If I give my son's hand to your daughter in marriage, your family will own half of everything that is the Castellammare estate."

Vittoria screamed and became completely hysterical at hearing these words and nearly blurted out the long-held secret she had in her own heart.

You murdered my father and stole the Castellammare estate from my family. And now you would offer back half of what is rightfully mine?

"Go on, get out of here," Paolo said with a wave of his rifle butt at Count Don Carlos.

He and Mario and several more of Ernesto's men were whipping the horses from beneath Count Don Carlos and his men, but he once again spun around to face the weeping Vittoria where she was being sheltered by the other women.

"Please consider this offer," Count Don Carlos called out. "I make it in peace."

"Go on, get the hell out of here!" Mario shouted.

"With one simple gesture, half of everything I own will be yours!"

Prodded again by Ernesto's men to leave, Count Don Carlos waved with his hat and galloped off with his men. Mario spat on the ground and helped herd everyone back into the church. Father Columba resumed the service. Vittoria continued wiping her tears, but it was a drone of words she hardly heard now, as that long-dormant part of her mind began to scheme. Half of Castellammare. And with that bastard one day in the ground, they would have all of it again.

The Lord is my light and my salvation; whom shall I fear?

That was all it would take. Sophia's hand in marriage and the wedge would be driven into the log.

The words of the Father continued while Vittoria was deep in her thoughts. *The Lord is the stronghold of my life; of whom shall I be afraid?*

Vittoria could not imagine how this foolish idea had gotten into Count Don Càrlos's head, but she accepted it as a divine gift right then.

I believe that I shall see the goodness of the Lord in the land of the living.

Wait for the Lord.

Finally, after all her anguish and handwringing, the Lord God was delivering Castellammare back into her hands.

She looked up at the cross and imagined Santino hanging there in place of Jesus and believed in her anguished sorrow that he had given up his life to bring Castellammare back to its rightful owners. Vittorio too had done his part and Vittoria had done all she could to keep the flame alive. Now it was up to Sophia to do what was required of her.

Tears flowed anew from Vittoria, and the women consoled her, not the least bit aware that Vittoria was now smiling somewhere deep inside her heart.

She followed the casket out of the church, scheming in her mind. She followed it through the cobblestone streets of the village, planning.

As Father Columba prayed over her son's grave, Vittoria stole glances at Sophia and planned her daughter's future.

Being shrewd, Vittoria did not speak a word of her plans over the following week. She let the sorrow pass and the drudgery of their lives to return. Then, at the end of a particularly difficult day, she dropped the bomb over their evening meal.

"Perhaps we are foolish not to consider Count Don Carlos's offer."

Sophia's head lurched up as if her mother was mad. Mario stared with rage in his eyes if she had committed a venial sin.

"Are you kidding?" Sophia said.

"Eh, for you alone I think this. It is a hard life we live, and what hope have you of ever escaping it?"

"You are mad."

"Say what you will, but it seems to me that you are foolish not to consider his offer."

Mario slammed his fist down on the table.

"Enough of this talk!"

Both women jumped a bit at the violent gesture and Vittoria fell silent. Cunning as she was, she knew enough to keep her mouth shut now. The seed had been planted. She would water it for a few days, let the roots sink in and take hold and prune things again at the appropriate hour.

That moment came the following week, while Sophia and Vittoria were walking together in the fields. The sun was high in the sky and the women wiped the sweat from their brows and across the land you could see the impoverished people laboring away on their land, tending to the olive groves, tending to the vineyards, tending to the tomatoes and wheat and corn. For Sophia, who had grown up in this life, it was nothing more or less than what you would expect, but for Vittoria, who had once been destined to be a baroness, it would always be a bitter pill to swallow.

"If only you had known Castellammare in its day," Vittoria said with a sigh.

"Please, don't start in on that again," Sophia said.

"Very well, but you cannot imagine."

Vittoria stood up and waved her hand across the countryside.

"To have all you see under your power. To manage the vineyards and fields. To operate the mills and olive presses. To own all the distribution. It was our family's destiny."

Vittoria stooped down and pulled at the weeds. It was a long moment before Sophia spoke.

"I have heard that his son is a tramp and a fool."

Vittoria smiled.

"All the better, then. With Count Don Carlos in his grave, you would soon own everything."

"And have fools for children."

"Not with our blood, no. You would have beautiful children."

"You sound so sure of yourself."

"The cream rises to the top, my child. The cream rises. Ah, but of course, you can stay here and work until your hands are hard and your back is crooked, and your heart is even more calloused than your hands, if that is what you desire. My story is already written, but the pages of yours are yet blank and you can decide how you would like to fill them."

"You are very cunning, mother, but don't think I am unaware of what you are doing."

Vittoria stood up.

"Do you think for one second that I don't despise that man, as much as you do? More than you could ever despise him. I would rather eat poisonous toads, but there is a simple truth here. The man is growing old. He has no other heirs. So, when he is dead someday, and thank God he will be, you will have only his idiot of a son between you and owning the entire estate. Now, you tell me. Could I possibly hope to present you with a better future in this world?"

Sophia went on working for a long spell before she spoke again.

"I am happy with my life here. This is all about you and your obsession. And I needn't remind you what that obsession has cost our family so far."

Vittoria's body tensed up at hearing those words and the bitterness of old spilled into her heart, but she checked herself. She felt the prize imminent and nearly hers now. All it took was patience. Let the plant grow further and at the exact right moment, she would harvest the crop.

Later that afternoon, on their way back to the house, Sophia spoke.

"I will consider doing this thing. But for you, not for me. Please never think that I have any desire to marry that worthless piece of rubbish for the sake of some land and a title. As you said, I would rather eat poisonous toads."

Vittoria put her arm around her daughter as they walked.

"You may say you are doing this for me, but someday you will see the wisdom of my words. You will stand upon the stage of the world, a great woman, and thank me for what I have done for you."

One day later that week, Vittoria arranged with Sophia to deliver their meat and produce into Castellammare. Vittoria and Sophia rode in their wagon. Paolo and three other armed men road alongside them on their horses. The journey required that they pass by the Castellammare estate and of course this had been precisely Vittoria's intention. Count Don Carlos was no less vigilant than Ernesto and would no doubt learn of their presence from his men.

They had been in the village less than an hour, bartering with store owners over their goods when a great commotion could be heard along the streets and Count Don Carlos was seen riding past, accompanied by his son Maximo and several armed guards. When Count Don Carlos tipped his hat at Vittoria, she very subtly nodded in return. Sophia looked up once at the staring Maximo and returned to her business. Maximo continued staring as they rode past until he nearly fell out of his saddle.

Vittoria returned to her business, knowing the signal had been sent. I am willing to tolerate you and consider your proposal. The next step is on you.

Two days later, several of Count Don Carlos's men rode up to the front of Vittoria's house, bearing a white stallion. They were met by Paolo and Mario and a handful of other armed men.

"What business do you have here?" Mario asked.

"We come with a gift for Signora Vittoria."

"Tell Count Don Carlos we do not want anything to do with his gifts."

Mario and the other men went to drive the horses away, but Vittoria appeared at the door and commanded everyone to stop. Count Don Carlos' men tipped their caps in her direction. As Vittoria stepped further out onto the porch, Sophia appeared in the doorway behind her. Every one of the men on horseback turned his attention that way. The man speaking looked back at Vittoria, but the others were unable to take their eyes off of Sophia, so Mario ushered her back into the shadows and closed the door.

"What is it that you wish?" Vittoria said.

"Count Don Carlos has sent you this horse as a gift. Like the white dove, he hopes that it will spread the spirit of peace across the land."

"Peace," Mario said and spat.

Again, Vittoria held up her hand.

"Tell Count Don Carlos that in the spirit of peace, I will accept it."

"Did you have any other words for his ears?"

"Tell him, thank you, and go in peace."

Vittoria took the reins of the horse. Count Don Carlos' men tipped their caps again and trotted off. Vittoria handed the reins to one of the men.

"Place it in the corral with Santino's white stallion."

"You're mad," Mario said.

"Am I mad to want peace? Is it better to live in fear as we have? That at any moment, you too might be killed? Or Sophia? Or me? Or any of us?"

Vittoria waved her hand across the group of armed men surrounding her. No one answered.

"Do not think that the anger is gone from my heart," she said. "Or the disgust, or my feelings of revenge, but I have had enough of war. As foreign as it sounds to these ears, perhaps in peace we will finally have what we could not find by warring with each other."

Vittoria looked from face to face, pulled up her dress, climbed the steps to the porch, and went back inside.

Two days later, while Sophia was gone to market, an invitation arrived for Vittoria and her entire family to join Count Don Carlos for dinner at Castellammare. When Vittoria hinted to Mario that she might accept, he went into a rage, first breaking things in the house and then out in the barn before he saddled his horse and rode off into the hills.

Having heard the ruckus, Francesca walked over to Vittoria's cottage as Mario was riding off. When Vittoria explained the invitation, Francesca shook her head.

"Getting into bed with Count Don Carlos? The people will abandon you, Vittoria. They will throw rocks at your windows. They might stone you to death."

"Then they will be fools. Do you think things will change under his rule? Never. Do you think we will run roughshod over the people, as he has? Of course not."

Vittoria paraded about the room, already feeling the power flow through her veins.

"No. We represent the people's only hope, Francesca, and I believe you know that too."

Francesca watched warily as Vittoria continued to stalk the room.

"What?" Vittoria said, seeing Francesca's look. "If I could convince you, I'd spit right here in my own kitchen floor, as if it were the grave of Count Don Carlos. I despise the man, even more than you do, but kings and princes have often held their own noses in these matters, in order to maintain peace and preserve their own blood."

"What?" she said again, seeing Francesca shake her head.

"What? Matters, you call it? Do you think I don't know where this game of yours is headed? You are playing with the life of your daughter, not your own. She is the pawn you are moving about in this game of yours. Have you asked her how she felt?"

"Of course."

"And?"

"She is willing to consider it."

Just then, they heard the wagon pull up out front and a moment later, Sophia came in through the front door. She kissed both women and set some things down on the table.

"Where's Papa?"

She looked from face to face.

"He rode off into the hills," Francesca said.

Vittoria stared for a long moment before handing the invitation to Sophia. Sophia read it without emotion and looked from face to face again, reading the situation quickly from the looks in Francesca and Vittoria's eyes.

"It will do no harm to go sit at his table and see what he has to say," Sophia said and set the invitation down.

Francesca stared at Sophia and finally looked at Vittoria.

"My God, I'd swear you have her hypnotized."

"I'm going to feed the animals," Sophia said and went back out the door without another word.

Vittoria and Francesca were left staring at each other.

"I'd swear it by God. You have that poor girl hypnotized."

Dinner with Count Don Carlos

Of course, Mario had refused any invitations to dinner at Count Don Carlos' home and had even gone to see Ernesto with his complaints, but ever the shrewd one himself, Ernesto had given the meal his blessing, advising Mario that sitting down to break bread with the enemy did not constitute a betrayal.

Enraged, Mario rode off to Palermo and was not seen for a week.

When the hour for the dinner actually arrived, a gilded carriage pulled up in front of Vittoria's house and a man dressed for royal courts climbed down and helped the two women inside. Count Don Carlos had agreed to allow six armed guards to accompany the women and Paolo was among them. The carriage rode out of the village and people paused to stare at it with suspicion and disgust.

As, with each passing mile, the carriage drew nearer to Castellammare, the memories and old emotions were rekindled in Vittoria. For, other than from afar, she had not seen the villa since that odious night when the Baron Castellammare had taken Vittoria and Vittorio up to confession and communion, only to be slaughtered at the hands of a mob, and though Vittoria had always imagined riding back to take possession of what was rightfully hers, she had never imagined it in quite this manner, so it required every bit of cunning and determination she could muster to swallow her pride and pretend that she did not want to take a knife to Count Don Carlos' throat upon seeing him on the porch of the estate as the carriage rode up.

He was there waving in a grand, ceremonious fashion and Maximo stood alongside him, looking as if someone had cloned a more benign version of Count Don Carlos. Maximo had the same long, square, handsome face, the same straight, strong nose, and the same sensuous mouth, but in the eyes, the two men could not have differed more dramatically. Count Don Carlos's eyes were forever narrowed as if you had just insulted his wife and he was considering how to gut you.

Maximo's eyes had the look of someone who had just been told a joke and did not understand it, or, in general, as if he was simply outwitted by life. He seemed pleasant enough, behind his dumb, mindless grin.

"Welcome, welcome," Count Don Carlos called out as the women were helped down from the carriage. Count Don Carlos came down the steps to greet them.

"Son, this is Vittoria and her daughter Sophia. Ladies, my son Maximo."

Both women shook Maximo's hand with a curt nod and without a smile. His grin slowly faded in response, until he was left staring dumbly at Sophia.

"Please, come inside," Count Don Carlos said. "I trust you won't mind if we do without the grand tour tonight. Dinner is ready and my hope is that we will have many more opportunities like this one to explore the entire estate."

Vittoria nodded respectfully and went into the house at Count Don Carlos's encouragement with Sophia beside her. Maximo followed along behind.

"Your coats, ladies?" Count Don Carlos said.

A servant came and disappeared with them in back. Vittoria had stopped in her tracks, taking in the estate, and in particular, all the changes Count Don Carlos had made. The place was at once consistent with Vittoria's distant memories of it, and unsettling different. She stood there as if compelled to restore the villa to its former state and ready to bark orders at a waiting work crew.

"Ladies?" Count Don Carlos said.

Broken from her spell, Vittoria looked at him and followed his gesture into the dining room. There, a large, rectangular table carved from oak, with a heavy top and thick legs, which sat in place of the table Vittoria had known.

"Please," Count Don Carlos said as he had her sit at one end of the table.

Sophia and Maximo were seated opposite each other in the middle and Count Don Carlos took the other end, far enough away from Vittoria to make it seem silly.

When the servants came, pouring wine, Count Don Carlos held up his glass.

"Let me just say what a great pleasure it is having you here."

Both women held up their glasses and drank without a response.

The meal arrived promptly and was consumed with Count Don Carlos speaking to Vittoria across the distances and she offered the occasional word in return, and with Maximo and Sophia eating in complete silence. Maximo kept stealing glances at the enchanting Sophia and looking away stupidly every time she returned his gaze.

With the meal soon over, Vittoria declined a walk, citing the need to get up early and deal with her chores in the morning, so the carriage was called. Vittoria and Sophia climbed into it, their armed escort gathered around, and Count Don Carlos stood on the porch, waving off ceremoniously the two women as they started on their way home.

"So, what did you think of Maximo?" Vittoria said after some distance.

"I have no idea whether or not to believe these tales of his debauched behavior down in Palermo, but I do know he's an idiot. The whole night and he said not one word."

"Eh. He was clearly overawed by your beauty."

"You are being generous."

"So, marry a bright young man like Paolo and be poor all your life."

"For you, money is everything."

"In this world, money is everything."

The women glared at each other and were silent the rest of the way home.

The following week, they accepted another invitation for dinner from Count Don Carlos and this time Vittoria agreed to accompany him for a walk after the meal, leaving Maximo and Sophia sitting alone on the porch together.

After several furtive but silent glances from Maximo, Sophia blurted out.

"Don't you ever say anything?"

Maximo looked over, blinking.

"I am sorry. You're just so beautiful, I don't know what to say."

"Then pretend I'm ugly."

Maximo smiled and appeared to relax a bit.

"I'm sorry but I can't imagine you being ugly. You do seem nice, though."

"Like your whores down in Palermo?"

Maximo blushed.

"I know. There are many rumors about me, but they're not true."

"Oh, so you've never been with a whore down in Palermo?"

"Well, my father sent me down there once. He told me it would help me to become a man. Now I go down into the city from time to time to drink with my friends, but not that. Not anymore."

Sophia nodded.

"So, what are your plans in life? How do you see your future here at Castellammare?"

"I don't know. I guess just to help my father run things."

"And when he is dead?"

"I don't know. Just to keep things going."

Sophia nodded and gazed out across the countryside in the sylvan light of dusk, the shrewdness she had acquired from her mother suddenly sparking to life. She recalled her mother's words.

One day you will be a powerful woman, with the world at your command.

And suddenly now she felt that power running through her veins.

Clearly, Maximo would be of little use in running this estate, but as her mother had also said, so much the better. With Count Don Carlos in his grave one day soon, Sophia would have command of an empire.

She looked over at Maximo, who was still staring at her helplessly.

"So, is it your wish to marry me?"

Maximo stared, his eyes wide open and with a dumb grin on his face.

"Yes. Yes, I would very much like to do that."

"Okay, good, because I see no point in wasting time. We will tell them tonight of our plans and arrange the wedding as soon as possible. Agreed?"

Maximo nodded.

"Good."

She kissed Maximo on the cheek.

"Let's go find our parents and inform them."

At hearing the news, Count Don Carlos was delighted and kissed Sophia's hand. Vittoria was both delighted and shocked by the transformation of her daughter. It was as if someone else had taken over her body.

Still, Vittoria wasted no time in arranging the wedding and gave no thought to the many whispers that went on behind her back around the village. Or to her husband's rage, or to the disbelieving looks of Francesca and Teresa. She knew that this marriage represented a Trojan horse. Count Don Carlos could live his life with a feeling of legitimacy now and die in peace, as was his hope. The more important point was, with Maximo as the witless husband, Castellammare would have been returned to its rightful owners.

There were moments when Vittoria paused to wonder. Had she been more patient and wiser, could the deaths of Vittorio and Santino have been avoided? She would never know the answer to that question for sure, and perhaps it would always haunt her, but at least she would not have failed in fulfilling the promises she had made to her brother and her son and all of their ancestors.

The wedding was held at the Castellammare estate and a truce was called for the occasion, so that both during the ceremony and over the course of the ensuing reception, a contingent of Count Don Carlos' men was gathered over here and a contingent of Ernesto's men gathered over there, with even a grudging nod of respect offered between the men from time to time, such that the event went off smoothly. Gino was there, dancing with and charming all the young women, including

Countess Sophia, everyone had a grand time and even the embittered Mario seemed to be taken in by this joyful moment for his daughter.

That night, in the newlywed's bedroom chamber at Castellammare, Countess Sophia soon discovered how true Count Maximo's confessions were about his escapades in Palermo, or at least how little he had learned from them. He was on and off in less than a minute, yet seemed quite satisfied with his efforts.

Disgusted and furious with him in equal measures, Countess Sophia refused Count Maximo's advances the following night, and the night after that, and for several weeks following. Count Maximo, angry and wounded by her refusals, told his father he needed to attend to business in Palermo and disappeared.

When Baroness Vittoria stopped by one day and queried, "Anything yet?" Countess Sophia answered incredulously. "You must be kidding. I won't let him near me."

Upon hearing Countess Sophia's explanation for why, Baroness Vittoria threw up her hands.

"What is wrong with you, child? Sometimes you have to teach these young fools."

"This marriage was your idea. You teach him."

Baroness Vittoria slapped her daughter.

"You don't talk to me that way. My brother did his duty. Your brother did his duty. I've done *my* duty. Now it is time for you to do yours."

Seeing her daughter cry, Baroness Vittoria felt remorse and reached out a hand, but Countess Sophia slapped it away.

"You talk of duty when you ran off to marry the man that you loved. And you now have the nerve to marry me to this idiot."

"Everything I have done has been with one purpose, child. To return this estate to our family, its rightful owners."

"And in the meantime, the earth is littered with the graves of your obsession."

Baroness Vittoria started to raise her hand again but relented, realizing that nothing could be accomplished by anger at this point, other than to sew more bitterness. Seeing her daughter's mind was hardened, she decided that patience was the proper course and departed with a final kiss on Countess Sophia's head.

With Count Maximo gone, Countess Sophia shared polite dinners with Count Don Carlos each evening, during which time she picked his brain for every bit of knowledge she could glean about Castellammare. How did the vineyards work? How did the olive presses work? Where did he sell his crops and products and to whom? By the time Count Maximo reappeared, Countess Sophia felt even more profoundly that he was a useless and unnecessary appendage.

He went to her room that night and begged.

"Please. You make me look like a fool."

"You are a fool. I won't bother telling you what else I think of you."

"You may think I'm foolish, but you are even more foolish to think that I am unnecessary. If we don't produce a child, my father will have no use for you either."

Countess Sophia harrumphed.

"Think what you want, but he knows who your mother is and your only use to him is the legitimacy of the Castellammare name. Without a child, he will quickly dispense with you."

"He wouldn't dare. The peasants would tear him and this place to pieces."

"Not if you are childless. A woman who cannot bear children loses her dominion. People will talk, but no one will raise a finger to protect you."

Countess Sophia considered his words in silence.

"Please. Let us try again," Count Maximo said.

Countess Sophia reviewed him coldly.

"What? Have you been practicing with your whores down in Palermo?"

Count Maximo sat there with his hands clasped, fidgeting with his two thumbs.

"You are such a jerk," Countess Sophia said.

"I went and asked questions. That is all. Because I wanted to please you."

Her nose went up, she did not protest further.

As before, it was over very quickly, but having satisfied Countess Sophia, she forgave Count Maximo this time and embraced him with a few tender kisses.

"We'll have to work on your part," she said and held his head.

"Did I please you then?"

Countess Sophia looked at him and nodded.

They lay there in silence for a long time and then suddenly Maximo was talking of his childhood and confessing his fears.

"I hate my father."

Countess Sophia looked over with interest.

"When I was a boy, I was terrified of bugs and snakes, so he used to laugh at me and make fun of me. Tell me I would never become a man in front of the others."

Countess Sophia stared, waiting, and expecting to hear more. It came.

"I don't think a day went by that he didn't talk of the need to kill off your family. He would tell me, 'You have to be strong and prepare yourself because one day they will come back and try to reclaim what they think is theirs.' When the castle was robbed and we found blood outside and learned that Vittorio had been killed, he told me, 'See, just as I warned you,' but I never believed you were bad people, the way he had said. And of course, I heard all the local stories about what had happened and felt it was all wrong that we were here in the first place, instead of you."

Countess Sophia stared for a long moment and kissed him on the cheek.

"I heard all the stories, too, but none of it mattered to me." Countess Sophia shrugged. "I guess it's all over with now. Too many people have died and I'm just glad there's peace."

"I'm just glad you're here with me."

Countess Sophia smiled insincerely and held his head, not ready to go that far. She had done her duty and was glad for the peace and even endured this man having his way, but she did not love Count Maximo and doubted she ever would. She assumed that for all her life, she would be left to wonder what young man might have come along to sweep her off her feet. She tucked those youthful dreams deep inside her heart somewhere and began to plot the other destiny she had been called upon to live.

In the spring of 1887, Countess Sophia gave birth to boy and girl twins. The girl was named Athena and the boy Santino, after his late uncle.

Count Don Carlos would sit on the porch on summer afternoons, as Baron Castellammare had done those many years earlier, and when men came to meet and talk business with him, he would point them in the direction of the new countess, Sophia. This was usually met with raised eyebrows, but these men were quickly stopped in their tracks by the combination of Sophia's beauty, her determined, no-nonsense nature, and her shrewd business dealings.

With her newfound wealth, Countess Sophia arranged for a private tutor to teach her twins so that they would have the finest education possible, a fact that did not make much of an impression on the impetuous Santino, but Athena took to her studies promptly and was soon seen toddling about the estate, giving orders in several languages.

In all this, Countess Sophia found herself so busy, she hardly had time for her husband, who responded to this lack of attention by disappearing for weeks on end in Palermo.

Count Don Carlos was overjoyed with his grandchildren running around the estate and the devotion and kindness his daughter-in-law, Sophia showed toward him.

As if all the boxes in his life had been checked, he passed away in his sleep. When a maid went to arouse him and found his cold, dead body, a great clamor arose and echoed across the estate. Count Maximo had to be dragged back from Palermo. News quickly spread across the countryside, too little sadness among the peasants and not a small amount of rejoicing.

Baroness Vittoria, who had remained estranged from Sophia for the most part, traveled to Castellammare as soon as she had heard the news, and Sophia received her coolly, but graciously. Sophia had wine brought to the porch and the two women sat there in the shade, gazing out over the rolling hills and fields of the Castellammare estate.

"I remember like it was yesterday," Baroness Vittoria said. "My father sitting here and fanning himself, that the last day of his life."

Countess Sophia spun her wine glass in her hand without commenting. Everyone had their memories, sorrows, and regrets. Perhaps Countess Sophia had failed to sympathize with those of her mother thoroughly enough. Had she lost her own mother early in life and then watched her own father slain at the hands of a mob, her view of life might well have been equally distorted.

In any case, though she had provided amply for her mother's well-being over the past three years, she regretted their differences and their failure to stay in touch.

"Why don't you come to stay here, mother," Countess Sophia said.

Baroness Vittoria glanced once at her daughter and back out over the estate. A tear formed and trickled down her cheek, then another one. Baroness Vittoria wiped at them and reached out for her daughter's hand without speaking.

Countess Sophia Meets Duke Don Vito

One day the following year, Giancarlo and Fidelio suddenly reappeared in Castellammare, dressed up in fine suits like dandies now and sporting a carriage. When they pulled to a stop in front of Ernesto's house, Ernesto came out, playing with his mouth and doing all he could to keep from laughing.

"What's the matter, boss?" Giancarlo said, stepping out of the carriage. "You don't like the color?"

"You son of a gun," Ernesto said and gave him a hug. He hugged Fidelio too. "So, you got rich. Why in the world did you come back to this dusty place?"

"Oh, America's good," Giancarlo said with a look at Fidelio. "We've got ourselves a couple of houses and some land there, but come on, this is home. Besides, our money is worth what, ten to one back here? We figure we'll set ourselves up as big shots in Palermo and travel back and forth."

"So, what do you want with me?"

"Jesus Christ, boss. We just came by to say hello."

Ernesto gave them a nod as a silent hello.

"Okay. So now you've said hello, get the hell out of here."

Giancarlo gestured with a look at Fidelio.

"Get a load of him. Come on, boss. Jump in! We'll take a ride around the village and show off."

"I wouldn't be caught dead with you sons of bitches. Come on in and have a glass of Castellammare wine before I run you off."

The two men had a look around while sitting down. Ernesto brought the wine.

"You know, we could bring our decorator down from Palermo if you'd like, boss," Giancarlo said.

"Shut up and drink."

Ernesto poured the wine and the men held up their glasses.

"Salute."

"Salute."

"Where's Constantina?" Fidelio said.

"Eh, probably at Castellammare with Baroness Vittoria. The women run the place now. You know Count Don Carlos passed away."

"Yeah, we heard," Giancarlo said.

"God rest his soul," Fidelio said satirically.

Ernesto drank again.

"So, tell me about it," he said.

Giancarlo and Fidelio looked at each other.

"There's the good and the bad," Giancarlo said. "Lots of money to be made, but if you don't have any? Jesus, the poor bastards. They're crammed into all the big cities like rats in a hole. Most of the cops are Irish so they won't even go into these slums. You live there and you're left to the mercy of the black hand."

"The black hand?"

"Yeah, boss," Fidelio said. "You wonder where all these two-bit cutthroats from Naples and Palermo have been disappearing to? Over there. They've set up protection rackets and are bleeding the poor dry."

Ernesto looked the two of them up and down.

"Is that how the two of you got rich?"

"Hell no, boss," Giancarlo said. "We made our money off the rich. You have to be scum to tax those poor bastards in the slums. They got nothing."

"We're like Robin Hood," Fidelio said.

"Sure, like Robin Hood," Ernesto said. "So, what else?"

"Oh, we were going to tell you," Giancarlo said. "Remember that Duke Don Vito from Palermo? From the old days?"

"Sure. I heard he was over there too."

"Yeah, big time. Only they ran him back to Sicily."

"What for?"

"For making trouble. What do you think? See, there's this Italian cop named Petrosino. Talk about Robin Hood. They say he's incorruptible. Anyway, he goes into these Italian slums and starts knocking the heads of all these guys mixed up in the black hand, and all of a sudden half the mob is on the run."

"Then he digs up sixty bodies in a basement up in Harlem one day," Fidelio added.

"They called it the Murder Stable. You don't pay up, bing, bang, boom and you're underground! Well, word is, Petrosino knew Duke Don Vito was involved but couldn't prove it."

"So, he trumps up some minor charge and gets him deported."

"And believe me," Giancarlo said. "He's mad as a hornet. Swears he's going to put Petrosino in the ground someday."

"So, he's back in Palermo now."

"Yeah, boss. Other than missing you so much, we came to warn you."

"Get out of here."

Giancarlo and Fidelio laughed.

"But seriously, boss. Duke Don Vito's got money coming out his ears and is planning to take over all of Sicily, so don't be surprised when he comes knocking at your door."

"Maybe I'll go over to America."

"If you got money," Fidelio said. "It's a great place. If not, better to starve over here."

"So, what are your plans?"

"Oh, we got it made, boss," Giancarlo said. "We'll sit around the cafés sipping wine and watching the girls go by."

"Always the playboy."

"Hey, life is short. I paid enough dues up there in those hills. Eating your crappy stew and using the woods as my bathroom. I'm going to enjoy life now."

"Like you ever suffered."

Giancarlo smiled.

"You keep me posted, yeah?"

"You bet, boss. You have any trouble, send a message over to Palermo and we'll see what we can do."

"Thanks."

The men stood up and shook hands.

"Sure you don't want a ride, boss?"

Giancarlo laughed and jumped out of the way as Ernesto tried to kick him.

Outside, Ernesto watched as the two men climbed into their fancy carriage, saluted a final time, and headed down the road.

Late that summer, as Countess Sophia attempted to arrange a buyer for her grape crop, she discovered that not a single one of the usual merchants would do business with her. This was a new development, though not entirely surprising to Countess Sophia. She had heard the whispers behind her back in the past and knew these men spoke of her with disdain. They bristled at the idea of doing business with any woman, however much they stood in awe of her beauty.

But at least they had always dealt with her. Now no one would come forward.

When Countess Sophia inquired further, she was told to go see a man in Palermo. This man turned out to be Duke Don Vito.

Countess Sophia went to meet with him immediately and was told she would have to pay a percentage of her profits, or there would be no deals. Sophia told Duke Don Vito what he could do with his deal.

With her crop ready for harvest and destined to rot in a warehouse, Countess Sophia dispatched an emissary to Naples, where she quickly found the necessary buyers. News of this deal quickly spread back to Palermo, and a furious Count Maximo rushed home to rage at Countess Sophia soon after. There were forces at work here that she did not understand, and unless Count Maximo was allowed to run Castellammare as he sought fit, it would be lost to both of them.

Countess Sophia scoffed at her husband.

"Shrewdness is in finding ways around an obstacle, not butting heads with it, and butting heads is the only tactic you seem to understand."

"I am only saying, let me make certain decisions and give the appearance of me running things."

"No. Either you run things yourself or get out of the way."

Count Maximo stormed back to Palermo and Countess Sophia got back to managing the estate.

A few weeks later, Countess Sophia received an ornate envelope in the mail, addressed from Palermo. She opened it and found a note inside, apologizing profusely for the inconvenience, even lamenting the very need for the note's existence, but certain sums would have to be paid in order to prevent certain buildings around the Castellammare estate from being burned to the ground. Of course, if after certain buildings were burned to the ground and certain sums were still not paid, then certain other buildings around the Castellammare estate would be burned to the ground, and so on until the monies were paid. In closing, those writing the letter apologized again profusely and made clear that they were only acting as intermediaries. Their only interest was in looking out for the rightful owners of the Castellammare estate. The note, couched in flowery prose as it was, would have made a poet from the Elizabethan Era proud.

Sophia's first impulse was to burn the letter, ornate envelope, and all, but discretion stopped her and she brought the note to Baroness Vittoria's attention.

"It's that bastard Duke Don Vito," Countess Sophia said.

"Of course it is," Baroness Vittoria said.

"So what?"

"So, you go along."

"So, we just give in to these crooks?"

"We do what is best."

"Giving in is best? Is that what you taught me?"

"My dear, there are forces at work here that you don't understand."

"And you do."

"I know enough not to be rash."

Sophia was beside herself.

"Look," Baroness Vittoria said. "I'll have Mario bring the letter to Ernesto's attention. Let's see what he says."

Ernesto read the note and sat there brooding in silence for a long moment. He was an old man now and little more than a respected figurehead, but no one was shrewder and Ernesto immediately knew what this meant. Duke Don Vito was finally expanding out from Palermo and flexing his muscles into the countryside, just as Fidelio and Giancarlo had predicted he would.

"Enzo," Ernesto called out.

Enzo got up from taking a nap and came over.

"Go to Palermo. Find Giancarlo and Fidelio and show them this letter."

"Why don't you send me?" Mario said.

Ernesto motioned with a hand for him to be silent.

"Find Giancarlo and Fidelio," he told Enzo. "They will help you to arrange a meeting with these people. Be humble. Don't make any trouble. Just find out what they want. Say that the Countess of Castellammare has asked us, as her intermediaries, to inquire discreetly into the matter."

"You know where to find Giancarlo and Fidelio?"

"Check the cafés. If you don't find them there, check the whorehouses."

Enzo started to leave.

"And don't get lost down there."

Ernesto made a lewd gesture with both his hands.

"Get back as soon as you can."

As soon as Enzo was gone, Ernesto eyed his son and stared off into space, scratching his forehead.

"When are you going to learn?"

Mario scoffed.

"I'm a grown man. Quit treating me like a kid."

"I treat you like a kid because you act like one."

Mario fumed in silence.

"Look, you don't use your head to scratch your ass."

Mario fumed some more.

"That's okay, but someday hopefully you'll be sitting in my place and you'll understand. What are you going to do? Run off every time there's a problem? No. You must learn to delegate."

Ernesto looked off, scratching the stubble on his cheek now.

"The important thing here is to exercise caution. As Bernardo once told me, long ago now, the world is growing smaller. So, eh, it was bound to come to this. Sooner or later, these big shots like Duke Don Vito were going to get restless and go looking for new Maggietory. So now we must determine just how powerful he is and decide on a course of action from there."

"And we all know what that course of action will be in advance. Kiss his boots rather than fight."

Ernesto eyed his son, picked up a big chunk of provolone off the table, sliced off a piece, and stuck it in his mouth. When he offered a slice to Mario, Mario declined, so Ernesto ate that piece too and set the cheese back down.

"You and your wars. You never seem to understand. If we hit these guys, there'll be no end to it."

Mario scoffed.

"He'll just think we're weak and hit us anyway."

"Always ready to spill blood, you."

Mario glared. Ernesto scratched by his nose and yawned.

"No, that's the last thing you do. We'll see if we can work with Duke Don Vito first. And if not, eh. You can have your damn war."

Ernesto looked out towards the mouth of the cave. Gino was sitting there in the pale afternoon sunlight. He was an old man too now. They were all growing old and a new world was coming. Ernesto had no illusions about what that meant. There was a new breed of people in this racket, whose first interest was in making money, not protecting the poor, and seeing justice done. You paid up, and if you didn't, they came around and put a bullet in your head.

He sighed.

"Go down and tell your mother that we're looking into it and tell her to convey the message to Sophia."

He patted his son on the shoulder.

"Go. Be with your wife and family. There is nothing more we can do for today."

Ernesto watched his son head off, worried that their days had come to an end. What would Mario and his men do otherwise? They had no skills, besides the use of guns. They would be down to tilling the soil or banditry or starving to death if things went on this way.

A few days later, Enzo returned with news from Palermo. Ernesto sat down with him in the cave, having made sure that Mario was not around to listen.

"It was Duke Don Vito behind the letter."

"Did you meet with him?"

"No, but I met with Giancarlo and Fidelio and they inquired for me and were told that this is how Duke Don Vito deals with people who don't pay up."

Ernesto nodded, listening, thinking, worrying.

"There's more, boss."

Ernesto motioned for him to go on.

"Maximo has been hanging around with Duke Don Vito's gangs up there and getting friendly with them. Can you believe that bastard?"

"What are you telling me? He's extorting money from his own family?"

"Hell if I know. All I know is," Enzo gestured with both hands, "They're in bed together somehow and I wouldn't put it past Count Maximo. He's incapable of putting two nuts together. Meanwhile, his wife has started an empire. You figure it out."

Ernesto made a face that said he wasn't entirely convinced of Enzo's logic, but he wasn't the least bit happy with what he was saying, either.

"What more do you know about this Duke Don Vito?"

"Oh, his organization is taking over everything. If you're a peasant, they come with a fancy wagon, pick up your goods and transport them to the village for you. Then they rent you a stall at the market and wet their beaks at every stage of the process. This is pizzu on a grand scale."

"And the old royal families. Where are they in all this?"

"Marrying their daughters off to Duke Don Vito's rich friends."

"It's come to that."

Enzo shrugged.

"Think about it, boss. It makes perfect sense. The families maintain their power. This Duke Don Vito acquires legitimacy, and all of it is done without one bullet being fired."

Ernesto shook his head. Enzo shrugged again.

"There's more, boss."

"What are you waiting for? Act two? Get on with it."

"It's a story, boss. It takes time to unfold."

"I'll give you a story. So what?"

"This Duke Don Vito wants you to come to Palermo and meet with him."

Ernesto nodded wearily.

"And you didn't tell me this at the beginning because?"

"I was getting to it."

"You were getting to it. You and your novellas. So, when does he want this meeting to take place?"

"At your convenience, but as soon as possible."

Ernesto nodded.

"He'll send a fancy carriage for you."

"I'm sure he will."

Ernesto sat there scratching the stubble on his cheek again.

"How powerful is he?"

"Boss, I say you bargain the best you can, but make the deal. These people are on another level altogether."

"So, we extort now . . . and bully . . . and steal . . . and kill anyone who gets in our way."

"It's survival, boss."

"Survival for what?"

Enzo shrugged.

"Go meet with him. It's all you can do."

Ernesto thought for a long moment.

"All right. Tell him to send his fancy carriage."

A week later, Ernesto was being escorted up the stone steps and in through the palatial front doors of a Palermo estate sitting above the Mediterranean Sea with gorgeous views and breezes. The living room led out to a stone terrace and a breeze fluttered in through the open doors. Duke Don Vito was there wearing a cream-colored linen suit with a sky-blue shirt. He had a broad forehead and receding hair that was combed straight back. His sage eyes were shrewd but not unkind. He had a good nose and a sensitive mouth. Overall, he was handsome in appearance, slightly over six feet tall, around 190 lbs., well-built, and gracious in style.

In greeting Ernesto, Duke Don Vito bowed slightly.

"Your reputation precedes you, Don Ernesto."

"As does yours," Ernesto said.

Duke Don Vito held up his hands in modesty.

"Men like me walk on the shoulders of giants like you."

Duke Don Vito smiled, snapped his fingers and a servant appeared.

"Bring us a chilled white wine, please."

The servant bowed and scurried off.

"Please, have a seat, my friend."

The two men sat in padded chairs. The terraced hillsides fell away to the city of Palermo and the sea below them. There were vineyards along the hillsides, the village was white, and the sea was the color of turquoise.

When the wine came, Duke Don Vito held up his glass.

"To peace."

Ernesto held up his glass and drank without answering.

"So, you wished to speak with me?"

"Ah, well. As I said, what we hope for is peace. Certain things must come to pass, but hopefully, there is no need for us to go to war over these changes."

"And who is deciding these things?"

"Don Ernesto, please. You have your domain and I respect that, but we cannot pretend to operate as separate little fiefdoms anymore. The world is rapidly growing smaller and we need to change with it."

"So, I am told."

"Trust me. There is no stopping these changes in the world. Take this new democracy and the vote, for instance. If we don't look out for our own interests, who knows what kind of idiots will be running the place."

"So, what do you propose?"

"It's not what we propose. We're doing it already. You see, we simply run our own candidates and get the people to vote for them."

"Then what is the point of the vote?"

Duke Don Vito smiled, picked up a ballot that had been lying on the table next to him, and showed it to Ernesto.

"At first, we tried to educate the people. Talk sense to them. Maybe twist a few arms. But let's face it, most people can't read or write and don't understand what's what, and in most cases don't want to know, so now we make it simple for them. We put an ox and a mule next to the candidates and tell them to vote for the mule."

"And if they don't?"

"They can go find themselves new jobs. Really, it's very simple this way. If there are 400 people in a village, you will find that all 400 of them have voted for the mule. So, they take care of us and we take care of them. It's that or they're left at the mercy of these politicians who are idiots, most of them."

"But who still taxes you from the other end."

"Leave that to us. We take care of everything."

Ernesto nodded.

"Please, drink your wine," Duke Don Vito said.

Ernesto did.

"So, what do you want from me?"

"Help us to institute our system in and around Castellammare, of course."

"Our people are mostly happy with the way things are now."

"Don Ernesto, please. I know otherwise."

"I said mostly. I can guarantee you that they will be far more unhappy with your system."

"So, that is your job. To make them understand and accept it."

"And what is it you would have me do regarding the Countess of Castellammare? Pay up or we burn her place down?"

Duke Don Vito shrugged.

"If you choose to work outside the system, that is the price you pay."

"I don't think you understand the people of Castellammare."

"And perhaps the people of Castellammare don't understand me."

Duke Don Vito organized the Castellammare area to become one of the strongest mafia organizations in Sicily, after Palermo.

Ernesto looked out at the sea. It was a very pleasant view. It was not a very pleasant conversation. Either he agreed to do as Duke Don Vito asked, or there would be war.

"Don Ernesto, I'll tell you what. As a gesture of goodwill, we'll forget this business with the Countess. It was in bad taste. My men, sometimes they get carried away. And if we can come to an understanding, my door will always be open to you. Any little thing that comes up that doesn't sit right with the people, you come to me and we'll make an accommodation. The only rule is, everybody pays for their protection. Then we take care of the politicians and everyone can go on about their lives without any trouble."

Ernesto looked back out at the terraced hillsides and the sea.

"I cannot say yes without talking to my people."

"Of course. I understand. Go explain things. And if there are any concerns, you are welcome to come back and talk to me about them further."

Ernesto remained, staring at the sea as he spoke.

"I have spent my entire life trying to do what is right by the people. The food and money we receive are given to us out of love and gratitude. We never demand a thing from anybody. These people are family to us. How can I go to them now and say, either you pay or we burn down your house?"

"You're taking the wrong attitude, Don Ernesto. Just explain to them, we're getting more organized now. That's all. We must. It's that or this new government and the times will trample over all of us."

Ernesto looked over at Duke Don Vito and nodded.

"I will do my best to explain it."

Duke Don Vito leaned forward and patted Ernesto on the knee.

"Trust me. I called upon you because you have always been reasonable and diplomatic. No one needs a war. Let's work together. I assure you that I am equally concerned about the needs of the people."

Ernesto gestured with his hands and stood up.

"We shall see."

"But Don Ernesto, you're not going to stay? I had hoped for us to have dinner."

"I appreciate the offer, but it is best that I get back. The sooner I can communicate your offer, the sooner I will have an answer."

"Very well. It has been a pleasure and I will hope for your success."

Duke Don Vito snapped fingers and the same servant appeared.

"The carriage, please."

The servant hurried off and Duke Don Vito walked Ernesto out to the stone steps in front.

"Have you ridden the trains yet, Don Ernesto?"

Ernesto shook his head.

"You must! My god, the speed . . . it's eye-opening. They say the line between Lercara Friddi and Leonforte will be completed sometime next year. Soon you will be able to travel from Palermo to Messina in four to five hours. Can you imagine it? There is no getting around this changing world, Don Ernesto. All we can do is adapt."

Ernesto nodded. The carriage came and he climbed in. Duke Don Vito shut the door and leaned his head in.

"For both our sakes, I hope you will be successful."

The two men stared for a long moment before Duke Don Vito stood up.

"Good luck," he said and waved to the driver.

Their eyes met one more time before the carriage lurched forward and away down the cobblestone driveway.

Duke Don Vito Takes Charge

The thirty-mile trip required a change of horses and took most of five hours going up over the mountain, leaving Ernesto plenty of time to consider what he had learned. Wanting his wife's counsel, he had the driver return him home and as always, found the place smelling of food. In fact, Constantina was just then pulling a pasta casserole out of the oven. She placed the food on the table, kissed her husband on the cheek, and served him bread and wine without saying a word. Only when he had fed himself well did she speak.

"What did this Duke Don Vito have to tell you?"

Ernesto explained.

"You tax the people on both ends and they will revolt."

"I explained this to Duke Don Vito and he assured me they will take care of everything, including the government."

Constantina stared at her husband and encouraged him to eat more. Ernesto held up a hand and finished his glass of red wine.

"The question is, do we have a choice, short of all-out war?" she said.

"You know the answer to that question. Why do you always ask it? Of course, there's a choice. There's always a choice."

Ernesto sat there drumming his fingers on the old wooden table.

"I think the only question is, can we convince your son to keep the peace."

"My son?" Constantina said, cleaning up. "Why is he always my son?"

Ernesto smiled a bit.

"I don't know. Where did he get this hot blood of his?"

Constantina stopped cleaning and stood there with a hand to her mouth.

"Wait here," she said suddenly and went out the door.

She was gone for five minutes. When she returned, Mario and Baroness Vittoria were with her.

"Sit," Constantina said and brought more glasses.

Ernesto shrugged and poured all four of them full.

"Salute," he said and drank.

"So, let me guess," Mario said. "You dragged us over here so you can tell us you sold out to this Duke Don Vito? I already figured that."

"I brought you over here so we could talk some sense into you," Constantina said. "Now both of you listen."

Mario looked at everyone around the table.

"So talk," he said to Ernesto.

"Show your father some respect."

"I said 'talk'. Let's not make a big deal of it."

"Show some respect," Constantina said once again and gestured at Ernesto to go on.

Mario sat there fidgeting restlessly throughout the entire explanation and shook his head when Ernesto was done.

"You're worried about me? Wait until the rest of your men get wind of this deal."

"We're here to talk about you. I'll take care of everyone else in good time."

"Good luck."

"Let's worry about you," Constantina said.

"You want to know if I'm going to make trouble?"

Mario looked at Baroness Vittoria and back.

"I'm no fool. I knew this was coming. I'm surprised it took them so long."

"So, what?" Ernesto said.

"I say we negotiate for some terms. We control the local politics. We control the local markets. We control the money and send a cut up to Duke Don Vito. He can think he has ultimate say, but it won't amount to much on the ground. In the end, all he wants is his money anyway, right?"

Ernesto looked at Constantina and back at Mario.

"Good. Now you're starting to make sense."

"Oh, like all of a sudden I acquired brains."

"Well, forgive me but you haven't displayed them a great deal in the past."

"You think I've been dumb because I wanted to get tough in the past. Well, think about it. If we had gotten tough in the past, we could have grown and gotten into these other things, in which case we would have been stronger and would have been in a position to stand up to this Duke Don Vito instead of having to lick his boots."

"And we would have been just like them."

"And here we are, about to become just like them anyway. Only licking their boots in the process."

Not having an answer for Mario, Ernesto turned to Baroness Vittoria.

"Are you all right with this?"

She shrugged.

"Do they leave my daughter in charge of Castellammare?"

"I have Duke Don Vito's word on that. He'll rescind the terms of the note, but she pays going forward just like everyone else. He doesn't want the estate. He's not foolish enough to make more trouble than necessary for himself."

"The question I asked is, is he a man of his word?" Mario said.

"Duke Don Vito may be many things, many of them ruthless, but he is a man of his word. I trust him that far."

"So, go tell him. These are our terms or my men will revolt. And then we'll see what kind of man he is."

"I will call for his fancy carriage tomorrow."

"Without talking to the other men?"

"There is no discussing this deal. We take it or leave it, and make the best terms possible, as you said."

Ernesto poured the glasses full again of the Castellammare wine and shrugged.

Two days later, a carriage arrived for Ernesto at dawn and delivered him to Palermo in time for lunch. Duke Don Vito had the meal served out on his terrace, and it was with the sort of flair that a man from the country like Ernesto was not accustomed. Ernesto watched warily as oysters were served, then pasta, then duck, then veal, then fresh fruits and cakes. At that time, he also refilled the glasses with the Castellammare wine he had brought with him. Duke Don Vito commented on the wine, its body and richness, its aroma, its distinct flavor and unique taste. This was a wine like none he had ever had, one befitting of the Castellammare name.

The two men had continued their talk of life, marriage and children, and the changing times, but not a word was said about their business until the meal was complete and the two men had retired to the veranda with snifters of brandy.

"So, what do you have to tell me about our business, Ernesto?"

"I can tell you that it doesn't go down easily."

Duke Don Vito nodded.

"And what does that mean to me?"

"It means, my men will not agree to this new regime without certain terms. And if these terms are not met, they will simply melt back into the hills. In which case, they will be a menace to both of us."

Duke Don Vito nodded while studying Ernesto.

"So, are you telling me you cannot control the men who work for you?"

"Duke, my world is a different one from the one which you inhabit. These men have submitted to my authority in the past, not because I have power or a heavy hand, but because we all believed that we were fighting for the same thing. Now everything is to change."

Ernesto shrugged in that Sicilian way of expressing skepticism.

"To do as you wish, the men want to control certain things."

"And what are these things?"

Ernesto explained as Duke Don Vito listened without the slightest hint of emotion. When Ernesto was through, Duke Don Vito scratched the back of his neck and looked out at the sea. He thought carefully about what he had been told and eventually gestured in a way that said, okay.

"That is fine. It is better this way, no? Your people are already well known. If I bring in all-new faces, I will only be making trouble for myself. I would only ask for some...shall we say...accounting clarity on your end."

"That will not be a problem," Ernesto said.

Duke Don Vito nodded.

"Yes, I think this will be good. You already have the organization on the ground. I will supply a few people. People for instance, who are familiar with how the politics and the other apparatuses of power work, how we collect the goods for the market and manage the stalls, but they will remain in the background. What we want is continuity. That way, no matter where you go in Sicily, the terms will be the same. It's only fair, right? Everyone should be on the same level. Then there is no reason for anyone to complain."

Ernesto did not like Duke Don Vito's speech, but maintained a poker face and nodded throughout it. It was all he and his men could do. Work with the situation as best they could and if things became untenable, there would be war. Nothing would prohibit them from going to war down the road, but peace was always preferable, so they would try that path first.

"Good," Duke Don Vito said at seeing Ernesto acquiesce. "A man named Bruno will be arriving at the Castellammare area in the next few days. He will help you with implementing the system."

"Perhaps it would be best if you gave us a few weeks to spread the word and smooth over the transition."

"Please," Duke Don Vito said. "As I told you, Bruno will stay in the background, but I would like to have someone there assessing the situation. And of course, clarifying things for you, as it becomes necessary."

Again, Ernesto nodded without revealing the least bit of emotion.

"Give me at least three days to round up my men and explain the situation."

"Very well. Today is Friday. I will plan to have Bruno there at your home on Monday morning. Not too early, but please be ready to receive him."

Again, Ernesto nodded and left that afternoon not liking the taste in his mouth, but he had learned long ago to place the interests of the people first and make his own feelings secondary. You did not start spilling blood because you disliked something. You only spilled blood when it became the last resort.

Upon arriving home, Ernesto sent out word to all the leading members of the gang. There would be a meeting at the cave the following evening. Ernesto had thought to make it earlier in the day but wanted to make sure there was ample time for everyone to get the word out.

As the hour for the meeting neared, the men called to attend it made their way up into the hills, and began to converge near the cave. As they arrived, Ernesto called for someone to relieve Gino and asked him to come inside. Ernesto wanted his sage presence if nothing else, and because he would go along, as would Paolo and Enzo. There was also a younger man named Martino now that Ernesto had advanced because of his good judgment and character, but he was young and his blood sometimes ran hot like Mario's, and Ernesto knew that with the wild spirit came a streak of independence. A man like Martino might go along initially, but bolt the minute there was trouble. Ernesto missed having Giancarlo and Fidelio around. Then, Fidelio had never been easy to control, either.

As these men and a few others gathered together, a bottle of Castellammare wine was passed around among them. Ernesto took his drink and passed the bottle on.

"Let's take it easy tonight. We have a lot of business to address."

"The chaperone now," Enzo said with a smile at Paolo. "All of you, make sure you're home by ten..."

Paolo gestured and most everyone laughed.

"If you're done screwing around," Ernesto said.

Enzo pretended to be scared, laughed again with the others, and gestured at Ernesto.

"You're on, boss."

"Then listen, all of you, before your blood boils hot over what I'm about to tell you, listen to the entire thing. Then we will discuss things. Hopefully in a civilized manner. Then we will vote. At this point, I have given my tacit approval to this plan, but I also made it clear that my men would have the final say."

"My blood's running hot already, just listening to you," Enzo said.

"Well, the point is, get hot all you want, but just listen to me first."

Enzo rolled his eyes and wanted to protest, but he shut up and listened without saying a word as Ernesto explained what Duke Don Vito had proposed. All the men listened and there was not a happy face among them.

"That's it," Ernesto said when he was done.

"Why don't we just cut off our you-know-whats, and hand them over to this Duke Don Vito right now," Enzo said. "He's going to own them anyway, sooner or later."

"So, you're saying we control everything on the ground," Paolo said. "The money, the markets, these voting polls you mentioned. Everything."

Ernesto nodded.

"They'll bring in their fancy wagons and the likes, but we have complete control on the ground."

"And go lick their boots in Palermo whenever we want something," Enzo scoffed.

"I can't see how it does any harm to try," Paolo said.

"Of course, you're from Palermo. What do you know about the way we do things here?"

"Are you calling me a traitor?"

"All right," Ernesto said. "We won't need a war with Duke Don Vito if we're going to start fighting amongst ourselves."

"I'm with Paolo," Martino said. "It does no harm to try. We can agree for the time being and if it doesn't work out, we run them all back to Palermo. In the meantime, we watch, we learn, and we grow stronger, so that we are prepared should that day come."

Gino and Ernesto nodded their heads in approval and there was a general assent amidst the murmuring of the men.

"What about you?" Enzo said to Mario. "You haven't spoken a word."

"That is because I've already had several days to digest these matters. And I do agree with what Martino just said. We run their system, we grow stronger and richer, and we cut off the head of this snake if it ever comes to that."

"You are forgetting," Enzo said. "This snake of yours, it will be growing stronger this entire time too. Don't think for a second that it will be easier down the road to cut off its head. It will only become more difficult."

That led to renewed bickering among the men. Ernesto held up a hand.

"I can't deny the wisdom of what you've just said, Enzo, but it neglects one thing. We might never need to cut off the head of this snake. So, one way, we have certain war, and the other way, there is a chance for peace."

Ernesto allowed the men a few moments to talk among themselves before he interrupted them.

"So, shall we vote?"

"What's the point?" Enzo said. "It's obvious how this is going to go and I'm not going to be the one to upend the cart. Is anyone here *unwilling* to give this thing a chance?"

No one raised a hand.

"There's your vote. Everyone went with the mule."

Some of the men laughed.

"I'm just warning you right now. The minute I see the people getting screwed in this thing, that's it. I'll go to war with these bastards. By myself if I have to."

A great murmur arose and Ernesto silenced it with both hands.

"If the people end up getting screwed in this thing, you will not be alone, Enzo."

"So, what now?" Paolo asked Ernesto as the men spoke among themselves.

"One of Duke Don Vito's men will be here to start showing us how things work on Monday, so in the meantime I want each of you to go to your people and spread the word. As much as you can between now and then. Make it clear. If we don't go along with this deal, there will be war. So, we give it a chance and if it doesn't work out, we go to war."

There was more talk and more Castellammare wine passed around before all the men departed and slipped into the night.

By Sunday evening, Ernesto had received several reports back from his people, most of it encouraging. However, any hopes he had of things going smoothly were dashed when Bruno showed up at his door on Monday morning. Three armed men were with him, one of them driving a nicely decorated market wagon. Ernesto introduced himself, along with Mario, Enzo, and Paolo, but none of Bruno's men showed the least bit of expression.

The eight men were left staring at each other in the street at dawn.

Bruno's cheerless face was that of a killer: flat, emotionless, and with lifeless black eyes that were forever furrowed up in a look of suspicion. The eyes were so devoid of human warmth that you could entirely forget Bruno was basically a handsome man with a good nose, chin, and mouth.

"Do you have everything arranged with the people?" Bruno asked Ernesto.

There was no talk of coffee or getting acquainted. Constantina came out with a dishrag in her hands, stared at the men, and went back inside.

"We will do the best we can today, but don't expect perfection. It will take time for the people to accustom themselves to these new ways."

Bruno nodded. Ernesto and his men mounted their horses and together they rode through the village with the wagon following along behind them. Having been warned, many of the peasants were ready with their goods and produce when the wagon came by, but when the procession arrived at the market, they discovered some of the peasants were already there setting up. Bruno sat on his horse, glowering first at these activities and then at Ernesto.

"I thought you had organized things."

"I told you it would take time."

"In Palermo, we have a simple way of dealing with insubordination. Shoot an insubordinate! It saves a lot of talk and time and suddenly everyone becomes very cooperative."

Ernesto stared at Bruno without saying a word.

"We don't shoot anyone around here. Now you and your men go over there by that tree and stay out of the way. That was part of the deal I made with Duke Don Vito. His people were to stay in the background and we were to run things on the ground."

Bruno stared back without a word, but eventually nodded at his men and retreated to a safe distance. Once they had, Ernesto dismounted and went out among the merchants, explaining to them again how things had to work now. It was that or war."

The merchants who had belligerently defied the new rules eyed Ernesto, and the other men on their horses and grudgingly gave in. Within the hour, all the merchants were in their assigned stalls and things went on smoothly for the rest of the day.

Early on, Ernesto pulled Paolo aside and told him to take a message to Duke Don Vito.

"Offer my apologies. I can't take another carriage ride right now, but you speak for me and this is my message. Something has to give. This Bruno is a bull. Send someone else to look over things or there's going to be trouble."

As Paolo rode off, Mario was eyeing Ernesto, and Ernesto was eyeing Bruno.

As hoped for, Bruno was relieved the next day, but the new men were if anything, less cordial and talkative. Still, Duke Don Vito clearly had said something because they had stayed out of the way and displayed greater discretion.

All through the course of that week, Ernesto and his men went from village to village, instituting the new program and utilizing this opportunity to educate the peasants about how the upcoming elections would work. You voted for the mule. That was all you needed to know.

Things did not go smoothly at every turn, but there were no major problems and by the end of the week, the wild horse had been broken and the transition complete. The merchants paid for their booths and a percentage of their profits, the money was divided up from there and a portion of it passed up the line to Duke Don Vito and his men.

Summers in the Italian Alps

The weeks passed and there were occasional skirmishes among various factions, but for the most part, peace prevailed across the countryside. One day that summer, Ernesto wearily mounted his horse and journeyed to Castellammare for a visit with Countess Sophia. Baroness Vittoria was there frequently now and Ernesto found them both sitting on the porch just like Baron Felix Castellammare used to do as he drank his ice-cold Castellammare wine in the afternoon heat.

"Don Ernesto, what a pleasure to see you," Countess Sophia said. "Please come sit with us and have a glass of wine."

He dismounted from his horse and joined the two women. Both of them gave Ernesto a kiss and a hug. A servant brought out another glass of wine and they drank in silence for a spell.

"So many memories," Baroness Vittoria said finally.

Ernesto nodded.

"Do you remember my brother and I at your cave?"

"Who could forget?"

"Dear Vittorio, God rest his soul," Baroness Vittoria said.

She crossed herself and Ernesto nodded sadly.

"I remember sitting right here with my father and Vittorio on hot summer afternoons, my father with his ice-cold wine."

"Ah yes," Ernesto said. "Do you still keep ice in the cellar, Sophia?"

"It seems like way too much trouble to me," Countess Sophia said. "Besides, I hear you can now buy refrigeration. Someday soon it will come to Castellammare."

"My God, already a new century," Baroness Vittoria said.

"It's a changing world," Ernesto said.

"But at least there is peace," Baroness Vittoria said.

"At least there is peace," Countess Sophia said.

She stole a glance at Ernesto.

"Another wine, Ernesto?"

"No, thank you," he said with a wave of his hand.

Countess Sophia studied him now.

"So, what was the purpose of your visit?"

"Ah, mostly to check on how things are going with you and Duke Don Vito."

He looked over at Countess Sophia. She shrugged.

"What choice do I have?"

"None that are very pleasant, I would think," Ernesto said. "Then, people make unpleasant choices all the time. But you do not strike me as someone who would willingly do that."

Countess Sophia smiled.

"If you are checking to see if I have a revolution in the works, you can rest easy."

"Good."

They sipped their wine again and enjoyed the breeze blowing up from the sea.

"You had said 'mostly'," Countess Sophia said.

"Ah, you don't miss a thing."

"I try not to."

"Yes, well I've received word that Duke Don Vito plans to visit the area next week and I am told that he has hopes to see you. He speaks of your beauty all the time and apparently will waste no opportunity to reconfirm the veracity of that observation for himself."

"You are being very poetic today, Ernesto."

"Well, when we speak of a woman's beauty, there is poetry."

The two women smiled to themselves. With peace, and with age, Ernesto had become more elegant and regal.

"Well, you tell Duke Don Vito that I will be happy to receive him and of course will insist on serving him dinner. Why don't you and Constantina plan to join us? We'll have Mario and mother and . . . who knows . . . Maximo might even be here. And if not . . . but do you know . . . will Duke Don Vito be traveling with his wife, Duchess Sabrina?"

"It is my impression that he will not."

"One of those kinds of wives."

Ernesto gestured to say that he did not wish to touch that bit of mischief.

"Well, if my fool of a husband does not come home, Duke Don Vito can be my companion for the evening."

Baroness Vittoria swiped at her daughter with a frown and Countess Sophia swiped back.

"In any case, I hope you will join us, Don Ernesto."

"It would be my pleasure."

He sighed, finished the last of his wine, and stood up.

"I will send word when I know what day Duke Don Vito plans to be here and we'll arrange an elegant classic Sicilian dinner, which he loves."

Ernesto bowed.

"Ladies."

"Be well," Baroness Vittoria said.

Once Ernesto was well down the road, the women looked at each other.

"He seems to grow frailer by the day," Baroness Vittoria said.

"Yes, it's been months since I saw him, and the change is obvious."

Baroness Vittoria shook her head.

"What, mother?"

"Oh, Ernesto drove me nuts with his caution for so many years, but in the end, I see he was right. It is always a more worthy battle, fighting for peace than riding off to war."

"He has done much for the peace of this land."

"He has done much for peace."

Two days later, Ernesto sent word that the dinner had been arranged for the following week. Then, before the dinner could take place, Ernesto passed away suddenly in his sleep.

As word spread, a great sorrow spread across the land. Women everywhere dressed in black and wore black shawls over their heads. They attended Mass with their prayer beads and watered the earth with their tears. Men were no less stricken and toasted to his name with their glasses of wine.

For the funeral, Duke Don Vito sent several gilded carriages over from Palermo and nearly flooded the village with flowers. Giancarlo and Fidelio showed up in their fancy carriage, the interior of it overflowing with more flowers. Gino was so old now, he had to be helped inside the church. Constantina had arranged for Duke Don Vito to sit in the front row with the other elevated members of Ernesto's old gang and he walked at the front of the procession as it left the church with the coffin, holding Constantina's hand.

The statue of Jesus went out ahead of everyone and the icons of saints followed along behind them as the drums beat and the trumpets played their sad, blaring music. The people wept and the weeping did not end, even after Ernesto had been placed in the ground and everyone had gathered for the memorial service hours later at Castellammare.

Upon seeing Sophia's beauty again, a thought immediately entered Duke Don Vito's mind that day, so when the opportunity to talk with her alone presented itself, he wasted no time in saying hello. With a bow, he greeted Baroness Vittoria first, then Countess Sophia, and sat down next to them. Some small talk ensued.

"My wife is with child again," Duke Don Vito said when there was a silence.

"Yes. In Sicily, you bear children until you become an old maid."

Baroness Vittoria elbowed her daughter, who laughed.

"Forgive me, Duke Don Vito. I have seen what it has done to my own skin."

"You are no less a beauty, my dear."

"Thank you for saying so, Duke Don Vito."

"You are welcome ... So, are you serious? You have no plans to bear more children then?"

"I had not thought of it, no."

"A shame."

"Why?"

"With your beauty and business sense, the more children you have the greater your legacy."

By the way, perhaps you and Baroness Vittoria would like to join us at our villa in the Italian Alps this summer."

"I had no idea you had a villa in the Italian Alps, Don Vito."

"Oh yes. They've even made me a duke up there too. It's quite a show."

"I see."

Countess Sophia was smiling. Baroness Vittoria was not.

Countess Sophia's daughter Athena ran up just then, out of breath.

"Mama, please, may I go up to the castle? I found some wildflowers up there yesterday and I wanted to go pick some more."

"Please, dear. We're honoring Ernesto today. Maybe later. Did you say hello to Duke Don Vito?"

Athena curtsied.

"Welcome to Castellammare, Duke Don Vito."

He smiled.

"Would you like to go to the Italian Alps this summer and escape the heat?"

Athena looked at Countess Sophia as though seeking permission.

"Well, maybe we'll all go to the Italian Alps this summer. Now go pay your respects, child, and we'll talk about going up to the castle later."

Athena curtsied again to Duke Don Vito and ran off. Countess Sophia looked back at Duke Don Vito.

"I suppose there's no refusing your offer now."

"We would love to have you. Please, and bring Maximo as well. It might facilitate our plans."

"Please feel free to invite Mario too," he said to Baroness Vittoria.

"It's something to consider," Baroness Vittoria said coolly.

"Ah, I sense my duties with the poor widow continue," Duke Don Vito said. "Please excuse me. I will look forward to the resolution of this conversation at the appropriate time."

These last words were said specifically for Countess Sophia. He bowed to both ladies and left. Baroness Vittoria waited until Duke Don Vito was well out of earshot before she spoke.

"You can't be serious, marrying our ancient blood with that scoundrel."

"Mother, you're never very becoming when you hiss."

"Never mind. You know what I mean."

Countess "What?" Baroness Vittoria said.

"You? Who had me marry this useless oaf? Daring to suggest to whom I should marry my twins and to whom I should not?"

Countess Sophia laughed.

"Well, for the very reasons you wished to marry me to Maximo, I would gladly marry my family with Duke Don Vito's. Only I will be doing it with class . . . and don't you ever think of interfering."

The following month, Duke Don Vito's wife Sabrina gave birth to a stillborn child. In grief, she fled to their summer residence in the Alps as soon as she was well.

Having remained behind to deal with business, Duke Don Vito made a point to stop by Castellammare and renew his invitation. When he rode up to the villa, he heard shouting within and hesitated. One of the servants must have seen Duke Don Vito, because Countess Sophia appeared at the door a moment later, straightening her disheveled hair.

"It's always a pleasure to see you, Duke Don Vito."

"Perhaps I have come at the wrong time."

"No, please, come sit down and have an ice-cold glass of Castellammare wine with me."

Countess Sophia gave instructions to the servant.

"Please, come sit," Countess Sophia said again.

Maximo appeared at the door as Duke Don Vito was dismounting and stood there staring in a surly mood. Duke Don Vito gave the reins of his horse to another servant and said hello to Maximo.

"Perhaps you will excuse us, Countess. I have a little business I'd like to discuss with Maximo alone."

He waved at Maximo in a way that said, you don't have a choice in this matter.

Having led Maximo far enough away so that Sophia could not hear them, she watched Duke Don Vito bark away at Maximo, in what appeared to be a lecture. Clearly furious over having received it, Maximo stormed off towards the stables. Duke Don Vito came back to the porch, smiling.

"So, that ice-cold glass of Castellammare wine you had offered . . . ?"

Countess Sophia smiled.

"Ah, here it is right now."

The servant placed them on the table and left. Duke Don Vito and Sophia toasted and drank.

"I was deeply saddened to hear of your loss."

Duke Don Vito nodded sagely.

"Thank you. My wife promptly fled to our place in the Italian Alps. In fact, that is why I stopped by to visit. Please, it would be my great pleasure to have you join us. My boat leaves in a week. You are welcome to bring your daughter and son and Baroness Vittoria and whomever you wish."

"And you're sure we wouldn't be too much of a burden given the circumstances?

"Not at all. This place, you could get lost in it and I'm sure my wife would enjoy the company."

"Well, I would hate to disappoint Athena. She has talked of nothing else since your invitation."

"Splendid. Then it is settled. I will send two carriages, one for you and one for your luggage."

Countess "I don't know that that will be necessary."

"No, you absolutely must be prepared. This is a grand affair."

They both smiled and drank. Then Duke Don Vito grew serious.

"Don't feel you are obligated to bring your husband. I have probably overburdened him with new business duties anyway."

"Is that why he stormed off."

"Yes. Certain things in this life just can't wait."

Countess Sophia smiled.

"Then to the Italian Alps."

The two toasted and drank and talked for some time before Duke Don Vito finally excused himself and rode off.

The following week, the carriages arrived to gather Sophia's entourage and their belongings, as promised, and a big white steamer sailed away from the harbor an hour later. In the end, both Maximo and Mario had declined to go, so there were only Countess Sophia, Baroness Vittoria, Athena, and Santino.

Athena and Santino were quick to rush to the front of the ship and leaned over the railing excitedly as the sea mist splashed up from the bow. Duke Don Vito showed the ladies to their cabin and the three of them retired to the foredeck for a glass of wine. The twins were running here and there breathlessly. The sky was clear, the sea was blue, and the wine was very pleasant in the shade of the castle.

The ship sailed north, passed through the Straights of Corsica, and docked in Genoa the following evening. They took an overnight train from there to the end of the line, where several carriages transported their belongings the remainder of the way to Duke Don Vito's estate on Lake Como.

When they arrived at around two in the morning, Duke Don Vito's wife, Duchess Sabrina, was there to meet them at the door and helped with getting the twins to bed. Thereafter, they shared an aperitif and everyone retired to bed. The mood of their brief gathering was tempered by Sabrina's ongoing grief.

In the morning, Sophia and Baroness Vittoria awakened to the vision of a brilliant blue lake below them and white clouds drifting across a brilliant blue sky. Duke Don Vito had breakfast served on a terrace surrounded by pine trees, where the temperature was a pleasant twenty degrees cooler than at Castellammare.

"I have died and gone to heaven," Countess Sophia said.

"Ah, wait until they make you a Duchess," Duke Don Vito said. "Then you will know heaven. Right, dear?"

Countess Sabrina, who had been gloomily playing with her food, looked up.

"This title business has gone to my husband's head."

"I do not deny it, but I tell you, when I snap my fingers now, people really jump."

Baroness Vittoria smiled. Sophia had started to laugh but stopped herself. Countess Sabrina looked away from the two women toward her husband, and then back at her food.

"What do you ladies think of going out to fish later on?" Duke Don Vito said.

"Fishing for what?" Sophia said.

"Whatever is beneath the waters of that lake out there, of course. I have a wonderful boat and the twins will have a delightful time."

"I'm willing to try my hand," Countess Sophia said.

"I'm willing to watch," Baroness Vittoria said.

"Splendid. We'll go out later on. Then tonight, I'm having my good friend Teodoro and his wife Theresa over for dinner. The Duke and Duchess of Brescia. You will love them." Duke Don Vito leaned in and pretended to whisper. "Talk of royalty. This is the real thing. Their family goes back a thousand years."

"Did they sell titles a thousand years ago too?" Sophia said.

Duke Don Vito smiled and shook a finger.

"Perhaps. I think more likely you had to slay a dragon. Why don't you ask Teodoro when he gets here?"

"Oh, you would love to embarrass me, wouldn't you?"

"No, of course not, dear. You do that so splendidly all on your own."

"You are a rogue."

"Perhaps, but among many other things."

Athena and Santino ran out onto the terrace just then and asked if they could go down to play at the lake.

"Fine," Countess Sophia said. "But stay close. Duke Don Vito is taking us out on his boat later on."

Further excited by this news, they hurried out to a nearby path and ran down through the woods to the water's edge, with the adults watching them.

The women spent the rest of the morning lounging around on the terrace, reading, chatting, and enjoying the pleasant sunshine. Duke Don Vito went off to deal with his business affairs, but returned for lunch and afterward, walked everyone down to the dock where they boarded his big white boat. Duke Don Vito had two old deckhands on board to help with baiting hooks and netting fish, in case someone actually caught something, which Countess Sophia and the twins did at various points during the afternoon, and which lead to a great deal of hilarity.

All in all, it was a grand time on the lake and their laughter was still echoing up into the mountains as they motored back towards shore late in the day.

That evening, a very royal looking carriage arrived before dinner, and the very royal looking driver, who was dressed in a blue camlet coat and pants, climbed down to open the carriage door and an even more royal looking couple climbed out. The man was wearing a black topcoat, a black top hat, and gray striped pants. The woman wore a burgundy colored velvet dress with Venetian lace underneath and a substantial string of pearls around her neck. He had a face that was almost feminine with its oversized eyes, cupid nose, and sensuous lips. His forehead was tall and draped with dark ringlets, his chin tapered and perfectly proportioned. The woman was exceedingly pale of skin but flushed with warmth. Her dark eyes were intense, her nose small and straight, her mouth petite and seemingly puckered from the contrast of its smallness and the fullness of the lips. All in all, they were truly regal-looking and exuded a grave, but gracious air as they ascended the steps to Duke Don Vito's grand villa.

"Teodoro! Theresa!" he called out as he went down to greet them. "How delightful to see you again!"

He kissed cheeks with Baron Teodoro and kissed Baroness Theresa's hand.

"Welcome. Come meet my other guests. Baroness Vittoria, this is the Baron and Baroness of Brescia, and Baroness Vittoria's daughter, Countess Sophia. Baroness Vittoria is the grand dame of Castellammare. For no less than 500 years have they and their family guarded over this land."

Baron Teodoro acknowledged their lineage with a bow and kissed both their hands. Baroness Theresa kissed cheeks with them.

"And Sophia's twins, Athena and Santino," Duke Don Vito said.

The twins curtsied and bowed.

Baroness Vittoria and Countess Sophia were left staring. They had always considered themselves royalty, but even they could see this was royalty on another level.

"And why are your hands purple?" Baroness Theresa asked Athena

"It's from picking flowers."

"She thinks she's going to make perfume," Santino said.

Athena dismissed him with a look.

"I am going to make perfume." She looked at her hands. "This is from lupus and gentian, but there are so many different kinds of flowers up in the hills. I don't even know their names, but isn't it wonderful? It is important that a woman smells pretty so I'm going to make my very own brand of perfume someday. Just like my great-grandmother Baroness Roseanna."

Baroness Theresa smiled graciously at Countess Sophia.

"Forgive me," Countess Sophia said. "My daughter is filled with fantastical ideas."

"No, this is wonderful," Duke Don Vito said. "She is very industrious. I'll tell you what, Athena, you make a line of perfumes and I'll help you to market them."

"Thank you, Duke Don Vito. I'm going to gather bunches of flowers tomorrow and start practicing."

Santino made a face. Athena punched him and off they went.

"Behave yourselves," Sophia called after them.

She offered the duke and duchess an apologetic smile.

"You do your best."

"Oh, it's fine," Theresa said. "Such beautiful twins. And to be young again."

"To be young again," Duke Don Vito said. "Well, come, let's go inside and proceed with the festivities."

He shepherded his guests into the villa amidst many conversations.

Duke Don Vito Helps Baron Teodoro

Over dinner, they talked of Italian unification and the possible war with Austria and disparity of wealth between north and south. Before long, Baron Teodoro and Duke Don Vito were retiring to his dimly lit study for snifters and cigars.

"So, how do your enterprises go?" Duke Don Vito asked.

"Not well, Don Vito. Not well."

"No? But how can this be? Your family has made the finest wines and sparkling wines in all of Italy for generations."

"I know, but I do not have your business acumen, Don Vito. I suppose it was never in my blood. I should have been a painter."

"Ah, but you have prestige nonetheless. A name. My god, you should be dominating the markets up here."

Baron Teodoro shrugged and put down his cigar.

"I am at the point of having to sell off some of my land."

"No, please. This is madness!"

"Yes, but it is true."

Duke Don Vito studied the baron.

"Teodoro, I have long thought of discussing certain business matters with you, but have never felt it was the proper time to do so. How could I, the upstart duke, pretend to broach such things? But Teodoro trust me, if I know one thing, it is how to make money."

"I know you do, Don Vito. And for that, I respect you greatly."

"So, if I may dare ask with all due humility, would it make sense for us to join our business interests together?"

"Duke Don Vito, I have long thought of asking for your help, but have been too embarrassed to raise the subject."

Duke Don Vito scoffed.

"Teodoro, please. It would be my honor."

"No, the honor would be all mine, Don Vito."

Duke Don Vito scoffed again.

"Teodoro, please. You embarrass me."

"But it is true. I think of business and grow faint. I grow sick, really. Sadly, I was not made for such things."

"Fear not, my friend. Put your trust in me and I'll make sure your fortunes are restored. My god, can you imagine the power of our two families combined? We'll own all of Italy."

"Just to see our financial house in order, Duke Don Vito, you cannot imagine the sleepless nights my wife has experienced. I have suffered sleepless nights just worrying about her. It has left me feeling like an utter failure as of late."

Duke Don Vito reached out and touched Baron Teodoro's hand.

"Trust me, my friend. Everything will be all right now. I envision you overseeing production and being the ambassador. I'll oversee sales and we'll find an equitable manner of splitting the profits. Does that make sense?"

"Of course. Whatever you say."

"Good, good." Duke Don Vito puffed on his cigar. "We are going to do great things together."

"Thank you. Thank you so much. I..."

"Please, Teodoro. I told you. You embarrass me. The honor is all mine."

"But, trust me, I will defer to your every judgment."

"I know. I know. So, let us plan to meet at your winery at the earliest opportunity and we'll set a plan in motion to take over Italy... There, I see a little smile on your face and I will take that as payment over all the money in the world."

"You are too kind, Don Vito."

"And you are too modest. More brandy?"

"Oh, I have not even touched the one you poured me."

Baron Teodoro drank and Duke Don Vito poured his glass full again.

The two men went on discussing their business ideas and eventually made their way back out to the parlor, where Baroness Theresa immediately sensed her husband's brightened countenance.

Baron Teodoro went over to stand by the side of her chair and she smiled.

"I don't know what you said to my husband, Don Vito, but thank you. It has clearly lifted his spirits. And in turn, mine."

"Ah, my dear Theresa, thank you for uplifting my spirits. If I did anything for your husband, it was to remind him of what a great and good man he is."

"He is," she said with an admiring squeeze of his arm. "And you are very kind to say so."

They continued talking for a short time inside and said good night before going their separate ways.

"We will see you for breakfast in the morning?" Duke Don Vito asked Countess Sophia.

"Yes you will. Thank you. Thank you for everything. It has been a most wonderful sojourn already."

"Made all the more wonderful by you, Baroness Vittoria, and your twins."

The next day, Duke Don Vito summoned Count Maximo from Palermo, instructing him to make his way to Naples by boat and take the train from there to the end of the line. One of Duke Don Vito's carriages would be waiting for him. Two days later, Baroness Vittoria, Countess Sophia and the twins rode down to the train station at the base of the mountains.

Count Maximo was his usual belligerent self upon arriving and remained sullen the entire way back, hardly saying a thing beyond one-word answers.

"What's the matter with you?" Duke Don Vito said upon Count Maximo's arrival at the estate.

"You said to come, so I came. What more do you want?"

Smelling trouble, Countess Sophia gathered the twins.

"Come, you two. Let's go read a story in Athena's room and leave the men to talk."

"You mean to argue," Athena said.

"Ssshhhh, you," Countess Sophia said with a face over her shoulder at Duke Don Vito.

Duke Don Vito watched Countess Sophia lead the twins off and waited until they were well out of earshot before he turned and spoke again to Count Maximo.

"Is it too much trouble to be pleasant around your beautiful wife and twins?"

"What do you want from me, Don Vito?"

"Eh. A smile, for starters."

"Do you smile when people order you around?"

Duke Don Vito gestured his exasperation.

"Is your wife unfaithful? No. Is she unpleasant or cold? No. If she were any of these things, I would understand. But no. You make trouble for yourself where there is none."

Over the next few days, Duke Don Vito came and went with business, but he was always there in the mornings for breakfast and back for dinner. and occasionally to have lunch. A few times, he heard a shouting match echoing out of the back rooms and knew that Count Maximo and Countess were going at it, and felt like taking the opportunity to knock Count Maximo around but checked his impulses.

Later that week, Duke Don Vito suddenly excused himself over pressing business matters down in Milan. He was taking the train and could be expected back to the villa in a couple of days. Before leaving, Duke Don Vito instructed Count Maximo to stick around until he returned.

It was almost a week before Duke Don Vito reappeared. When asked about the details of his trip, he gave vague answers and changed the subject. "More wine? Shall we all go out for another day of boating on the lake?"

A few days later, Countess Sophia took Duke Don Vito aside.

"I think you can send my husband back now."

"Yes? You're sure?"

Countess Sophia laughed.

"I'm sure. You can send him back to Palermo now. Please. He's driving me mad."

"He's driving everyone mad."

"Good. Then let's enjoy the rest of our sojourn in peace."

"I'll send him on a little business mission first thing in the morning."

"Make it a big business mission."

This time it was Duke Don Vito who laughed.

As September drew near, Duke Don Vito made arrangements to shut down the villa and everyone made the return trip to Sicily. Duke Don Vito's carriages were waiting there in Castellammare when they docked and Duke Don Vito rode with Countess Sophia and Baroness Vittoria and the twins back to the Castellammare estate.

When the horses pulled to a stop in front, the twins immediately ran off.

"I'll take care of them," Baroness Vittoria said.

Duke Don Vito got out and gave the driver a hand with all the luggage. Then he walked Countess Sophia to the door and they stood there facing each other. Countess Sophia took Duke Don Vito's hands.

"I can never thank you enough. Somehow, I had never thought to escape Sicily in the summer. What a wonderful time."

"Then we will do it again next summer, and the summer after that and for all the years to come."

"If you'll have us."

"Of course, my dear. It was my pleasure. It will be my pleasure."

Back Home at the Castellammare Villa Estate

Countess Sophia turned and walked into the Castellammare villa estate, sitting and relaxing for a while before heading up to her room to unpack and assure that everything was in order after their long summer sojourn. She listened to the laughter and joy of her twins as Baroness Vittoria stayed outside watching them running and playing, and capturing every minute of freedom they could grasp, knowing their summer vacation was coming to a close.

The twins' tutors were preparing their lessons for the upcoming year and their time of learning was soon to begin. Athena, although she had enjoyed her summer in the Italian Alps, was eager to get back to her studies and longed to learn more of everything her tutor had to offer. Santino on the other hand, was consumed with the memories of the summer he had just spent in the Italian Alps and was anxiously awaiting their visit that Duke Don Vito promised them next year and the year after that and the year after that . . . He remembered in awe, the beauty of the lake where they would go out on the boat to fish and swim. He looked out at the vast Mediterranean Sea which surrounded the Castellammare villa with its sparkling water and most recently, hearing the sound of the lapping waves caressing the shore as they rode past in their carriage up the mountain. Even though he was being given one of the finest educations available, one only a royal could afford, he decided he wanted to live in the fishing village with the peasants and become a fisherman.

"Mama," Santino said as he rushed into her room, "I'm going to become a fisherman. I'm going to move down to Castellammare and live with the peasants and catch fish with them."

Countess Sophia looked at him in horror, "You think you're going to do what?"

"Yeah mama, that's what I'm going to do."

"Ohhhhh, absolutely not! No son of mine is going to be working and living like a peasant. I don't know what you're thinking!"

Santino sadly hung his head and walked back outside, his mother still raging on and on in the background. He knew what his mother said, and he knew better than to argue with her.

He walked over and sat at the side of the cliff staring out into the glistening sea, feeling the cool salty air caressing his face and tucking his dream away inside his heart.

A few days later, summer vacation was over, the tutors arrived, and Athena and Santino began their lessons. As the weeks passed, Athena grasped every bit of knowledge she could, while Santino started plotting a way to sneak down the cliff right after his lessons to be near the sea and maybe see some of the fishermen at work. One day, his tutor was not feeling well and had to leave early to rest and tend to her illness. She left Santino some assignments to complete and instructed him to let his mother know she had to go home for the day and she would be back tomorrow. Santino decided that this was his opportunity. He knew that it would take some time, but he still had most of the day to execute his plan. His mother, occupied with running her business and the estate, believed that he was working with his tutor. She didn't see them working in the library, so she thought perhaps they decided to work on his lessons outside to enjoy some of the brisk fall weather, which was not uncommon.

Santino began his trek down the path, slipping into the woods if he thought someone was approaching. As he neared the bottom, he could hear the water lapping at the shore and saw its sparkling beauty. He sat down and took off his shoes and rushed to put his feet in, feeling the cool water as it splashed up his legs, he stood there peering out at the open sea and a net floating in the water caught his eye.

"It's not that far," he said under his breath, "I can go in the water and get it and then I can catch fish. Maybe when mama sees how good I am, she'll change her mind. I'll dry off when I go back up the path and she won't even know."

He proceeded to go into the water and reached out for the net. Something was holding it, so he pulled and tugged at it to no avail. He dove down into the water, hoping to untangle the net from its snare. He came up for air and went down again tugging at the net, section by section, wrapping it up his arm pulling up the loose sections as he went, to see where it was caught. He needed to come up for air again and didn't want to let go of the net he had gathered, but it was too heavy and he had to release it. As he began to rise to the surface of the water, he was abruptly stopped. While he had let the net slide down off of his arm back into the sea, it had become tangled into his shirt buttons. He tried frantically to free himself, but was losing strength and slowly slipped into unconsciousness. The beauty and call of the sea and the dream Santino had tucked into his heart had become his watery grave.

It was dinnertime and while Althea was still busy with her lessons, Santino was nowhere to be found. Sophia went out onto the front porch, calling for him to come in and clean up for dinner. Moments passed and Countess Sophia, Baroness Vittoria, and Athena found their places at the dinner table.

Countess Sophia looked around and Santino had still not come to the dining room.

"Has anyone seen Santino?" she asked her mother and daughter, obviously annoyed.

"No. Not since he was with his tutor this morning." Athena answered.

Baroness Vittoria shook her head.

About that time, they heard a horse galloping toward the estate.

"Countess, Countess!" the rider yelled out as he approached the castle, "Your son!"

Countess Sophia bolted out the front door. "What about my son?" She frantically cried out.

"I found him tangled in a net offshore. I'm sorry Countess, Count Santino is dead. The villagers are working to free his body and get him out of the water."

"No, my god, no!" Countess Sophia screamed as she collapsed to the ground. Baroness Vittoria rushed to her daughter's side to console her. Athena stood there, shocked, not wanting to believe what she had just heard. Not until she saw Santino's limp body being carried up the path could she accept the news, and she silently began to cry.

The villagers carried the lifeless boy to his overwrought mother and she sat on the ground holding him in her arms gently rocking him, and she began to quietly sing him a lullaby. After a while, Baroness Vittoria came and gently helped her daughter to her feet as she finally released Santino's body from her embrace.

Duke Don Vito, upon hearing the news, rushed to Sophia.

"I will take care of the funeral and all of the arrangements," he told her.

Two days later, Santino's funeral took place. Duke Don Vito had arranged a funeral befitting royalty. Carriages filled with flowers lined the streets and the church, as he had for Sophia's brother years earlier. The church was filled beyond capacity and mourners lined the street dressed in their black attire and wailing in their grief.

At the conclusion of the Mass, they all proceeded to the cemetery to lay Santino to rest near his other family members his mother Sophia's fraternal twin brother Santino, and his grandmother Baroness Vittoria's fraternal twin brother Vittorio.

Baroness Vittoria, once again feeling the grave pain of loss, slipped into a dark depression.

Countess Sophia threw herself more deeply into her business affairs to try and dull the numbing pain of losing her son. Count Maximo came for the funeral and went back to Palermo as soon as he could, which was in no way unusual and a relief to Countess Sophia. In all of her grief, his anger and bitterness at life were more than she could bear right now.

Countess Athena Weds

The year was 1905, and with the passing of time and busyness of life, the pain of their loss had somewhat subsided.

Duke Don Vito went to visit Countess Sophia and Athena at the Castellammare villa estate and when he arrived, they both came out to greet him.

"It has been too long," Countess Sophia said, kissing cheeks with him.

"Eh, business. Your fields look rich," Duke Don Vito said, surveying the countryside.

"Yes, Athena's doing a wonderful job," Countess Sophia said. As Athena had matured into an independent young woman, Countess Sophia had turned many of the duties at Castellammare over to her.

"It has been a good crop. Please, come sit on the porch and have a glass of wine. We have something to tell you. Athena's engaged and the wedding is planned for next month."

"My god. Are you crazy? You waited so long to tell me?"

Duke Don Vito jumped out of his motor carriage and swept Athena up off the ground.

"Who's the lucky man?"

"My tutor's son, Marco."

"The same one?"

"The same one."

"You didn't want to fish around a bit?"

She slapped at Duke Don Vito and struggled until he set her down.

"I love him. He's smart and handsome and good to me and . . . he's also a Count." Athena blushed, looking at Duke Don Vito with a shy smile.

"Oohhhhh. So, who's going to pay for the wedding?"

"Stop it."

He laughed and picked her up again.

"Well, congratulations. I can't believe you two were keeping this a secret."

"We planned to tell you."

"But when?"

"Well, you know now. So there."

"Okay. Well, I'm going to have to give you half of Sicily or something."

"Some nice dishes will do."

"Dishes?! Are you kidding? Maybe a little villa in the Italian Alps or something."

She slapped at him again.

"You don't have to do anything like that. Maybe an apartment in Florence."

"Florence?"

"Yes. Marco is planning to teach there."

"And what of your mother's business? So, you're done with business now?"

"No, but I want to do other things."

"Very well. So, I'll see about that apartment and..."

He gestured at Sophia.

"It's on the fourth of next month. The first Saturday."

"Well, I can't wait to meet this professor of yours."

Duke Don Vito smiled.

"Ladies," he said and drove off.

When the day of the wedding arrived, people poured into Castellammare from all over the countryside. They came in motor carriages. They came in carriages. They came in wagons, on horseback, on mules, and on donkeys. Knowing there would be so many, Baroness Vittoria, Sophia, and Athena had concluded early on that there was no way to hold the ceremony in a church.

Instead, canopies had been set up on the huge cobblestone courtyard to one side of the villa with tables and chairs arranged in perfect lines underneath, and a stage was placed in front to serve as the altar. A horn and string band was playing Italian love songs and a bar was already serving up beer, liquor and Castellammare wine to get the crowd in a celebratory mood.

Duke Don Vito had personally sent a motor carriage to pick up Gino, who had to be wheeled to his table in a chair. He was withered with age, but lean and alert and still smiling as always.

Baroness Vittoria went over to say hello.

"Ah, Vittoria, the love of my life."

"Dear old Gino, how are you?" she said with a kiss on his cheek and her arms draped around his neck.

"My little school girl. Did you ever grow up?"

"I've tried. I'm not sure I did."

"Maybe it's best not to."

"Maybe it's not."

"I was going to get him something to drink," Duke Don Vito said.

"I'll take care of Gino while you visit the other guests."

"Thank you, Vittoria," Duke Don Vito said as he turned to walk away.

"So, what will you have, young man?" Baroness Vittoria asked Gino.

"Castellammare wine. I need something to fortify the old blood."

"You wait right there and I'll be back."

Baroness Vittoria ran into Giancarlo and Fidelio along the way.

"Hey, I'm a-gonna dance," Giancarlo said as he swept Baroness Vittoria off her feet.

She laughed and swatted him away.

"I'm getting Gino a drink."

"Is that old bastard still alive?"

"Don't talk like that," Baroness Vittoria said with another swat at him.

"Come on, Fidelio. Let's go give the old man some crap."

By the time Baroness Vittoria returned, Gino was surrounded by Enzo, Teresa, Paolo, Francesca, Giancarlo, and Fidelio.

"It's all the old crowd," Giancarlo said, trying to dance with Baroness Vittoria again.

"Will you stop it," she said, setting the glass of wine down in front of Gino.

"What's the matter? Only one glass!" Giancarlo said.

"You've got two legs. Go get your own."

"Come on, Fidelio. Let's go and bring everyone some wine."

Giancarlo pinched Baroness Vittoria as she passed by and she shrieked. A few minutes later, the eight of them were touching their glasses. Where they were all once like children in Gino's lap, they were now in their sixties and aging.

"To all the fallen," Giancarlo said.

"To Ernesto," Enzo said.

"To Santino," Teresa said.

"To Vittorio," Gino said.

"To Vittorio," Baroness Vittoria said, wiping at her tears.

"I remember him crying up a storm when they took you away," Gino said to Baroness Vittoria. "Then the next day he was going to save the whole world."

Baroness Vittoria was crying now.

"Hey, let's drink our wine and be merry," Giancarlo said. "We all got to go someday."

"But not so soon," Baroness Vittoria said through her handkerchief.

"Come on, cheer up everybody. It's a wedding."

They toasted again and drank together and slowly started to drift their separate ways.

"Anything else I can get you before I go?" Baroness Vittoria asked Gino.

"Another kiss."

"Aw, I love you, Gino," she said with her arms around his neck again. "I'm so glad you're here."

"I'm glad to be anywhere. Now, go take care of your duties."

She laughed and kissed him again and went off to attend to the wedding.

When the moment came for the vows to be exchanged, Athena stood there staring intently at Count Marco, as if asking with her young tender heart. "Do you promise to take good care of me? Will you be there until the end?" With her long, thick auburn hair, pale skin and stunning beauty, and Count Marco's tall, straight physique, curly blonde hair, and blue eyes, they could have passed for an Austrian couple. Surrounded as they were with a sea of dark-haired Sicilians, they seemed out of place but when they finally kissed, everyone understood the sincerity. It was a kiss for today and all time.

With the ceremony over, the band struck up a tune and the newlyweds were swarmed by well-wishers. Then they took to the dance floor and all the men took their turn with the bride, including her father Maximo.

Finally, the cake was cut, and Duke Don Vito enjoyed a quiet moment, eating his cake and watching Athena throw her bouquet. As he took another bite of his cake, he smiled and winked at Countess Sabrina. Countess Athena and Count Marco were dancing to a slow tune and the entire wedding was watching.

As the silky light of dusk fell over the festivities, Duke Don Vito's personal motor carriage whisked the newlyweds away to Palermo, where a private yacht awaited to take them on a tour of the Mediterranean for their honeymoon, a personal honeymoon present to them, courtesy of Duke Don Vito.

Mixing Blood

Countess Athena and Count Marco had a splendid honeymoon travelling the Mediterranean aboard Duke Don Vito's yacht. They returned to Castellammare and were greeted by Countess Sophia, Baroness Vittoria, and Duke Don Vito.

"You two are just glowing," Duke Don Vito said.

"Oh, yes," Countess Athena responded, "We had a wonderful honeymoon. Thank you so much Don Vito." She leaned to embrace him and kiss him on his cheeks.

"So, what do you think about our yearly tradition of the Italian Alps? Are you both going to join us this year?"

Athena looked at her new husband hoping he would say yes. He looked at his beautiful new bride and said, "How can I say no?"

Duke Don Vito stood up, slapped his knees and said, "Fine, fine! I will make arrangements for all of you to be picked up around our usual time and we will continue our yearly tradition. We'll speak again to confirm the time as it draws closer."

"Thank you, thank you," Countess Athena said as she reached over to embrace and kiss her husband, "We will have such a wonderful time there. It is beautiful!"

The time came and they all travelled to the grand villa estate.

"It's everything you said it was . . . and more," Count Marco exclaimed.

That evening they all sat out on the terrace sipping the Castellammare wine they had brought over with them.

"Tomorrow night, Teodoro and his wife Theresa, the Baron and Baroness of Brescia will be joining us for dinner." Duke Don Vito said.

Countess Athena leaned over to Count Marco and said, "You will love them. They are such wonderful people."

The next evening, the royal carriage arrived carrying Baron Teodoro and his wife, Baroness Theresa.

Duke Don Vito rushed out to greet them both as he kissed Baroness Theresa's hand and kissed Baron Teodoro on both cheeks.

"It is so wonderful to see you both again. Come and meet our newest guest, Athena's new husband Marco."

"Oh, my goodness Athena, you look radiant. It is a pleasure to meet you Marco." Baron Teodoro said as he reached out his hand.

"Well, let's go inside and enjoy our dinner."

When the meal concluded, the men proceeded to the study to talk of business and of life.

Teodoro said, "Athena has grown up to be a beautiful young woman, and she has married well. A Count!"

"Yes, it's good blood. In fact, Athena is as shrewd as she is beautiful."

"Perhaps I would do well to mix my blood with hers."

Duke Don Vito held up both his hands.

"Teodoro, that is a splendid idea."

"You think?"

"Of course. You see, their line is prone to twins. Usually fraternal, a boy and a girl. Occasionally two girls or boys, but it is likely there will be two of them, either way."

Duke Don Vito gestured and laughed.

"So, you get busy. I'll get busy. We'll make sure Countess Athena gets busy and we'll mix our blood altogether."

"You think?"

"Of course. I've already discussed the subject in the past with Sophia in passing, and now that Athena is married, trust me. She would be honored to have your bloodline in our family. I'm sure Sophia will easily convince Athena"

"Well, if Athena is as shrewd as you say she is, I will be honored. There is no question as to her beauty."

"No, they don't come any more beautiful, do they?"

"She could have been a queen."

"In the olden days, when things were as they should be, she would have been in line to be a queen."

The two men continued discussing their business ideas and eventually made their way into the parlor.

"So, it looks as if you two gentlemen have been busy slicing up Italy," Countess Sophia said.

Actually, we could not get as far as we would like."

"How do you mean?"

"We ran out of troops..."

Duke Don Vito gestured and let the thought hang there in the air.

Countess Sophia stared for a long moment before laughing.

"Ah, I see. So, we are in need of reinforcements."

"There went a few more troops," Countess Sophia said as they disappeared.

"Yes," Duke Don Vito said. "But it's all in the timing, my dear. It's all in the timing.

"I see. Well then, I had best have a conversation with my daughter and have her get to work."

"I see. Well then, we'd all better get to work."

Duchess Sabrina looked down sadly. Baroness Theresa seemed to blush.

"Come, ladies," Countess Sophia said. "This is where you show some backbone."

"Or thighs," Baroness Theresa said.

When everyone laughed, she blushed even more so, but smiled, then encouraged her friend Countess Sabrina with a gentle hug as she went to speak with Countess Athena. Their conversation went well and Countess Athena was in agreement with their plan. Countess Athena had a great love and respect for Duke Don Vito and Countess Sabrina, and also for Baron Teodoro and Baroness Theresa. She came into the parlor where they were all sitting and sipping on their Galliano. Duke Don Vito handed Countess Athena a glass as they all raised them to toast.

"To our success."

"To our success," Countess Sophia said and everyone toasted.

"Perhaps we should retire then, my dear," Baroness Theresa said.

Following another toast with the Galliano, Baron Teodoro had Duke Don Vito call for the carriage and they went outside to wait in the cool, summer evening. The night air was alive with crickets and the trill and twitter of a treecreeper. The moon was out and splashing its white light on the lake.

"Thank you so much for the wonderful evening," Baron Teodoro said. "All of you. I look forward to what our future holds."

In the stillness of the mountains, they heard the clip-clop of horse hooves and the carriage arrived a moment later from the stable area behind the villa. There were kisses and hugs and farewells and finally Baron Teodoro and Baroness Theresa were seated in their carriage looking out.

Soon enough, our families will be drawn together in all things, God willing. For my wife's sake more than anything, I pray she is successful this time."

"She will be, Don Vito. Be gentle with her and I will say my prayers for the success of all the parties concerned."

"God will hear my prayers too."

"Good. It's a regular conspiracy we have going."

"But for all the right reasons," Duke Don Vito said.

He kissed Countess Athena on both cheeks.

"Let us talk about business in the meantime. I have plans to expand our wine and olive oil interests to America."

"America?"

Countess Athena raised her eyebrows.

"Yes. Perhaps we'll even market your perfumes over there. We will talk. And thank you again."

Duke Don Vito bowed, and retired to his bed chambers with his wife.

Two days later, Giancarlo and Fidelio showed up at Mario's front door in their carriage. Baroness Vittoria was there, and after the usual greetings, the two men took Mario aside.

"We need to talk," Fidelio said. "Perhaps we should get Enzo and Paolo involved too."

"What's the problem?"

"Come," Giancarlo said. "We don't want to be telling you this story twice."

Mario joined them in the carriage and they rode over to the far side of the village, where Enzo and Paolo lived on opposite sides of the road. They found Paolo eating while Francesca and Teresa worked together in the kitchen.

"Giancarlo! Fidelio!" Teresa said. "My god. Look at you. I heard you two were big shots now."

They hugged.

"Big fish in a little pond."

"But you've done well. I hope not in any bad way."

"No. We are still stealing from the rich and giving it to the poor."

"I hope so. God, it's so good to see you. I feel so old in comparison."

"Eh," Giancarlo said. "You're still as beautiful as ever. You too, Francesca. If this is growing old, I could market it."

Francesca smiled and gave both men a kiss on the cheek.

"Something to eat?"

"Thank you. Perhaps a bit later," Giancarlo said. "Right now, we need to steal your husband to discuss some business."

"Ah, more secrets."

"Better that, so we don't soil those pretty ears."

Paolo wiped up the rest of his pasta with a chunk of bread and chased the last bite down with a gulp of red wine.

"Come back for something to eat and to talk before you leave," Teresa said.

"We will," Giancarlo said.

"Promise me."

"I promise."

Outside, Fidelio asked where they could find Enzo.

"I think he's with the horses," Paolo said.

The three men walked around in back and over to the stables. Enzo was inside.

"What brings the dukes of Palermo this way?" Enzo said with a smile.

"Trouble," Fidelio said.

"I might have guessed."

"Come," Giancarlo said, "We need to talk."

The four men sat on the bales of hay with the sunlight filtering through the cracks in the boards and the place smelling of horse sweat.

"So, what is it?" Enzo said.

"Did Ernesto ever tell you about a man named Petrosino?" Giancarlo said. "A cop from America?"

Paolo and Enzo looked at each other and shrugged.

"He mentioned something, yeah?" Paolo said. "He's the one who ran Duke Don Vito back to Sicily, right?"

"Right. So, guess what? Petrosino was gunned down in the Piazza Marina in Naples a few weeks back."

"What the hell was Petrosino doing in Naples?" Enzo asked.

"We were wondering the same thing and cabled a friend of ours in America."

"And the story is," Fidelio interjected, "When a black hander named Enrico Alfano arrived in America, the authorities over there soon figured out that he had killed a young couple in Naples just before getting on the boat. So, they put him on a boat back from where he had come. Only Petrosino gets to thinking now. 'Why don't I go search the records over in Italy? Maybe I'll dig up all kinds of interesting things on these slimy bastards'."

"So? What does this have to do with us?" Paolo said.

"Well, who do you think might have shot Petrosino?"

"I give up," Paolo said.

"Don't be so stupid," Fidelio said, "Duke Don Vito, of course."

"How do you know that?"

"How do I know anything?"

Enzo looked at Paolo.

"Duke Don Vito was up at his place in the Italian Alps two weeks ago, right?"

Paolo nodded.

"As far as I know."

"Well," Fidelio said. "My sources are telling me that he was in Naples when Petrosino got hit."

"It sounds crazy," Paolo said. "So what? He gets a wild notion that Petrosino's in Naples and takes a train down to shoot him."

"Don't be stupid."

"Say that again and I'll get stupid with that pitchfork over there."

"Well listen up."

"Well, come on and just finish your story."

"I'm trying," Fidelio said. He looked over at Giancarlo. "Jesus, you need a bottle of wine to deal with these guys."

"I'll give you a bottle of wine. Right over the head."

"All right, look," Giancarlo said. "Petrosino shows up in Naples and starts digging around. That's what we know. And he digs up some pretty serious stuff. Now the wise guys get wind of this and set him up with a supposed informer. 'I've got something that you're dying to hear.' That sort of thing. And apparently, this Petrosino is just dumb enough, or fearless, to walk into the trap. Boom! Only, in the meantime, these guys had gotten word to Duke Don Vito. I don't know how or where. I just know that ever since this Petrosino deported him, Duke Don Vito's had an overwhelming urge to put a bullet in his head."

"So, you're saying Duke Don Vito rode all the way down from the Italian Alps just to shoot this Petrosino?"

"I'm not saying he rode from anywhere. I don't know where he was or how he got there. I'm just saying he was there and boom, a bullet in Petrosino's head."

"Just like that? Everybody's standing around watching and Duke Don Vito shoots him?"

"No, Petrosino was already dead. Duke Don Vito had arranged for his people to shoot him and when he saw the corpse, he took out a little frustration."

"Jesus, what a story," Enzo said.

"And you believe all this," Paolo said.

Giancarlo and Fidelio both shrugged.

"We don't have pictures to show you, but do I believe these guys? Yeah. 100%. I can tell you this much. The police may have kept this kind of hush hush over here, but it's all over the papers in America. The whole city of New York is weeping. And of course, they're calling for revenge."

"Okay, so we're back to square one," Enzo said. "Why the hell do we care?"

"You care because if you're doing business with Duke Don Vito, you're in somebody's crosshairs." Giancarlo held up his hands. "Fair warning."

Both Paolo and Enzo sat there staring.

"Okay, we owe you thanks for coming down," Enzo said. "Did you want us to get those clothes cleaned for you before you get back in that carriage?"

"Thank you, but I will take care of that later," Giancarlo said. "Although, an ice-cold glass of Castellammare wine will do . . . if you can afford it," he continued with a smirk and slight chuckle.

"Maybe. The ladies wanted to say goodbye to you anyway, remember?"

At the door to the stable, Giancarlo stopped them again.

"Make sure Sophia knows. We hear stories about ..." Giancarlo made a gesture. "You know. So, before they start mixing blood, she should give it some thought."

Enzo nodded and the men went back into the house.

In good time that day, Enzo and Paolo told Teresa and Francesca what they had learned, and they told Baroness Vittoria a few days later, and Baroness Vittoria told Countess Sophia, but Countess Sophia was unfazed.

"I have business interests with Duke Don Vito," she said. "What he does in his spare time is none of my business."

Baroness Vittoria was furious, but for Countess Sophia, that was the end of it.

Arranged Marriages

Within a month of their return from the summer sojourn, both Countess Athena and Duchess Sabrina had confirmed that they were pregnant, so word was sent by telegraph to Baron Teodoro and Baroness Theresa. Word came back from them that Baroness Theresa too was with child. Corks were popped, sparkling wine spilled, and more oaths made.

All this time, Duke Don Vito had been working furiously to promote their mutual business interests. For a company logo, he used an image of Baroness Theresa in her royal robes, with cherubs and fountains and various other images around her and Baron Teodoro's last name for the brand.

"It inspires confidence and trust, right?" Duke Don Vito said upon revealing it.

Everyone agreed. Duke Don Vito couldn't look at his handiwork enough.

"For those in America, it will remind them of the old country," he said and again, everyone agreed.

Duke Don Vito used the same brand for their line of sparkling wines but the Castellammare name for their wines because it had been long associated with both the common people and good vintages.

Leaving Countess Athena to deal with Sicily and the south, Duke Don Vito departed for the north and by that winter, sales of their products had ballooned all over Italy. Baron Teodoro's fortunes were quickly reversed and everyone prospered. Duke Don Vito's only frustration was that he himself could not go to America. He was left to dream of a time when his son could go in his place to further the family's interests.

In the immediate, he called for one of his lieutenants named Ruggio. Ruggio was middle-aged, and despite his bony brow and sloping forehead, his long, hooked nose and sagging, deeply lined skin, he was not painful to look at. Perhaps it was the sincerity in his steel-blue eyes that overcame all the other drawbacks to his appearance.

Duke Don Vito was waiting for him on the veranda and explained what he wanted. Ruggio was to take a boat to America. He would be given enough money to be comfortable. His job was to look into things, assess the current market and products, see where and how they might establish their own niche, and report back.

Ruggio was not particularly bright, but not stupid either; clever but not ambitious. In short, he was just the sort of man that Duke Don Vito had in mind for the job; someone who could be counted on to be creative and industrious, but remain loyal, no matter the circumstances

With that set in motion, there was nothing else to do but wait. The three women could not give birth fast enough for Duke Don Vito's tastes and Ruggio could not report back from America fast enough.

As always, Duke Don Vito was more than happy to assist Countess Athena with her ideas and industriousness and indeed her line of hair dyes, like her perfumes, were an instant success.

It was the spring of 1907. Within weeks of each other, Countess Athena, Duchess Sabrina and Baroness Theresa all gave birth to healthy children; Duchess Sabrina to a boy they named Vito, Baroness Theresa to a boy they named Antonio, and Countess Athena to twin girls, she named Florence and Maria. Things could not have worked out more fortuitously and the anticipated celebration was arranged that summer at Duke Don Vito's villa in the Italian Alps.

With sparkling wine in hand, he offered a toast.

"To our success."

They drank.

"It only remains to decide who gets whom."

"Can't we let them decide for themselves?" Countess Athena said. "My mother's life is a testament to how these prearranged marriages work out."

Baroness Vittoria bristled. Baron Teodoro and Baroness Theresa looked at each other and down.

"Oh, I am sorry," Countess Athena said. "You...but of course, I didn't know."

"We were lucky," Baroness Theresa said. "But it's true what you say."

"But it will only become more difficult as they grow older," Duke Don Vito said.

"How so?" Countess Athena said.

"Well, their interests may run here and there and anywhere. It's best if they know from the start that it's already decided."

"But what if we arrange for Florence to marry Antonio and she falls in love with Vito?"

"Let's put names in a hat," Duke Don Vito said with all his charm.

"Oh you," Countess Athena said.

"But it's perfect," Duke Don Vito said.

"Perfect? As if we know how they'll feel in fifteen years?" Countess Athena asked.

"We never know how things will turn out in life. Let's choose at random and leave it in God's hands."

"As long as you agree that if one wants the other, we won't stop them."

"Of course not, Athena. What do you think I am, a brute?"

"Sometimes, yes," Countess Athena laughed.

"You don't mean that," Duke Don Vito replied, pretending that his feelings had been hurt.

"Yes, well, as long as you meant what you said."

"Of course. I may be a brute, but this brute is a man of his word."

"All right."

Baron Teodoro had a hat with him and Countess Athena gestured at it.

"Oh, of course," he said and handed it to her.

"So how shall we do this?" she asked.

"Well, Antonio was born a few days earlier," Duke Don Vito said. "So, let's put the twin girls' names in the hat and whichever one you pick out, Athena, she will be married to Antonio, and the other to Vito."

Still not entirely pleased with the enterprise, Countess Athena scribbled both names on a small piece of paper, tore it in half, folded those two pieces, and dropped them into the hat.

"You do it," she said to Baroness Theresa.

"Oh, I couldn't."

"I'll do it," Duke Don Vito said.

"No, you brute. Teodoro, will you please do the honors?"

"Certainly," he said and reached his hand in without looking.

Countess Athena took the piece of paper from him and unfolded it.

"Maria," she said.

"Perfect," Duke Don Vito said. "I've always had a thing for Florence."

"Oh, you are a brute," Countess Athena said, slapping him.

"Well, I meant for the name. My god, where your mind goes."

"Oh, stop it." Countess Athena chuckled at Duke Don Vito.

Countess Athena looked down at her two baby girls, clearly still uncertain about their enterprise.

"It will be fine," Duke Don Vito said.

"It will be fine." Countess Athena kissed both her babies on their foreheads.

Countess Sophia looked at Baroness Vittoria. "I only pray they find the love that I've never had."

Baroness Vittoria stared for a long moment and walked out of the room."

"You shouldn't be too hard on her," Duke Don Vito said. "She returned your family to Castellammare."

"And so, I keep my peace. Mostly."

"So, I'll send Maximo to America on business and we'll find you a new boyfriend."

"Just send Maximo to America on business and I'll find my own boyfriend. Remember, people finding mates for other people is how I found myself in this situation."

"Every life comes with its burdens, Sophia."

Baroness Theresa came over and held Countess Athena's hands.

"Please. Accept my gratitude. Both for your beautiful children and your friendship in my life. What we do today will be remembered in a hundred years, and for that, I would sacrifice much."

"Oh Theresa, you are so much wiser and more gracious than me. Thank you, too."

Countess Athena looked down at her twin daughters.

"If I complain, do not doubt that I feel grateful every day. I have been blessed with much goodness. All of us have been blessed with much goodness."

"Here, here," Duke Don Vito said. "Let us set aside our troubles and toast to our good fortunes."

Countess Athena focused her attention on raising Maria and Florence, and no expense was spared in doing so. As was the case with Antonio and Vito, Maria and Florence were tutored in all the academic disciplines and at an early age had already learned multiple languages. They were taught etiquette and the idea that they were royalty was drummed into their heads from the very start.

Each year, the tradition of summer in the Alps continued, and with all the three families present, the four children, who had been bound together by a secret pact, were allowed to play freely with each other, with no idea of their destinies, and never a word said about it.

By the time the children were five and six years old, their characters and nature were already becoming evident. Florence had dark hair, dark eyes, and olive skin, and had the seriousness of a saint about her. Maria, conversely, was pale and delicate and exquisite in her beauty, even more so than Countess Athena, with light hair, green eyes, and the spirit of a sprite. Whereas everyone seemed to be in a room, Maria seemed to be above and outside it, in another world. Similarly, Antonio was short, dark, thick and brooding; while Vito was tall and fair and cerebral. None of this escaped Countess Athena's attention – Florence seemed to belong with Antonio and Maria seemed to belong to Vito – but she held her tongue in front of the others and never said a word.

By this time, Duke Don Vito had come to be known throughout all of Italy as the godfather of godfathers. Not only did he control his own business, but every other member of the Cosa Nostra was obliged to come to kiss Duke Don Vito's ring and consult with him before conducting any major business of their own. Admittedly, his was a fiefdom within the larger fiefdom of the government, but in most cases, the government kowtowed to him and not the other way around.

There were ongoing whispers when it came to Duke Don Vito's business, of threats being made and things being wrecked, and people being shot, but Countess Sophia and Countess Athena refused to acknowledge this dark side of Duke Don Vito's existence. When they heard such things, they ignored them. After all, Duke Don Vito had always dealt fairly with the business associates and peasantry they knew, and to meet him was to be charmed. Besides, the women's aspirations to wealth and power were not going to allow anything to get in the way, not even Duke Don Vito's purported savagery.

Beyond the question of Duke Don Vito's personal foibles, there were far more troubling things to worry about across the land—drought, famine, and the recurring political upheaval associated with them—so that hundreds of souls crushed the docks each day, hoping to reach America and find new dreams. Even many of Duke Don Vito's fellow mobsters were fleeing to America, seeing at once an opportunity to make their fortunes in a new, golden land and escape his all-controlling hand.

For those who remained behind, the new, unified Italy was dominated by a corrupt government, an increasingly effete and decadent royalty, the Cosa Nostra, and an anarchist movement. The Cosa Nostra had long aligned itself with the royalty, looking for stature and legitimacy by association, the anarchist movement took aim at everyone but the peasants, and the government was mostly hapless to do anything about any of it.

One autumn, when the destined children were nine years old, Duke Don Vito received a telegram from Teodoro, requesting his immediate presence. There was trouble and Teodoro needed Duke

Don Vito's help. When Duke Don Vito arrived at his castle in the foothills of the Italian Alps, Teodoro met him personally at the door. His smile was strained. He worked nervously as the two men sat down to talk.

"A brandy? Anything to drink?"

"A brandy will do."

Baron Teodoro had asked the servants to leave them alone in his study and poured the two drinks himself.

"What can I do for you, my friend?" Duke Don Vito said, taking his glass.

"I don't know. I wonder if anything can be done."

Baron Teodoro sat down, his hands still working nervously.

"I fear for the safety of my family and need to ask for your help."

"What on earth is going on?"

"Mobs. Insurrections. My rivals. God knows what else."

"Please be more specific, my friend. Mobs could mean anything and the insurrection? It is everywhere."

"When I say insurrection, I mean the socialists. You know. . . Italian Labor. The Italian Revolutionary Party. All the workers' associations and all parties associated with them. They want to take my land, all my holdings. They make mischief with my commerce."

"My friend, what else is new? Every week, I find my goods being raided on the way to market. My exports and imports are spilled on the docks. Just the other day, it turned out that some religious relics I had acquired were fakes. These anarchists raided the warehouse where I kept them stored, dragged the entire cache to a field in front of the local church, and torched the whole lot."

Duke Don Vito shrugged.

"How was I to know? How do you deal with these people? I would have let them go at a bargain rate. Instead, thousands of liras go up in smoke. So, you absorb your losses and move on. What are you going to do?"

"But this is different, Don Vito. Have you ever heard of this Mussolini?"

"Vaguely, yes. There are so many of these idiots. How do you keep track?"

"Well, this man presents a new level of concern. He's risen the ranks of the Socialist Party and now has the whole Italian government worked up into a fervor of redistribution. There's talk of taking my land and giving it to the peasants. A thousand-year legacy destroyed just like that."

Duke Don Vito shook his head sadly.

"It is a tragedy, what's going on. What is wrong with these people? They should emulate England. You have democracy but you still maintain the tradition of royalty. Otherwise, there's nothing but chaos."

"I know," Baron Teodoro said as he looked away from Duke Don Vito, fearing he would insult the man. He cleared his throat

Duke Don Vito stared, seeing his friend's troubled look.

"Listen, Teodoro, if worse comes to worse, we'll simply buy more land and build you a new villa and to hell with them."

"I know, Duke Don Vito. And that would all be well and good, but there is this other element. I guess you would say your rivals. Our rivals. They have threatened the safety of my family."

Duke Don Vito nodded, understanding now.

"Did you receive a note?"

Baron Teodoro nodded.

"How much?"

"Fifty percent of all my profits."

Duke Don Vito cursed under his breath.

"Look, Teodoro. Don't worry. I will deal with these bastards. And provide you with security in the meantime. They know enough not to mess with me."

"Duke Don Vito, I understand and appreciate what you're telling me but I truly fear for the safety of my family."

"So, what do you want from me?"

"I would like to send them to America."

Duke Don Vito's eyes got big.

"To do what?"

"Well, surely you know people who can keep them safe. And find a place where Antonio can continue his education. Then perhaps one day it will be safe to bring them back. Or I can join them in America."

"And what about Antonio marrying Maria?"

"We can send her over there and the two of them can start a new life. I don't care, as long as I preserve the family legacy."

"Frankly, Teodoro, I think you are going a bit overboard but..."

"...but you will help me, yes?"

"Of course. If you insist, I will do whatever I can."

Duke Don Vito shrugged.

"I'm sure if it's done right, all will be well. There are certainly fine schools to attend in America."

"So, you will help."

"Of course, my friend."

Baron Teodoro reached out to touch Duke Don Vito's hands.

"Thank you. I feel every day as if barbarians are at my gates."

Duke Don Vito patted Baron Teodoro's hand back.

"I'll look into this business about America. In the meantime, I'll make certain your family is safe."

"Thank you."

The two men talked of business for another hour before they stood up.

"So, let's have a look at Antonio before I'm on my way," Duke Don Vito said.

As they made their way out of the study, Baron Teodoro called to a servant and asked her to bring his wife and son. A minute later, Baroness Theresa and Antonio appeared. Baroness Theresa looked worn but exuded a gracious smile, as always.

"Don Vito, how good to see you."

"And, as always, a delight to see you."

While they kissed cheeks, the boy stared. He was handsome but short and squat. He was observant, but his dark eyes suggested an innate suspicion of the world. As Countess Athena had observed a few years earlier, he seemed to be more of a match with Florence than with Maria, but as Countess Athena had also done, Duke Don Vito said nothing of his thoughts. Instead, he patted Antonio on the head with a smile.

"Such a handsome young man."

Antonio did not seem to appreciate either the compliment or the pat on the head and said nothing in return.

"Say thank you," Baroness Theresa said.

He did so, but without any enthusiasm. Baron Teodoro nodded and Baroness Theresa led him away with a final goodbye to Duke Don Vito.

"I fear all this upheaval has made him wary," Baron Teodoro said.

"Teodoro, wariness is not the worst trait to have in this world."

"I suppose not, though I must admit. It is not what I had envisioned for him. None of this is what I had envisioned for him."

Baron Teodoro sighed heavily and put a hand to his forehead.

"My friend. Be of good cheer. I will make some arrangements to ensure that you and Theresa and your entire family are safe. And as soon as I'm back in Palermo, I will put this other plan into action."

Duke Don Vito patted him on the back.

"And everything else? It's fine?"

"Well, whatever is left."

"Oh come."

Duke Don Vito smiled and started for the door with a hand at Teodoro's back.

Young Love & The Massacre

Before leaving northern Italy, Duke Don Vito contacted some of his business associates in the mafia, explained the situation and was assured that Baron Teodoro and his family would receive whatever protection was necessary. Satisfied, Duke Don Vito headed home to Palermo.

Immediately upon his return, he sent for Ruggio. Ruggio had recently returned from his first trip to America with good news and bad news. There was much opportunity in America and a lot of money to be made, but it required money to start and organization to flourish. Of course, Duke Don Vito had the money, but he had no organization.

The fact that he could not go to America himself was consuming him like a caged lion.

Settling in on the veranda with Ruggio, Duke Don Vito explained the possible plan to safeguard Baron Teodoro's family in America.

"It is all arranged. We sail from Genoa on Wednesday. A man with the Fiore people will be posing as the husband. He's very stately looking. You would think he was a prince."

Duke Don Vito pulled his head back.

"Even when he opens his mouth?"

"Even when he opens his mouth. He speaks several languages."

Duke Don Vito nodded and leaned his head in again.

"We have all the papers to show that he's a professor going to lecture in America with his family. With the money, there should be no problem with immigration. I know from watching and going through twice now that they quickly separate the herd, and the well-off go right through."

Duke Don Vito nodded and looked up.

"Fine, but I want you to go along and watch over them the whole time. Nothing can go wrong with this. If something happens to that family, I will have broken my bond."

"I understand, Duke Don Vito. I will watch over them the entire way."

"I know." Duke Don Vito patted him on the hand. "I will take the train with you to Milan. I want to reassure Teodoro before he parts with his family."

Ruggio nodded.

"Good," Duke Don Vito said. "Let's meet in Palermo on Monday night. We'll take the night boat to Naples and the train from there to Milan."

Ruggio nodded again.

"Good. Now allow me to enjoy this wedding."

Ruggio stood up, bowed, and left.

"Do you have any ideas where we can put them? Where Antonio can receive a proper education, if necessary?"

"Sure. Don Gallo has set up operations in New Haven. It's a safe place. Much safer than New York, and Yale is there."

"And this is a fine school?"

"They don't come any better. The boy would have the finest education."

"Good. I have a feeling this whole thing will blow over and come to nothing, but just in case, make tentative arrangements for getting the family to America safely and into the protection of Don Gallo. Your passage will be first class of course, and you'll have all the money you need. Your only job will be to make sure that everyone gets there safely."

"I will guard them with my life, Duke Don Vito."

"Good. Reach out to Don Gallo. Make sure he is receptive, and I'll arrange everything for your passage."

Ruggio nodded.

"How goes everything else here in Sicily?"

Ruggio shrugged.

"You know Ernesto's old hand, Martino?"

"Not intimately."

"You know what I mean."

"Of course. What of him?"

"He's joined the anarchist movement and his zeal knows no boundaries. The church, the wealthy, to him, the one is the pawn of the other."

"So, get rid of him."

"It's not that easy, Duke Don Vito."

"Of course it is. Why the hell do I expand my private army to hundreds of men, if not to get rid of mischief like this?"

"I understand, Duke Don Vito but . . ."

"But nothing. Get rid of him."

Ruggio sighed.

"What?"

"What? Well, for one thing, the man turns out to be as shrewd as we can be ruthless. We corner him and he manages to escape."

"So, use more men."

"It's not that simple. To the peasants, he's a hero. You try to suppress this rebellion and it's like throwing gasoline on a fire. You kill Martino and you will have made him a hero."

"Well, better a dead hero than a live nuisance."

"So, we kill him and you will find out how much better."

"All right. Capture the bastard and bring him to me. I don't care. I just want this theft and burning of my goods to stop."

"Shall I focus on that or getting the family to America?"

Duke Don Vito gestured and rubbed his forehead in thought.

"Find someone to take care of this and you concentrate on the family."

Ruggio stood up.

"I will reach out to Don Gallo, arrange a new thrust against this Martino, and report back."

"Thank you. You're a good man, Ruggio. Take care of this and I'll buy you a house on the shore in America. Wherever you want."

"Thank you, Duke Don Vito."

Ruggio went out and Duke Don Vito sat there staring at the turquoise sea, lost in thought. He yearned to be in America himself and to take advantage of the great business opportunities there, but thanks to Petrosino, this was an impossibility. Duke Don Vito's frustrations were made all the greater by the reports he was regularly receiving from America. There was little in them to make him happy. The old bosses who once kissed Duke Don Vito's hand had grown increasingly independent now that they were removed from his authority.

Duke Don Vito had concluded that to go legitimate was the best course of action and envisioned sending Vito in his place, but Vito was several years from being old enough and mature enough to undertake the enterprise.

Duke Don Vito sat there drumming his fingers.

After some minutes, he called for a servant and instructed him to send word to Countess Athena. Duke Don Vito wanted to meet with her at the Castellammare Villa the next day. A full-fledged assault on America might have to wait, but there was nothing to stop them from laying the groundwork.

The next day at noon, Duke Don Vito was disembarking from his new car in front of the Castellammare Villa. It was an open-air Mercedes, burgundy in color, with black fenders and sideboards. Overall, it was very elegant looking and both Countess Athena and Countess Sophia came out to greet him, laughing at the sight.

"It has been too long," Countess Sophia said, kissing cheeks with him.

"Eh, business. Your fields look rich," he said, surveying the countryside.

"It has been a good crop. Please, come sit on the porch and have a glass of Castellammare wine."

"Thank you. My god, Athena. Your hair's the color of wine."

"It's good to see you too, Don Vito."

"Come. You know it is always good to see you."

As they too kissed cheeks, the twins came running out of the villa and threw themselves at Duke Don Vito's legs. Maria was as bright as polished glass. Florence stood there staring in silence, as dark and impenetrable as Antonio. Duke Don Vito tickled Maria and patted Florence on the head.

"Uncle Don Vito," Maria said. "Can we take a ride in your new motor carriage? Can we?"

Duke Don Vito smiled at Countess Athena.

"No, you're not taking a ride in Uncle Don Vito's motor carriage right now," she said. "Now the two of you go get cleaned up. We'll be sitting down to lunch in a few moments."

Maria groaned, but grabbed Florence's hand and ran off. Duke Don Vito and Duchess Sabrina joined Countess Sophia and Countess Athena on the porch and the four of them were soon sipping their ice-cold Castellammare wine together.

"This place, it always brings me such peace," Duke Don Vito said.

"I am glad to hear that. So, what is it you came to discuss?"

Duke Don Vito looked.

"America."

"What about it?"

"I'm planning to expand our business interests there, of course, with your help and involvement. If only Vito and Florence would hurry and grow up. I think it would be ideal to send them as our emissaries."

Countess Athena sipped her wine and nodded her head in agreement. The issue of Duke Don Vito's banishment from America, and for that matter, the question of whether Vito should marry Florence, as opposed to Maria, lingered silently between them.

"However we do it, I think this is the best path for us now," he concluded. "To hell with Sicily, and Italy. The government is more of a problem than these anarchist bastards. At least in America, they know how to deal with these types. Shoot them!"

Both Countess Athena and Countess Sophia sat staring at Duke Don Vito. He shrugged.

"I must tell you, Athena. Vito has expressed his...affection...for Maria."

Countess Athena nodded.

"I suspect we have thought the same thing."

"That they are a better match?"

"It's obvious, is it not?"

"So, what shall we do? I don't dare insult Teodoro and Theresa."

Countess Athena shrugged.

"As you said, we have years in which to decide things, and perhaps the four of them will decide the matter for us."

"Perhaps. So, what do you think of my plans to expand our business interests to America? Whichever way they marry, once it is done, we will send them over to America and let them lay the groundwork for our export business."

Countess Athena looked at Countess Sophia, who seemed to understand and stood up.

"I'll go take care of lunch."

Countess Athena waited until she was gone.

"Don Vito," she said. "I have never thought to raise this subject with you before, but I do not want my daughters mixed up in this other business of yours. With all due respect."

Duke Don Vito stared in the way that only a man of ruthless character can stare. Then he smiled.

"But of course. The idea of America is to have a clean break, right?"

"As long as we understand each other."

"Trust me. I want only the best for my son too."

"And still I worry," Countess Athena said. "This naïve young couple, thrown to the wolves over there?"

"They will not be alone. And I have no doubt that Maria or Florence will be every bit as shrewd as their mother, Countess Athena. And grandmother, Countess Sophia. And great-grandmother, Baroness Vittoria. With our help, how can they fail?"

"Still, I will worry. Perhaps I will go over there with them. At least initially. That would make more sense, don't you think?"

Duke Don Vito was tiring of his America problem and smiled in a way that wasn't really a smile.

"The point is, with all these Italian immigrants fleeing to America, we have a captive audience. How can we fail? All we need to do is set up our own network over there and make our brand synonymous with the old country and quality. That way, every time an Italian goes to the market in America, they're looking for our name, and if they don't see it, they're asking the store owner where it is."

Duke Don Vito waved a hand with a big flourish.

"I have no doubt it will be a great success."

"And is that it?" Countess Athena said. "A line of olive oil and nothing else?"

"No, of course not. We start with that, then move on to our wines and sparkling wines, and keep growing our line of exports until we own the place."

Countess Athena stared at him with the same suspicions.

"I have no doubt this export business of ours will be a great success. What I doubt is the ability to separate one business from the other over there. I fear it will be my daughter's ruin."

Duke Don Vito stared off for a moment, then said, "Remember, Sicilian women are more dangerous than shotguns and can take care of themselves, and you know they'll be protected."

"When I give my word, that is sufficient. After all, in America, I will not be dealing with corrupt governments. When you have a level playing field, these other things you speak of are no longer a necessity."

Duke Don Vito sipped his wine, annoyed by Countess Athena's badgering, but otherwise satisfied with things. He was very eager to see Vito marry Maria, not Florence and at least they had discussed that thorny subject.

"Let us go have lunch," Countess Sophia said.

Duke Don Vito slapped his knees and stood up.

An hour later, Duke Don Vito was pushing away from the table.

"My God, what a meal. I don't know if I can stand."

Maria got up and dashed to his side.

"Can we go for a ride in your new motor carriage now, Uncle Don Vito."

Duke Don Vito looked at Countess Athena.

"You go," she said.

"No, you come with us."

"No, I have other things to do. I no doubt should start planning things for America."

"Oh come," Duke Don Vito said.

Countess Athena still refused but watched from the porch as Duke Don Vito and the twins did circles out in the yard. As the ride finished, Duke Don Vito joined his wife back on the porch.

Duke Don Vito touched Sabrina's hand and pointed. Off to one side, among some trees, Maria and Vito were holding hands and staring intently at each other.

Duchess Sabrina averted her eyes and put a hand to her face.

"My god, they're going to kiss."

Duke Don Vito laughed.

"So. It's a good sign. Look at them. It's like they were made for each other."

"At eight years old?"

"What are they going to do at eight years old?"

Duke Don Vito held his head back and smiled at his wife.

"Sometimes I think you were never a kid."

She waved a hand at him and he laughed

Antonio Escapes to America

Back home, Duke Don Vito spent the next few days greatly frustrated by what he liked to call his Petrosino curse. It had become like a prison sentence to him, this waiting for Vito to grow up and mature. If it had been possible to marry children and have them breed at such a young and tender age, Duke Don Vito would have done so. If it would have done any good to drag Petrosino's corpse out of the grave and fill it full of more bullets, he would have done that too.

About midmorning the next day, Ruggio came rushing into Duke Don Vito's study, completely out of breath. Duke Don Vito looked up from his work, sensing trouble.

"Boss, there's been a catastrophe up at Vezio."

"What kind of catastrophe?"

"I don't know for sure, but the word I got is someone in the family insisted on going out for a ride and they were ambushed."

Duke Don Vito jumped to his feet.

"Is the family alive?"

"I don't know, boss. The telegram I got from Luigi said that his men had been ambushed and a lot of them were dead so..."

"But did they save the family?"

"I don't know, boss. Luigi didn't say."

"What kind of idiot would send you a telegram and not tell you the most important thing?! And how the hell do you know that someone insisted on going out for a ride in the first place?"

"I'm trying to tell you, boss. The telegram said 'Family ambushed. Many dead. On my way to find out.' That's it."

"So how did you find out the rest?"

"This happened yesterday. Sometime early - and Luigi sent one of his men down on the afternoon train to fill us in on what he could."

"And he knows all this, and he doesn't know if the family's alive?"

Ruggio shrugged.

"Maybe some of them. I don't know. I guess you can figure the chaos, boss. If the men had to fight their way out, they're probably still in hiding."

"My god."

Duke Don Vito paced the room.

"All right. Get the motor carriage out and give me five minutes. We'll drive to Messina, take a ferry to the mainland, and catch the nearest train. It's the fastest way."

"I think it comes all the way down to Palmi now."

"Good."

Duke Don Vito shook his head and looked to the heavens.

"What a disaster. I told that fool never to leave the house, didn't I?"

"I know, boss. I heard you many times."

"All right, get the motor carriage out. I'll be down in a minute."

Five minutes later, they were on their way to Messina. Three hours later they were on a ferry to the mainland. At Palmi, they learned the next train did not leave for eight hours so they drove north to Cosenza and intercepted a train coming out of the east.

The following day at dawn, they were finally pulling into the end of the line at Como. Ruggio had sent a telegram from Naples and Luigi was there to meet them. More than a dozen of his men stood nearby. Luigi shrugged remorsefully without saying a word.

"Are they alive?" Duke Don Vito asked.

Luigi shook his head.

"None of them?"

"I think maybe the boy, Antonio."

"You think."

"Well, we had to fight our way through an angry hornet's nest to get up there and when we finally arrived at the scene, we found everyone dead except for one of my men, Miguel. He was shot in the chest and lived long enough to tell us that he gave his life trying to protect Antonio. He thinks he got away, but we've searched everywhere and we can't find him."

"If he's alive, the peasants will know. They're probably hiding him."

"Yeah, that's what we figured too, but no one's talking to us."

"All right, look. Let's find out who the village elder is. The mayor? A magistrate? I don't care who, but explain to them that we're here to protect the boy and get him to a safe place. Throw money around if you have to, but find him. And if they want credentials, just mention my name."

"All right."

The men stood there looking at each other.

"I'm going to ask you right now, Luigi," Duke Don Vito said. "Did you do everything in your powers to protect them?"

"Duke Don Vito, I had twenty men around them. Eighteen of them now dead. And those two would have given their lives, but the family was already gone and they've been off trying to find the boy."

Duke Don Vito nodded.

"All right. Twenty men should have been enough. They must have come with an army. Anyway, the fools never should have gone out."

"I warned them boss, but the woman, Theresa, said she had had it up to here with being cooped up inside that villa," he said, raising his hand above his head.

"What a disaster . . . All right, let's get things into action. We've got to find that boy. And we're going to need more men."

"I took the liberty of stationing about thirty men around your villa. We can leave some there and take the rest with us to Vezio."

Luigi had four motor carriages with him and the dozen-plus men squeezed into the seats. Duke Don Vito rode in one of the middle cars with Luigi and Ruggio.

At Duke Don Vito's villa, they stopped long enough for Duke Don Vito to refresh himself and to reorganize the men. Ten were left at the villa. The rest piled into another half dozen motor carriages and the caravan started up alongside the lake.

When they arrived in Vezio, Duke Don Vito secured lodgings at the one hotel while the men spread out across the countryside, looking for word of the boy.

Late that afternoon, Luigi returned to the hotel. Duke Don Vito was seated in his room, sipping a glass of brandy when he came in.

"We found him."

Duke Don Vito jumped to his feet.

"You have him with you now?"

"No. The magistrate wants you to come personally. They won't reveal the boy's exact location until they speak with you personally."

Duke Don Vito downed the rest of his brandy and grabbed his coat.

"Let's go."

Ten minutes later, they were being welcomed into the magistrate's home on the outskirts of Vezio.

"Something to drink?" the magistrate asked after the introductions.

"No, no. Let's talk about the boy."

"Well, he's not in a good state."

"You mean he's been injured?"

"No, not in the way you're thinking. No, he's..."

The magistrate gestured at his head.

"I'm sure what he witnessed must have traumatized him. Apparently, he hasn't said a word since they found him."

"So, when can I take possession of the boy?"

The magistrate stared.

"You understand. Your name proceeds you, Duke Don Vito, but I have never met you personally. I have never seen your picture. How do I know you are who you say you are?"

"How well did you know the baron?"

"Well enough."

"Then you will know his wife's nickname for him was Doro. The boy was born on April 13th. His nickname is Tonio."

Duke Don Vito rattled off a number of other facts that only someone intimate with the family would have known.

"And of course, you know he was my business partner."

"Yes, yes. No, I am satisfied now. And forgive me. One cannot be too cautious under the circumstances."

The magistrate snapped his fingers and a servant disappeared. A moment later, he reappeared with Antonio. As if in a twilight sleep, but yet recognizing Duke Don Vito, he immediately ran to the one person who was familiar to him. Duke Don Vito knelt down holding out his arms to Antonio who ran into them and held him tight, putting his head on Duke Don Vito's shoulder.

"Oh, you poor boy. You poor boy. Don't worry."

Duke Don Vito kissed his head.

"You are safe now and we will take care of you."

Duke Don Vito met the eyes of the magistrate and the two men stared.

"I would say, be safe but I'm sure you know how to take care of yourself, Duke."

The magistrate waved.

"You are free to go."

"Thank you. And please, I want to reward the family who protected him. If I send a reward, you will make sure it gets to them."

"I will. I can't guarantee they will accept it, but I will try."

"Please. You tell them that I could never repay them enough. In the name of..." Duke Don Vito waved with his hand. "Please insist that they accept it."

"As I said, I will try."

Duke Don Vito stood up and put his arm around the boy.

"Well, we'll be off, and thank you again."

Duke Don Vito stopped at the door.

"Has he eaten?"

"Nothing here. I don't believe so. Not since..."

Duke Don Vito nodded and went out the door.

Back at his villa, he had a servant offer the boy food and make sure he was comfortable in his room. Meanwhile, Luigi tended to the security outside and Duke Don Vito sat down with Ruggio in his study.

"The question is, do we still send him to America now?"

Ruggio shrugged.

"If word gets out that he's alive, and it will, the boy will never be safe here."

"Perhaps with me in Palermo."

"He will be safer, but you will only be dragging trouble along with you."

Duke Don Vito nodded and drank his brandy, not liking what he was hearing, but knowing Ruggio was right. The people who had done this would never rest knowing the boy was alive.

Duke Don Vito sighed.

"All right. The boy goes to America as planned. The next question is, how do we get him out of here and down to Genoa?"

"I'll work on it."

"All right but we leave in the morning. Final question. How and when to hit these bastards back."

"I know how Luigi feels. With his men dead like that? He won't rest until half the country's in their graves."

Duke Don Vito nodded.

"No, we'll hit them hard, but it must be proportional. And we must make sure we have the right people. My feelings and Luigi's feelings aside, we don't need an all-out war on our hands."

Ruggio nodded.

"And of course, you make sure you and the boy are on the boat before Luigi hits them."

"Okay, boss. So, what now?"

"Check on everything. I'll make sure the men are fed. And have something set out for you. I'm going to try and eat with the boy alone."

Duke Don Vito stood up and walked Ruggio to the door.

"God, what a disaster. And all because the fool woman wanted a ride in the country. She forgot that the monarchy is dead."

Duke Don Vito patted Ruggio on the back.

"Thank you for everything, Ruggio. Did you decide on which coastline yet?"

"Don't worry about it, boss."

"No, it's okay. I hear New Jersey's nice. I'll put you right there on the waterfront."

"Let's make sure the boy is safe first."

"I'm afraid it might not be so easy, getting down off this mountain."

"We'll manage. I'll discuss it with Luigi and report back later on."

Duke Don Vito had a quiet meal served in his private dining room and had the lead maid, Leona, dote over the boy, but he mostly played with his food and wouldn't say a word. Duke Don Vito nearly shuddered to think of what he had witnessed and what was going on in his little brain. Both his parents and his older brother gunned down before his eyes. What a horror.

Later, once the boy had been put to bed, Duke Don Vito called for Ruggio and sat down with him in his study.

"So, what does Luigi think?"

"He thinks we should have a peasant take him down the mountain hidden in a wagon full of hay."

"This is insane. What for? We get a hundred guns, go down in a caravan and anyone gets in our way, we send them to meet their maker."

"I thought the same thing, but Luigi pointed out, 'let's say we do win the gun battle, then we've got the authorities all over our asses. Plus, then those bastards know the boy is still alive'."

Duke Don Vito nodded and scratched his head with just his pinkie and ring finger. He gestured and nodded again.

"All right. I'm glad to know somebody's thinking around here."

"So, you agree?"

"Yes, but I'm going to be the peasant."

"You, boss?"

"I'm not leaving a single thing to chance. And you tell Luigi, I want men stationed all along the way, should something happen. Maybe even set up roadblocks and pretend to be checking the wagon. That way if some son of a bitch is watching, they think I've already been checked. Arrange for a caravan with my motor carriage to go down the hill. Pick somebody that's halfway . . . you know . . . good looking to impersonate me."

"Sure, we can do that boss, but I still don't think you should be doing this."

"I'm doing it, so get busy. And get me some proper clothing."

Duke Don Vito looked at his manicured hands.

"I'll find some dirt outside . . . Go on! You know what to do. Have everything ready and we'll leave first thing in the morning."

Duke Don Vito hardly slept that night and slipped out before dawn in his under-cover peasant clothing. He was wearing black pants, a soiled white shirt, a black vest, loose-fitting boots, a scarf, and a soiled floppy hat. He had soiled his hands and made sure to soil his face too.

Just to be safe, they explained everything to the lifeless boy and told him not to say a word, no matter what. The men constructed an air cavity around him with branches and loaded the wagon with hay. The motor carriage caravan went down the mountain first, to make it look as if Duke Don Vito had already left.

As he made his way down the mountain, armed men followed along, but well back among the trees, to keep themselves invisible. Then, every few miles, there were men manning checkpoints and stopping everyone who came by. When they got to Duke Don Vito and his wagon, they stabbed their bayonets into the hay here and there as he muttered and cursed, pretending to be furious.

It took most of the day to reach Como, where Duke Don Vito quickly changed his clothes, and the boy was transferred to the trunk of a motor carriage. The caravan of motor carriages then raced the final one hundred and fifty miles to Genoa. Luigi had arranged for lodging at the villa of one of his friends. Just to be safe, the motor carriage with the boy was driven around back and the boy shuttled in through the back door of the villa.

After some discussion, it was agreed that they would transport the boy onboard the ship to America in a steamer trunk. The woman of the house had him bathed and doted on him, but Antonio still had not said one word. He hardly looked at anyone, and when he did, it was with a lifeless, blank expression that crushed your heart.

"I wonder if he will ever be the same," Duke Don Vito pondered before going to bed.

Knowing that they had to move him quickly, the following morning they packed up a few of Antonio's belongings and slipped him back in the trunk of the motor carriage and headed to the dock where a steamship was boarding passengers for America.

First class passengers had deckhands taking their trunks and placing them in the bottom storage area of the ship, whereas immigrants, who were known as second-class passengers or steerage passengers were sent to the middle deck of three-deckers called the steerage where the admiral's cabin was located. They often placed hundreds together in a single large hold. White bread, potatoes, and soup were the only foods that were good. If they did have any meat or fish, it was old, tough, and rancid.

Although the conditions on the boat would be a great challenge, emigration was fueled by dire poverty. This also included the islands of Sicily and Sardinia, with the landless peasants experiencing hardship, exploitation, and violence. The soil lacked nutrients and contained a lot of salt, causing crop failure, while malnutrition and disease were widespread.

While everyone was busy getting the passengers on board and checked in, one of Duke Don Vito's men who had hired on as a deckhand to watch after the boy, slipped him into a steam truck and loaded him onto the boat with the rest of the trunks and supplies. Antonio remained in the bottom of the ship, hidden from everyone. Duke Don Vito's deckhand, Elio, found a concealed corner and filled it with hay for the boy to hide in. He took care of Antonio, bringing him food and clothing for the month-long journey to America.

When the day had finally arrived and the ship docked at Ellis Island, Elio took Antonio out in the steamer truck and placed it with several others that were stacked. When no one was near, Elio knocked on the trunk twice, so that Antonio would know the coast was clear. Elio quickly opened the trunk, just enough for him to slip out and Antonio rushed over to blend in with a family who was disembarking from the ship.

Realizing that Antonio was alone, he was placed in a detention center where he remained for two months until the next steamship would be returning to Italy. Unaccompanied children who had no family members to receive them were sent back to their country. The occupants of the detention centers were fed three meals a day and slept dormitory-style. Less than two percent of immigrants were held for any length of time while they were awaiting money to be wired, or until they could supply an address of where they would be living.

Knowing that he would be departing back to Italy the next day, Antonio climbed out a window and hid in the shrubs. As he observed his surroundings, he noticed people boarding a boat heading to New York City. Being the clever young boy that he was, he blended in with a crowd of people who were speaking the language he knew so well. He slipped between them and boarded the boat, and when they disembarked, he followed them into the Italian neighborhood known as Little Italy.

Having not eaten since the previous day, Antonio was famished. As he walked around the neighborhood, he noticed an Italian Market and slipped in and stole some fruit. Before he had a chance to get away, the store owner grabbed him.

"Why do you come in and steal from my store?" he fumed at the boy as he shook him. "Where are your parents?"

Antonio was shaking and had tears in his eyes, "I'm sorry sir. I am so hungry. My parents . . . my parents . . .," he said sobbing now, "are dead."

The store owner, Nicolo took pity on the boy and said, "It's alright. Come over here and sit. I'll get you some food."

"Josephine," he called out, "Bring me out some salami, provolone, and bread."

Josephine came walking in, "You had dinner already, you're hungry - -?"

She didn't finish her sentence as she saw the sobbing boy sitting in the chair. "Oh, my little bambino," she sympathetically said as she looked at the boy sitting in the chair, his tears soaking his face, "Come, I will get you something to eat."

Antonio sheepishly followed Josephine to the table and sat there silently, scoffing the food placed before him.

Nicolo looked at Antonio who hadn't lifted his head, 'So, where do you live?"

"I don't know."

"Who are you running from?"

The boy looked up at him in silence, his countenance was of mortifying agony. As the memories flooded his mind, he again began to weep and slowly started to unwrap the horrors of losing his parents and his brother. He told them how Duke Don Vito had sent him over to America from Italy on a steamship to hide him from the men who killed his family.

Antonio was finally able to speak about what had happened, and recounted every detail as he told it to Nicolo and his wife, Josephine, often telling his story with his voice shaking as he cried and wiped his tear-stained face. As much pain as it was costing his young mind to relive this consternation, it was also the beginning of healing.

Nicolo understood that Antonio's young life depended on him remaining hidden.

"I'll tell you what I'm a gonna do." He told Antonio. "I'm a gonna give you a job. You clean the store and stock the shelves at night when no one is around, and you can live in my basement. Josephine will make sure you eat, have a bed to sleep in, have clean clothes and we'll pay you a little money too. And we will call you Tony. No one will be looking for Tony."

Tony looked up at Nicolo and Josephine, nodding his head.

"Yes sir, thank you sir. I will do a good job."

At night, every night for five years, Tony cleaned the store and made sure all of the shelves were stocked. He was very diligent, working hard, and earning an honest living. During his time living in the basement, he had become very close to the storeowners' son, Michael who was close to his age. Michael shared his schoolbooks with Tony and became like a brother to him. Although he was not able to receive any formal education, Tony was a very clever and intelligent young man.

One evening as Nicolo was about to close up the market, the neighborhood *padrone* known as "Joe the Boss" walked in with another young man. Nicolo stopped what he was doing and looked up at him, wary and untrusting.

"Nicolo, you look like you could use some help in the store."

"Well, I . . ."

"My nephew," he said as he waved a hand towards the young man, "needs a job. You need some help, don't you Nicolo? He's a fine worker."

Nicolo, knowing he had no choice in the matter responded, "Well, um . . . sure. When can you start?"

"He'll be here tomorrow morning." Joe said as he turned and walked away.

As he locked the door behind them, Tony came up from the basement.

"What was that all about?" he asked Nicolo.

"I've had to hire someone else to do your job. I won't need you to work for me anymore."

Tony looked at Nicolo and wanted to ask why, but by the way he was hanging his head and the fear he saw in his eyes, the answer was clear with no words needing to be spoken. He understood that it wasn't his choice.

Tony packed up his belongings and took the money he had saved and left the basement he had called home and used as his safe space, his refuge for all these years. He headed back up the stairs to leave and Josephine stopped him.

"Tony, you don't need to leave!" she said as she choked back tears.

"I think it would be best. Thank you for everything. Thank you for being my family." He said and he walked out the door.

The year was 1920, and by this time, the men who had killed his family had forgotten about Tony and moved on to other matters. Duke Don Vito knew that Tony had arrived in New York, but his men were never able to find him.

Tony walked the streets that he hadn't walked for many years and stopped at the rooming house for a temporary place to stay, unsure where his life may take him. The next day, he met up with a guy named Al Capone and they began running the streets together. Al taught Tony how to survive by trading loyalty for favors and selling stolen dresses and other goods. As their business began to thrive, Tony was met in a back alley by a couple of the men who worked for the Don of the neighborhood, the same who had forced Nicolo to give his nephew a job, "Joe the Boss".

"So, you're doing business in our neighborhood?" the men said to Tony, "The Boss says you need to pay him a percentage of the take."

"I'm not giving him anything," Tony replied as he turned and saw the guns pointed at him.

"Eh, you may want to reconsider our offer. The Boss has some cop friends who would be very interested in your illegal "business".

Knowing they had no other choice, Tony and Al complied, but began plotting their revenge. Al Capone took him under his wing and taught Tony the techniques of guns and shooting them effectively on the streets of New York and later on in Chicago. Joe the Boss was no friend to anyone in Little Italy. He was ruthless and demanded his percentage from all of the business owners, even though most were very poor.

The annual tradition of the Feast of Saint Rocco was approaching, and Tony decided that this was the time to take his revenge. As the people processed down the street honoring the saint, Tony was following along shadowing his victim and ready to strike at the perfect moment. That moment was not to come, but he continued watching him and realized Joe the Boss was walking home. Tony forged ahead and slipped inside the house and as Joe entered, he lifted his gun and shot him three times, killing him.

Tony earned the respect of the neighborhood and ended up taking it over and treating it and the people far better than they had ever experienced under Joe the Boss.

His business of selling stolen dresses became a legitimate business in what is now known as the New York fashion district. Tony purchased fine clothing and materials for buyers of impeccable taste. He had the finest tailor in the area making custom suits for men who insisted on a perfect fit. Tony was sitting in the shop one morning when a customer walked in with his newly tailored suit.

"Good morning Mr. Gallante. How can I help you?" the tailor asked.

"This suit is perfect, until I sat down to my mother-in-law's lasagna last night. She kept bringing out more and then salad, bread, dessert! 'Eat, eat!' she kept saying. I had to unbutton my pants!"

Tony and the tailor laughed as Mr. Gallante rubbed his still-engorged belly.

"Well, I can let them out and you can just wear your belt tighter."

Tony was looking at the items sitting on the tailor's table and saw a roll of elastic over to one side.

"How about . . ." Tony said, thinking aloud, "You put a piece of this on either side of the waist band?" as he held up the elastic and began to pull and stretch it, "And it won't show or change the look of the slacks."

"That just may work," the tailor said. "What do you think Mr. Gallante? Should I try it? I have to take the waistband apart anyway."

"Yeah, let's give it a try. I think you may be a genius Tony." He said as he was walking out the door. "See you tomorrow."

The next afternoon, Mr. Gallante came back to pick up his slacks which still fit perfectly, but now had some give in the waist. They were more comfortable when he sat, bent over, and of course, ate more of his mother-in-law's cooking! All thanks to Tony and his brilliant idea of stretch-waist pants!

Antonio is Found

When Vito was between 12 and 14, he and his dad, Duke Don Vito, had developed a secret code that no one knew except them. As he grew, he would take these messages to places his father could not go and decipher them for the people who were to receive them. This remained helpful to Duke Don Vito for many years.

During that time, Countess Athena was continuing her production of wines, perfumes, and hair dyes, and working closely with Duke Don Vito. Sofia continued to live with her at the Castellammare Estate and helped raise Athena's twin daughters, Maria and Florence and with running the estate. The girls were growing into distinguished young ladies, not lacking in beauty, charm, intelligence and wit. Unchanging from childhood, Maria was still more outgoing and business-minded than her twin sister, Florence, but both were being groomed to continue Countess Athena and Duke Don Vito's legacy.

Baroness Vittoria continued to live at the Castellammare Estate as its grand dame until her passing.

Duke Don Vito felt that it was time for Vito to become more involved in the business, but his mother, Duchess Sabrina thought otherwise.

"No, Vito you cannot get him involved in the business. He will end up getting killed." Duchess Sabrina pleaded with her husband. "It is far too dangerous here. You can't even show your face for fear of having your head blown off."

Duke Don Vito wanted to tell her to stop. She knew why this child was born. She had agreed! But as he looked into her eyes and saw her aching heart filled with fear for the son she so deeply loved, he softened. "Perhaps, we can think of something else . . . somewhere else. Maybe it's time for a fresh start in America."

Vito, now a man, was sent to New York to begin marketing Countess Athena's wine and olive oil in the new country. He visited several markets, and her products became very coveted by merchants and consumers. Their American business was beginning to flourish, but suddenly trouble erupted. Word had somehow gotten out that Duke Don Vito was Vito's father and other "mobs" were going to have to deal with them. Al Capone heard of the unrest and decided to go and help out with the situation. He sent word that he wanted to meet with Vito and have a talk. Tony told Al that he thought it would better if he joined them so that he'd have his back in case of trouble. As they walked into the room, Vito turned and said, "Can I offer you gentlemen some Castellammare wine?" Before they could answer, he began pouring three glasses.

"So, you're Duke Don Vito's son?" Al asked.

"Yes, I am," Vito responded.

"Why are you here and not your father?"

"My father was unable to come to America at this time, and he has sent me to have everything in place so that we can begin importing our products in New York and then throughout the country."

"Where is your wife?" Al asked.

"I am not married. My marriage has been arranged to one of the Castellammare twin daughters of Countess Athena. Our marriages were arranged right after we were born. I was to marry one of the twin daughters and the son of the Baron and Baroness of Brescia was to marry the other. Unfortunately, the baron and baroness were brutally murdered, and we do not know the whereabouts of their son. My father has had men searching for him for many years."

Tony looked at him and memories came rushing back, "Duke Don Vito." He said under his breath. "What is his name?" He asked aloud as he looked up at Vito.

"Who's name?" Vito asked.

"The missing son."

"Antonio . . . they called him Tonio. Why? Have you seen him? Do you know him?"

"Yes, I do. I am Antonio!"

Vito looked at the young man he hadn't seen since they were boys. His exterior had hardened, but he looked into his eyes and knew this was Tonio. The two men stood up and embraced, kissing each other on both cheeks.

"I must get word to my father. He will be so pleased to know you are alive and well. He was so worried about you and had men searching for you for years!"

Vito sent word to his father telling of his meeting with Antonio, who was now called Tony. Tony, being the son of a baron and baroness was now given his rightful title as Baron Antonio. Duke Don Vito quickly went to Countess Athena and told her the news and she agreed it was getting close to the time to send her daughters to America to be married and fulfill their pact made so many years ago.

Maria, upon hearing the news absolutely refused to marry Tony. Even though the arrangement had been made, Duke Don Vito and Countess Athena knew from the time the children were eight years old that this may happen and were in agreement that they would allow Maria to marry Vito. Their kindred spirits were undeniable with both of them being vivacious and lively.

"Mother," Maria said to Countess Athena, "I am happy that Antonio has been found alive, but I will not marry him." By now she was in tears, "I cannot! You know I love Vito!"

"Maria, my darling, don't fret," her mother assured her with a calming voice while she gently hugged her and patted her back, "Duke Don Vito and I knew this was a possibility from the time you were children, and if your sister is in agreement, you may marry Vito instead."

Both Maria and Florence were quite beautiful, a trait passed down from generation to generation of the Castellammare women. Although their beauty was apparent at birth, they only grew more beautiful as they aged and matured into aristocratic royalty.

Maria was 5'6" tall and weighed around 120 pounds and Florence was around the same height, but slightly heavier. Unlike Maria, she was easy going, calm, and patient.

Florence was very close to Maria and felt compassion for her. She knew how much Maria was in love with Vito, so she agreed to marry Tony. Tony stood about 5'6" tall, except for when he was wearing the two-inch heels on his shoes, and he carried around 170 pounds on his large frame.

The date was set, and Maria & Vito and Florence & Tony were wed in a beautiful double ceremony. Although their marriages had been arranged before their births, both grooms were delighted that day as their beautiful brides were walked down the aisle to join them. At the close of the ceremony, Duke Vito and Duchess Maria were introduced as man and wife with the introduction of Baron Tony and Countess Florence immediately following. The wedding reception continued deep into the night with Castellammare wine continuing to flow, music and dancing, and food and spirits all remaining abundant throughout the celebration, as was Duke Don Vito's custom.

Duke Don Vito offered to send the couples anywhere in the world for their honeymoons. The two newlywed couples decided that they wanted to honeymoon together in New Orleans. Both Maria and Florence loved history and old southern charm which was rich at their beloved Castellammare estate. New Orleans not only boasted of these, but the weather was also similar to that of Sicily. Of course, Duke Don Vito made sure all of the arrangements were in place with the finest accommodations and every luxury available to them.

Duchess Maria & Duke Vito and Countess Florence & Baron Tony continued to be very close often living together in the same houses. Unlike Baroness Vittoria and Countess Sophia, the twin girls' husbands were good and loyal to their wives and their families remained very close in life and in business for over 60 years.

Prohibition, Bootlegging & Concrete Boots

Prohibition and bootlegging were looming in the wild 1920s and early 1930s. Vito worked with Joe Kennedy to transport a shipment of liquor from Canada by truck, travelling through New Hampshire, Concord, Nashua, Lowell, and then into Boston on Route 3. During their trip, they reached Concord at around midnight when the dual-wheel Model B, Ford broke down on a back rural road close to a farm near Concord, New Hampshire. The truck driver went up to the door of the farm and knocked.

"Who's there?" the farmer asked curtly, "Do you know what time it is?"

"Sorry, sir, our truck broke down and we were hoping you could help."

The farmer opened the door and saw the truck illuminating in the moonlight off in the distance. He looked at the men and immediately knew they were transporting illegal goods.

"What do you want from me?"

"We see you have an Abbott-Downing truck over there and thought you might like to sell it."

"Maybe, if the price is right."

The driver took a roll of cash from his pocket and offered it to the farmer and added, "This, along with our new truck."

"And a case of that liquor you're hauling – we've got a deal."

The men moved the liquor from the broken-down truck to the farmers truck and went on their way.

The farmer went back into his house and poured himself a nightcap before heading back to bed.

Joe Kennedy was never officially tied to bootlegging and official records have never been found. However, his father Patrick Joseph Kennedy, was originally a saloon-owner in Boston and also imported whiskey prior to the Prohibition in 1920. He was allowed to keep the storage of liquor that he had already purchased, but could not sell, transport, or manufacture the illegal spirits. In 1933, when he knew Prohibition was ending, he continued to bootleg by importing expensive Scotch and gin from the United Kingdom to avoid paying government taxes. By December of 1933, the 21st Amendment was ratified and Prohibition was lifted, and customers bought the expensive liquors by the case. Later, Kennedy sold his liquor franchise for $8.2 million, which is around $157 million in today's dollar, which was financed by Duke Don Vito.

Duke Vito's storefront in New York had become a very successful and thriving business while Baron Tony continued working the streets maintaining mob law.

Baron Tony had become enamored with the new Packard sedan and decided to purchase one but wanted to have it customized. He had a secret compartment installed between the dashboard and the motor which he was able to access from the outside of the car. He never had reason to use it until one night at the New York Harbor.

Illegal bootlegged liquor was being imported into the harbor from the islands and this was by far, their most lucrative business. Baron Tony had heard rumors and decided to visit the dock one evening and oversee the shipment. A foreman from a rival family who was working on the dock had been skimming for himself. Baron Tony stood out of sight and watched the man as he stashed liquor in a steam trunk hidden behind trucks waiting to move the shipment. Baron Tony walked around the corner and stood behind him as he continued to bury his stash in the straw-filled trunk.

"What are you doing?" Baron Tony blurted out as the foreman slammed the lid and spun around, obviously startled by Baron Tony's presence.

"Nothing!" the foreman blurted out, "I wasn't doing anything."

"Oh, what's in the trunk?" Baron Tony asked.

"Just some straw. I was wondering how it got here," the foreman frantically lied, trying to pretend he was shocked at the presence of the straw in the trunk.

"Well, I've heard . . ." Baron Tony wasn't even able to finish his sentence when the guilty foreman began yelling at him.

"Yeah, what have you heard?" he screamed.

An argument ensued and Baron Tony decided the argument was finished. He reached into his vest and drew one of his .38s and shot him. The foreman dropped over dead and Baron Tony slid him into the secret compartment of the Packard. Before long, the police arrived and walked around the pier looking for something or someone. They walked past the trucks and Baron Tony's car with their flashlights glowing into each of the vehicles windows, and they looked underneath.

"I don't see anything," one of the officers said to the other.

"Someone called and said they heard what they thought was a shot," the other officer answered.

"Probably one of the fishing boats unloading and banging stuff around," the first officer said, "Nothing here. Let's go." Both officers got back into their car and left.

The foreman's body was disposed of and never found, but the rival family knew that Baron Tony had killed the foreman and it was time to teach him a lesson, so they carefully plotted out their plan.

One night, Baron Tony stood alone at the pier for a while watching the boat being unloaded. Being alone was very unusual occurrence since he never went anywhere without his bodyguard. He walked back to his car where two of the rival family members were hiding behind the large Packard sedan and ambushed Baron Tony placing a sack over his head, blinding him from his captors. They took him back to a warehouse, where other family members were waiting to carry out their vengeance.

"Eh, big shot!" the lieutenant of the family jeered at Baron Tony while they dragged him into the warehouse and threw him into a chair. "Who's the big shot now?" he continued taunting Baron Tony.

"This is going to be your last lesson!" he said as men placed his feet and lower legs in something cold and wet, which was cement. They left him sitting, tied to the chair for quite a while as they continued to taunt and curse him. Finally, he was lifted, and Baron Tony could feel the weight bearing on his lower limbs as he was carried and thrown into the back of a truck and driven back to the pier. By this time, the pier was void of any people and silence cut through the night as they lifted Baron Tony and threw him into the frigid water. They rushed back to their truck to get away before being seen.

Near the dock where Baron Tony's body had been thrown into the water sat a crane that Baron Tony's crew used to unload bootlegged liquor from the boats at night. Although everyone had left, the crane operator was still sitting in his crane, not working, but chugging a bottle of the bootlegged liquor. The crane cable and net, which was now submerged deep in the water since the tide had come in, was completely invisible from the dock. When the truck had driven up, he vanished into the darkness of the night and sat quietly in the crane watching the men as they threw Baron Tony into the harbor water off the dock. As soon as the truck drove away, he started the crane and pulled up the net to see if he could see Baron Tony in the water. To his surprise, when he pulled up the net, Tony was in it! He quickly got him out of the net and broke the concrete off of his legs and feet. Baron Tony thanked him and went about business as usual.

Although Baron Tony seemed cool and composed, his focus now became retaliation and revenge! It wasn't long before Tony abducted the lieutenant from the family and returned the favor by imitating what was done to him. The lieutenant was placed in concrete and dumped into the pier, although Tony was successful in his endeavor. It was about five years later when the New York port authority was dredging the harbor and pulled up a concrete block with boots imbedded in it and leg bones sticking out. The dock workers started the phrase "Concrete Boots."

Al Capone had met with a man named Torrio, who convinced him to come work with him in Chicago where he brought his expertise as a numbers man, as well as his street smarts to Torrio's business of bootlegging, gambling, and prostitution. In a short time, Torrio made Al his partner.

Al Capone wanted total control of the streets of Chicago and rival gangs needed to be eliminated to make that happen. Al and Tony had continued to keep in contact even after Al moved to Chicago. Tony, being Tony, was more than eager to help Al with his problem.

"I think it's time for a little vacation." Tony said to Al. "I hear Chicago is nice this time of year."

"Nice?" Al responded as if questioning Tony's sanity. "I'm going to be heading to my home in Florida in a few days to warm up!"

"Perfect! We'll talk when I get there."

Tony began collecting all of his things together for his trip, including his pistols which were as important as his wardrobe. He carried six on his person wherever he went with two in his front vest harnesses, two in his vest harnesses in the back, and two in his boots. In the event of a shootout, he would never run out of bullets and would have the upper hand while his enemies were reloading.

The phone rang and it was Duke Don Vito. "I hear you're taking a trip to Chicago."

"Yeah, I need to take care of some business with Al and his men. They're having trouble with the North Side Gang and I'm going to help him with his problem. You know, he did me right when I had nowhere to go – I owe him."

Duke Don Vito knew that Al had helped Tony after he had to move out of the store, but never felt that Al Capone should be in charge since he was nothing more than a renegade and needed to be put in line. He was smart and an asset to the organization, but he was also egotistical and too indiscreet and hasty in his dealings. Duke Don Vito respected and trusted Tony, knowing that he would carefully consider his options and never act on impulse. After their conversation and contemplating what Duke Don Vito had said, Tony began devising his plan of action and its players.

Baron Tony boarded the train from New York headed for Chicago. As they approached the station, people on the train were buzzing about the police and FBI agents all standing on the platform. "They must be looking for someone." "Who do you think it is?" "I wonder if they're dangerous! Are we safe?"

Baron Tony looked out and saw Elliot Ness standing amongst the crowd and knew that he was there for him. Ness had been promoted to Chief Investigator of the Prohibition Bureau for Chicago to bring the end to bootlegging activities. He had to have found out that he was going to be on the train. As the train began to stop, Tony got up from his seat and went in to use the restroom. When he came out, he was dressed as a woman and proceeded to get off the train and walked through the crowd of people undetected. Elliot Ness and the agents believed that Tony had decided to change his plans and nixed their operation of looking for him in Chicago, which worked out to Tony's benefit as he proceeded with his plan.

He met with Al Capone's proteges and others who would be key to carrying out what would become one of the most high- profile events in history, **The Valentine's Day Massacre**, which took place on February 14, 1929.

At 10:30 on a cold, blustery Thursday morning, seven members and associates of the North Side Gang had gathered at a Lincoln Park garage when two of Tony's men dressed as police officers burst in and ordered the men to line up against the wall. The men, believing that this was a police raid, and they were going to be arrested, did as they were told. As they lined up against the wall, two assassins wearing overcoats, suits, ties, and hats ran in shooting Thompson submachine guns, one having a 20-round magazine and the other a 50-round drum, and thoroughly sprayed the men, continuing to shoot them as they fell to the floor in their own pools of blood. As the explosion of the guns ended, the two men dressed as police officers escorted the assassins out with their hands up and guns pointed at them to make it appear as though everything was under control to the several onlookers who were now lining the street. They all got into a black Cadillac touring car that resembled a police car, complete with siren, gong, and rifle rack and fled the scene with no one ever knowing their true identities.

The actual police arrived at the bloody scene and found only two survivors, one being a German Shepherd named Highball, who belonged to one of the victims and the other was a man named Frank who was still conscious, although he had sustained fourteen bullet wounds.

"Who did this?" the police asked as he was loaded onto a stretcher. "Who shot you?"

Frank looked up at the officers, his very life pouring from his wounds onto the blood-soaked sheets of the stretcher where his body was lying, but refused to give up any names and said, "No one shot me!"

The police officers blankly looked at one another as Frank was put into the awaiting ambulance and driven to the hospital where he died three hours later.

Some of Tony's people had contacted Chicago newspapers and publicity of the massacre was huge – the people were outraged and blamed Al Capone. The Chicago police and citizens always believed that Al was to blame, but with his airtight alibi of being at his home in Palm Island, Florida, and his claims that he knew nothing of the attack, they couldn't charge him and there was never enough evidence of who the actual shooters were. Some of the freelance reporters continued writing about the story, adding their opinions and hypothetical facts which added to public fear and was causing problems for all mob bosses. These freelance reporters were always Tony's enemies, selling their fabricated stories to whoever would pay the most for them, and he knew he needed to finally address them and put this story to rest. Never being aware that he felt that way about them, they were elated to meet with him.

It was five years to the day of the Valentine's Day Massacre and Baron Tony was finally going to give these freelance reporters the facts of what happened on that bloody day. He had offered to portray a reenactment of the Massacre so that they would finally know what had really happened, but none of this was to be publicized since he had only allowed a select few to participate. The day arrived and the freelancers showed up with their notepads and cameras, eager to finally find out who had done it and why. Baron Tony walked in dressed in a police officer's uniform, something he did often when doing a hit, and proceeded to reenact and tell the story. Cameras were flashing, hands were busy writing as they grasped every detail, eager to present their story to the world, coveting the prestige and honor that it would bring to their careers. Baron Tony allowed them to reel in their glory for a while - and then he lined them up against the wall as he had five years earlier and shot them. No one ever knew!

Although Al Capone was never charged with the St. Valentine's Day Massacre, he nonetheless found himself in trouble because he refused to pay a percentage of his take to the family and ended up being turned in to the IRS for tax evasion. Tony had connections in Chicago and tried to get Al off, but to no avail. One of his ideas was to have the juries changed, but in the end, Al ended up in jail where he served eight years of his eleven-year sentence. His wife appealed to the courts to release him due to his lack of mental capacity and the rapid decline of his health from syphilis and gonorrhea. Upon his release, he returned to his home in Palm Island, Florida, where he lived out his days as an invalid.

As per Duke Don Vito's instruction, Baron Tony took over the Chicago Outfit, mimicking Duke Don Vito's style of remaining behind the scenes and laying the foundation for generations to come.

While Duke Vito continued business in his storefront and with his imports and sales, some became aware of Duke Don Vito being Vito's father and began asking for favors. Duke Don Vito had a reputation of being firm in his dealings, but loyal. Vito was being lured into the mafia life he had watched and grown up in his entire life. Prohibition, gambling, prostitution, bootlegging - money was flowing, and the New York Mafia was out of control.

Duke Vito was closing up the store for the day when the phone rang.

When he answered, he heard the familiar voice of his father. "Vito my son, how are things going?"

"Well papa, the business is going very well, but . . ." Before he could finish his sentence, Duke Don Vito stopped him and said, "How 'bout you come for a visit? Your mother and I are heading to the villa in the Italian Alps and would love to have you come for a while."

"I would love to, but with the store and things going on, I don't know if it's such a great idea right now."

"My son, I think now is the right time."

Duke Vito knew that he was going and there was going to be no more discussion on the matter, "I will be there soon, Papa."

Vito looked at the villa where he, Tony, Maria, and Florence had loved to spend their summers as children. Duke Don Vito had built airstrips on the property where he could travel in his Bi-Plane to and fro without having to make plans and arrangements with anyone. When Duke Vito arrived, his belongings were unloaded by the attendant and placed into an awaiting car where Vito was driven up to the villa. He was barely out of the car as his mother rushed out to greet him, hugging and kissing him on both cheeks.

"Oh, my son, I miss you so!" she exclaimed with tears in her eyes. "Let me look at you!" She held his shoulders back to look at him and hugged him again.

Duke Don Vito walked out onto the front porch, "Sabrina, let him be!" he chuckled, "You're smothering him."

"Oh, you!" she laughed wiping away her tears. "Let me go in and see if lunch is about ready."

"Papa," Duke Vito said as he walked over and embraced his father. "You're looking well."

The two men continued their conversation about the trip and family as they walked into the house for lunch. Duchess Sabrina, Duke Don Vito, and Duke Vito sat around the dinner table enjoying their meal with continued pleasantries, several refills of Castellammare wine and plenty of good food. Both men knew the conversation to come but did not want to mention anything in front of Countess Sabrina knowing how she felt about Duke Vito being in the business.

"Vito, come - let's go for a walk and settle that delicious lunch," Duke Don Vito said as he leaned over and gave Countess Sabrina a kiss on the cheek.

Both men arose from their seats and Countess Sabrina began clearing some of the dishes from the table and one of the servants quickly rushed over to finish the task.

"So, tell me, what's going on?" Duke Don Vito asked his son.

"Prohibition, bootlegging, money, power . . . they're out of control! Everyone wants in - members threaten other members to eliminate competition - some gangs are hijacking each other's shipments of alcohol and forcing others to pay for protection to leave their goods alone. Shipments can only go out with armed guards. Some have found out that you're my father and are looking for favors."

Duke Don Vito continued to walk with his son, listening intently with his head tipped to one side and tapping the tips of his fingers together with both hands. Obviously disturbed by what he was hearing, but composed, he knew that Duke Vito could not be the front man organizing this chaos. He knew the danger - he knew the promise he had made to Duchess Sabrina – he knew what it had cost him. He was a target and always had to look over his shoulder. They stopped walking and Duke Don Vito turned to his son, "We need organization." He said to Duke Vito, shaking his head. "You know the men, who will they respect – who'll respect them. Loyalty, respect, not quick to react - the keys to a good leader."

"Papa, you know . . ."

"Not you, Vito – Absolutely not you! I met a guy a while back – he's running the Five Point Gang, Charlie, uh . . ." Duke Don Vito snapped his fingers as he tried to recall the name.

"Yeah, I know him. His name is Charlie Luciano, but they call him Lucky. Not sure if he got his name because he's lucky in gambling, or if it's because he survived getting beaten and his throat slashed when he wouldn't go work for one of the bosses. He isn't into petty crime like the others. He's into bootlegging and makes his money by protecting some of the Jewish and Irish gangs – he charges them each ten cents a week!"

"That's exactly who we need, someone who the people trust and respect – someone loyal. That's good! We'll get this taken care of. Now, let's get back and have some of your mother's cannoli."

The two men headed back to the villa talking about the store and the imports and how well the wine and olive oil sales were going as they walked in.

Countess Sabrina said, "Work! Is that all you men talk about?"

Duke Don Vito said, "Yes, that and your cannoli!"

The three of them went out on the front porch and enjoyed their espressos and cannoli, knowing that their time together would soon be over as Duke Vito headed back to America.

When Duke Vito arrived back in America, Duke Don Vito's plans were already in motion. It was 1931, and The Commission was established with Lucky Luciano becoming the dominant crime boss in the United States. Tony, having been groomed and taught by Al Capone, wanted to be enforcement in The Commission and formed a branch he named Murder, Inc. Luciano set up policies and governed activities along with other Mafia bosses who believed in the "old world" principles of tradition, respect, honor and dignity. Al believed he should have been the one chosen instead of Lucky, but Duke Don Vito had never even considered him for the position. Within a short amount of time, The Commission consisted of seven family bosses, the leaders of New York's Five Families who would oversee all activities and mediate family conflicts. Their agreement was to meet every five years or anytime a family problem needed to be discussed.

A few minor meetings had taken place during the five-year span, but the formal meeting was due as per their agreement. A rustic spaghetti dinner was prepared for The Commission meeting, where the men convened in a New Jersey warehouse. A long table was set up with fresh Italian bread and Countess Athena's imported olive oil lining the center of the table along with antipasto. Each of the ten men and their bodyguards came and sat around the table ready to enjoy their meal and Castellammare wine.

Lucky sat down at the head of the table, Duke Vito sat to his left, and Baron Tony sat at his right.

Duke Vito lifted his glass and said, "Salute!"

Everyone at the table raised their glasses saying, "Salute!"

They proceeded to enjoy their appetizers before the primo course of spaghetti was brought out to be served. The aroma filled the air as the bowls were walked around the room and served each of the diners. Each of the men was relishing his meal, reminiscent of the old country, when . . .

"Come out with your hands up!" they heard someone yelling outside.

"We're asking you again - come out with your hands up!"

The men said nothing and looked at each other, and then over at Tony who was still eating his spaghetti. The building had one door – one way in – one way out - and the police were at that door!

"Throw your weapons out the door and come out with your hands up," the police again yelled. "This is your last warning! Come out or we'll shoot!"

The gunfight began! The men and their bodyguards were shooting through windows that they had broken out and the police were returning gunfire.

Duke Vito, who was obviously panicked said to Baron Tony, "If we don't go out, they're going to kill all of us!"

Baron Tony calmly sat at the table eating his spaghetti as bullets whizzed past him.

"Tony, are you crazy? What are we going to do? How can you sit there just eating?" Duke Vito was angry, but Baron Tony appeared unconcerned. In his silence, he was planning on how to get Vito and himself out.

When Baron Tony finished his meal, he said to the men, "Shoot out as many of the streetlights as possible."

They shot out almost all of them which made the street dark.

"Are you ready?" Baron Tony asked Duke Vito.

"Ready as I'll ever be!"

Baron Tony donned his bullet-proof vest which was meticulously made to perfection by a leather craftsman. They had chosen different leathers to combine until the perfect ones were paired for their strength and ability to protect him. The craftsman then sewed two harnesses inside the vest to carry his pistols and keep them in close range for quick access. He also donned four extra guns to avoid reloading, which gave him an advantage over his opponents who would have to stop and reload. He carried a gun in each of his boots which had custom holsters installed, and also his jacket vest pockets. Baron Tony picked up two Tommy guns and Duke Vito already had his in hand as they proceeded out the policed door, back-to-back – tightly as possible – with their Tommy guns firing at the police as they trudged down the sidewalk trying to dodge the shots being fired at them.

Suddenly, Baron Tony felt fire burn through his body – he had been shot in the neck. He dropped to the ground still firing his two Tommy guns at the police as he laid there. Duke Vito reached around and grabbed Baron Tony by the back of his jacket with one hand, still shooting with the other as he attempted to pull him to safety. Within seconds, their driver pulled the car up to the sidewalk and Duke Vito climbed in pulling Tony up onto the running board. As the car peeled away, there sat Tony on the running board with Duke Vito holding him by the neck of his jacket, still shooting both of his Tommy guns as they disappeared into the darkness of the night escaping the police.

When they had driven a while and knew the coast was clear, the driver stopped the car. Duke Vito helped Tony inside and saw that the bullet was not fatal and one of their doctor associates could fix him up. Tony survived and his wounds healed, but he always talked in a low-raspy voice because of the damage from the bullet near his vocal cords.

Duke Vito was thinking back on the shootout and how Tony was sitting there eating his dinner in the midst of chaos and said, "My God, Tony! How could you be so calm?"

Tony looked up at Duke Vito and gave him a nod, "When a situation presents itself, you stop, assess it, and plan your course of action. I was going to finish my dinner - could be my last meal, you know - and I was going to enjoy it!"

Duke Vito just shook his head and knew that Tony was the right man for the job.

After this mafia shootout, they always made sure that they had two ways in, and two ways out. In public places, they always kept their backs to the wall.

Tony stayed at home with Countess Florence during his recovery and Duke Vito also felt it was good for him to follow his father's advice and keep a low profile, especially after the shootout with the police.

A few weeks had passed, and Countess Florence invited Duke Vito and Maria over for dinner so that the men could catch up, as well as Maria and herself. They pulled up to the house and Countess Florence ran out to greet them.

"It's so good to see you." Countess Florence said and she embraced and kissed her sister and then Duke Vito. "Come in the house and relax. Tony is pouring us all some Castellammare wine and we can sit and chat. It's been too long."

"How is the old guy?" Duke Vito chuckled.

"Back to his ornery self!" Countess Florence said as they walked in the front door.

"Vito, Maria!" Tony said as he walked over to them first embracing and kissing Maria and then Duke Vito, "It's so good to see you."

"You look well Tony," Duke Vito said. "Better than when I was dragging you down the road with your butt on the running board."

Both men laughed and went into the parlor to catch up and enjoy their wine.

"I need to go and see if dinner is about ready," Countess Florence said.

"Oh, let me help you." Maria said as they both headed toward the kitchen.

The women were finishing up with the final preparations before serving dinner and Maria looked over at Countess Florence and said, "You know what we need?"

"I have several ideas," laughed Countess Florence, "But what do you have in mind?"

"Remember our honeymoon? I can't get that place out of my mind. The beauty, the history, and the weather remind me of home, back in Sicily."

"We should go back. A second, or in our case, fourth honeymoon." Countess Florence laughed.

"We'll mention it to the boys at dinner and see if they'll take us!"

The women proceeded to take dinner out to the table and called to their husbands, "It's ready!" They both chimed. "Come on, let's eat before it gets cold."

Both men made their way to the table, following the aroma of the dinner as it wafted down the hall.

Tony proceeded to refill the wine glasses and they all sat down to eat.

"Florence, this is delicious." Maria said, "It's almost as good as mine." She chuckled as she looked at her sister who was smirking back at her.

They all continued eating and when they had finished their salad, Maria looked at the men and said, "Florence and I were thinking . . ."

"Oh boy, that means trouble." Duke Vito said as he and Tony began to laugh. Both women looked at them and sighed. "Okay, okay, what were you thinking?" he asked.

"We want to go on a second honeymoon back to New Orleans. It's so cold and we miss the beautiful weather back in Sicily and . . ."

"Alright, we can go!" Duke Vito said.

The women were elated and immediately started making plans, while the men returned to the parlor to have a brandy and smoke cigars.

"You're such a pushover," Tony said, laughing.

"I didn't see you saying we couldn't go, tough guy!"

"You cannot say "no" to the people you love very often. That's the secret. And when you do, it has to sound like a "yes" or you have to make them say "no." You have to take time and trouble."

"You don't have to tell me, I'm right here with you."

They all enjoyed each other's company and conversation, then as evening came to an end, Duke Vito and Maria said their goodbyes and headed home.

Second Honeymoon in New Orleans

Duchess Maria and Countess Florence were busy packing and making sure everything was in order for their trip to New Orleans while Duke Vito and Tony were making preparations for their absence from daily business. Duke Don Vito had offered to send his plane to take them to New Orleans, but they decided to take the train and enjoy the scenery. Of course, Duke Don Vito had arranged the finest accommodations for every aspect of their trip, from having the finest cabins on the train to hotel accommodations, and dining. Cars and drivers were on standby to take them anywhere they wanted to go and at any time.

Tony walked into the bedroom and by the door were two large trunks and a couple of smaller ones.

"What is all this?" he asked Countess Florence.

"My luggage!" she answered, looking surprised that he didn't know.

"What? Are we going for a year?" he laughed, "and they do have stores there if you need anything."

"I just want to be prepared."

The maggiordomo knocked on the bedroom door, joined by the under-butler to take Tony and Countess Florence's trunks to the awaiting car where they would meet Duke Vito and Duchess Maria at the train station. As they arrived, passengers, dressed in their finest apparel were standing in line with their luggage waiting to board the train. Their driver opened the door for Tony and Countess Florence to exit their car and Duke Vito and Duchess Maria's driver pulled up next to them. The women excitedly greeted one another as porters came to carry the luggage up to their first-class cabins.

"Please, come with me," the transport official said to the two couples.

As they followed, he whisked them ahead of awaiting passengers to their first-class cabins, which were furnished like living rooms complete with armchairs, drapes, carpeting, and radio gramophones where they could listen to radio and radio programs.

"Isn't this so much better than flying? We can see the country as we travel." Duchess Maria said.

"It's beautiful, but five days to get there and five days back!" Tony said.

"Oh, just relax for a change." Countess Florence said as she gave him a peck on the cheek, "After all, it's our second honeymoon."

Both couples proceeded into their luxurious cabins where the porters had already placed their luggage and were standing by awaiting their guests.

"Sir, madam - may I assist you with unpacking?"

"No thank you, not right now. Perhaps in a little while."

"Anything you need, please don't hesitate to ask." The porters said as they exited the cabins.

Both couples made themselves comfortable as they heard the conductor shout, "Aaaall aboard!"

Within minutes, the train's whistle blew, and it began to move slowly at first, and then began to pick up speed. At the station, those who had said their good-byes and wide-eyed children who were fascinated by the huge steel locomotive frantically waved as the train pulled away. Passengers waved back until the people had become smaller and smaller in the distance and their journey was underway.

During the five-day trip, Tony and Duke Vito finally had time to relax, but Tony was always looking over his shoulder and on high alert to his surroundings. Both women were soaking up the beautiful views, the fine dining, and just the time they were able to spend together. The time on the train had gone by very quickly and they were at their destination.

The train pulled into the station and Duke Don Vito had a 1933 black Packard Limousine and their private driver, Pasquale, waiting to take them to their hotel - the finest in New Orleans, the 16-story Baronne Street Tower which boasted of boutiques, a barbershop, and other amenities, all within the hotel. Their luggage had been unloaded from the car onto a cart and was loaded into the service elevator to be brought to their suites.

"Would you like to see your rooms?" the bellhop asked.

"Yes, that would be wonderful." Answered Duchess Maria.

"Please, follow me."

They all stepped into the elevator and the bellhop told the elevator attendant, "16th floor."

The women got out of the elevator first and the bellhop stepped ahead of the couples to open the doors to their suites, which looked more like luxury apartments. Maids were standing at attention, ready to assist them with their every need.

They had not yet closed the doors to their facing suites and Countess Florence and Duchess Maria were in their doorways chatting about places they wanted to visit. Duke Vito and Tony were just about to take off their coats and hats when Countess Florence said, "I'm famished!"

"I certainly could sit down to a nice dinner," Duchess Maria responded.

They went into their rooms to freshen up and joined each other at the waiting limousine and proceeded to Toney's Spaghetti House, which was operated by Sicilian newcomers to the area. Their menu was gaining attention with veal or eggplant parmigiana, artichokes stuffed with breadcrumbs, olive oil, and bacon, and the New Orleans-style spaghetti served with "tomato gravy".

"Spaghetti?" Duchess Maria said. "We can have that anytime. Seafood! That's what you eat in New Orleans!"

"But we need to support our people. And there was no spaghetti on the train. And – tomato gravy? We need to find out about tomato gravy. How about we have seafood tomorrow night?" Duke Vito said.

Both women were laughing at Duke Vito and his "tomato gravy" comment. "Alright, tomato gravy it is – but tomorrow night, seafood!"

They arrived at the restaurant, the driver stopped the limousine in front, got out, and opened their doors. The two couples proceeded to enter the restaurant and sat down at a vacant table. Several patrons watched them as they came in and some of the staff was whispering, wondering who they were receiving such royal treatment.

The waitress came over to the table and welcomed them, handing them each a menu.

"Good evening, my name is Leah, and I will be your waitress this evening. May I get you something to drink while you look over the menu?"

"We'd like four glasses of your finest red wine. Do you have Castellammare wine?" Duke Vito asked.

"I'll have to check. Please give me a moment." Leah responded and went to the back to ask the owner.

"Do you know who these people are? Are they some kind of royalty?" the owner asked Leah.

"No, I've never seen them before. I don't know if they're royalty, but they seem very nice and they're asking if we have Castellammare wines."

"I'll go talk to them," he said as he walked towards the table.

"Good evening gentlemen, ladies," he said, nodding his head at the couples. "Leah told me that you were asking if we had Castellammare wine. I am so sorry, but it's very difficult to get here."

"Really?" Duke Vito asked.

"Yes, we used to buy it all the time in the old country – it was the best wine I ever had, but they just don't import it to New Orleans. There are a few boats delivering merchandise to the docks on the Mississippi River, but the boats are usually here for export. Mostly sugar and some cotton," the owner said as he shrugged his shoulders. "Where are you from?"

"We're from New York, just visiting," Duke Vito answered.

"Yes, we're on our second honeymoon," Duchess Maria said smiling at Duke Vito.

"No, where are you from originally?" he asked again.

"Oh, we're from Palmermo originally," Duke Vito didn't offer any further information on who he was or his family background of royalty.

"I knew that accent! Well, it was a pleasure speaking with you. Enjoy your meal," the owner said as he walked back to the kitchen.

Duke Vito sat there quietly pondering and finally said, "You know, this would be a good place to import Athena's products."

"No business Vito," Duchess Maria said. "This is our vacation!"

"Okay, okay. You're right," he said. But his thoughts continued.

They enjoyed their dinners, several glasses of wine and finished up with espressos.

"When Leah brought the bill to the table, Tony said, "Our compliments to the chef! The dinner reminded us of home-cooked meals in Sicily."

"Thank you. I will be sure to let him know," Leah responded.

The owner, seeing that they had finished their meals and were getting ready to leave came back over to the table to thank them for coming.

"Thank you so much for coming to our restaurant. It was our pleasure to serve you. I hope you will come back again."

"Everything was delicious," Countess Florence said. "I'm sure we'll be back before we head home."

They left the restaurant and proceeded into their awaiting limousine; the driver opened the doors as they approached. Countess Florence and Duchess Maria got in first with Duke Vito and Tony getting in behind them.

"So, what are the plans for tomorrow?" Duke Vito asked. "I know you girls planned everything out."

"Well, first we want to see the French Quarter and then there are some cute boutiques . . ." Duke Vito and Tony were half-listening, but Duke Vito's mind was still on the opportunities for importing Athena's products to New Orleans. It would open up a whole new area of opportunity for marketing in the south.

Pasquale turned and asked, "Is there anywhere you'd like to go?"

Tony answered, "Maybe just a drive around the village this evening. Or does anyone else have anything they'd like to do?"

They all nodded 'no', and Duke Vito said, "We'll just drive around tonight and see where we may want to go tomorrow. You know the area, so we'll leave it up to you."

The driver took them down several streets where nighteries, also called night clubs, were filling with their exclusive patrons dressed in their finest attire. Nighteries were quite new and the concept of them had recently come from Paris with the French population growing in the area. Patrons either had a membership or paid a cover charge and entered through the velvet curtain barrier where they experienced high prices and a hat-and-coat-check. Some of these nightclubs were more than just a drinking spot and had restaurant service which earned them the name "supper club" or "dinner club". They also would have entertainment with comedians, dance acts, and other performances.

Other means of entertainment that they passed as they cruised the streets of the city were concert saloons, dance halls, multiple theaters with live performances, and also several motion-picture theaters.

"This place is hopping!" Tony said. "I think there's something for anyone and everyone to do after the sun goes down."

"Maybe we'll check out the supper club tomorrow night," Duke Vito said.

"Great idea, but I think that I'm ready to call it a night," Tony said. "Take us back to our hotel."

"Yes sir."

Pasquale pulled the limousine to the front of their hotel and immediately opened the doors for them to step out. As they walked toward the entrance, the porter opened the door and nodded. "Good evening," he said as they entered.

Both couples went to their suites and enjoyed a quiet and pleasant evening, cherishing their time alone together away from the business and traveling that always pulled them apart.

The next morning, they woke up to a beautiful sunny day and were ready to head out and see the sites. They dressed and made their way down to their awaiting limousine and Pasquale drove them to their first stop at Café Du Monde to enjoy Café Au Lait and beignets for breakfast. The women chatted endlessly about where they wanted to visit that day, while Tony and Duke Vito read the morning paper, The New Orleans Item-Tribune.

Tony whispered to Duke Vito, "Nothing about me in today's paper, so I guess it's a good day."

Duke Vito said, "No one knows anything about us or the family here. We'll just keep low and enjoy our time. Look at them - they're more excited and happier than I've seen them in a while."

They finished their coffee and made their way to historical sites, bayous, and churches. The city, being so rich in history and places to see, was barely skimmed as they decided it was time for lunch.

"Any suggestions?" Duchess Maria asked their driver.

"It depends on what you'd like to eat," he answered.

"Seafood!" Countess Florence quickly answered.

"Do you like oysters?'

"Oh yes," Duchess Maria and Countess Florence said in unison.

"I have just the place," the driver said, "Casamento's Restaurant on Magazine Street. They've been open since 1919 and are known for their seafood, but especially oysters."

They arrived at the restaurant and looked around at all of the tiled surfaces which resembled the buildings in Italy. The waitress came to the table and offered them menus.

"Can I get you something to drink while you look over the menu?" she asked.

"We'd like four glasses of your finest white wine," Tony answered.

"The décor in here reminds me of Italy, so much tile work," Duchess Maria said to the waitress.

"So much tile," the waitress laughed, "that my father needed to use four different tile companies to complete it."

"Your father is the owner?" Duchess Maria asked. "Your oysters came highly recommended by a friend."

"They are good! We serve them several ways. Let me get your wine and give you a chance to look over the menu."

A few minutes later, she came back with the wine and they placed an order for a full oyster loaf that they all shared, along with a few more glasses of white wine.

The waitress returned, "Can I get you anything else? Dessert?"

"Oh, no thank you," Tony replied. "I may need to put my stretch-waist pants on after this."

"Absolutely delicious!" Duchess Maria said.

They paid their bill and walked out to their awaiting limousine to visit a few more sites before dinner. Their driver, Pasquale, offered information on several of the historical sites as they drove past. Some, they wanted to stop at and see; others they decided to wait and visit, perhaps another day.

They visited shops and parks until evening was drawing near and dusk was upon them. Pasquale took them back to the hotel to give them time to change and freshen up before they went to the supper club for dinner and an evening of entertainment. The couples met at the doors of their suites, dressed in some of their finest attire, ready to embark on an evening of new experiences. They arrived at the supper club and stepped into the crowd of elites, the wealthy, the upper crust of the city. Most of the women were pompous, vain, and intentionally poised, but as Duchess Maria and Countess Florence walked into the room, eyes turned upon them. They were beautiful, regal, and graceful and it flowed from them naturally, without the need to put on airs. They were escorted to their table where they had dinner, several glasses of wine, and thoroughly enjoyed listening to Satchmo's unique singing voice and trumpet playing.

As the evening drew to a close and turned into the wee hours of the morning, they readily looked forward to a good night's sleep and headed back to the hotel.

The next morning, they went down to their awaiting car and Pasquale asked them where they would like to go today.

"Let's take it a little easy this morning," Tony answered. "Let's just drive and sightsee for a while."

"Yes sir. Would you be interested in viewing some of the plantation homes along the Mississippi River? There is a lot of history about slavery, sugarcane and cotton export and . . ."

"Yes, yes!" Duke Vito answered enthusiastically and abruptly. "There's a lot of opportunity in that area. I think we should check it out. Everyone agree?"

"Sure!" they each said.

Pasquale proceeded towards the Mississippi River where several plantations had been built along its banks in the late 1700s and into the mid-1800s. Most of the plantations still had several acres of sugarcane fields and a few had acres of cotton fields. Slaves had worked tirelessly during the eighteenth and nineteenth centuries on these fields, ensuring that their owners continued to make money for their very comfortable lifestyles. Although slaves worked hard, Louisiana's slave trade was governed by the French *Code Noir* which offered them certain privileges such as the right to marry, married couples could not be forced to separate, nor could they separate young children from their mothers. Under some circumstances, even though cruel, corporal punishment was allowed, but slave owners were not permitted to torture their slaves, and owners were required to teach them the Catholic faith. By 1863, the Emancipation Proclamation had set slaves free and a significant number started running businesses and owning property, but most left Louisiana.

They continued viewing plantations, which ran through several counties, and as they passed the Glenfield Plantation, while Pasquale interjected about a civil war battle that had ensued on the property and a bullet hole was still in the front door. Duchess Maria and Countess Florence were thoroughly embracing the historical facts and knowledge they were gaining and yearned for more.

As the couples peered out at their surroundings, they each were enamored by the beauty and charm of each plantation's history and the land where it sat. Although most were occupied by their owners, they were able to view a couple of them up close. As they continued traveling, a plantation placed in the background of massive, majestic oaks sat before them. Duke Vito could vaguely see in the distance a large sugar cane boat docked on the Mississippi towards the back of the sprawling grounds. Two large trucks were pulling into a long driveway leading to the dock with goods loaded in the back, ready to take to the awaiting ship.

"Let's follow them," He said.

"Are you sure we can go in there?" Duchess Maria asked nervously.

"I don't see why not. The trucks are going in with their loads."

Pasquale followed the trucks up the driveway and the grand plantation home came into full view. It had seventeen, twenty-foot-high columns that were each twenty-four inches in diameter, twelve-foot-deep porches on three sides, with the front facing the Mississippi River. The front and back were identical, with two grand eight-foot staircases rounded to meet at a landing, and one branching off to the upstairs balcony.

Duchess Maria stared in awe at the beautiful home, "Isn't it grand?"

Countess Florence answered, "Yes, it is beautiful."

They parked near the dock and walked down towards the dock and sat on a bench facing the water. Duke Vito and Baron Tony watched the men busy at work loading the containers of sugar onto the boat.

"This place would be perfect for importing Athena's products and Duchess Maria really loves it. I'll have to see who owns it and if they'd be willing to sell." Duke Vito said to Baron Tony.

They sat for quite a while, unnoticed by the busy workers when the double doors facing the river at the back of the plantation home opened. An older gentleman appeared and gazed out at the workers on the dock and then turned and sat in one of the many rocking chairs on the porch.

Duke Vito continued to sit on the bench for a few moments and then turned to Baron Tony and said, "I wonder if he's the owner. I think I'll go and talk with him and see if he's interested in selling."

He proceeded to walk over to the seated man, who stood up as Duke Vito approached. In the distance, Baron Tony watched as the man reached out to shake Duke Vito's hand. They talked for quite a while and then again shook hands as Duke Vito turned and walked back to the bench where they were still sitting.

Baron Tony said, "Well? What did he say?"

Duke Vito looked down and said, "He said he's not interested. I told him that I would make him a worthwhile offer, but he still said he doesn't want to sell."

The boat was finished loading, deck hands were undoing the ropes and the water began to flow through the paddlewheel of the boat as it slowly pulled away from the dock. They watched for a while and then headed back to the limousine to go back to the hotel and dress for dinner. As they left the driveway, Baron Tony looked back at the plantation and saw a sign bearing its name, Seventeen Oaks.

They spent the next couple of days visiting historical sites, enjoying the culture and cuisine of the area which consisted of French, Italian, Creole, and of course, seafood. Their time in New Orleans would be coming to a close within a few days and the women decided to do some shopping before they had to get belongings together for the train ride home. As they arrived at the hotel after dinner, Baron Tony quietly asked Pasquale to arrange the convoy to pick him up the next morning around the corner from the hotel so that he could take care of some business. He slipped Pasquale a note with the details, ensuring that the convoy was fine-tuned for the impending mission. Knowing that Countess Florence and Duchess Maria would be busy shopping, Baron Tony would be able to slip away undetected.

Early the next morning, Baron Tony walked around the corner where two black Packards were waiting with the black Packard limousine between the two parked cars. When Baron Tony reached the limousine, Pasquale opened the door for him to get in and the procession began.

They drove up the long road past several plantations before reaching Seventeen Oaks where the convoy drove up the long driveway to the front of the plantation home where they saw a servant sweeping the front porch. The servant, seeing the convoy, turned and ran into the house to the library where the owner was sitting.

"Sir, sir, I believe the president is coming up the drive." He said trying to catch his breath. "Three black Packards just drove up the driveway, the one in the middle is a limousine."

"The president?" The owner questioned. "Why would the president . . ..?"

The servant walked back to towards the front door and saw Baron Tony walking up the long, wide brick pathway to the grand front doors. His driver was standing by the limousine and two bodyguards were standing at each of the cars in the front and back of it. They were all standing at attention, dressed in suits and ties with overcoats, and wearing fedoras. The servant opened the door and said, "May I help you, sir?" By now, the owner was coming from the library and caught a glimpse of Baron Tony standing in the doorway. As the wind caught Baron Tony's unbuttoned overcoat, it flew slightly open, allowing a brief view of his vest and the .38s tucked into their holsters.

"I'd like to speak with the owner."

"May I give him your name, sir?"

"The name is Tony."

The servant turned to retrieve the owner who had already made his way into the entryway and stretched out his hand to greet Baron Tony.

"Tony. Maxwell." He said while shaking hands. What can I do for you?"

"I am here to discuss some business."

Maxwell, thinking Baron Tony was interested in shipping from his dock said, "Come into the library where we can talk." Baron Tony followed him through the large walnut doors into a room filled with walnut shelves and every book and genre imaginable. A rolling ladder was attached, which allowed access to even the highest placed literature. In the center of the room sat a large walnut desk with an appropriately sized leather desk chair sitting behind it, two chairs facing the front, and a matching leather sofa over to one side of the room.

"Would you like to have a seat?" Maxwell asked. "Cigar?" he said opening his humidor filled with domestic and imported cigars.

"No, thank you. I'll get right to the point. My friend is interested in buying your plantation and I came to talk with you about it."

"Ah, the man I spoke with yesterday. As I told him, I am not interested in selling."

"Well, I'm thinking you should be. He is ready to make you a great offer."

"There is no offer that is that great. I am not ready to sell."

Baron Tony turned and looked straight into the man's eyes, his hand reached up and rested on the pocket of his vest, and he said, "Well, I'm going to make you an offer you can't refuse."

Fear immediately crept over Maxwell, sending chills down his spine as he recalled his brief view of Baron Tony's vest and holstered pistols which were poised for immediate access when Baron Tony was standing in the entryway. Maxwell realized he wasn't dealing with just any ordinary man.

The blood drained from his face, causing him to become a ghostly white, "I, I, um I think I may be willing to consider an offer. Since my wife's passing, the house is too big for just me. Perhaps he'd like to meet and discuss the matter further?" Maxwell, who was visibly shaking said in a quivering voice as he handed Baron Tony a business card.

"I'll have him give you a call." Baron Tony said. "I'm glad we are able to do business . . . I don't want to have to come back."

"No, no – a deal is a deal." said Maxwell, who was more than eager for Baron Tony to leave.

Baron Tony reached out and shook Maxwell's hand, then turned and walked out the solid walnut door of the library towards the front door.

"Good day, sir," the servant said with a nod as he opened the door.

"Good day," Baron Tony replied as he walked out of the plantation house and stepped into his waiting limousine. The bodyguards followed Baron Tony's lead and got back into their cars, driving up the long driveway and onto the main road.

"Is there anywhere else you'd like to go?" asked Pasquale.

"No. I'd better get back to the hotel before the wife notices I'm not there. Take me back to where you picked me up."

"Yes sir."

Baron Tony sat in the back seat gazing out the window and quietly pondering as they drove. He knew that once Duchess Maria moved to New Orleans, Countess Florence would be wanting to be near her sister, and soon, New Orleans would be his new homestead as well. He traveled back and forth from New York to Chicago for business often, so it was very important that the family remain close to one another. Duke Don Vito was always adamant about staying in the background, quiet but observant, and Duke Vito would have his own dock to import Athena's products from Sicily. This was new territory, and gangs and families wouldn't be competing at every turn. Countess Florence and Duchess Maria loved New Orleans and Duke Vito knew without even mentioning anything to Duchess Maria, that she would be thrilled about purchasing the plantation. By the time the driver stopped to let Baron Tony out, he was ecstatic to tell Duke Vito about his visit to the plantation and the owner's 'eagerness' to meet with Duke Vito and talk about selling, as well as with Countess Florence to suggest that they move here with them.

As the convoy stopped in the same place where they had met Baron Tony earlier that day, Duke Vito came walking up the street with the morning newspaper in hand. He looked at the convoy and knew Baron Tony had something to do with its presence. Duke Vito walked slower and watched as the bodyguards emerged from their cars - standing in place, and then Pasquale stepped out of the limousine and opened the door for Baron Tony. People who were driving by and those who were walking stretched their necks to get a glimpse of who this important person could be. When Baron Tony got out of the limousine, he saw Duke Vito walking up the street in his direction and proceeded toward him.

"Keep it on the down-low? Don't draw attention to yourselves?" Duke Vito scoffed at Baron Tony.

"So, I'm a rebel!" Baron Tony said. "But I have news for you."

"Who's swimming with the fishes now?" Duke Vito asked, looking down and shaking his head.

"Nobody. He saw it my way." Baron Tony smirked. "You know that plantation you were eyeing? Well, he's decided to sell."

"He said he wasn't interested!" Duke Vito said with shock but excitement in his voice.

"Well, I made him an offer he couldn't refuse!" Baron Tony said as he handed Maxwell's business card to Duke Vito. "Give him a call. He's ready to talk."

The Purchase of the Plantation

Duchess Maria and Countess Florence headed to their hotel suites, two bellhops followed – their arms filled with the treasures the two women had purchased from each and every store they had visited.

Duke Vito was sitting in their suite awaiting Duchess Maria's return, anxious to present her with the great news about the plantation owner being willing to sell. He could hear the women walking down the hallway chatting and laughing and going their separate ways as the bellhops opened the perspective doors to their suites.

Duchess Maria entered their suite, bellhop in tow, packages hanging from both arms and piled to where he could barely see over the top.

"Where would you like for me to put your packages, ma'am?" he asked.

"Just set them on the bed, thank you," Duchess Maria said. As he turned to leave, she handed him some folded money.

"Thank you, ma'am," he said, exiting the suite.

Duchess Maria smiled as she looked at the packages sitting on the bed, obviously pleased with her purchases. Duke Vito looked over his newspaper at her and in a stern voice said, "I think we need to talk." Duchess Maria didn't reply, but looked strangely at him and thought to herself, "Is he upset that I spent so much money? He never cared before. It's my money too, how dare he tell me what I can and can't spend." She was completely caught up in her thoughts and becoming annoyed when he said, "What would you think of moving to New Orleans?"

Duchess Maria spun around, "What? Are you kidding?"

Duke Vito smiled at her obvious shock and said, "Remember that plantation we visited where we sat at the docks watching the boats loading sugar and cotton? Baron Tony spoke with the owner and he's willing to sell. I thought I'd give him a call and we can look over the house and see if you like it."

"Oh, yes! The grounds are so beautiful, and I'd love to see the inside."

"I'll go and make the arrangements." Duke Vito said, grabbing Maxwell's card that Baron Tony had given him and some change from the dresser to use at the phone booth downstairs.

As Duke Vito walked out the door of his suite, Baron Tony and Countess Florence were coming out of theirs, Countess Florence was obviously overjoyed with the news Baron Tony had just shared with her. The two men walked to the elevator, while Countess Florence went to see Duchess Maria who was going through her packages. When Countess Florence walked into the suite, neither of them could contain their excitement. Although they both lived a good and happy life in New York, New Orleans was a quiet and rich culture, and away from the business.

"Oh Maria, I'm so happy for you. Baron Tony told me that Duke Vito is going to buy the plantation."

"I can't wait to see the inside! You will come with us, won't you?" Duchess Maria asked. "But I'm going to miss having you close by." Her excitement began to wane as she thought of how far she would be moving away from Countess Florence. They had always done everything together and even though their personalities were polar opposites, they had always been inseparable, and their differences brought them balance.

"Of course, we'll go with you! – And maybe you'll go looking at homes with Baron Tony and me when we start looking. After he told me the great news about you and Duke Vito buying the plantation, he asked me how I would feel about moving here too."

Duchess Maria and Countess Florence hugged each other, excited for the new chapters of their lives, eagerly planning and talking about their future in New Orleans and anxiously awaiting the return of their husbands. Within minutes, the door to the suite opened and Baron Tony and Duke Vito entered. Duke Vito said, "We will be meeting with Maxwell at ten o'clock tomorrow morning! Now, let's go and have some lunch?"

They went downstairs to their waiting limousine and spent the rest of the day enjoying the sites and visiting a couple of their new favorite local restaurants and looking forward to their impending meeting the next day.

The following morning, everyone got up early and Pasquale drove them to Café Du Monde for Café Au Lait and beignets. Duke Vito and Baron Tony picked up the morning paper and casually read through it as Countess Florence and Duchess Maria talked about the places they had visited, people they had met, and their hopes of moving to New Orleans.

"Is everyone about ready?" Baron Tony asked, as he folded up his newspaper and set it on the table.

"Yes," Duke Vito responded, also folding and setting down his paper and finishing up his Café Au Lait, "we should get going."

They all made their way to the limousine and proceeded to the plantation for their meeting with Maxwell. They arrived at the long and winding driveway lined with oak trees and stopped at the front of the plantation where a servant was waiting for their arrival.

Pasquale opened the door to the limousine and the two couples exited, walking toward the house and up the steps. The servant, Edmond, opened the door and said, "This way, please. Mr. Claiborne is expecting you."

As they entered the plantation, the head housekeeper Allain, was standing in the entryway ready to take Duchess Maria and Countess Florence on a tour of the plantation. Baron Tony and Duke Vito followed Edmond to the library where they met Maxwell.

Duchess Maria and Countess Florence looked around at the grand staircase and the ornate woodwork with the rich finishes.

"Oh, this is exquisite!" Duchess Maria said to Countess Florence.

"It's just beautiful!" Countess Florence agreed.

Allain showed them each room of the house filled with pre-civil war furnishings and boasting of rich historical décor. She continued their tour by taking them out onto the wraparound porch built along three sides of the house. They walked onto the front porch which was overlooking the Mississippi River and the dock. Several rocking chairs were lined up along the front porch where some of the chair arms were visibly worn. It was apparent that many hours had been spent in these chairs while their occupants enjoyed the magnificent views of the acreage and the sparkling river.

While Duchess Maria and Countess Florence were viewing the plantation, Baron Tony and Duke Vito were negotiating the particulars of the sale with Maxwell. Not only would Duke Vito be purchasing a home; he would also be purchasing a business since the dock was leased by several plantation owners to ship their goods. When Baron Tony left Maxwell the day before, after convincing him to sell, he told him to come up with a fair price. Baron Tony was admittedly surprised when Maxwell set up the meeting for the following day, expecting him to need some time to get his figures together. Maxwell wanted to come up with an inflated figure because of Baron Tony's threat, but thought it would be in his best interest to be fair. He presented a number of $25,000 to Duke Vito who readily accepted and counteroffered at a higher price of $30,000. Maxwell was taken aback by Duke Vito's generosity and saw an unexpected kindness in him. Baron Tony sat back quietly and allowed Duke Vito to take care of business as he saw fit.

"I realize how hard this must be for you," Duke Vito said to Maxwell.

Maxwell replied, "I'm going to be honest with you, it is. My wife and I moved into the plantation house when we were newly married and raised our family here. We built the dock to ship our sugar and then several of the plantation owners asked if they could use our dock for their exports and it became a thriving business."

"The dock drew my interest in the plantation for importing goods from Sicily. My wife's mother, Countess Athena, exports olive oil, wines, and other items to the United States which I now sell in New York and I am wanting to bring her goods to this area. And, my wife absolutely loves history and historical sites, so it appears to be a perfect fit."

"It appears so. My children are grown and have families of their own and after my wife's passing, the house has become very lonely and empty. None of my children want to move here and take over the business; they are content with their lives the way they are. I wish you and your family well and pray you fill the house again with the laughter of children!"

"Thank you, Maxwell," Duke Vito said, reaching out to shake his hand. "We will bring life back into the plantation and continue running your business with the integrity that you have always shown."

"I need to find a new place, so how soon will you be moving in?"

"It won't be for around six to eight weeks. We need to take care of business in New York. Will that give you enough time?"

"I don't foresee any problem," Maxwell answered, feeling more at ease with the two men.

"I will have a car bring your money within a couple of days. We'll talk again before we head back to New York."

Both men again shook hands, Baron Tony stood from his chair and they proceeded out the doors of the library as Duchess Maria, Countess Florence, and Allain were walking in from the back porch. Duchess Maria looked straight at Duke Vito who gave her a wink and a smile, letting her know that this was going to be their new home.

Edmond opened the front door and they walked down to their waiting limousine. Before stepping into its open doors, they turned to gaze back at the plantation and admire its grandeur and the vastness of the several hundred acres where it majestically sat. They were all somewhat spellbound by their surroundings.

"So," Baron Tony said, breaking the silence, "where do we want to go for lunch?"

"Ladies?" Duke Vito asked. "Where would you like to go? I'm famished!"

Duchess Maria said, "Let's go back to Toney's Spaghetti House and tell him the great news about buying the plantation and that you'll be importing Castellammare wines and olive oils. I think he'll be pleased!"

"Great idea. I'd like more of their tomato gravy before we head back to New York!" Duke Vito replied.

Pasquale drove down the long driveway away from the Seventeen Oaks Plantation and headed to the restaurant. Duchess Maria and Countess Florence were busy talking about décor and furnishings, while Duke Vito and Baron Tony were discussing business and imports. They arrived at the restaurant and were greeted by the owner as they entered the door, "Ciao. Che piacere vederti!"

"Ciao, it's nice to see you again too!" Duke Vito replied.

"Come right this way. The best table in the house - i miei amici, la mia famiglia."

"Toney, we have some wonderful news – we purchased the plantation house and will be importing Castellammare wines, as well as olive oil, and several other products from Countess Athena. I will bring you the first bottle that comes off of the boat!" Duke Vito said.

"Aaaahhh, that's wonderful news! For you, lunch is on the house."

"Thank you, but that's not necessary." Duke Vito replied.

"I insist, my friends – my family!" Toney said as he waved his hand, calling over the waitress. "Take good care of my friends. Anything they want!"

They enjoyed a wonderful lunch, wine glasses were kept full thoughout the meal.

When they were finished, Toney came back to their table to say good-bye before they left.

"When will you be moving?" he asked.

Duke Vito replied, "In about six to eight weeks. I have to make sure business and the imports in New York are managed by people I can trust. You know what I mean?"

"Yes, yes! You don't need any sticky fingers in the till."

"That is very true, although any man can turn traitor," Duke Vito replied.

The men embraced, "Ciao!" they all said to Toney as they left the restaurant.

After they arrived back at the hotel, Baron Tony and Duke Vito left to make some calls and have the cash sent for the purchase of the plantation before they headed back to New York. Within a couple of days, the money arrived in a black leather briefcase. Pasquale drove Baron Tony and Duke Vito, along with two black Packards, one in front of their limousine and one in the back and delivered it to Maxwell at the plantation.

As the cars drove up the long driveway, Edmond informed Maxwell that they had arrived. Maxwell came out of his study as Baron Tony and Duke Vito were coming up the steps toward the plantation's front entrance.

"Good afternoon, gentlemen," Maxwell said as he reached out to shake their hands. "What can I do for you?"

"We came to take care of our business with you." Baron Tony replied.

"So soon?" Maxwell said, rather shocked. "I didn't expect you to be back so soon. I haven't found a new place yet and . . ."

"No, no. We told you six to eight weeks. We wanted to take care of everything before we headed back," Duke Vito said. "You'll find it is all in there." Duke Vito handed him the black leather briefcase.

Maxwell opened it and found stacks of one-hundred-dollar bills, as well as a few five-hundred and one-thousand-dollar bills. His eyes grew wide at the sight.

"We have the contracts here for you to sign and we will be moving in around six weeks from now. Agreed?"

"Yes, yes. Perhaps your wife would like to keep some of the furnishings. I am sure I won't be needing everything."

"I will speak with her about it and we'll take care of the details after her decision," Duke Vito replied.

The men shook hands and left the plantation, getting into the limousine as Pasquale signaled the armed men standing by the Packards that they were ready to leave.

On their drive back to the hotel, Baron Tony was talking to Duke Vito about buying a home nearby so that Duchess Maria and Countess Florence would be close to one another.

"It's hard when we're at home in Chicago, she really misses Duchess Maria, especially when I'm traveling."

"Baron Tony, we stay with you in Chicago and we all have more than enough room, why don't you just stay with us in New Orleans. The plantation gives everyone plenty of space and we're both away with the business often. I think Duchess Maria and Countess Florence would be pleased with that arrangement. We're family!"

They arrived back at the hotel and Duke Vito went to get Duchess Maria to meet in Baron Tony and Countess Florence's suite, so that they could discuss the furnishings that Maxwell was willing to leave with the plantation house and living arrangements that he and Baron Tony had just spoken about.

Needless to say, both Duchess Maria and Countess Florence were thrilled with their idea and both of them loved the furnishings in the plantation house and decided that they would like to keep whatever he was willing to leave. The décor of the plantation was exquisite and perfectly fit the era of when the home was built.

Duke Vito said that he would call Maxwell and make all of the arrangements. Meanwhile everyone else stayed at the hotel to get their belongings together for the trip back to New York.

When they arrived home, much needed to be done in preparation for their move and in the time frame they had set. The domestics were assigned their tasks for closing up the New York house and packing up the items that were to be moved to the New Orleans plantation house. Although six weeks seemed like ample time, much needed to be done on the home-front and with Duke Vito's storefront and imports to continue running smoothly, along with Baron Tony making sure the operation of Murders, Inc. continued without a glitch in the New York area.

Moving companies who would travel across the country were relatively new in 1936. Typically, a move of this distance would be made by ship. Duke Vito and Duchess Maria chose to have their household items delivered to New Orleans by moving trucks, since their furnishings and other items would be packed in the trucks one time and then transported to their new home and unloaded. Had they chosen to ship their items, they would have needed to be loaded and unloaded several times, it would have taken up to three times as long to arrive, and with handling, damage could be done.

The movers arrived and carefully wrapped and placed their items in the moving trucks. Within a few hours, the house was emptied of what they had chosen to take, the moving trucks were closed and latched, and then headed down the dusty road where they watched as it faded into the distance. Duchess Maria and Countess Florence headed back into the sparsely furnished house and sat down to a cup of tea.

"I can't believe we're really moving to New Orleans," Duchess Maria said, as she sipped her tea.

"On to new adventures," smiled Countess Florence. "Are you keeping the house in New York?"

"Well, we haven't decided what we're going to do right now. Duke Vito will be coming to check on the business from time to time and he'll have the house to stay in while he's here, and we'll keep some of the domestic staff on to make sure the house is kept up."

"That's a wonderful idea!" Countess Florence replied as she finished her tea. "I think I'll go and make sure everything is packed up for the flight tomorrow."

"I should go and take care of that also. I don't think Vito has anything ready to go!" Duchess Maria said, shaking her head.

The following day, a Packard limousine pulled in front of their house to drive them to the airport. They walked out the door and the driver took their luggage and placed it in the trunk.

"Do you ladies have everything?" Baron Tony asked. "Tickets?"

"Of course," Countess Florence replied in an indignant tone. "How could I possibly forget the tickets? They're right . . .," she frantically patted the pockets of her coat. "Duchess Maria! Did you grab the tickets?"

"No, you put them in your purse!" Duchess Maria laughed at her sister who was always so organized, so calm, and on top of everything.

"Oh, here they are," Countess Florence said with a sigh of relief. "I don't know why I'm so nervous."

Everyone chuckled at Countess Florence, who was obviously not her typical self. They stepped into the limousine and headed for the airport to board the newest TWA Douglas DC-3 daytime airplane owned by Howard Hughes and invested in by Duke Don Vito. Duke Vito, representing the mafia, traded four mafia owned hotels in Las Vegas with Howard Hughes in the 1960s for his interest in TWA. [2] The airplane traveled non-stop from New York to Chicago in only four hours. The daytime airplane had 18-21 seats, whereas the transcontinental sleeper flights also offered curtained berths with goose-down comforters and feather mattresses for the long journey from continent to continent. The previous version, the Douglas DC-2 took 25 hours and stopped three times to refuel when traveling across the United States.

When they arrived at the airport, the driver carried their luggage to the plane where stewards received it and placed it onboard, while the two couples boarded along with a few other passengers.

Flying aboard a commercial flight was for the elite. Each passenger paid three-hundred dollars for the flight, which would be close to five-thousand dollars today. Once the flight was airborne, cocktails were offered, followed by entrée choices of sirloin steak or Long Island duckling, served on China dinner plates with silverware. Flight attendants and cabin boys were available for the ultimate comfort of each guest.

When the plane arrived in Chicago, a limousine was waiting to take them to Baron Tony and Countess Florence's home where they spent a few days before boarding the train bound for New Orleans – the final destination of their journey.

---

[2] Story in Book 3 of series

Life on the Plantation Begins

The motorcade pulled up the long driveway to the beautiful plantation house. The bodyguards fanned out to check all surrounding areas and inside the house before Duke Vito, Duchess Maria, Baron Tony and Countess Florence entered.

"Can't be too careful," Baron Tony said. "Never know who or what could be waiting around the corner."

The women were anxious to go inside and get started making the plantation house their own, but knew Baron Tony was right. In their lifetime, they had seen way too much – way more than anyone should ever witness. As they stood next to their limousine waiting for the signal that all was clear, the warm air flowing across the Mississippi River brushed their faces while they watched the paddle boat at the dock being loaded with sugar. As they gazed around the property, it was apparent how Maxwell and his domestic help had kept the plantation house and the grounds in pristine condition.

A nod of approval was given, and Baron Tony said, "We're good to go!"

They entered the house, and to their surprise, the moving trucks had already delivered their furnishings and other items that they had sent from New York and Maxwell's servants had made the house ready for them to move right in upon their arrival. The furnishings that they had chosen to purchase with the house looked even more regal and elegant with their own personal touches added.

"Oh my gosh, it's beautiful," Duchess Maria said as she gazed around the room.

"Not as beautiful as you! Are you happy?" Duke Vito asked.

Duchess Maria threw her arms around her husband's neck and kissed him passionately. "Yes, I am. This whole place is like a dream! Thank you."

Duke Vito smiled at Duchess Maria and said, "You can thank me later."

Baron Tony came into the house and said to Duke Vito, "Let's go down to the dock and introduce ourselves. After all, this is your business now and they should get to know you."

"Good idea," Duke Vito said as he walked out the front doors with Baron Tony.

"Maria, they even have the bedrooms ready for us." Countess Florence said. "Of course, it's not exactly the way I would have done it, but it'll do for now."

Duchess Maria shook her head, smiling at her twin sister who had to have everything meet her perfect standards and ideals.

"Well, you'll have plenty of time to get everything in order. Right now, let's have a cup of tea. It's been quite a journey and it's good to be home."

The days quickly turned into weeks and everyone had finally settled into their new surroundings. Countess Athena's imports were arriving at the plantation dock and being distributed to many stores and restaurants in the area. Baron Tony was taking care of business from New Orleans with occasional trips to Chicago for meetings and updates.

Their fifth wedding anniversary had arrived, and Duchess Maria and Countess Florence were busy making an elegant Italian dinner and organizing a beautiful evening to spend with their husbands. The staff had been given the night off and they were looking forward to a quiet evening celebrating.

Duke Vito came into the plantation house with a bouquet of roses for Duchess Maria and bottles of Castellammare wine to serve with dinner.

"Oh, it smells great in here!" Duke Vito said. "What's the occasion?" he asked pretending to forget it was their anniversary.

"You better know what the occasion is," Duchess Maria said in a scolding voice.

"Oh yeah!" Duke Vito replied, handing Duchess Maria the roses he had hidden behind his back and giving her a kiss. "Happy Anniversary my love. I put the wine on the table."

Countess Florence came down the stairs wearing her new dress and ready for her evening with Baron Tony. She looked around the room as she reached the bottom stair but didn't see him.

"Vito, where's Tony?" she asked.

"I don't know. I haven't seen him since this morning."

"Dinner's ready," Duchess Maria said, coming out of the kitchen. "Oh, Tony's not here yet?"

"No!" Countess Florence replied.

Baron Tony came bursting through the front door, "Sorry I'm late!"

Countess Florence looked at her husband's empty hands, "Why were you late? Did you have to turn around to get me some red roses for our anniversary?"

"I'm so sorry darling. I was going to buy you some, but it was too late, and everything was closed. It's the thought that counts!"

"Yes, thoughts count, but what really counts are red roses!"

Baron Tony leaned over and kissed Countess Florence, "I really am sorry. I'll make it up to you. Would you like diamonds? Gold? Furs?"

Countess Florence pretended to be angry, but then sweetly looked into Baron Tony's eyes and smiled, "Oh, let's go eat dinner you crazy fool!"

"Yes, it smells wonderful!" Baron Tony replied. "Magnifica cena."

They enjoyed their dinner along with several glasses of Castellammare wine as they reminisced about their wedding day and adventures they had shared over the past five years.

Don Vito sat and pondered as he listened while the conversation continued. Duchess Maria looked over at her husband and said, "A penny for your thoughts."

Don Vito looked at her with a smile, "You know what's missing right now? A nice evening drive."

"Did you need to go somewhere?" Baron Tony asked. "I'll send for the cars."

"No, I have been thinking about sending for the Mercedes." Don Vito had a 1936 Black Mercedes Roadster Special that was still in New York. He had been tossing around in his mind where he would enjoy it most, Chicago or New Orleans. Don Vito had his entourage available whenever he needed to go somewhere, but sometimes he enjoyed getting behind the wheel of his Mercedes and taking off on his own. Of course, his bodyguards were always following not too far behind.

"I believe I've finally decided to have it brought here. Chicago would be great, but with the winters and snow . . ."

"I think that's a wonderful idea," Maria chimed in. "The plantation roads are so beautiful here, I think New Orleans would be the best choice."

"Well, the decision has been made! We'll send for her tomorrow," Don Vito replied, smiling as he rose from his chair.

Duchess Maria and Countess Florence both loved Mediterranean cuisine with all of the fresh herbs and vegetables, so Countess Florence decided that she would like to have a garden at the plantation so that they would have fresh produce daily.

"Tony," Countess Florence said, "I think I'd like to have a garden."

"Okay, where would you like to put it?" Baron Tony replied.

"Come outside and I'll show you."

They both walked around a couple of areas of the grounds and found the perfect spot. It had plenty of sunlight and would be easy to water.

"I'll tell you what. I'm going to go into town to the local dealer and buy a tractor to get the ground ready for you to plant."

Baron Tony called for his car to take him to the dealer and as they arrived, he saw a new John Deere Model-B tractor sitting on the side of the building. He walked into the dealership and the salesman walked over to Baron Tony, "Can I help you?"

"I'd like to buy that tractor on the side of the building. Here's five-hundred dollars - cash."

"Sir, that tractor sells for much more than that, let me talk to my boss."

He walked into the back of the shop where his boss, a small local gangster and his cronies were smoking, drinking, and playing cards.

"Sir, I have a man out front who wants to buy the tractor for five-hundred dollars."

"Don't bother me – I'm not selling it that cheap. You handle it," he gruffly replied to the salesman.

"Sir, I think you need to take care of this. This guy, his driver, and some other guys who were with him. They drove up in a brand-new Packard sedan and . . . I really think you should take care of him."

The salesman was visibly nervous, so the owner went out to see who this was and saw it was Baron Tony. The owner knew of Baron Tony and his reputation.

"Good afternoon, what can I do for you today?" he asked, straightening his shirt and smoothing his hair.

Baron Tony responded, "I'll give you five-hundred dollars for the tractor on the side of the building."

"Five-hundred dollars? That's a fair deal and listen, I'll throw in the attached plow!"

With the purchase made, Baron Tony hopped on the tractor and headed down the road, as his Packard followed behind.

He arrived back at the Seventeen Oaks Plantation where everyone was sitting in Adirondack chairs sipping tea and enjoying the beautiful day. Baron Tony pulled up the driveway, excited about his new tractor and waving at everyone as he drove. They were frantically waving back, not because they were excited, but because the plow had dropped, and Baron Tony was plowing up the lawn. Not realizing what was happening and with all of the attention he was getting, he continued waving until he was abruptly stopped after colliding into a tree. Everyone jumped up from their chairs and ran over to Baron Tony who was still sitting on the tractor, stunned by what had just happened.

"Tony! Tony!" Countess Florence yelled as she ran toward her husband. "Are you hurt?"

"No, I'm okay," he replied sheepishly.

Duke Vito was at the scene by now, checking for any damage other than the lawn Baron Tony had dug up, and of course, admiring the tractor at the same time.

Nothing besides a small piece of bark from the tree had been damaged in the collision - *except* Baron Tony's ego.

Within days, Baron Tony had the area for the garden plowed and Duke Vito had the yard repaired where Baron Tony had destroyed the lawn. Countess Florence was busy at work in her garden, tilling, planting, watering, and within a short time, sprouts were beginning to pop up out of the ground. Not only was Countess Florence excited about her garden, but so were the crows. She would run out and shoo them away, but they seemed to come right back as soon as she walked away.

"These horrible birds are eating my plants," she angrily told Baron Tony.

Baron Tony didn't say much - what could he say? He decided to go and sit outside and watch the crows. First, one appeared, then the next, then a flock - he reached into his vest, pulled out his two .38s and began shooting.

The birds scattered, except for a few casualties.

Countess Florence came running outside to see what all the commotion was, and Baron Tony said, "Well, you have a few less to worry about."

"Yes, but what about the plants that you also shot up?"

"Oh, they'll grow back. Maybe we should make a scarecrow. I'll make it look like me. They won't come back then. They're scared of me!"

He stuffed one of his old suits with straw and put a fedora on its head, then stuck it out in Countess Florence's garden. It seemed to work. Countess Florence was soon reaping the rewards of her labor with fresh produce.

As summer approached and the heat became blistering, the couples decided to spend a few months in Chicago at Baron Tony and Countess

Florence's house. This became their yearly tradition, reminiscent of their childhood when they spent winters in Sicily and summers in the Italian Alps.

This year, they had much to do back at the Seventeen Oaks Plantation House. They were hosting the Plantation Ball and Duchess Maria and Countess Florence were already making preparations before leaving Chicago. They wanted everything to be perfect. Lists and menus were made, décor was discussed, and everything was being started before their mother, Countess Athena, would arrive to help them and finalize everything.

"I don't know why I'm so exhausted," Duchess Maria told Countess Florence while they were going over the list. "I think I'm going to go on to bed."

"So early?" Countess Florence asked.

"I'm just not myself," she answered. "Maybe after a good night's sleep, I'll feel better in the morning. Good night."

"Good night."

The next morning, Countess Florence was up bright and early and ready for her day. She, Duke Vito, and Baron Tony sat down for breakfast, but Duchess Maria did not come down.

"Vito, where's Maria?" Countess Florence asked.

"She's a bit under the weather. She thinks she may have eaten something that didn't agree with her. She's feeling a bit nauseous. I'm going to have tea and toast sent up to her in a bit."

"Yes, she told me last night she was exhausted and went to bed quite early. And now this morning she's feeling nauseous?"

"The last few days actually," Duke Vito replied. "Maybe we should call the doctor."

"Or, maybe a midwife," Countess Florence replied with a smirk.

"What? No, can't be!" Duke Vito sounded shocked.

"Can't be what?" Duchess Maria said as she came down the stairs.

"Why are you up?" Duke Vito asked. "You need your rest."

"I'm feeling much better now." Duchess Maria replied, looking strangely at her husband. "I think the tea and toast settled my stomach."

"I think we should call the doctor for you to get a checkup," Duke Vito said.

"Why? I'm fine. It's just a little bug or something." Duchess Maria suddenly turned ghostly white and abruptly ran into the bathroom.

"Or something is right!" Countess Florence said.

Duke Vito sent for the doctor and after checking Duchess Maria, confirmed Countess Florence's suspicions. Duke Vito and Duchess Maria were going to be parents.

The warm days were soon turning brisk and chilly and snowy days were in the near future, so they decided that now was a good time to head back to the Plantation house. Duchess Maria was feeling much better and was eager to return home and start the preparations for the Ball and get the house ready for her parents and Duke Vito's parents who were coming to stay with them for an extended visit.

Countess Athena was eager to see the dock where her goods were arriving from Sicily, and she planned on helping her twin daughters with the preparations for the Ball. Duke Don Vito and Duke Vito had business to take care of. World War II had just begun in Europe. Duke Don Vito had missions to accomplish and Duke Vito would be his vessel and voice to the American government.

Once their families had arrived, the Plantation was buzzing with the preparations and the staff was kept infinitely busy with cooking, decorating, and cleaning. Baron Tony rehearsed his entrance and everyone's hard work paid off - everything went off without a hitch. The Ball and evening were a huge success and talked about for many, many years to come. Duchess Maria's perfect shot was always the highlight of the story.

Everyone was exhausted after the affair, especially Duchess Maria with her ever-growing stomach.

"You must rest, Maria," her mother, Countess Athena said. "Why don't you take a little nap. I am going to go down to the dock to watch my shipment coming in. Countess Florence is in the garden. It will be nice and quiet for you."

"That's a good idea, Mother, I am rather tired."

Countess Athena walked down to the dock where they were unloading wooden crates of olive oil and Castellammare wine. The water sparkled as the sun bounced off the slight waves. Duke Don Vito walked over to Athena as she stood watching the men and said, "I'm glad I invested in you. I could see your vision when you were a mere child running out to greet me with your brightly colored hair. You were a sight!" He began to laugh.

Athena began to laugh too, "Even if I was the sight, I had a vision!"

"And you've done well."

They continued to watch the workers and while they gazed out at the Mississippi River, in the far distance they saw a huge paddle riverboat cruising along in the horizon.

"What kind of boat is that?" Athena asked Duke Don Vito.

"I believe it's a paddle riverboat cruise," Duke Don Vito replied. "Vito told me that they have actually docked here on a couple of occasions.

"Oh, we should go on a cruise. We have a while before Maria is due and it would be wonderful to relax and spend some time travelling together. Let's talk to everyone about it tonight over dinner."

Duke Don Vito shook his head in agreement, "Sounds like a good idea."

The rest of the day went on as usual and as dusk enveloped the daylight, everyone arrived back at the Plantation for the evening and each went their separate ways to dress for dinner.

At seven o'clock, everyone convened in the dining room where the antipasto, fresh bread with olive oil, and Castellammare wine was served. Laughter and conversation were not lacking as everyone enjoyed their meal and each other's company. The main course was ready to be served, but Countess Athena motioned the servants to wait. She stood up and cleared her throat to draw everyone's attention. As they became silent and looked at Athena, she began to speak.

"Don Vito and I were down at the dock today and we noticed a paddle riverboat out on the horizon and were thinking about taking a family vacation. All of us! We could get away and relax for a couple of weeks. What do you think?"

"I think it's a wonderful idea," Duchess Maria replied before anyone else. "I would love to get away for a vacation before our new addition arrives."

The couples each looked at each other and shook their heads in agreement and confirmed they would like to go, one by one.

"I think the paddleboat will dock at the Plantation and pick us up," Duke Vito said. "I've let them use the dock on occasion and I'm sure they'd reciprocate."

Duke Don Vito and Duke Vito took care of the arrangements and confirmed that this would be a business trip for themselves. They were to board the paddle riverboat within a few days, so the ladies needed to plan a shopping trip for new outfits and visit the salon before they left.

The days went by quickly and the day had arrived. The servants took their luggage out to the dock where the paddle riverboat docked soon after.

The captain came down to greet them as they boarded, "Duke Vito,' he exclaimed, as they embraced each other, "So good to have you aboard. Enjoy!"

He turned to the stewards, "You take good care of my friends! Make sure they have everything they need for a pleasant trip."

They boarded the paddleboat and walked past the deck lined with lounge chairs to the interior where they were shown the salon, the dining area, the saloon, and smoking bar prior to arriving at their cabins. Each couple was assigned their own personal steward who would take care of their every need while onboard the paddle riverboat.

The ladies had planned to meet out on the deck while the men had decided to visit the smoking bar where they would indulge themselves on a variety of imported cigars over the course of their journey. The bar would also be where Duke Vito and Duke Don Vito would be spending hours planning and discussing how and where they would import the codes that Duke Vito had been taught since he was a youth.

Mussolini was growing in power and Hitler had taken notice. By 1939, Mussolini and Hitler had signed a military alliance known as the "Pact of Steel." Mussolini had stretched his military finances to capacity and felt that by joining with Germany, it would give Italy time to regroup. In a short time, Mussolini emulated Hitler's hatred of the Jewish people and discriminatory policies were implemented in Italy.

After bribing members of the fascist party, Duke Don Vito had become friends with Mussolini's son-in-law and contributed four-million dollars to the party over the next few years. This would amount to around $78 million in today's market. He had become a trusted commodore of the Italian army and was privy to inside information and plans.

In the end, his allegiance would be to the United States and Duke Don Vito and Duke Vito were forming their strategy on how to carry out their plans undetected and get the pertinent information to President Roosevelt.

With Duke Don Vito and Duke Vito spending all of their available time together, Baron Tony stayed close by the women who spent much of their time out on the deck. He was sitting in a lounge chair and gazing upon the banks of the Mississippi as the ship cruised past and pondering one of his favorite books, "Tom Sawyer and Huckleberry Finn," by Mark Twain, he had always loved to read as a boy. He had recently watched the movie and memories began to flood his mind. Baron Tony remembered sitting on the Hudson Bay as a young boy and reliving the pain of his parents and brother's deaths. He remembered the terror and the feeling of having no one and being completely alone. He was so grateful to Duke Don Vito for saving his life and sending him to America where he would escape certain death at the hands of these vicious savages who took his family and his life. It was on the banks of the Bay where Baron Tony met a young man who reminded him of a caricature he had seen of Rasputin and the Imperial couple of Russia, so Baron Tony gave him the nickname, Rasputin.

Rasputin was a large man, broadly built with a large muscular frame and standing close to a foot taller than Baron Tony. But, even with his large stature, he was a quiet man who also felt like an outcast of society. For many years, while they sat at the banks of the New York Harbor, they plotted their revenge on those who murdered Baron Tony's family.

Rasputin and Baron Tony became lifelong friends and in time was employed as Baron Tony's bodyguard and assisted in many jobs of Murders Inc. being carried out. Rasputin's hands were large and with a single jerk, he was able to snap the necks of his victims. Without any external wounds, their murders would often be thought of as a death by natural causes.

Baron Tony had made a decision! He was going to write a book about his life. Over the next couple of days, Baron Tony sat for hours writing about some of the highlights of his life. He gazed at the small wakes of the river as the paddle riverboat slowly parted the water as it travelled through.

He was deep in his thoughts when suddenly, a shadow overtook the sunshine where he was sitting.

"Hey Tony, what are you up to?" Count Marco asked.

"I am writing a book about my life," Baron Tony answered.

"An autobiographical account or fictitious?" Count Marco asked.

"No! My story." Baron Tony answered, confused by Count Marco's question.

"No, I meant . . . Oh never mind. If you need any help, I am a Literary English professor," Count Marco replied.

"Hey! That's a good idea. You know, I only went to school for three years. The rest of my learning I did in a basement using a friend's books. He taught me to read, write, and do arithmetic."

"Of course!" Count Marco replied. "May I see what you've written?"

Baron Tony was proud of his writing and enthusiastically handed Count Marco his great masterpiece. As he began to peruse Baron Tony's story, Count Marco's eyes grew wide at the childlike writing. Understanding that Baron Tony had not received the privilege of a formal education, Count Marco continued to work with Baron Tony throughout the rest of the cruise and continued to work with him once they arrived back at the Plantation and over the course of several years.

Baron Tony penned the story of several highlights in his life and Count Marco edited and embellished his writings. An author, who had grown up in New York and was a friend of Duke Vito's, created a bestselling novel based off of these writings and then followed up with the production of a trilogy of award-winning films which became a box office sensation and changed cinema forever. Still today, these films are considered a cult classic.

The Twins are Born

The time had come, Duchess Maria was in labor. Duke Vito began to nervously pace the floor as Duke Don Vito and Sabrina began to chuckle at their son's nervousness, but at the same time Duke Don Vito reminisced about his own nervousness the day Duke Vito was born.

"Vito, should we send the cars to pick up the midwives?" he calmly asked his pacing son.

Duke Vito turned to his father, his face rather pale, "Yes, I guess we should."

Normally, only one midwife would be necessary to assist with the delivery but looking at Duchess Maria's girth on her petite frame and the family history of twins, they agreed that two midwives would be safer for the delivery and the mother.

Countess Athena walked into the room and overheard the two men talking and said, "We have some time. The contractions are ten minutes apart and the midwives prepared the room for the delivery at their last visit when they checked on Maria."

"Vito, go ahead and give them a call and let them know that a car will be sent to pick each of them up. I would feel better having them here sooner than later. Do you agree Athena?"

"Yes. Her labor could progress more quickly, so I think that would be best."

Duke Vito came out of the library after calling the midwives, "Should I boil water or something?" he asked in a shaky voice.

Both sets of grandparents laughed and assured him that everything would be taken care of and not to worry.

"Can I go see her?" he asked.

Countess Athena replied, "Of course. Florence is with her, but I'm sure she would be happy to see you."

As Duke Vito walked up the stairs, he could hear Duchess Maria talking to Countess Florence. Her voice was rather intense, and the pain of her labor was obvious.

Duke Vito reached the bedroom and knocked on the door as he walked in. Duchess Maria looked up at Duke Vito as another contraction came and her face grimaced in pain.

Duke Vito rushed to Duchess Maria and clutched her hand, "Oh, my love, what can I do for you? Can I get you anything?"

Duchess Maria squeezed his hand tightly, causing Duke Vito to gasp in pain with his wife's crushing grip, "No darling, you have done quite enough," she replied through gritted teeth.

"The midwives will be here soon," Duke Vito said. "Maybe I should go outside and wait for them. If you need anything . . ." Duke Vito was backing out of the bedroom door as he spoke, quickly closing the door behind him.

Countess Florence had been sitting in the chair, silently laughing at Duke Vito's nervousness and lack of control in this situation. Duke Vito was a man who possessed the ability to run his business with skill and expertise. His demeanor was one of a man who was calm and in control of each situation he found himself in, until now.

Duke Don Vito, Duchess Sabrina, Count Marco, and Countess Athena were sitting in the parlor having tea when they saw Duke Vito come down the stairs and head outside onto the front porch. Duke Don Vito got up from the couch and followed his son outside, while Countess Athena went back upstairs to her daughters.

Duchess Sabrina looked over at Count Marco and said, "I think I'll join them to see if there's anything I can do."

Count Marco said, "Good idea, I'll go outside and check on Vito."

He opened the door to hear Duke Don Vito speaking to Duke Vito.

"Everything okay?" Duke Don Vito asked his son.

"I guess. I think Maria is really angry with me."

Duke Don Vito and Count Marco laughed out loud. Duke Don Vito said, "No son, she's not angry. She's in pain and right now, you're the one to blame! The pain will be over soon, and all will be forgotten."

"I hope so! Where are those midwives? Shouldn't they be here by now?"

"They'll be here soon. Come on, let's go for a little walk. Before you know it, you're going to be a Daddy!"

Duke Don Vito, Duke Vito, and Count Marco walked around the property and down to the dock when they saw one car pull up with the first midwife and shortly thereafter, the second car pulled up with the other midwife.

As the light of the day disappeared into the darkness of the night, the men walked back into the house to pour themselves a brandy when they heard the cry of new life coming from upstairs. Shortly after, the midwife came down the stairs to the waiting new father and grandfathers, "It's a boy!" she told them as she opened the blanket to show them the baby.

The men stood in awe, looking at the perfection of the baby when they once again heard a cry coming from up the stairs. Moments later, the other midwife came down the stairs, "It's a girl!" she said, as she opened the blanket for Vito to see his new daughter.

"She's beautiful," Vito said with tears in his eyes. "A boy and a girl! How's my wife?"

"She's fine! She wants to see you."

Vito cautiously walked up the stairs to see his wife who had seemed angry with him the last time he had seen her. He approached the bedroom door and quietly knocked before opening it. Duchess Maria was sitting up in the bed sipping on a glass of water that Countess Florence had just given her when she saw Duke Vito entering the room.

"Did you see them?" she asked him. Her voice was excited, but tired.

"Yes, they're beautiful. You're beautiful! I love you so much!"

"I love you too!" Duchess Maria said as she reached out to embrace and kiss her husband.

Duke Vito laughed, "You had me wondering for a while!"

They both laughed and Duchess Maria said, "I'm sorry, I . . ."

Duke Vito put his finger to her lips and said, "Shhhh, it's all over and we have two beautiful babies. Now, you need to get some rest." He leaned down and kissed Duchess Maria and left the room.

He went downstairs and saw Duke Don Vito holding his new granddaughter, with Duchess Sabrina leaning over his shoulder while baby Marie grasped her finger. Countess Athena was holding her new grandson, Vito Jr., while Count Marco sat next to them, staring at the precious new Castellammare twins. The grandparents were enamored with their grandbabies. Duke Vito beamed with pride as he stood in the doorway watching them coo and cuddle his children, putting aside their properness, all formalities, and tough exteriors; they melted with love into their new roles as Nonnas and Nonnos.

The twins, Vito Jr. and Marie, were the beginning of the fifth generation of Castellammare lineage.

About the Author

Lewis Barton

The Bartons settled in Salem, Massachussetts in 1632, and were the first family to settle in Barton Cove, Maine.

In 1643, Marmaduke Barton was condemned of stealing a pig and sentenced to 14 years. As punishment for his crime, he was sold into slavery and branded with an "S" on his forehead. At the time, since there were no prisons, slavery was deemed the punishment for crime regardless of race or religion.

Lewis Barton's ancestor, General William Barton, was a deemed a hero in the Revolutionary War under George Washington. The Barton Family has a history of serving in the United States military, with the author Lewis Barton serving in the army during the Vietnam War. Mr. Barton is a Corps of Engineer service connected disabled veteran. He graduated MCI in Pittsfield, Maine. In 2004, he was a "Presidential Point of Light" recipient presented by George W. Bush for his TV broadcasting and humanitarian acts during the 2004 hurricanes of Francis and Jeanne on the Treasure Coast of Florida. A film documentary, "The Eye of Two Sisters" was produced and received international recognition.

As a teenager in 1960, Lewis built a Street Rod (a Ford Model A, 5-window coupe), which after 60 years, he still owns and drives.

In high school, Lewis and his buddies played baseball in a flat field that his dad farmed. He later found out that it was this same field where his third great-grandfather, Josh Barton, had trained prior to mustering and being wounded at Bunker Hill during the Revolutionary War. He recovered from his injuries and wintered at Valley Forge. Returning to battle, he fought at Yorktown until the battle was over. He then walked 700 miles to his New Hampshire home carrying his musket.

A funny story about Lewis's great-grandfather, David Barton.

David Barton built a barn on his property in New Hampshire. A few years after the barn had been built, two separate towns, Pittsfield and Epsom were established, and the town line ran right through the middle of his barn. In those days, you were taxed on the livestock you owned and when the tax collector was coming, he would move the oxen from one end of the barn to the other, depending on which tax collector was going to visit.

Author Lewis Barton is also related to Clara Barton. Clara Barton began collecting supplies and worked to get them to the soldiers during the Civil War. She received official permission to bring supplies to the battlefields and was at every major battle in Maryland, Virginia, and South Carolina, where she also tended to the wounded and became known as the "angel of the battlefield." It was Clara's idea to have battlefield hospitals. When the Civil War ended, she started the Missing Soldiers Office with a small staff. They located 22,000 of the 63,000 requests for missing men, some were still alive. In 1881, Clara founded the American Red Cross where she served as president until 1904, when at the age of 82, she started the National First Aid Association of America, an organization that emphasized emergency preparedness and developed first aid kits.

Lewis describes how the story began:

On a Saturday morning, around eight o'clock, Labor Day weekend, 1972. I was sitting on a pile of 16 inch water pipes by the river at the base of Mount Washington in Brentenwoods, New Hampshire, reviewing engineering plans for my construction company on how to lay this pipe across the river, when an elderly man, by himself walked up and said, "Good morning, may I sit and rest?" We talked for over an hour and he said, "Would you meet me here tomorrow at the same time?" I said, "Yes." The next morning, he came with a thermos of hot chocolate and a bag of bran muffins. We ate, drank, and talked for over two hours. When he was leaving, I asked, "When will I see you again? How do I get in touch with you?" He said, "I will see you again someday, sometime," and walked away.

In 1980, Pope Paul II had been ordained and Ronald Reagan was the new U.S. President. I was living on Plum Island in Newberryport, Massachusetts. In the middle of the night, my old friend's relative who was working for my father, woke me up in the middle of the night and asked me if I had a thousand dollars cash that I could lend to my old friend for a few days. I asked, "Who is this old friend you are referring to?" and was told, "Your old friend who you met eight years ago at Mount Washington, Duke Vito Cornino, one of the world's most powerful men." Later I learned that he was in the New Hampshire White Mountains to chair The Mafia Council meeting of Godfathers, as Godfather of Godfathers. In that meeting the mafia council approved the plan to ordain a new pope and elect a U.S. president who were sympathetic on creating conflict in the USSR and allow the American/Italian Mafia to develop the Russian Mafia.

Several years of research continued and after the disappearance of the Castellammare and Cornino family members along with their staff and crew, Lewis Barton felt their story must be told.

Countess Athena and the Godfather's Twins is the first book of a four-book series.

We are working on the upcoming books which will cover the years and subjects as listed below:

Volume 2: 1940-1959

The United States and Don Vito made a deal for the U.S. to enter Europe through Sicily during World War II. Don Vito built a secret airstrip for ally spy planes at his summer home in the Italian Alps, where he also housed some Air Force pilots and personnel as they were passing through. This also allowed the allies to spy on the Germans and Italians.

Countess Athena formed a group of spies for the allies and sent information to the United States in secret compartments built into her wooden wine crates which were shipped to New Orleans.

Tony joined the military and promoted himself to Captain, taking leaves from duty at his discretion. No one is really sure if he ever actually joined, but . . . that's Tony!

When the war ended, Tony decided to use women as hitwomen based on Duchess Maria's actions at the Plantation Ball.

Duke Vito and Duchess Maria's twins were kidnapped when they were nine years old. They were abducted, tied up, put in burlap vegetable sacks, and then flown to Cuba in a C-47 military airplane. Once they were in Cuba, they were confined in a chicken coop with armed guards for 10 days until Tony and Vito found them.

In 1947, while Bugsy Siegel sat in his Beverly Hills home, an unknown assailant, Tony, shot and killed him with a .30 caliber military M1 carbine.

In 1948, the mob had President Truman re-elected in an unexpected victory over Thomas Dewey. An infamous front page photo of Truman holding the Chicago Daily Tribune, which stated, "Dewey Defeats Truman" will forever be etched in history as an embarrassment for Dewey.

In 1959, a deal was made between Joe Kennedy and the Godfather of Godfathers, Duke Vito, to have his son, John F. Kennedy elected as the 35th President of the United States.

After Castro took over Cuba, the mafia planned for Orlando, Florida to become the Las Vegas of the east, so they moved all of their gambling equipment there. Their plans were thwarted when Walt Disney bought up the land to build Disney World, so they once again moved their equipment to a place know today as Atlantic City.

Volume 3: 1960-1979

Fulfilling the deal with Joe Kennedy, in November of 1960, Tony ensured John F. Kennedy's election win in Chicago.

The plans were executed from the plantation in New Orleans to have John F. Kennedy assassinated because of the broken promises that his father Joe, had made with Godfather Vito. This book also discusses how Lee Harvey Oswald and Jack Ruby fit into the plan.

In 1964, Hubert H. Humphrey decided to run for president and sought financing for his election from Hoffa, Tony, and Vito while dining together.

The fifth decade meeting of the mafia godfathers chaired by Godfather Duke Vito in 1972, was held in the White Mountains of New Hampshire near Mount Washington. Vito proposed a plan as Godfather of Godfathers to have a favorable president and pope elected who would be sympathetic and join in the conspiracy to overthrow the USSR. Although approved by the Vatican, the wrong pope, John Paul was elected and ordained. After his assassination, John Paul II was elected as pope in 1978 and Ronald Reagan as president in 1980.

Lewis Barton tells the story of his first meeting with Vito. Their casual meeting and conversation began a friendship, although for seven years, Lewis had no idea who Vito was. A short time later, Tony decided to vet Lewis at a Boston Red Sox – Chicago White Sox baseball game at Fennway Park in Boston, Massachusetts. Vito arranged for Lewis and his daughter Marie's marriage. Lewis didn't know anything about her family and childhood for some time. Now after forty years, Lewis is still learning!

Lewis talks about the difference between he and Marie's upbringing. He grew up in a farming and lumbermill town on the Merrimack River in Pittsfield, New Hampshire. On Sundays, he and his siblings would pile into the back of Dad's 1939 Ford pickup and head up the hill to the Quaker meeting house for church, while Marie was chauffeured in a private limousine with guards to the private entrances of the Cathedrals she attended while in her summer home or winter home.

Tony came to Nashua, New Hampshire to visit Lewis on a hot, sunny Sunday morning and ask him for a favor. Soon Lewis and Marie married. Not long after, they found out that Marie could never have children, so "the family" met with some of the finest doctors and the surrogate mother program was conceived.

Volume 4: 1980-1999

Vito suffers a heart attack. Tony quickly has him boarded onto his own private medical airplane and "convinces the doctors" with his two .45s drawn, that he is not dead and to make sure he remains alive. With his own private medical team, Vito receives the first successful, but undocumented, heart transplant.

In 1982, the surrogate program blessed Lewis and Marie with their first set of twins, two boys. During the course of the 80s, Lewis and Marie's surrogate mothers delivered four more sets of twins. Countess Athena Marie and her fraternal twin brother who were born on June 13, 1985, were the first set of male and female fraternal twins in history. Duke Vito had planned their birth to coincide as a Father's

Day gift for Lewis. Lewis had no knowledge that a surrogate mother was expecting these children, and Lewis was delighted with his Father's Day surprise.

Lewis, unaware that he even had one, met his double in Newberry Port, Massachusetts 1982. In 1983, his double was assassinated. Lewis had three additional assassination attempts on his life, but survived

For Lewis's 50th birthday, Vito and Tony gave him a $50 million investment in Nigerian oil wells. Unfortunately, he never was able to get a return since the oil wells became nationalized.

Tony Jr., the leader of the Italian-Russian Mafia, attempts to take over the American mob.

Also in this book, Lewis talks about growing up in Pittsfield, New Hampshire in the 1950s. He adds stories about his family and ancestors. Once example: In the early 1800s, David Barton, Lewis' second great grandfather was one of the shooters in a gun battle, where three men were killed and the location in Pittsfield, New Hampshire became known as "Bloods Corner."

At the time of publication:

Fragrances are being reproduced from
Countess Athena's collection which she began as a child,
mimicking her great-grandmother, Baroness Roseanna.
She began exporting her fragrances, olive oils,
and wines to the docks of the Plantation in New
Orleans where they were distributed and
highly desired throughout the United States.

At the time of publication:

Lewis Barton, along with Nick Lucca,
President of Lionstone International in the USA
are preparing for the production of Sicilian wines
that will represent the heritage and quality
of those wines produced over a century ago
by Countess Athena, the Castellammare family,
and Duke Don Vito Cornino.